The Affair
of the
39 Cufflinks

Also by the author
The Affair of the Bloodstained Egg Cosy
The Affair of the Mutilated Mink
Assassin
The Alpha LIst
The Abolition of Death
Appearance of Evil
Angel of Death
Assault & Matrimony
Auriol
Additional Evidence

The Affair
of the
39 Cufflinks

James Anderson

Poisoned Pen Press

Copyright © 2003, 2006 by James Anderson

First Trade Paperback Edition 2006

10 9 8 7 6 5 4 3 2 1

Library of Congress Catalog Card Number: 2003111699

ISBN: 1-59058-291-8 Trade Paperback

Poisoned Pen Press
6962 E. First Ave., Ste. 103
Scottsdale, AZ 85251
www.poisonedpenpress.com
info@poisonedpenpress.com

Printed in the United States of America

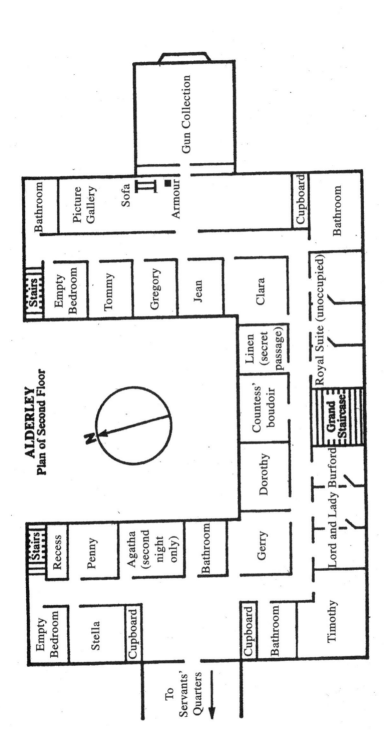

ALDERLEY
Plan of Second Floor

Author's Note

Money values

At the period in which this story is set, money in Britain was worth approximately fifty-three times its value in the early 21st Century. So to get an idea of their present day equivalents, all sums mentioned should be multiplied by fifty-three. For example, £1,000 then would have had the purchasing power of £53,000 in the year 2001.

Those wishing to get an idea of the value of a sum in another currency, such as US dollars, have two choices:

1. They can convert using the rate of exchange as it was at the time of the events in the book. This will turn £1,000 into just under $5,000, and £53,000 into about $260,000.

2. Alternatively, they convert at the rate of exchange at a more recent time. In 2001, for instance, this would have made £53,000 the equivalent of only about $78,000.

The matter is further complicated by the fact that the inflation rate has been lower in the USA than in Britain, so that $5,000 then would have had the purchasing power of about $63,750 in 2001.

Readers who find all this as confusing as the author does should seek help from their friendly neighbourhood economist, or any good international currency dealer.

(Figures from Economic History Services website: http://eh.net/hmit)

Chapter One

"I want to make one thing absolutely plain," said the Honourable Mrs. Florence Saunders. "After I'm dead, I will not come back."

Jean Mackenzie, her companion, blinked. "I don't quite…"

"You know perfectly well what I mean. I don't want you trying to get in touch with me at one of your séances. I'll have far more interesting things to do than potter around down here, spouting a lot of platitudes about peace and love. Understand?"

"Now, dear, you mustn't talk like this. It'll be many years yet—"

"Jean, don't talk nonsense. I'm ninety-six. It cannot possibly be *many* years. And I don't mind at all. My husband's dead. My only son is dead. I've had enough of this world now. I've repented of my sins and I'm ready to meet my Maker. So I want it made clear that there must be no long faces at my funeral. Let people enjoy themselves. I've taken one step in that direction already. Charlie Bradley has it in hand." She chuckled richly.

Jean looked doubtful. She was a thin, nondescript woman of about fifty, invariably clad in a tweed skirt and twin-set. Mostly her face wore an expression of doubt, or sometimes of anxiety. Doubt was now dominant as she didn't know whether to take Florrie seriously. How could her solicitor ensure people enjoyed themselves at her funeral?

But then, Florrie had never been serious. Even the name. She should be called Florence, a properly dignified name for the widow of an Earl's son. Jean had never felt quite comfortable calling her by her first name at all. But from the time she had come to her, Mrs. Saunders had been quite clear. "Call me Florrie," she had said. "Everybody else does."

It was her background, of course. Stage people were notoriously lax about such things. And although it must be seventy years since she had last trodden the boards, the music hall artiste, the old vaudevillian, was still there, struggling to get out.

Jean, though, wished she wouldn't talk about her death. For that made her think about what was going to happen to her when Florrie passed over. She had hardly any savings and it was many years before she would qualify for a small state pension. With no qualifications, she would have little chance of getting any job, except one as companion. And most paid companions were really no better than nurse and housemaid combined. But otherwise, what would she do? After twenty-three years in this lovely detached house, on the river, just outside London, it would be very hard to settle in some pokey bed-setter, even if she could afford the rent. Oh, if only she knew whether Florrie—

"Penny for 'em," Florrie said suddenly.

Jean gave a slight start. "I was just thinking what a remarkable life you've had," she said, untruthfully. "Tell me, would you change anything?"

Florrie shook her head firmly. "I had a wonderful time on the halls. Never made the West End, but might have done, if I hadn't got married. And I certainly don't regret that. People thought I was just Bertie's little bit of fluff and I craftily trapped him into marriage. Not so. It was a love match, even though he was a good bit older than me. And I worked hard to make sure he'd never be ashamed of me. In a few months I could speak and dress so you wouldn't know the difference between me and a Duchess. And I gave him a son. John was the apple of his eye. May sound shocking, but I'm always grateful Bertie died when he did. He saw John happily married to a lovely girl like Emma, with two daughters of his own. Then he passed away, less than nine months later Emma died, eighteen months after that John remarried—and within a few months was killed himself. It was a—a terrible time."

Her voice quavered and stopped. Jean wisely remained silent while Florrie collected herself. She had, of course, listened to all this many times before. Florrie would reminisce for hours. But it didn't bore Jean, who never tired of hearing about an early life so different from her own ultra-respectable middle-class upbringing.

Florrie was continuing now, talking almost to herself. "Worst choice John ever made, marrying Clara. I can understand why he did it: he thought Agatha and Dorothy needed a mother. And Clara could really turn on the charm, when she needed to. I don't know why she cut herself and the girls off from me completely after John's death: jealousy, maybe, or snobbery. Yet I was always nice to her. I never let it show that she was a disappointment to me, after Emma. Then, when the girls are grown up, she suddenly realises I'm getting on, and she ought to make sure I don't get my own back by cutting them out of my will. So she brings them to see me, and fawns all over me, saying how fond she is of me. Lying cat. And Dorry just sits there, staring at the carpet and fiddling her thumbs, and Agatha is red in the face and fuming. Very painful. Only happened once, though."

"Well, you did tell her you found three visitors rather tiring."

"I was hinting it would be nice to see the girls on their own. But she wouldn't have that."

"Still, you do see Agatha regularly now. I was amazed later on when I answered the door one day and there she was, in jodhpurs and all her motor-cycling outfit."

"Yes, she's one of a kind, is Agatha. But imagine having to come secretly, so her stepmother doesn't find out! And Dorry so cowed she never comes at all and from what Agatha says is not much more than an unpaid skivvy."

"Agatha seems to have made an independent life for herself."

"As far as she could. She ought to get out of that house. But, of course, she's got no money. What they get under my will is going to make a difference, though."

Chapter Two

"You're not going to get away with it, you loathsome old woman," said the voice on the phone.

Clara Saunders gasped and nearly dropped the receiver. She was about to slam it down, but some instinct stopped her. Managing with great self-control to keep her voice steady, she said coolly: "Who is that?"

"Oh, this is nobody at all. Nobody of any importance." The words were slightly slurred, the voice husky. It could have been a man or a woman.

"Obviously true. Equally obviously you're drunk."

"Oh yes, I'm drunk. And you know why? Because you've ruined my life."

"You're insane."

"Don't play the injured innocent. You sent that piece to the paper about me, you bitch."

Clara drew her breath in sharply. But she wasn't going to take this sort of thing lying down. "How dare you speak to me like that, you uncouth, insolent creature!"

"Insolent? How can one be insolent to a slimy toad like you?"

"I am not going to stand here and listen to insults from a contemptible, cowardly drunk. And let me warn you that if you call again—"

"No, let *me* warn *you*, my fine lady, that you're not going to get away with it." The voice got louder. "You'll pay, yes, you'll pay. I'm going to get you. I'm—"

At this Clara did ring off. She stood quite still in the hall of the old, rambling house in Hampstead. Her heart was pounding and her legs felt weak. Never before had she been spoken to in that ghastly way. Old, indeed! She wasn't sixty yet. But she did feel she'd handled the person with considerable dignity.

Suddenly she needed to sit down. She turned, to make her way back into the drawing-room, then gave a jump. Standing just two feet from her was a young woman. Clara clasped her hand to her heart. "Oh, Dorothy, don't creep up on me like that!"

"I didn't. I just came to answer the phone," Dorothy Saunders said defensively. She was in her early thirties, painfully thin, with short, mousy brown hair, and a deathly pale complexion. She was wearing a drab brown dress, about ten years out of date, thick stockings and flat shoes. At the moment her eyes were big with alarm. "Mother, who *was* that?"

"I don't know. Just some drunk."

"He threatened you, didn't he?"

"Certainly not!"

"But I heard him say, 'You'll pay, I'm going to get you.' "

"He didn't know what he was saying. He was totally out of control."

"It was terrible. It's the way Al Capone and those other Chicago gangsters talk to their enemies."

"I'm pleased to say, I wouldn't know. And I don't know how you do."

"Only from the talkies. It was one of *them*, wasn't it?"

"A gangster? Don't be ridiculous!"

"No—one of those people you've told the papers about."

"I tell you I don't know who it was."

"Aggie's always said something like this would happen—that one of them would try and get revenge."

"Your sister is absurdly melodramatic sometimes."

"But he did threaten you. Mother, you must tell the police."

"No. What could they do? Besides, it was only empty bluster."

"It might not be. And at least if he rings again you could tell him the police had been notified. It might just frighten him off."

"Well, I'll think about it, if it'll keep you quiet. Now I don't want to hear another word on the subject. Go and do something useful. Clean the bathroom."

"I cleaned it this morning."

"Well, clean something else!"

And Clara strode into the drawing-room and slammed the door behind her.

Chapter Three

"I wonder how many people will come to my funeral," Florrie said reflectively

Jean Mackenzie gave a tut. "There you go again, dear. You really must not think about these things."

"I like thinking about it. I want it to be a good one."

"I'm sure it will be, if a funeral can ever be good. And no doubt there'll be lots of people there."

"Hardly any family, though. All my generation long gone, and John's, too—all my nephews and nieces. Happened everywhere, of course. First the Great War, then the Spanish Flu."

"But you've got lots of great nephews and nieces, and great-greats."

"Four great nephews, one great niece and two great-great nieces. Yes, I expect they'll come. I think they're all in my will, aren't they? Let me have another look at it, will you, dear?"

Jean got to her feet and carefully navigated her way between the many stools, pouffes, chairs and occasional tables to the big Victorian bureau. She had no difficulty in locating the will, as this was a routine which was gone through at least once a week. Florrie knew quite well who was in her will and who would be coming to her funeral. But she enjoyed the little ritual, it helped pass the time and at her age such harmless whims could be indulged.

Jean glanced down at the envelope wistfully as she made her way back. If only she knew whether *she* was mentioned in it. She had never liked to ask; it would seem such bad form. And Florrie hadn't ever given the slightest hint. It would be so easy, she thought for the umpteenth time, just to come in one day, when Florrie was in bed, and look. But it wouldn't be right. The mere fact that Florrie gave her the opportunity would make it wrong to take advantage of it. Though it was such a temptation…

She handed the envelope to Florrie, who opened it.

"Now, let me see. Well, George and Lavinia will come. I'm sure of that. They've always kept in touch. Never any snobbery with the *real* aristocrats you know, the one's who've got aristocratic natures, not just a title."

"Oh, I know. And that time we stayed at Alderley was so wonderful. I'll never forget it. Even now, when they visit, I can't believe I'm actually talking to the Earl and Countess of Burford. They treat me just as though I were, well, one of them."

"That's precisely what I mean. And Geraldine's a lovely girl, such a live wire. So interesting, all she had to tell me about those terrible murders they had there. I do hope she'll be happy with that young man." She gave a sigh. "It must be lovely at Alderley now. I wonder what they're all doing at this moment. Keeping very busy I'm sure."

The August sun beat upon the half-drawn curtains of the mellow, oak-panelled room. Through the open French windows wafted the smell of roses and the faint hum of bees. In a large, well-worn black leather easy chair an untidy-looking man with wispy grey hair, a pink complexion and a straggly moustache whistled softly and not unmusically as his chest rose and fell rhythmically. *The Times* crossword puzzle, half finished, was open on his lap. George Henry Aylwin Saunders, twelfth Earl of Burford, was enjoying his usual post-prandial snooze. It was a peaceful scene.

It did not long remain so, as the double doors were thrown open and a girl breezed into the room. She was in her mid-twenties, petite, red-haired, with a tip-tilted nose and deceptively innocent large hazel eyes. She seemed to ooze energy. "Hello, Daddy," she said loudly.

Lord Burford awoke suddenly and blinked pale blue eyes several times before focusing on the speaker. He gave a grunt. "Oh. You've arrived."

Lady Geraldine Saunders looked hurt. "What happened to 'My darling daughter! You're home at last! It's been so long!' "

"It seems about three hours. How's London?"

"Big. Noisy. But fun."

"It's the noisiness—and the smelliness—that always strikes me most these days. Which is why I go up as little as possible. Is that *Peepshow*?" He pointed incredulously to a garishly coloured magazine she was holding.

"Yes. A little present for you."

She held it out to him. Lord Burford took it gingerly and gazed at it with distaste. "Why the deuce did you bring me this? It's an appallin' rag."

"There's something in it that will interest you."

The Earl read the caption to the picture on the cover: "'Shirley Temple: America's Little Sweetheart.' You surely don't—?"

"No, no—page twelve."

The Earl reluctantly flicked through the pages and opened the magazine out. Then his eyes bulged. "Good gad!"

A banner headline, across two pages, read:

IS ALDERLEY CURSED?

The rest of the pages consisted mainly of photographs, but there was a small block of text. The Earl read it.

> Twelve months ago this week two sensational murders were committed at Alderley, the 17th-Century Westshire home of the Earl and Countess of Burford. Amazingly, less than six months later, another, completely unconnected murder took place. Involving, among others, a government minister, film stars, American

millionaires, European aristocracy, foreign diplomats and an Olympic athlete,
with the murder weapons valuable firearms
from Lord Burford's world-famous collection, these crimes have led many people
to ask if an ancient gypsy's curse is
still exerting its malign influence over
the beautiful, stately home, and if this
could lead to further tragedies. See the
following pages for the full astound-
ing story.

The Earl looked up. "This—this is preposterous!"

"I know."

"It's absolute nonsense! It's ridiculous! It's—it's—" He groped for words.

"How about balderdash? That's a good strong word."

"Claptrap," said the Earl defiantly.

"Yes, claptrap's good, too."

"This business about a curse, I mean. The eighth Earl turfed some gypsies off his land and one old woman swore at him a bit and told him he'd regret it."

"And within twelve months he and his younger son were both dead."

"The Earl had apoplexy—probably what they'd call a stroke today—and the boy most likely got pneumonia. There wasn't anything mysterious about it. Since then there's been nothin' out of the ordinary. Most of my ancestors died peacefully, usually at a ripe old age."

"You don't have to convince me, Daddy. I'm not scared of any gypsy's curse."

"And those murders didn't involve the family. The people just happened to be here. I shall complain to the editor."

"I don't honestly think you've got any grounds. The story *has* appeared in a couple of books, after all."

Lord Burford turned the page to reveal a page of text broken into many short paragraphs and headed THE ALDERLEY MURDERS: FULL STORY. "You've read this?"

"Skimmed through it. Nothing that wasn't in the papers at the time. They seem to have got the facts right, and they don't libel anybody, so we'll just have to grin and bear it."

"Bear it I may. Grin I will not."

"The pictures aren't bad."

"Didn't look at 'em." He turned back the page. "My word, they've really gone to town. That's your mother and me when she opened the County Show last month. Nice photo of you."

"It's the one that was in *The Tatler.*"

"Oh yes. But they've put you in a line with all these other girls. 'Beauties Involved in Murder.' You, Jane Clifton, Anilese de la Roche, Laura Lorenzo, the little Dove—and Mabel Turner, for heaven's sake! This picture of her must be twenty years old, at least."

"That 'involved in' is a bit rich. You'd think they'd have had the decency to distinguish between the victims, the criminals and the innocent bystanders."

"Well, *you* weren't a bystander, either time. You were gettin' mixed up in the investigations."

Gerry nodded, a wistful expression on her face. "You know, in spite of all the horrible things that happened, it was fun, wasn't it—looking back?"

"I look back as infrequently as I can. Reckon those weekends put twenty years on my life."

"There's even a photo of Chief Inspector Wilkins—see."

"Oh yes. 'The Man Who Solved Both Cases.' Looking as bewildered as ever. He came up trumps, though. Er, did you just get the one copy of this?"

"Two. Mummy's got the other."

"Oh, you've shown her. How did she take it?"

"As you'd expect: phlegmatically."

"Good. I was just thinkin', rubbish as it all is, might be a good idea to get a few more copies. I can think of quite a few people who'd like to see it—some of the others who were here, apart from anybody else."

"OK, I'll get another half dozen."

"Better make it a dozen. So, what you doin' here? Row with the boy friend?"

"Of course not! And he's my fiancé, not just my boy friend; remember?"

"Thought you youngsters preferred these new-fangled terms. Anyway, why are you home?"

"I explained in my telegram. He's had to go away on family business. You know there was a death in his family—which is why we had to postpone the wedding. Well, it's led to a lot of legal and financial complications and he's had to go and help sort it all out. It was going to be lonely until he got back and I wanted a break."

"Why didn't you go with him?"

"I felt I'd be in the way."

"Lor, you've got sensitive all of a sudden. Anyway, it's nice to have you home, sweetheart. Place seems pretty empty sometimes, without you."

Gerry looked surprised and pleased. "Why, thank you Daddy. Anyway, I'm going to have a shower." She started towards the door, then stopped and turned round. "Oh, while I remember, I saw Great Aunt Florrie last week. She sent her love to you both."

"Oh, good. Your mother and I called to see her for a couple of hours back in the spring. How is she?"

"Perky as ever. Apart from my wedding, all she wanted me to talk about was the murders—much to Miss Mackenzie's disapproval. I filled her in on all the undercover stuff that never came out publicly. I think I'll send her a copy of *Peepshow*. I'm sure she'll enjoy making Mackenzie read it to her."

"Suppose I ought to read it—just to make quite sure they have got their facts right."

"Oh, absolutely," Gerry said.

She went out. The Earl buried his head in *Peepshow*.

Chapter Four

"Then there's Gregory," said Florrie. "He's certain to come when he learns he's in the will. Don't suppose his wife will bother, though. She's never been here."

"That's Alexandra, isn't it?"

"Yes. Don't think it's much of a marriage. She's very politically ambitious, and I imagine the fact Gregory's not exactly had a dazzling career has been a disappointment to her."

"But he's very respected as an MP, isn't he?"

"I believe so. I can't trust him, though. Maybe just because he's a politician. I don't believe a word one of them says. Frankly, I'd never be surprised to learn…"

She tailed off.

"To learn what, dear?"

"Oh, nothing," said Florrie.

"Greggy, darling, I saw an absolutely too divine dress in Bond Street today."

Gregory Carstairs, MP, who was pouring himself a gin and tonic at the time, gave a grunt. His companion, a sinuous dark-haired girl with pouting, scarlet lips, who was lounging artistically back on the sofa, displaying very long and shapely legs, clad in black stockings of the purest silk, went on: "It's chiffon, the palest shade of blue, with these delicious little pleats…" She prattled away, but Gregory wasn't listening. He gazed out of the window over the roofs of St. John's Wood to the famous Father Time weather vane of Lord's cricket ground, just a few hundred yards away. Useful, at least in the summer. If anybody should happen to see him in the neighbourhood, it provided the perfect excuse. Watching cricket was something nobody objected to a Member of Parliament doing; it was almost expected.

He was a heavily built man of about fifty with closely cropped grizzled hair, a florid complexion, the beginnings of a double chin and a neatly trimmed moustache, which he fondly believed gave him a military appearance. He always refused to talk about his war experiences, leading many people to assume he must have had a good record. In fact, he had been rejected because of flat feet, and had spent the whole of 1914 to 1918 in a Whitehall office.

He turned round and surveyed the chicly furnished, ultra-modern sitting-room of the flat, with its sharp angles and chromium fittings. 'Strewth, but this place was costing him a fortune. How long would he be able to keep it up? Or Poppy, for that matter? He was going to have to do something about it. But what? Poppy was such a clinger. And she wouldn't forgive easily if he just dumped her. He had to keep her sweet. It wouldn't be so bad if it wasn't for that damned letter he'd written her. What a fool he'd been! Tipsy at the time, of course, and in those days he'd been really smitten by her, but that was no excuse. He had to get out of this entanglement soon. But how?

"...and it was only ten pounds—well, guineas, actually. It would really suit me."

Gregory dragged himself back. "I'm sure you'd look absolutely breathtaking in it, my sweet. We must certainly think about getting it for you, er, sometime."

"Sometime?" There was a suspicious edge to her voice.

"Yes, Christmas perhaps."

"*Christmas?*" This time the voice was an octave higher. "But that's months and months away. And this is a summer dress!"

"But you've got dozens of summer dresses. And look so perfectly ravishing in all of them."

Poppy gazed at him, a disconcertingly acute and appraising expression in her large violet eyes. "Greggy, you're not getting hard up, are you?"

"Good lord, no! Whatever gave you that idea?"

"You haven't bought me anything nice for weeks and weeks."

"Well, I am a bit short of the ready just now. But it's just a temporary thing. Hold up in funds, lots of expenses, have to take the old woman to Monte later this month, as I explained."

"You've never taken *me* to Monte Carlo."

"I know, my sweet, and I'd like nothing better, believe me. But we did have that weekend in Brighton a month ago."

"That was no fun, not with you peering over your shoulder all the time, in a blue funk in case someone recognised you."

"Well, I do have to be careful, sweetheart. I mean if we were seen together, it would cause the most awful scandal in my constituency. I've explained what a provincial backwater it is, and how narrow-minded they are there. Any hint of what they'd call impropriety could cost me my seat. Do you know what my majority was last time?"

"Five hundred and sixty-eight," Poppy said in a bored voice.

"Oh. Then you can see how easily I could be kicked out."

"Would it really matter if you were? You seem totally fed up with it half the time, and there's all these late-night sittings and asking questions you know the answers to already and having to write letters to all those silly little constituents. And you're never going to get into the Government, are you? You're always going to be a back-bencher."

"I say, that's a bit below the belt. Besides, it's not true. One of the Whips was only saying to me a month ago that the Prime Minister's always got me very much in mind." He straightened his shoulders and unconsciously straightened his tie. "Anyway, it's a matter of duty. Family's got a long history of public service. Men from my background have a responsibility to serve this country." He took hold of the lapel of his jacket with one hand and gazed out over the rooftops. His voice took on a more resonant tone. "I often think, when I gaze at a view such as this, and look down at the people going peaceably, freely and unafraid about their business, how greatly blessed we are to live in a land like ours."

He turned round and addressed her earnestly. "Across a mere twenty-six miles of water, storm clouds are gathering and tyranny is raising its vile head. Yet how often we in Britain tend to take our blessings for granted. It has been wisely said that the price of liberty is eternal vigilance. Such vigilance is the duty of us all, but particularly of those happy few of us called to serve in the front line of liberty's defence, in the Mother of Parliaments. We—"

Poppy raised her hand to her mouth and ostentatiously stifled a yawn. Gregory gave a blink and came back to earth. "Well, you do see, don't you?"

"But do you really enjoy, it Greggy—all this defending liberty? Wouldn't you rather be spending your time with me?" The tone was wheedling.

"Well, of course I would, precious. You know that."

"Then why don't you chuck it in? After all, you've done nearly twenty years of public service. You could get your divorce and never have to worry about who saw us. And it's not as though the salary is up to much. You told me once it only made up a teeny bit of what you earned."

"Yes, but you don't understand. I'm on the Board of six companies, five of whom only want me because it looks good to have an MP on their letter heads. I'm an adviser to two business associations, simply because the idiots believe I can influence Government policy, or at least know what it's going to be. Then there's the odd bit of journalism. I'd lose all that if I gave up my seat. Besides, what would I do outside politics?"

Poppy gave a pout. "So I suppose that means you'll be going off to your dreary old constituency more and more, does it?"

"'Fraid so: make a few speeches, shake a few hands, kiss a few babies. And don't worry—I mean the sort that guzzle milk, not the kind that quaff champers." Gregory gave a forced chuckle.

"Will *she* be going with you?"

"Alex? Yes. She's dam' good at that sort of thing, I will say that. Worth a good few hundred votes."

"I could do all that sort of thing."

Gregory tried unsuccessfully to imagine Poppy earnestly discussing child welfare or old age pensions with the wife of his constituency party Chairman. But he wasn't forced to make a response, because she changed the subject.

"So, when you going next?"

"Tomorrow, actually."

"How long for?"

"Rest of the week."

"Oh, Greggy!"

"Frightfully sorry. But it can't be helped."

Poppy gave a sigh. "What about next week?"

"Not sure. Monday and Tuesday I've got speaking engagements. I'll phone you sometime Tuesday. Perhaps we can arrange something for Wednesday or later in the week."

"I won't budge an inch from the phone, darling," said Poppy.

Chapter Five

"Timothy will come, I'm sure," Florrie said. "I think he'd want to, but he'd come even if he didn't. Always does the right thing, does Timothy."

"Such a distinguished-looking man, I always think. And a very clever barrister, I believe."

"Oh, Timothy's all right. Terrible stick, though. How he came to have such a flibbertigibbet daughter as Penny I'll never know. She's a pretty little baggage, with no thought in her head apart from finding a husband."

"So sad her mother dying as young as she did."

"Yes. Can't have been easy for Timothy, bringing up a girl on his own. Still, he always seems completely in control of every situation."

"Thank you, Mr. Jackson," said Timothy Saunders. "I have no further questions. I'm sure his lordship and the jury will now know just how much weight to attach to your evidence."

He sat down, as Jackson, looking decidedly shaken, hurriedly left the witness box. A cross-examination by one of the sharpest forensic minds of the English bar left few people unscathed.

Timothy's face showed no expression. It hardly ever did. He felt no pleasure at having demolished one of the opposition's most important witnesses: just the quiet satisfaction of a professional at a job well done. He gathered his papers together as the judge announced the end of the day's proceedings. His junior counsel gave him a sideways glance. It had been a ruthless performance, one that made him feel slightly uncomfortable. But undeniably effective. "Nearly over, do you think?" he asked quietly.

Timothy nodded shortly. "We can expect an offer in the morning."

He was a slim man of no more than average height, with small, regular features, a neatly trimmed toothbrush moustache, a pale complexion and thinning light brown hair, concealed now under his barrister's wig. A man who would never be noticed in a crowd, whom most people would have difficulty in describing, even after spending half an hour in his company. He recognised that it was probably the constant experience of being unnoticed and ignored when young that had driven him relentlessly on in his determination to make an impact of some kind on the world.

He strode rapidly back to his chambers. It was only four thirty. Time for a full three hours' work on the opinion he was preparing for Hargraves & Hargraves. Not that there was any urgency. He could go home now. But the house would be empty, apart from the servants, tucked away in their quarters. Penelope would certainly be out. What would he do? Read a law book? He sometimes envied those men who had some all-consuming interest or hobby—gardening or golf or, like his distant relative, Lord Burford, gun-collecting. But he had never left time for things like that. And now he was surely not far away from achieving his life-long ambition: elevation to the Bench, leading, in all probability one day, to the position of Lord Chief Justice, and the opportunity not merely to practise law but actually to influence it, to change it. He knew that that was what his fellow lawyers expected. Even if none of them liked him very much, they all held him in the highest respect. And what was more important than respect?

Arriving back at his chambers, he sent his clerk home, poured himself a small glass of very dry sherry and sat down at his desk. He took out the case containing his pince-nez, thoroughly polished them with a clean linen handkerchief and put them on. He refolded the handkerchief and replaced it in his pocket, then opened his brief case, took out the papers—and saw It. His stomach gave a lurch. For a while he had managed to forget about it—this thing that clouded all his horizons, that threatened to shatter all his hopes for the future.

The Photograph.

Against his better judgement, he had to obey the impulse to look at it again. It was like the urge constantly to exert pressure on a painful tooth, just to see if it still hurt. His eyes gave the slightest flicker and his lips tightened momentarily—the closest he would ever come to wincing—and he hurriedly put it back in his case. He could not leave it in the office safe, as his clerk knew the combination, while Penelope knew that of the one at home. So he had been carrying it round with him. He ought really to deposit it at his bank. But then he would not be able to indulge the lacerating, but to him very necessary, urge constantly to stare at it, searching for some minute indication as to where or who... He knew when, but there was no clue, obviously, as to why. Was it a prelude to blackmail? If so, why was the demand delayed? Or was some enemy, someone he had destroyed in court, just playing with him, waiting to release it to the gutter press the moment his advancement was announced? The first he could put up with. And he would pay, unquestionably—provided he could think of some method to be sure he got the negative and all prints back; easier said than done, but it ought not to be beyond his wit. He just wished the demand would come tomorrow, so he knew where he was. But it was entirely out of his hands. And thinking about it at this time would serve absolutely no purpose.

With the strength of will and concentration which made him such a formidable lawyer, he thrust all thought of it from his mind, got out the Hargraves papers and commenced writing in a quick, neat hand. Every few seconds his eyelid twitched irritatingly, but Timothy ignored it.

Chapter Six

"Now the one who I think's really going to miss me is Stella," Florrie said.

"Oh, I'm sure she will. I do like Stella. And she's so smart and sophisticated."

"I suppose working as a fashion journalist in New York for ten years does that for you."

"I do enjoy her stories."

"Yes, she's a wonderfully entertaining girl. I love her sense of humour. I'm sorry her magazine went broke, of course, but I am glad it brought her home."

"But she seems to be doing just as well with this London magazine."

"Don't suppose she earns as much, though. She's a very ambitious girl, and I wouldn't be surprised if she moved on fairly soon. Ah well, we'll see. Or at least you will."

"She's the granddaughter of Margaret, your husband's younger sister, is that right?"

"I sometimes think you know my family better than I do. Yes. Margaret was pretty cool at first, but she came round in the end. We became quite good friends. And it's nice that her grandson keeps in touch, as well as her granddaughter."

"Stella and Tommy are first cousins, aren't they?"

"Yes. I'm fond of Tommy—even though he's not the brainiest lad you could hope to find."

"He's so charming, though. And funny. He really makes me smile with all those tales of his pranks."

"Bit too funny and charming sometimes, perhaps, but his heart's in the right place."

"He's such a good listener, too. He always seems really eager to hear the little stories I am able to tell him about communications with the Other Side."

Florrie strongly suspected that Jean's little stories were secretly a source of great amusement to Tommy. But she said nothing.

The richly carpeted and gracefully appointed car showroom had the hush of a great cathedral. Here and there among the multi-coloured and glistening graven images, elegant and expensively attired young men, the priests of this secular religion, conversed in low and earnest tones with equally well-dressed but clearly timid acolytes. Occasionally a single word or phrase wafted, like a mantra, above the low hum: "torque," "compression," "power-to-weight ratio."

Tommy Lambert, an exceedingly tall and slim young man of twenty-three, with a pink complexion and a mop of unruly sandy-coloured hair, stood gazing out through the plate glass window at the sunlit bustle of London's Park Lane, his normally amiable expression replaced at this moment by one of profound gloom. No eager enquirers after truth had approached him that morning, perhaps sensing that he was as much a noviciate as they themselves. And no enquirers, to be promptly converted into cash-paying customers, meant no commission this week. And no commission meant no—what? Champagne cocktails? Tickets to the new Rodgers and Hart musical for himself and Ginny or Susie or Joanie? No afternoon at Epsom on Saturday? He could put up with that, though, if it wasn't for the other business. The day suddenly darkened as he thought of it again. What the deuce was he going to do? For the moment Benny seemed reasonably content with ten shillings a week. But that was just interest. It could only be a matter of weeks at the most before he demanded payment in full. And when he didn't get it he'd probably turn very nasty. Confound the fellow who'd given him that "sure-fire" tip. Nothing seemed to have gone right since.

"Hello, Tommy," said a soft and slightly breathless voice behind him.

Tommy spun round and his face lightened. "Penny, old bean, what a surprise!"

The girl standing there was a few years younger than himself. She had bobbed, platinum blond hair, done in lots of tight curls, and enormous pale blue eyes, set wide apart. She was wearing a cream cotton suit with peak lapels and patch pockets, and perched slightly to the side of her head was a light green Tyrolean hat, decorated with a pheasant tail. She looked extremely fashionable and very pretty. She was smiling rather tentatively at him.

"How are you, Tommy?"

"Oh, spiffing, really, you know."

"I saw you through the window. You were looking a bit in the dumps."

"Was I? Well, suppose I am, really."

"Oh?" She stared at him sympathetically. "Something wrong?"

"Nothing more than usual. It's just that I think that Lagonda might be exactly the car you're looking for, madam. Let me show it to you." He ushered her towards a scarlet two-seater Tourer.

Penelope Saunders looked somewhat bewildered. "I'm sorry, Tommy, I didn't really come in to buy a car."

"I know, but the Lord High Sales Manager was approaching. Got to pretend you're a customer." He stopped by the Lagonda. "Look at the car, not me."

"Oh, right. I thought I'd just pop in and see how you were getting on at the new job. Sort of cousinly interest."

"Jolly decent of you. That is the trouble, really. I'm not much good at it. I've only sold three cars in four weeks."

"Is that bad?"

"Well, they don't expect you to be a super salesman in a month, but I am starting to get some rather old-fashioned looks."

"Oh, I am sorry. I was hoping this time you might have found something that really suited you. I mean, you've always been keen on cars, haven't you?"

"Keen on driving them, not selling them."

Penny was staring intently at the sleek lines of the Lagonda. "It is awfully pretty, isn't it? I wish I *could* buy it."

"It's not all that expensive," Tommy said hopefully.

"It is for me. Daddy keeps me most horribly hard up. My allowance is positively laughable. Only I don't laugh. You'd think he'd want me to have a good time. But no. And it's always 'don't do this, don't do that.' He doesn't like me smoking in public. He won't even let me paint my toenails. And he thinks night clubs are dens of iniquity. He's like one of those Victorian fathers you read about."

"Well, I suppose he is, really, isn't he? Victorian, I mean. How old is he?"

"Forty-six."

"Well, there you are. He was born in the nineteenth century, so he *is* Victorian."

"But he doesn't have to behave like it. It's the nineteen thirties now."

Tommy said: "Get in the car—look as though you're really interested."

He opened the driver's door and Penny got in. Tommy went round to the far side, gathering up a couple of brochures from a nearby stand on the way, and sat in the passenger seat. "I'll pretend to be going through all this technical stuff with you."

"It's really comfy," Penny said, leaning back in the seat. "You'd think he'd let me have a car, wouldn't you? I mean, just because I gave his Daimler the teeny-weeniest dent the only time he let me drive it, he uses that as an excuse—says he's frightened I'd have an accident. It's the money, really, I'm sure."

"He must have oodles, too."

"He's absolutely rolling. And it's not as though he's got anyone—or anything—else to spend it on."

"So, what's he do with it?"

"Just invests it. I think he gives a lot to good causes, as well."

"Well, I'm a good cause. Wouldn't slip a few quid to me, would he? I've got all sorts of ripping ideas, that just need a bit of capital."

"There's not a chance of that, darling."

"He doesn't like me, does he?"

Penny wriggled awkwardly. "It's not that he doesn't like you. But he doesn't really approve of you. Thinks you should have trained for some proper profession."

"It's all very well for brainy geezers like him. Can you see me as a lawyer or doctor or architect or something?"

Penny tried for a moment and failed.

"I think I'll turn to crime," Tommy said gloomily.

"Don't be silly."

"I'm not being silly. I've seriously thought about it. Oh, not anything that would hurt anybody, but where would be the harm in pinching something from somebody who'd never miss it? Just to put me on my feet."

"You mustn't say things like that. *I* know you're joking, but other people wouldn't—people who don't know how you're always kidding and playing pranks and practical jokes. That's something else which puts Daddy off you."

"That's just fun! They never harm anyone."

"I know that. I think some of them are screamingly funny. But Daddy's got no sense of humour at all."

"I say, I brought off an absolutely terrific wheeze a couple of weeks ago. This old chum of mine was working for a company owned by an absolute bounder. Name of Hodge. Frightfully rich, and he and his wife are the most appalling snobs. Anyway, he had an application for a job from the son of some marquis or other, old Etonian, and all that, but totally useless. Old Hodge-podge, though, couldn't resist having a gen-you-ine aristocrat on his staff, so to make room for him, he sacked my pal. No excuse, no apology, just a month's salary and out on his ear."

"How rotten."

"As you can imagine, he was pretty browned off and wanted to get his own back. He asked me if I had any ideas. So I put the jolly old brain-box to work and made a few enquiries. These people have got a big place in Sussex, swimming pool, acres of grounds. And it's on a main road to the coast. I found out they were planning a big garden party for the next Saturday—lavish open-air buffet, marquee, and so on. Asking all the toffs of the county. So I went to a sign writer and got a lot of big placards done. The Saturday was a super day and my pal and I drove down. We got there just before the party started and we stuck these placards up about every fifty yards at the side of the road for the quarter of a mile leading to the house. They had things on them like 'Open Day,' 'No Charge,' 'Everybody Welcome,' 'Free Refreshments,' 'Beautiful Gardens,' 'Swimming Pool,' 'Bring the Kiddies.' And the ones nearest the house had big arrows, pointing through the gates. Then we beat it, pronto."

"What happened?" Penny asked, wide-eyed.

"I found out all about it later, from a johnnie who was at the party. As you can imagine, on a beautiful Saturday, the roads were jam-packed with people on their way for an afternoon at the seaside, and within minutes cars started to roll in. The Hodges didn't realise what was happening at first, thought they were invited guests. The climax was when a charabanc, with about forty people on board, arrived. They twigged then, but it was too late. There were already about twenty cars parked on the drive, people were helping themselves to grub and drinks from the buffet, kids were trampling all over the flower beds, changing into their bathing costumes in their cars and jumping in the swimming pool. Some people actually went in the house and started poking round all over the place, using the bathrooms, what have you. The butler was trying to get rid of them, which led to a lot of nasty arguments. And the most topping thing of all was that one of the real guests was an eccentric old baronet, who always dresses in the most disreputable togs and hardly ever shaves or has his hair cut. The butler thought he was one of the gate-crashers and forcibly ejected him. By which time, most of the toffs were pretty fed up, and started to leave, *en masse*. Hodge was running round in circles, trying to get *them* to stay and the intruders to leave, all at the same time. Mrs. Hodge was having hysterics in her boudoir. I'm delighted to say that their great day was totally ruined. And serve them bally well right."

Penny gave a sigh. "Oh, Tommy, you're so clever! To think of that!"

Tommy endeavoured unsuccessfully to look modest. "I do seem to have a flair for that sort of thing." Then he became gloomy again. "Good to have a flair for something, I suppose. Certainly haven't got one for selling cars."

"What would you like to do?"

"Dunno, really. Used to think I'd like to be a reporter. Must be terrific fun, going round interviewing film stars and racing drivers. I'm not much of a writer, but that doesn't really matter: you just put down what they say. It was Stella getting her first job in that line that put the idea into my head. Incidentally, I hear she's back."

"Stella who? Back from where?"

"Stella Simmons. Cousin Stella. Home from the US of A. A pal of mine ran into her. Seems she's working for some fashion mag, but I don't know which one and her number's not in the phone book, so I haven't been able to get in touch with her. I thought she might have given me a call, actually. I used to have quite a crush on her, when I was about thirteen."

Penny gave an almost inaudible sniff. "Really?"

"And she was jolly nice to me."

"Really?" said Penny again. The temperature in the Lagonda had dropped a degree or two.

"Girls of that age haven't usually got much time for young lads."

Penny frowned. "What do you mean: 'that age'?"

"Well, she must have been twenty-three or more then."

"Oh." Penny's face cleared. "Then she's quite old?"

"Mm, that was ten or eleven years ago."

"I see." The atmosphere was suddenly warmer again. "She sounds very nice," Penny said condescendingly.

"You never met her, then?"

"I've never even heard of her. And I don't understand. If she's your cousin and I'm your cousin, she must be my cousin, too, mustn't she?"

"You're not my cousin."

"Don't be silly, Tommy, of course I am."

"Not my full cousin—first cousin, nor even second. We're different generations."

Penny looked quite blank. "How do you mean?"

"Well, let me see. Your grandfather and my father were first cousins. So I'm second cousin to your father. I think that makes you my second cousin once removed."

"Removed where?"

"That's just what they call it. Means a generation younger."

"I'm nothing like a generation younger than you, only three or four years."

"That's got nothing to do with it. But if we were looking at the family tree, you'd be one level lower down."

Penny was looking totally bewildered. "I don't know anything about the family, really. Daddy never talks about them. So where does this Stella girl come in?"

"Ah, well, my father and her mother were brother and sister. So she *is* my first cousin. And you're her second cousin once removed, too, as well as mine. Aren't you a lucky girl?"

"Mummy had some first cousins. I used to call them Auntie or Uncle."

"Oh, that's just an old convention. You needn't call me Uncle."

"I wasn't going to," Penny said blankly.

"We'd better get out. Can't sit here all day."

"Tommy, you were joking, weren't you? About taking up crime."

"What? Oh yes, of course. You know me. Here, take these." He handed her the brochures. "I'll give you my card. Look at it, say loudly: 'Thank you, Mr. Lambert. I'm very interested in the car. I'll come back and see you when I've had a few days to think about it.'"

"Say that again."

Tommy did so, and Penny carefully repeated the words under her breath.

He got out, hurried round the car, opened the driver's door for her and with a flourish handed her his business card. "Please don't hesitate to contact me, if you have any further questions, madam."

Penny concentrated furiously. "Thank you, Mr. Carr," she said in a loud voice. "I'm very interested in you. I want to think about you for a few days and see you again."

Chapter Seven

"I suppose Clara will let the girls come," Florrie said.

"Surely she will! And come herself, I should hope."

"Hypocrite if she does. But be criticised if she doesn't, I suppose. Unless she could claim pressure of work."

"Work? What do you mean, dear?"

"I told you what Agatha told me about Clara's nasty little money-making scheme. I put in a guarded reference to it when I made those little changes to my will last month. Anyway, Agatha should be here again any day now. I must find out if it's still going on."

Clara reached forward and took the rough-skinned hand of the plump young girl, who was sitting on the edge of the hard upright chair in the coldly furnished and immaculately tidy drawing-room, an expression of acute doubt on her pale, unattractive face. Clara's claw-like fingers tightened in what was meant to be a reassuring, clasp, but which only made the girl wince slightly. Clara hastily let go.

"Now, Martha," she said gently. "I know you're a good, loyal girl. But when you learn of some terrible deceit, you do have a duty to make sure the truth comes out. It's not right that your master should deceive your mistress in this way. Don't you think she should know about it?"

Martha nodded.

"Then can you tell her yourself?"

"Oh no, madam, I couldn't."

"But she'll never find out unless somebody tells her. You tell me and I'll make sure she learns just what's been going on."

Martha twisted her hands together. "I don't know, I'm sure."

"You came to me, remember, my dear, not the other way round. All you've told me so far is that your employer is deceiving his wife with another woman, but you haven't even told me his name. Why did you come, by the way? We've never met before, have we?"

"It was Lily suggested it, madam, Lily Watson. She was in service with Dr. and Mrs. Forbes-King."

"Ah yes, of course. And in that case, it was the mistress who was carrying on."

"That's right, madam, and Lily said that after she told you about it, it all came out. They're divorced now, of course, and Lily had to look for another position, but she said that wasn't your fault."

"Of course it wasn't. How can it ever be wrong to tell the truth? Now, I can see you're an honourable girl and you hate carryings-on. They go against everything your mother ever taught you, don't they?"

"Yes, madam."

"And she was a good woman, wasn't she?"

"Oh yes, madam. She still is. She's still alive."

"I'm so glad. The world can ill afford to lose women like your mother. Now I'm sure you want to be a credit to her—speak up fearlessly and uncover all this lying and deceit."

"Oh yes, madam, but…" Martha ran her tongue round her lips. "Lily did say as how you made it worth her while, like."

"But of course. Virtue should always be rewarded."

She opened her clasped left hand to reveal the crisp £5 which was folded in her palm. She made it crackle temptingly. "Well." Martha took a deep breath. "The master is Mr. Terence Leigh."

Clara's eyebrows shot upwards. "The novelist?"

"Yes, madam."

"Really? Right, now tell me exactly what happened."

"Well, it was Wednesday last week. That's me usual half-day—the mistress changed it this week. Anyway, the mistress had gone to visit her parents and wasn't expected back until late and the master was going to be working in his study. Now, he'd said he'd go out for a meal in the evening and told cook she could have the afternoon off, as well, which was very unusual. She went out about one. I went out about quarter past, and I noticed this big red and white American car parked a little down the road, with a lady sat in it. I didn't think nothing of it, really. I 'adn't gone very far when I found I'd left me purse behind, and I 'ad to go back. The car was still there, but the lady weren't in it. Well, I went in through the servants' door at the back and started up to me room. But when I was passing the main bedroom I heard voices coming from it."

By now Clara's long, narrow nose seemed to be almost visibly quivering. "What voices?"

"One was definitely the master, and the other a lady."

"Could you hear what they were saying?"

"Just a few words. I heard the lady laughing, and then she gave a sort of little scream. And I heard her say: 'Terry, you're a wicked man, you know that?' And the master, he said: 'And you're absolutely wonderful, Marigold.'"

"Marigold? Had you ever heard a mention of that name?"

"No, madam. And nobody ever calls the master Terry."

"Go on."

"Well, I would have liked to have seen who the lady was, if she was the one in the car, but they might be in there some time, and when they did come out, it wouldn't be likely I'd see her face, 'cos I'd have to keep out of sight myself, and anyway, it was me afternoon off, and I knew my friend would be waiting for me, so I just went on up, got me purse and scarpered. The car were gone, though, when I got back that night."

"What did the lady in the car look like?"

"Real glamorous. Very blond hair, lots of make-up."

Clara nodded to herself. "Yes, it could be…" She fell silent for a few moments, then stood up. "Well, thank you, Martha. You did quite right in coming to me." The £5 note rapidly changed hands. "Now, if at any time you have any further information, about this or any other matter, you know where to find me. And please pass the word among your friends." She ushered the girl into the hall, opened the front door and practically shooed her out. Then she returned to the drawing-room.

What was the name of that girl in the new review? Marigold Green—that was it. She was blond. Clara grabbed up a copy of the *Evening News* and turned to the theatre page. Yes, *Keep Smiling* at the Star Theatre. Curtain up at eight. It was just ten past seven, so Marigold Green ought to be there now. It was worth a try.

She went into the hall, picked up the directory, found the Star Theatre's number and picked up the telephone receiver. As she did so the kitchen door opened and Dorothy came along the hall. Clara looked up irritably. "Oh, go away, Dorothy. I told you I did not want to be disturbed."

Dorothy gave a nervous jump, like a frightened filly. "I'm sorry, Mother. I heard the girl go, so I thought—"

"Don't think so much. Just do as you're told. Go and do the ironing."

"I've finished it."

"Well, start getting the meal ready."

"The joint is in the oven."

"Are the potatoes done?"

"No, not yet."

"Well, go and do them."

"Very well, Mother."

She started back to the kitchen. "And scrape them, don't peel," Clara called after her, and lifted the telephone receiver.

"Star stage door," a rough Cockney voice answered, when she got through.

Clara adopted a gruff tone. "Marigold Green, please."

"Who wants her?"

"Terry."

"Hang on."

For a minute or so Clara heard distant snatches of conversation, footsteps and various bumps and bangs. Then a female voice, slightly breathless, came on the line. "Terry, darling, you're not supposed to call me here."

Clara rang off.

Her thin lips formed into a smile. That settled it. If only it could always be so easy. She put through another call. It was answered quickly.

"*News of the Week.*"

"Saucy Snippets column, please."

A male voice spoke next. "Saucy Snippets."

"This is C. S."

"Ah, dear lady, how nice to hear from you. It's been some time." He had an exaggerated, plainly bogus upper-class accent.

"I have something for you."

"Splendid."

"One of the country's leading writers—married—is having an affair with a well-known young review artiste."

"Excellent. What would we do without these people? Let me have the names."

"Just a moment. How much?"

"Usual. Thirty."

"No, I want forty. He's a very big name indeed. I can tell you exactly when and where they last met and what his wife was doing at the time."

"Oo, I'm not sure about that."

"I can easily go somewhere else. I came to you first."

There was a pause before he said: "Well, OK—provided he is as big as you say."

Clara hesitated for a moment, remembering that awful phone call she had received. Suppose… But forty pounds was forty pounds. "Terence Leigh," she said.

There was a whistle.

"Big enough for you?"

"All right, it's a deal. Let's have the rest."

"The girl is Marigold Green, who's in *Keep Smiling* at the Star." She gave a summary of what Martha had told her.

"Is this one hundred per cent reliable?"

"Absolutely. If you want to confirm it yourself, find out what sort of car Marigold Green drives. I guarantee it's a big red and white American one. It was seen parked outside his house on Wednesday afternoon, by someone who couldn't possibly have known Marigold Green's car."

"Sounds good. OK, if that checks out, I don't see any problems. You'll be paid within a few days."

Clara rang off.

"And that's just about all my family" said Florrie. "All the ones who matter, anyway." She looked suddenly wistful. "I do wish I could be there for the funeral. And for the reading of the will. There are going to be some surprises when it's read. I'd love to see the reactions." She seemed to brighten. "Perhaps I will. Perhaps, after all, I will come back, just to see my funeral and what happens after. And it wouldn't be because one of your mediums tries to conjure me, or whatever you call it. But because I choose to. I might even be able to cause a bit of a rumpus."

Chapter Eight

The public hall was dingy, dusty and ill-lit. Nevertheless, the hundred or so seats were each occupied. The atmosphere was intense and all eyes were fixed on the man standing on a dais at the front. On the face of Jean Mackenzie, sitting in the third row, was an expression close to awe. Mr. Hawthorne really was wonderful.

There was nothing in the appearance of the speaker to account for the effect he was having. He was insignificant-looking, with a receding chin and a few sparse hairs carefully spread across his scalp, and was wearing an ill-fitting suit. When he spoke it was with a pronounced London suburban accent. He was standing now with his eyes closed, making small clutching movements in the air with his hands.

"Now, I have a spirit here who wants to pass a message to a lady whose first name begins with—with, er, J. Jane? Joan?"

There was no response.

"Or perhaps Jean. Is there a Jean in the audience?"

Miss Mackenzie's heart missed a beat. She timidly raised her hand. "My name is Jean."

"The spirit is a woman who passed over at the age of about forty. Does that mean anything to you?"

"It could be my sister. She was forty-eight. Her name was Marion."

"Marion, yes. I'm definitely getting the name Marion. Marion sends her love to you, Jean, and she has an important message for you. She says that you're going to be given a great opportunity. A chance that is vouchsafed to few. You must seize the moment when it comes. Be resolute. Do not be afraid."

"I'm sorry, I don't understand. What sort of opportunity?"

"I cannot say. You will know when the time comes."

"When will this be?"

"Soon. Very soon."

"Will it be to do with the Message? The Work?"

"I'm sorry, the Spirit is fading. There is no more. Another appears. A man. He wishes to pass on a message to his daughter. Her name I think begins with S."

But for once Jean Mackenzie was not listening. A message actually for her. It was thrilling. But what did Marion mean? "A great opportunity." It could mean so many things. And "do not be afraid." Afraid of what? It sounded rather frightening. She was not at all resolute, as Marion had very well known. It, whatever "it" was, was going to be soon. How soon? Tomorrow? Next week? Next month?

Oh, dear, it was worrying. She almost wished Marion hadn't send her a message. But no, she shouldn't think that. She had been greatly privileged. So many others in the hall would be envying her. During the tea and biscuits afterwards she would be a centre of attention. A very unusual occurrence. She could at least make the most of that, while it lasted, before getting back to Florrie. With only Mrs. Thomas, the housekeeper, for company, she would be getting bored and ready for a long chat. Probably about her funeral and her will again—

Then it suddenly hit Jean. Oh no. Surely Marion couldn't have meant that. Surely not.

Chapter Nine

Dorothy Saunders was engaged in her perennial task of scraping potatoes, when she heard the front door open and close. She hurried out to the hall. The young woman who had entered was tall and sturdily built and had a brown, weather-beaten face and untidy, short-cropped hair. She was wearing a fur-lined leather jacket and jodhpurs and carrying a motor-cycling helmet and goggles. She saw Dorothy and mouthed the words: "Where is she?"

Dorothy pointed towards the drawing-room, then went back to the kitchen. The other followed her in and closed the door.

"Did you see Grandmamma, Aggie?" Dorothy asked, with as much eagerness as she ever showed about anything.

Agatha Saunders nodded. "Yes, she seemed jolly bucked to see me, too."

"How is she?"

"Well, frail, of course, but still got all her wits about her. She sent her love. And Mackenzie sent her regards."

"Did Grandmamma like the chocolates?"

"Yes, she said they were her favourites. She was sorry she didn't have anything in return, but she said that both you and I can look forward to receiving something from her in the not too distant future." She hoisted herself onto the table and lit a cigarette.

Dorothy frowned. "What did she mean?" She started scraping potatoes again.

"That we're remembered in her will, I think."

"Oh, we are, then. That's nice. Though I hope it's not for years yet, of course. I wonder how much."

"Well, I shouldn't expect too much, petal. I doubt if she's all that well off. Anyway, it might be just things: ornaments, jewellery, paintings, stuff like that."

"All the same, it's nice that she doesn't hold it against us that we didn't see her for all those years."

"Well, I blame myself that I didn't think to go and see her long before ever Mother suddenly got it into her head that we should all go. I told Grandmamma that. She understood. 'It's water under the bridge,' she said. Anyway, I've kept in touch pretty regularly since then."

"I haven't, though. Oh, Aggie, you're so lucky just to be able to jump on your motor-cycle and go all that way, whenever you feel like it."

"I'll take you one day, I promise."

"Did Grandmamma tell you anything more about Mummy and Daddy?"

"A bit, including a few things about Daddy when he was a boy. I'll tell you all about it later."

"Oh, lovely. I'll come to your room tonight, when Mother's asleep."

"What's she been doing today?"

"Well, there's been another girl here."

Agatha gave a groan. "Somebody's maid?"

"Looked like it."

"Another little fool throwing her job away for a few quid, I suppose. That's two this week!" She banged on the table with her fist. "It's not right, Dorry! How would she like it if her secrets were being offered for sale to the highest bidder?"

"She hasn't got any secrets."

"She must have. Everybody has. You know that. She's never talked about her family. I've often thought there must be something there she's ashamed of."

"Well, if there is, nobody knows it but her."

"She couldn't be absolutely sure of that, though, could she?"

"What do you mean?"

"It ought to be possible to hint that one knew something. She just might give something away. Be fun to try, at least."

"Oh, Aggie, don't cause any unpleasantness."

"There's enough unpleasantness around as it is; a little more won't make any difference."

She got down off the table and moved toward the door. "I think I'll make a start now."

"She may not have finished."

"Too bad."

"Aggie, the cigarette!"

"Oh." Agatha turned, expertly flicked the stub into the sink and went out.

Clara was writing busily when Agatha entered the room. She looked up crossly, then said: "Oh, it's you. Where have you been?"

"Just riding."

"You'll be getting yourself killed one of these days, careering round on that machine."

"Which will solve a few problems for you, won't it, Stepmother?"

"Why do you call me that?" Clara asked sharply.

"I've decided to call you that in future. Because that's what you are. Dorry can call you Mother. I'll call you Mother in company. But my real mother is dead and I don't want ever to forget that."

"I've been more of a mother to you than she ever was."

"Only because she died," Agatha shouted in a sudden temper.

"Keep your voice down!"

"Sorry." Agatha looked abashed, but only for a second. "I hear you've had another little visitor."

"Er, yes. I did not invite her. She just showed up."

"Seeking your advice, I suppose?"

"In a way."

"And you told her just to dish the dirt to Auntie Clara and everything would be all right."

"What a horrible expression!"

"Accurate, though. And which of your seedy journalistic friends did you peddle it to this time?"

"They are not my friends. Just people I do business with."

"Some business. Breaking up marriages, ruining people's reputations, humiliating others, losing silly little maidservants their jobs."

"I have never revealed a source. People sometimes guess who's been talking about their affairs, and they dismiss them. But if these servants are too stupid to foresee that possibility, it's not my fault. I only ever report the truth."

"And that makes everything all right?"

"I have to supplement my income some way. Your father did not leave—"

"Don't blame Daddy for this. He'd turn in his grave if he knew what you were doing."

"He did not leave us well off, Agatha."

"That's what you always say. But you'll never tell us how much he actually left. And because there was no will ever found, we can't check up."

"That is a private matter. But I assure you, financially it's been a very hard struggle."

"Well, if you'd allowed Dorry and me to get jobs it wouldn't have been so hard. We could both have trained for something properly if you hadn't put your foot down. Just because you wanted a couple of unpaid housemaids."

Clara sneered. "And just what would you have trained for, my girl? Nursery governess?"

"Women are doing all sorts of jobs these days they've never done before—lawyers, doctors, even. I don't say I could have done that, but at least I could have gone to secretarial college and become a shorthand-typist."

"People of our class do not become shorthand-typists."

"Our class? What do you mean *our* class? Dorry and I are the great granddaughters of an Earl. What was your great grandfather? You always keep very quiet about that. And that's not the only thing you keep quiet about, is it?"

"What do you mean?" The question came just a bit too quickly.

"I think you know quite well what I mean."

"I have absolutely no idea."

"I see. Well, then, let's just leave it at that, shall we? For the moment."

"You're a spiteful, ungrateful girl. Well, if you so despise me, you can leave any time you like."

"You know I can't do that. I'm thirty-three and I've never had a job. Who'd employ me? Besides, this house was bought by my mother and father. I was born here. Why should I have to leave?"

"You don't have to. You're welcome to live here as long as you like. But while you do, I expect proper respect. Why can't you be more like your sister? Whatever her failings, she is always polite and obedient."

"Because she's scared to death of you, that's why."

"Nonsense."

At that moment Dorothy put her head round the door. Clara rounded on her. "Is the meal ready?"

"Not quite, but—"

"Don't come in here again until it is! Now go and finish."

"Yes, Mother." And Dorothy's head disappeared.

"I'll come and help, Dorry," Agatha called. She walked to the door. Just inside it she turned and made a clumsy curtsy before going out.

A hit, a palpable hit, she thought with satisfaction.

Chapter Ten

It was a few days after Gerry's return, and she and her parents were at breakfast when Merryweather, Alderley's august and imperturbable butler, entered the room, bearing a silver salver. He crossed to the Earl. "A telegram, my lord," he murmured.

"Ah." Lord Burford swallowed a mouthful of bacon, laid down his knife and fork, tore open the envelope and read the enclosed message. "Oh, dear," he said. "Oh, dear, dear."

"What's the matter, George?" asked the Countess.

"Great Aunt Florrie's dead."

"No? Oh, I *am* sorry. When?"

The Earl read from the telegram. "'Deeply regret inform you the Hon. Mrs. Florence Saunders passed away peacefully in her sleep during night.' Signed Mackenzie."

"Miss Mackenzie will be terribly upset. She must have been with her for about twenty years."

"At least that, Lavinia. Glad now we went to see her, back in the spring. And had 'em both to stay for a couple of weeks a few years ago. Probably the last time Florrie went away anywhere. I think Miss Mackenzie enjoyed it even more." He looked at Gerry. "And you said you went out to see her quite recently?"

"Yes, a couple of weeks ago. Florrie was very chirpy. Said she hoped she lived long enough to come to my wedding. Sad she didn't. You know, she was talking about her childhood in the East End. It suddenly hit me that at the period she was talking about, Dickens was writing about people like that. She might actually have met him! It made me realise just how old she was. Did you know her father drove a Hansom cab?"

"Oh yes."

"How did Bertie's parents react to him marrying her?"

"Well, I don't think they were actually overjoyed, but mainly because she'd been on the Halls, which was considered highly disreputable. But Bertie's elder brother, Aylwin, my grandfather, took their side, and did all he could to get her accepted in society. And as he was the heir to the title, that carried a lot of weight. Plus, of course, she apparently transformed herself remarkably quickly."

The Countess said: "When I first met her, it was quite impossible to tell she hadn't been born into the aristocracy."

"But probably the most important factor in her being accepted was that it was impossible not to like her," said the Earl.

"I thought she was terrific," Gerry said. "I'm really sorry she's gone. Still, she had a wonderful life, lived to be nearly a hundred and died peacefully in her sleep. What more could anyone want?"

"Not altogether wonderful," said Lord Burford. "Lost her husband, which was only to be expected; he was several years older than her. But to outlive your only son must be awful. And then John's first wife, Emma, died, too, and for years after that, she hardly ever saw her granddaughters, thanks to their stepmother."

"You mean Clara cut them off from her entirely?"

"Yes. I think she was determined to keep them completely under her thumb and didn't want anybody else to have influence over them. Wasn't that it, Lavinia?"

"I'm sure it was. She loves to control people. Even when the girls had reached their teens and we invited them here in the summer once or twice Clara made it virtually impossible for us not to include her—instead of just enjoying the break and going off for a holiday on her own."

There was a pause, which Merryweather, who was still standing impassively by, was quick to utilise. "Will there be a reply, my lord?"

"Oh. Yes, suppose so. Let me see. Say 'Very sorry to hear sad news.' No, that sounds as though somebody's cat has died, or something. 'Deeply saddened by tragic occurrence.' No, dammit, that's what you'd say about a shipwreck. Oh, you decide, Merryweather, you're so good with words."

"Thank you, my lord. I will endeavour to compose a suitable missive." Merryweather glided from the room.

As the door closed behind him, Lady Burford said: "Really, George, you leave too much to Merryweather these days. Surely you can compose your own telegrams."

"He enjoys doin' things like that, so why not let him?"

"An excellent excuse for mental laziness."

Gerry said hurriedly: "So I've met Agatha and Dorothy, have I?"

"When you were little," the Countess said, "but they were eight or ten years older than you, so you wouldn't have had a lot to do with them."

"I seem to remember the stepmother. A bony sort of person. Long, pointed nose. Rather like a witch. But very gushing."

Lord Burford chuckled. "Yes, that's Clara, to a tee: a gushing witch."

"You've got to hand it to her in a way, though, haven't you?" Gerry said. "I mean, you marry a widower with two kiddies, and then he kicks the bucket and you're left to bring them up on your own. It's quite a responsibility."

"They were very polite, well-behaved children," said the Countess. "I will at least say that for Clara. Though I believe it was achieved more by fear than kindness. I'm quite certain they were afraid of her."

"Is that why you dislike her so? I mean, it can't be just the long nose and the gushing manner."

"I did not say I dislike her."

"Oh, Mummy, it's as clear as daylight."

Lady Burford hesitated, before saying reluctantly: "Well, there are certain things. Things she's done."

"What things?"

"Things that I—we—people think, well, dishonourable."

Gerry's eyes were round. "Crikey, this is fascinating. Spill the beans."

The Countess hesitated. Lord Burford drained his coffee cup. "We might as well tell her, Lavinia. Fact is, Clara has a big circle of friends, or at least acquaintances. People she's cultivated. She can be very winning, when she remembers not to overdo it. She's a very good listener, and she's got a highly sympathetic manner. She gets people to tell her things. Things they wouldn't want known. And then she uses the information for her own ends—financial ends."

"You don't mean blackmail?" Gerry said incredulously.

"No, no, no. At least, I don't think so. No, she sells it to the papers: the gossip columnists and the gutter press. Must have made quite a useful additional income, over the years."

"Oh, is that all?" Gerry sounded quite disappointed. "Well, I think that's rather enterprising of her."

Her mother looked aghast. "I hope you don't mean that, Geraldine."

"Well, if a person's going to be so stupid as talk about their affairs to anybody they don't know they can trust, they've got only themselves to blame if it gets out. Of course, if it's something she's actually been told in confidence, I agree that is not quite-quite. But you don't know she's done that, do you?"

"Well, one thing I do know she's done is bribe servants for information about their employers."

"Really? Mm, that I agree is going too far." She gave a start. "Golly, you don't mean—surely she didn't try to bribe Merry, did she?"

The nickname was one only ever used by Gerry, and went back to when, as a very little girl, she had been unable to pronounce "Merryweather." During one stage she had driven everyone nearly to distraction by wandering round the house chanting "Merry'n'Gerry, Merry'n'Gerry" over and over again.

"I don't think even Clara would have had the nerve to try that," said the Earl dryly.

"Would be lovely to see his reaction, though. Did Florrie know about what Clara was doing?"

"I'm pretty sure she did, aren't you, Lavinia?"

"Yes. From Agatha, I imagine. She didn't refer to it precisely, but she did mention something about Clara's 'activities' in a very grim voice the last time we were there."

"I suppose the girls will do pretty well from Florrie's will, won't they?"

"I doubt Florrie'll leave much," said the Earl. "Great Uncle Bertie was never very practical and I remember being told made some pretty unwise investments. Florrie's had to live quite modestly. I mean, she only kept about three servants. There's the house, of course. Good area, but it's not all that big and a bit dilapidated. I'm not sure, though, that Clara would be too happy if the girls came into a lot of money. She still likes to keep 'em under her thumb, Dorothy especially, who didn't used to be much more than Clara's dogsbody. 'Course, we haven't had anything to do with them for years."

"I doubt if things have changed," said the Countess.

"Well, no doubt we'll see them at the funeral and maybe get some idea then."

Late that afternoon the Earl was going over some accounts in his study when the telephone rang. He lifted the receiver.

"Burford."

"Ah, my lord, I'm so glad to have caught you," said a deep and somewhat fruity voice. "My name is Bradley, Charles Bradley. I am the late Mrs. Florence Saunders' solicitor and executor."

"Indeed? How d'you do? And what can I do for you, Mr. Bradley?"

"Firstly, I want to inform you that I have been told by Miss Mackenzie, Mrs. Saunders' companion, that shortly before her death my client expressed a wish to be buried in the family plot at Alderley parish church."

"Really? That's surprisin'. Always thought of her as very much a townee. Never showed much interest in Alderley, that I can recall. It's not as though her husband's buried here; he was cremated, I seem to remember."

"Yes, indeed, and I suppose he not having a grave elsewhere made her feel that somehow she would be closer to him there. You have no objection, I trust?"

"Good gad, no. She has a perfect right to be buried here. And at least it'll save me and my family a trip to town."

"Of course, though it will not be so convenient for the other mourners. However, I understand there are frequent trains to Alderley Halt."

"Yes, and they stop here if requested. That's an old right we have, going back to the days when the first railway company got permission to run the line through our land. And the church is only a hundred yards or two from the station. D'you expect many to come?"

"Impossible to say at this stage, but I should imagine a fair number. Although most of her contemporaries have passed on, she was held in high esteem. I imagine, however, that they will be mostly personal friends and relations, and it may perhaps be possible, at some later date, to arrange a memorial service in London, which members of Society and representatives of the various organisations and charitable institutions that she and her late husband, and indeed your family generally, have been associated with, might attend in order to pay their respects."

Managing, with some difficulty, to hack his way through the dense undergrowth of this sentence, Lord Burford nodded absently, then, remembering that Bradley could not see him, said hastily: "Yes, yes indeed."

"There is one other thing, my lord. I have to inform you that you, Lady Burford and Lady Geraldine are beneficiaries under Mrs. Saunders' will."

"Oh, that was kind of her."

"Now I have a great favour to ask you. To the best of my knowledge, the other major beneficiaries—nine in total—will be attending the funeral, and as it might present some difficulties for them all to be gathered at the same place at any other time, I am wondering if it would be convenient, after the funeral, for the reading of the will to be held, er—" Bradley hesitated.

The Earl came to his rescue. "To be held here, you mean, at Alderley?"

"Precisely, my lord. I realise it is a great imposition."

"Not at all. I see no problem."

"That is a great relief to me, my lord. I do appreciate it."

"Not at all. Glad to help. Nine other beneficiaries, you say? Possible to know who they are?"

"Of course. I have a list here, somewhere. Bear with me for a moment, if you please." There was a few seconds' silence, punctuated by the sound of rustling paper, before Bradley came back. "Here we are. Apart from yourselves, the principal beneficiaries, in alphabetical order, are Mr. Gregory Carstairs, MP, Mr. Thomas Lambert, Miss Jean Mackenzie, Miss Agatha Saunders, Mrs. Clara Saunders, Miss Dorothy Saunders, Miss Penelope Saunders, Mr. Timothy Saunders, KC, and Miss Stella Simmons."

The Earl, well aware that his wife and daughter would be interested in this information, was scribbling furiously.

"I see. Well, thank you, Bradley. We'll look forward to seeing them and you on—oh, I suppose the date hasn't been fixed yet?"

"Unfortunately not, my lord. I will, if I may, telephone you again as soon as I have finalised the details with your rector and the undertakers."

The Earl said good-bye, rang off and went to find the Countess.

◇◇◇

"Of course, we are going to have to invite them all back here."

"*All* of them, Lavinia? Not just the beneficiaries?"

"No, all the mourners—all who come to the funeral."

"But d'you think that's really necessary? There might be dozens of 'em."

"It can't be helped, George. Most of these people will be coming from London, I imagine, though perhaps some from even farther afield. There's no decent restaurant or hotel for miles. The village has Miss Clatworthy's tea shop, which seats about a dozen, and *The Rose & Crown*, which is just a small public house. And we can't expect people to travel all this distance and then afterwards just to traipse back to the station and catch the first up train, without some proper refreshment. After all, she was your relative, and many of them will be coming as a mark of respect to the family."

"Yes, of course, my dear, you're quite right. It's the least we can do. I'd better get Hawkins to have a word with Jenkins at the village garage about laying on some transport. Some taxis from Westchester—or perhaps a charabanc."

"This will not be a factory outing, George."

"Maybe you're right: not very suitable. Taxis, then. How many, I wonder…"

Gerry was scanning the list of beneficiaries. "I've never heard of most of these people. Who are they? I mean, what relations are they to Aunt Florrie—and to us?"

"Well, actually, I'm not quite sure myself, offhand. I'm familiar with some of the names, and I know Timothy and Gregory slightly. But I can't place Thomas or Penelope or Stella. I'll try and work it out—go back through some old papers and photo albums and *Debrett*."

"Don't bother on my account," Gerry said. "It's not all that important."

"No, no, I want to do it. We're all going to be sittin' round a table together, and it could be embarrassing if I don't know who they are. Now, what was I going to do?"

"Taxis," said the Countess.

"Ah yes. I was just tryin' to work out how many…" And the Earl wandered out, counting on his fingers.

◇◇◇

The following morning there was a telegram from Bradley informing them that the funeral had been fixed for twelve noon on the Wednesday of the following week. "That's really very convenient," said Lord Burford. "The last train to town from the Halt goes at four twenty-five. So if the service takes an hour, they can all come back here and have a bite at a civilised hour, then wander round the house and grounds for a bit, while those of us who're involved can listen to the will being read. Then we can have tea and get 'em back to the station in plenty of time."

However, in the afternoon, there was another phone call from Bradley. "Disaster, my lord," he began dramatically.

"My word, that sounds serious. What's the trouble?"

"I spoke to your rector and then to the undertakers first thing this morning, sent the announcement to *The Times* and then wired or telephoned the legatees. No sooner had I completed everything, when I received notification that a very important court case, in which I am deeply involved, has been called for the morning of the day of the funeral. There is no way of obtaining a postponement and I simply have to be there."

"I see. That's bad luck. So it means you won't be able to make it to the funeral."

"Unfortunately, no."

"Or be here for the reading of the will."

"Well, I do not anticipate this case going on well into the afternoon. It is important, but not unduly complicated. So I am virtually certain that I could be there by 5 p.m. Unfortunately, as you are aware, by then it would be too late for the legatees to get back to London that night. It is really most unfortunate."

"Yes, it is." The Earl hesitated. "No offence at all, my dear fellow, we would be delighted to meet you, and all that, but is it strictly necessary for you to be here in person? Is there nobody you could send in your place?"

"I'm afraid not. It really has to be a lawyer, as there are always legal questions asked. But my partner, whom I could in theory ask to do it, will be on holiday next week. Then again, I am the executor of the will. There are numerous things which I can explain. People are frequently hurt or disappointed by the provisions of a will, and the executor can often smooth ruffled feathers, as it were, or explain and elaborate any conditions which might be attached to a bequest. It's really not satisfactory if the executor is not present."

"Yes, I can see that. Well, I really don't know what to suggest."

"Of course, and I hardly like to mention this, but if it were possible for the other beneficiaries to stay at Alderley overnight..." Bradley tailed away in a series of tentative little throat clearings.

Lord Burford did not reply for a moment. Eventually he said: "Don't think that'll be possible, actually."

"Oh. Then I'll just have to try and make other arrangements for some later date."

They spoke for a few more seconds, then the Earl went to find the Countess.

◇◇◇

"So naturally, Lavinia, I told him it wouldn't be possible. You agree, of course."

"No, George, I do not. I think you should telephone Mr. Bradley and tell him they are welcome to stay overnight."

"But Lavinia, I don't *want* to have people staying here. After the last two house parties, we both agreed no more."

"This wouldn't be a house party, George, it's nine guests for one night. By ten o'clock on Thursday morning they'll probably all be gone."

"But the last two times we've had people here it's been disastrous."

"This is quite different. These people are family, not spies and jewel thieves and blackmailers and film stars," the Countess said, blithely grouping the four occupations in the same category. "And when one occupies an historic house such as Alderley, where some of the most eminent men and women in the world have stayed, one cannot just shut its doors, because of a few unfortunate incidents."

"I know you enjoy entertaining, Lavinia. And you do it jolly well."

"I see it more as an obligation. And this will be a very good way of breaking the ice and getting back to normal again. After all, we do need to put an end to this stupid nonsense about a curse once and for all."

"Yes, you're quite right, my dear, as usual. I'll telephone Bradley back and tell him we'll give 'em all a bed for the night."

"I think perhaps you'd better make that nine beds, George, not just one." It was unusual for the Countess to attempt a joke, however mild, and she looked quite pleased with herself.

"Oh, very good, Lavinia. Of course. Though it'll be ten, as I suppose Bradley himself will be staying as well. I'll go and put the call through now."

"Ask Mr. Bradley to tell them not to bring evening clothes. We will not dress for dinner that night. We do not want them all to have the bother of bringing large suitcases with them. This way most people should be able to manage with a small overnight bag. I'll have a word with Merryweather. I expect he'll be pleased. I'm sure he's missed all the organising."

"Well, of course," said Lord Burford, "if I'd realised *that* I'd've arranged a house party months ago."

He went out. Lady Burford considered. Ten people, most of whom she did not know. No couples, so ten bedrooms. Where would she put them? Ten very different people…

Chapter Eleven

The phone rang in Tommy's flat. He answered it in his usual way. "What-ho."

"Tommy, it's Penny."

"Oh, hello, old girl. Nice to hear you. How's tricks?"

"OK. Tommy, did you hear about Great Aunt Florrie?"

"Yes. That's the one thing that's been helping me keep my pecker up."

"Tommy!" The voice was reproachful.

"Oh, I don't mean her dying. I'm sorry she's gone, and all that, but, after all, she was about a hundred and fifty. It's just that apparently I'm remembered in her will."

"Are you? So am I."

"Really? You don't know what for, I suppose?"

"No."

"Nor me. It's maddening. I mean, it might be only some old family heirloom, or something, but there's just a possibility it might be cash. Just a hundred smackers would be jolly useful."

"Same here," said Penny wistfully.

"Or even forty-seven," he added unguardedly.

"Forty-seven? What a funny amount."

"Oh, I meant fifty. Just saw forty-seven on—on a bus going past."

"I see. So you're going to the funeral?"

"Gosh, yes, you couldn't keep me away. I've got two days off. A funeral's one thing they can't refuse it for. You?"

"Yes, me and Daddy."

"And staying overnight?"

"Yes. I've never been there, have you?"

"Once, years ago. I'm really looking forward to it. I want to see where all the murders were committed."

"Don't! Those are the last places I want to see."

"They were the last places the people who were murdered wanted to see, but they were." Tommy gave a subdued chortle.

Penny giggled. "Tommy, you are awful!"

This had been so frequently said to Tommy that he had come to take it as a compliment. He smiled to himself.

"Anyway," she said, "you will be on your best behaviour, won't you?"

"What d'you mean?" he said indignantly.

"Don't do anything Daddy would disapprove of."

He was about to say that that left very few things it was possible to do at all, but stopped himself in time.

"Butter won't melt in my mouth, Pen."

"Good. So I'll see you there Wednesday, then."

"You bet."

"'Bye, Tommy."

"Toodle-pip."

Penny rang off. She looked thoughtful. Surely, No. 47 buses didn't go past Tommy's flat.

"All right, all right," Poppy muttered, as she hurried to answer the furiously ringing door bell. She opened the door, with a cross expression on her face, which was instantly transformed when she saw the visitor.

"Greggy, darling, what a lovely surprise!"

Gregory cast a quick glance behind him before hurriedly stepping inside.

"Sorry about the bell, but I haven't got my key and I could hear someone coming up the stairs."

"I didn't expect to see you today. You said you'd phone."

"I know, but I had to see you." He threw his hat onto the couch, crossed to the cocktail cabinet and poured himself a gin and tonic.

"What about?"

"Well, just to apologise, really. Fact is, I won't be able to see you for the next few days, after all."

"Oh, Greggy, you promised!"

"I know and I'm frightfully sorry. But tomorrow I've got to go to a funeral. Old great aunt of mine just died, aged ninety-six."

"But that'll only take a couple of hours!"

"No, it's down in Westshire, and I won't be back till Thursday."

"Oh Greggy, do you have to go?"

"I want to."

"Want to? But she's only a great aunt!"

"I know, but it seems I'm in her will."

"For a lot?"

"I don't know. I don't even know how much she was worth. But I am hopeful. Anyway, they can't hold the reading until five o'clock for some reason, by which the last train back will have left, so I'm going to have to stay overnight. The rest of Thursday I'll be catching up and then Friday evening Alex has invited a few quite important people round for drinks."

"But if you're staying in a hotel, couldn't I come with you? Nobody's likely to recognise you down there. I'd love a trip out of town—no matter where. I get so bored sometimes."

"I know, my sweet. But I'll be staying at Lord Burford's place."

Poppy's eyes grew large. "Alderley?"

"That's right. I told you he's a sort of cousin of mine."

"But that's where they had all those murders. There were dozens of pictures of it in the papers at the time. Alderley's absolutely divine. Oh, you are so lucky! I'd give anything to stay there. Do you think one day…?"

"My dear, when we're married I'll wangle an invitation for us both. That's a promise." One, he thought, he could safely make. "Anyway," he went on, "we've got this evening."

"Can we go out—do a West End show? You know, I've got this friend, who can always get tickets for anything."

"That would be lovely," he said enthusiastically. Then he looked doubtful. "But perhaps it would be better if we stayed in. Or maybe a local cinema, eh? If we slip in before the second feature's finished, there shouldn't be too many people around."

Poppy pouted.

Stella Simmons stared at her face in the mirror. She was quite pleased with what she saw. Not delighted. There was much room for improvement. But, on the whole, not bad. She looked, she thought, if not beautiful, at least attractive. And her training meant that she did know how to make the best of the face she had been born with. Her hair was good: thick, auburn, naturally curly and hanging loosely to her shoulders. Was that style a little too young now? Should she consider a more mature cut? Something to think about. Her brow and eyebrows were good, too, though the eyes were not as large or as deep as she would like—but eyes were something that you really could improve with make-up and false lashes. Her nose was on the large size, but at least straight; the mouth a trifle wide, but only a trifle, the jaw firm—but too square? No, on consideration, not really. She smiled mirthlessly at herself. Her teeth weren't absolutely straight and could do with a little cosmetic work, only she was such a coward when it came to dentists. And they were, at least, very white.

Yes, generally speaking, she would pass.

She got up from the dressing-table and looked at herself in a full-length mirror. She was wearing the smart black suit, which, together with a black straw hat, she had bought especially for the funeral. She was pleased with the cut and style. There was no reason why a funeral outfit had to be unfashionable. And, she, of all people, had to put on a good show: Florrie would have appreciated that.

She started to take the outfit off, thinking deeply as she did so. She wished she had known Florrie better. How many times had she seen her since arriving from America? Six? Seven? She certainly couldn't have hoped for a warmer welcome. Florrie had been genuinely delighted to see her. And her own stories about New York, the fashion scene there, and the Broadway shows had been a real hit with the old girl.

Everything Florrie had told her about the other relations had been useful, too, as they were, really, strangers to her. How would they receive her? The Earl and Countess and Geraldine sounded nice. She doubted there'd be any problems there. Clara, though, unless Florrie was exaggerating, which was possible, seemed to be a real witch.

She hung the suit in the closet. Now, who else would there be? Well, Jean Mackenzie, of course; she knew her quite well. And then the other relations. The second cousins: Gregory, the politician, and Timothy, the attorney. Timothy's daughter. And Tommy. Would he recognise her, she wondered? He was the only comparatively close relative among them and in his early teens had had, she fancied, quite an intense admiration for his older first cousin.

Anyway, this was a great chance to get to know them all. She had no close relatives, and kin were important, particularly to someone in her situation. After so many years in New York, she was making a fresh life for herself. Apart from a few colleagues on the magazine, she did not yet know many people in London. So it was going to be vital to create a good impression at Alderley. For some of these were important people and could be very useful to her, especially if she was to fulfil her ambition and break out from the fashion world into a wider sphere of journalism.

In fact, it suddenly occurred to her, this funeral might in itself be a way to start. There had been the usual formal obituaries of Florrie in the more serious papers, but no human interest stuff at all. After all, the old biddy had had quite a life. And her funeral was taking place within a mile or two of a house now famous or notorious for a series of lurid murders. The host and hostess on that occasion would be among the principal mourners. There must be chance that some magazine or paper would be interested in a short piece. And Florrie herself would surely have approved of her taking advantage of their relationship, if it gave her a leg up.

The most important thing, though, was really to get to know these VIP relations.

"Nepotism for ever," Stella said out loud.

Of course, it all depended on nobody in this country ever learning the real reason she had had to leave New York so suddenly. That would really be disastrous. But there was little danger of that.

Was there?

◇◇◇

"No," Clara said fiercely. "We've had this argument before. The house cannot be left empty. Burglars always prefer unoccupied premises. Mrs. Hopkins would be bound to tell her husband we were all going away, and he has some very disreputable friends."

"If we had a maid or two, like everybody else I know, and didn't rely on just a cleaning woman, three times a week, the problem wouldn't arise," said Agatha.

"A maid—or two, as you so vaguely put it—would be a totally unnecessary expense."

"As long as you've got Dorry and me, you mean."

"This is irrelevant. We do *not* have a maid. We do have Mrs. Hopkins. And Mrs. Hopkins has Mr. Hopkins, and Mr. Hopkins has friends. Which means you must stay home. Dorothy can accompany me."

"I don't *want* to go," Agatha said. "I loathe funerals. In a way, I'll be very glad not to go. But it'll look most odd if I'm not there, especially considering that I am one of the beneficiaries."

"We're *all* beneficiaries. I'll explain that one of us always has to remain behind and that you volunteered."

"That's rich!"

"It will show you in a better light than if I explain how you objected to doing this one thing for me, just to set my mind at rest."

"I've done it dozens of times for you—flitting around the house, turning lights on and off and playing gramophone records loudly until the early hours of the morning, but this is different."

"I don't know that 'flit' is quite an apt word to describe your movements." Clara eyed her large and somewhat ungainly step-daughter meaningfully.

Agatha's already rather ruddy complexion took on an even deeper hue. "That's damned unfair, Stepmother."

"Do not use that sort of language in this house, Agatha! I won't have it."

"Oh, please, don't quarrel!"

Dorothy spoke pleadingly, her hands clasped together, as if in prayer. Her face wore an imploring expression.

The words which had led to her speaking hardly merited the name quarrel, but to Dorothy even the slightest hint of what she always called "unpleasantness" was a major crisis, liable to lead to hysterics. Agatha immediately took a grip on herself and managed a forced smile. "Don't worry, petal. No quarrel."

She turned back to Clara. "Why, for once, can't you stay behind and the two of us go?"

"I am not letting you take your sister away, even for one night. Heaven knows which of your godless and immoral ideas you might fill her head with."

"That is totally absurd. Why don't you admit the real reason: that you're not prepared to forgo several hours of potentially very profitable gossip and prying and pumping, among some of the cream of society?"

This hit home and Clara could think of no better response than: "That is unworthy of you, Agatha."

Dorothy said desperately: "Look, Mother, I don't want to go either. I dread having to meet all those people. Couldn't I stay home and Aggie go with you?"

"Wouldn't help," said Agatha. "It's the look of the thing I'm concerned about. We should both be there."

"Besides," Clara said, "you know you'd be far too nervous to stay here on your own. Suppose some villain did break in? You'd be totally useless. He might murder you in your bed."

"Whereas I'm expendable," said Agatha.

"You know I did not mean that. But you are more capable of taking care of yourself."

There was a sullen silence for a moment. It was broken by Agatha. "You can't stop me going," she said sullenly.

"No, I cannot physically stop you. But you would be unwise to go against me in this. It is my house you're living in, remember."

"And you'd throw me out, just because I went to my grandmother's funeral?" Agatha sounded incredulous. "This is unbelievable. I—"

"Please!" This time Dorothy's voice was almost a scream. "Aggie, darling, do what Mother wants. Just once more. Please—for me."

Agatha looked at her. She was plainly seething, but at last muttered: "Oh, all right."

"Oh, thank you."

"That's more like it," said Clara with a satisfied air. "And if you like I'll tell everybody that you've got a bad cold or a sore throat or something. Would you prefer that?"

Agatha took a deep breath. "Tell them what you bloody well like," she said. And she strode from the room.

Clara gave a screech of horror.

Chapter Twelve

"I've worked it all out," said Lord Burford.

"What?" Gerry, sprawled inelegantly on the sofa, looked up from her copy of the new Edgar Wallace mystery.

"The family relationships you asked about." He brandished a sheet of paper, covered with handwriting.

"Oh, you shouldn't have bothered. It wasn't all that important."

"You asked about it and you're going to hear it. Make room."

Gerry moved up about six inches and the Earl flopped down beside her. "I've just concentrated on the people who are in the will and their immediate families, so this isn't complete, by any means."

"What a bitter disappointment."

"Just shut up and listen." He cleared his throat. "My great grandfather, the ninth Earl, had three boys and a girl. The eldest was Aylwin, my grandfather, who became the tenth Earl. You know all about him. The second son was Bertie and you also know about him."

"Yes, and about Florrie and John and Emma and Clara and Agatha and Dorothy and Old Uncle Tom Cobley and all."

"Right. We can now proceed. The third brother, after Aylwin and Bertie, was Thomas. He had a daughter, Phyllis, and a son, Harry. Phyllis married a man called Carstairs and had a son,

Gregory, and a daughter, whose name I've forgotten and who won't be here for the reading."

"I thought you were only bothering with the ones who will be here."

"Quite correct. My mistake. Forget Phyllis' daughter."

"And I was just getting fond of her."

"Gregory, an MP, is married to a woman called Alexandra but has no children. Harry had a son, Timothy, a KC, who is a widower and has one child, a daughter, Penelope, who will be here. Finally, Aylwin's, Bertie's and Thomas' younger sister, Margaret, married someone named Lambert and had a daughter, Henrietta, and a son, Philip. Henrietta married a Mr. Simmons and had Stella, who lived a good number of years in America, working on some New York fashion magazine, but who's presumably home now. Philip had a son, Tommy. All those branches of the family tended to marry late, incidentally, which makes all the ages out of alignment with us; my father and I both married young, as you know. Is that all clear?"

"Oh, absolutely." Gerry picked up her book again.

"Now," said the Earl, deftly removing it from her hand and at the same time consulting his piece of paper, "Bertie and Thomas being my great uncles, and Margaret my great aunt, means the following—I think I've got the terminology right: John, Phyllis, Harry, Henrietta and Philip were my first cousins once removed upwards, making their children, Agatha, Dorothy, Gregory, Timothy, Stella and Tommy my second cousins, and your second cousins once removed upwards, even though, Tommy, at least, is probably a bit younger than you. Penelope is my second cousin once removed downwards, so of course your third cousin."

"I feel so close to her already."

"Clara, as will be obvious, being the second wife of my first cousin once removed upwards, is the second wife of your second cousin once removed upwards, or, in other words, your second cousin once removed upwards by marriage—meaning,

I believe, that you can legitimately call her your second-cousin-once-removed-in-law."

"Gosh, can I really? How exciting!"

He frowned. "Or should that be twice removed? Anyway, as I said, there're lots of other relatives but they won't be here, so we can safely ignore them."

"It's so nice to feel safe. To summarise, then, we can say that the people who are going to be staying here are a bunch of distant relations."

"You could put it like that."

"Rest assured, Daddy, that is how I shall think of them, now and always."*

"You have no sense of family history," said Lord Burford.

He started to stand up, then froze in mid-movement. "Oh, lor."

"What's the matter. Hurt your back?"

"No." He sank back down. "Just remembered something. Gregory and Timothy aren't on speaking terms. They quarrelled years ago. They might have made it up, I suppose, but they're a stubborn couple of coves, so probably not."

"What did they quarrel about?"

"Well, my memory's a bit shaky. It must have been shortly after Gregory first got into Parliament. Some little revolutionary magazine wrote something libellous about him: said he'd voted for a bill only because he stood to make money from it, or something like that. Gregory decided to sue them, and got Timothy to represent him. Stupid, really, much better to have simply ignored it. Anyway, the case had just started, when it fell apart. Gregory dropped the suit. I don't know exactly what happened, but I heard a rumour that Gregory had wanted Timothy to do something that Timothy thought unethical and after a big row refused to represent him any more."

"Do you believe it?"

---

*Author's Note: Readers need have no qualms about doing the same as Gerry.

"I dunno. I don't say Gregory wouldn't do anything unethical; on the other hand, Timothy might well think something was unethical that nobody else would think was. He is a bit of a prig."

"It's not a problem for us, though, is it?"

"No, but they ought to be kept apart. Rooms in different wings, so they don't keep running into each other, have to use the same bathroom, and so on."

As he was speaking Lady Burford had entered. "Ah, Lavinia, I was just telling Gerry about Gregory and Timothy. They must—"

"I heard, George, and it's all right. I remembered about the quarrel. Gregory is in the east corridor and Timothy the west. And they will be well apart at dinner."

"You think of everything, my dear," said the Earl.

Chapter Thirteen

The Wednesday of the funeral was a cloudless and bakingly hot day. "Makes a change," said the Earl. "Practically always rains at the funerals I go to. Not the sort of day, though, you feel like getting togged out in a mornin' suit." He ran a finger round inside his stiff wing collar.

Everything was ready for the guests, just nine rooms having eventually been prepared, after Bradley explained that he had friends living not far away, with whom he had arranged to spend the night. In the dining-room, the servants were busy laying out the buffet.

At eleven forty-five the Earl, the Countess and Geraldine set out in the Rolls on the short drive to the church, just the far side of the village. On the way they saw the smoke from the London train approaching in the distance. When Hawkins pulled up at the church, there were a number of cars already parked in the vicinity, together with eight taxis, brought in from the county town of Westchester by the efficient Harry Jenkins. The hearse, which had borne Florrie's coffin from London, was parked immediately outside the church. Twenty or so spectators, including a number of children, were standing around. For the sleepy village of Alderley, this ranked as quite a show. The village constable, P.C. Dobson, a stout, red-faced man, whose uniform always seemed too small for him, self-importantly tried to appear to be keeping order.

They alighted from the Rolls. Some of the children cheered and Gerry gave them a cheery wave. Then she looked down the road in the direction of the station. "Here they come," she said.

Her parents followed her gaze. Quite a procession was approaching. All garbed totally in black, and looking, from a distance, like a disciplined army of beetles, they strode determinedly towards the church. As they drew closer, Lord Burford tried to count them. He made the number at least seventy. "By Jove," he muttered. "Never thought there'd be so many."

"There won't be enough taxis," Gerry said.

"Then they'll just have to run a shuttle service."

Fifteen minutes later everyone was seated in the little church, which had not been so full for many years, and the coffin had been brought in and placed in position. After the first hymn, "Abide With Me," and a prayer, the rector said: "I did not have the pleasure of knowing the Honourable Mrs. Florence Saunders, or Florrie, as I believe she insisted on being called by practically everybody, but I am assured that knowing her was indeed a pleasure. It is sad, though, if on occasions such as these, the priest has no recollections of the deceased, which can be passed on. I have, therefore, asked Mr. Gregory Carstairs, MP, Mrs. Saunders' great nephew, to deliver a eulogy."

Lord Burford groaned under his breath. "We'll be here for hours," he muttered.

Gregory went forward and turned to face the congregation. "Thank you, Mis—" he began, then quickly corrected it to "Thank you, padre."

Gerry stifled a giggle. "He was just going to say 'Mr. Speaker,'" she whispered to her mother.

"Ssh!"

The Earl had misjudged Gregory. One thing the MP could justly claim was to be a fluent speaker, and, when there were no votes at stake, when he tended to portentousness, a witty and interesting one. It was an ability that had given him the edge over his opponents at four general elections, and frequently in the House of Commons. Now he spoke entertainingly and at times quite movingly about Florrie, recounting several amusing anecdotes and referring to numerous kindly acts of hers. He went on for just twelve minutes before sitting down. A barely audible murmur of approval went round the church. Only Timothy remained stony-faced.

After this, the service proceeded in the usual fashion, ending with the interment in the Burford family's section of the church-yard.

As soon as he could decently do so, Lord Burford went across to Hawkins, who had been placed in charge of the transport arrangements. "Everything under control?" he asked.

"I think so, my lord." The chauffeur touched his cap. "Harry and I made a rough count as people were going in, and we think we can get everybody there in two trips per car. He has a couple of cars in the garage we can use, as well as the taxis. Some people will have to wait, though."

"Oh well, it won't be for long."

Lady Burford and Gerry had already reached the Rolls, which Gerry on this occasion was to drive. The Earl hurried to catch them up. They had to get home before the first of the guests arrived. Two of the church's sidesmen had been deputed to usher the mourners to the taxis and within minutes the process was under way.

The Countess and Gerry had barely time to remove their hats and gloves before the first of the taxis rolled up. In it were Clara, Dorothy, Timothy and Gregory. The Earl felt a stab of annoyance with himself; he had forgotten to give instructions that Timothy and Gregory should be sent in different taxis. He also noticed that there was no sign of Agatha. The four alighted from the taxi and the Earl and Countess greeted them in the porch. After expressing the usual commiserations to the two women, the Earl asked: "Er, Agatha comin' in one of the other cars, is she?"

"She isn't here, er—" Clara had obviously forgotten how she used to address him, and settled finally on "Cousin George."

She ostentatiously dabbed at her eyes with a handkerchief as she spoke.

"Really? I didn't spot her at the church, but with so many people there... Anythin' wrong?"

"She woke up this morning with a severe sore throat. I suspect tonsillitis. We thought it would be highly unwise for her to attend. She is devastated, of course, isn't she Dorothy?"

"Yes." Dorothy's eyes were cast down, her voice totally expressionless.

"So I should imagine. Poor girl."

The occupants of the second taxi were approaching, so the Earl and Countess had time only to shake hands briefly with Gregory and Timothy, who had been standing side by side studiously avoiding looking at each other. A footman had carried in the small cases which the overnight guests had brought. The Countess beckoned him across, spoke quietly to him for a few seconds; he nodded and then conducted the four upstairs.

The second group to arrive included a tall, thin young man, a blond girl, clinging firmly to his arm, and Miss Mackenzie. Gerry, who was standing a little apart, watching everything with keen enjoyment, saw Timothy, halfway up the stairs, turn and eye the boy with an expression of clear disapproval—of which he, however, seemed quite unaware. Miss Mackenzie was genuinely red-eyed, and Lady Burford devoted more time to her than any of the others. A second footman was still in the act of taking the bags from the second taxi, and the young man and the blonde stood waiting, gazing round them, seeming somewhat in awe of their surroundings.

The next car contained four people totally unknown to the Burfords. One of them was a young woman in her mid-thirties, wearing an extremely chic suit and hat. After shaking hands with Lord and Lady Burford she moved on a few feet and stopped, looking a little lost. Gerry approached her.

"Would you be Stella Simmons, by any chance?"

The young woman looked surprised and pleased. "Why, yes."

"I'm Geraldine Saunders." Gerry held out her hand.

Stella took it firmly. "It's a real pleasure to meet you, Lady Geraldine. I've heard so much about you." She had a very slight American accent.

"That sounds ominous."

"How did you know who I was?"

"It was a guess. From your outfit. It's by far the smartest one here and I heard you were a fashion journalist."

"Why, thank you. It's nice when someone notices. The magazine positively insists we always dress up to the nines when we're on public display. And it can be quite a bore. One day I swear I'm going to turn up at some do dressed like an old washerwoman."

"I can imagine how you feel. But I'm glad you didn't do that today."

"Oh, I couldn't do that at Alderley. Though I think Florrie might have liked the idea, don't you?"

"She probably would," Gerry agreed.

"Stella?"

The tall young man had approached from behind her. She spun round and looked at him for a second or two, a puzzled expression on her face.

"Don't you know me, dear cousin?"

Her face cleared. "Tommy?"

"The very same."

"Oh, Tommy, I am sorry. But you were just a school kid when I saw you last. And now look at you! You're so tall!"

"And skinny. I'd have known you anywhere, Stella. You haven't changed a bit."

"I'm sure I have but I love you for saying it. Here, give your old cousin a kiss."

Tommy was nothing loath. After disengaging himself, he suddenly remembered his manners. "Oh, this is another cousin, Penny Saunders." He drew the blond girl forward.

Penny, whose suspicions had been immediately re-aroused when she had first laid eyes on the "old" Stella at the church, had been looking at her wearing exactly the same expression that her father had worn when looking at Tommy; and her greeting was far less effusive than Tommy's had been. She shook hands with very stiff fingers, saying formally: "Pleased to meet you."

However, Stella smiled with the utmost warmth. "So at last I meet the famous society beauty," she said.

"Oh." Penny clearly did not quite know how to react. "Oh no, not really, it's nice of you to say so but—"

"You know something, Penny? You should be a manne-quin."

Penny's eyes widened. "Do you really think so?"

"I sure do. You've got everything: looks, figure, poise."

"Oh my, I never thought... It would be just wonderful. But Daddy'd never let me."

"Ah, he must be Timothy, the great lawyer, is that right?"

"He is a lawyer, yes."

"I do want to get to know everybody," Stella said. "I'm so out of touch with the family after nearly eleven years. Whether they'll want to know me is another matter, of course."

"I can't imagine there'll be any doubt about that," said Tommy.

"Thank you darling. Oh, you both know our hostess, Lady Geraldine, do you?"

"Actually, no," Tommy said. "Though I think we did meet when we were very small, Lady Geraldine."

Penny said: "I've wanted to meet you for many years, Lady Geraldine."

Gerry smiled. "I know—please don't say it—you've heard so much about me."

They all shook hands. "Now, two things," Gerry said. "First, I'm not the hostess. That's my mama. I'm really just a hanger-on here. Second, it's Gerry, OK? Now, I'm sure you'd all like to freshen up, so if you'll follow William, he'll show you your rooms, and then you can come down and have some grub."

Meanwhile, in the doorway people were now arriving in a rush, with a queue already forming outside. The taxis were positively tearing off the second their passengers had alighted. "Hawkins has certainly got 'em moving," Lord Burford whispered to his wife during a rare free moment.

What he did not know was that there was keen competition between the drivers. Harry Jenkins had started a book on which of them would be the quickest to get to the house, unload his passengers and return to the church, and was carefully timing the cars with several stopwatches. With each of the drivers having bet on himself, there was no likelihood of any of the second wave of passengers having to wait a moment longer than necessary.

After the first dozen or so arrivals, Lord Burford gave up all attempts to work out who they were. Earlier, there had been some discussion about the possibility of having Merryweather take people's names at the door and formally announce them, but the Countess had considered that this would give the proceedings more the atmosphere of some grand reception or ball and was hardly suitable for a funeral. The Earl, however, had begun to wish that they had gone ahead with the plan—though he had eventually to admit to himself that in most cases it would not have made a great deal of difference, as even when the guests introduced themselves, the names usually meant as little to him as the faces did.

Eventually the last of the guests had been delivered and the Earl and Countess followed them to the dining-room, where the magnificent cold buffet was waiting. The taxi drivers, who were to remain and later convey all but the beneficiaries to the station, were conducted by Hawkins to the servants' dining-room, where an equally good spread was to be served.

Among the guests, quite a party atmosphere was already developing, which, Lord Burford had often noted, was usually the way when people relaxed after the strain and solemnity of a funeral service. He and the Countess separated and moved around, at last beginning to learn the identity of some of the guests. Gerry introduced Tommy, Penny and Stella to her parents and then drew her father aside.

"Who are the old girls?" She indicated with her head.

Six ladies, all clothed in long black dresses and black hats, with veils covering the top halves of their faces, were gathered together in one corner of the room, appearing somewhat ill at ease. Apart from their sizes, which ranged from tiny to quite large, they looked practically identical.

"Haven't the foggiest."

"You should go and have a word with them, Daddy."

"Me? That's your mother's job."

"Mummy's got her hands full. Anyway, I'm sure they'd much rather talk to a man. Probably all old maids or widows."

"But if I don't know who they are, what shall I call them?"

"Don't call them anything. See what they call you. That may give you a clue as to who they are."

"Oh, very well." Lord Burford made his way across to the group. "How good of you all to come," he said. "I know my great aunt would greatly have appreciated it."

Gerry watched him engage them in conversation for a few seconds, then turned away to survey the room. She was surprised to see that Miss Mackenzie, a glass of wine in one hand and a smoked salmon sandwich in the other, was talking animatedly to Tommy, who was listening closely and nodding, as if fascinated by what she had to tell him. Then he smiled, but shook his head firmly, as if regretfully turning down a pressing invitation.

Five minutes later the Earl returned. "Well?" Gerry asked.

"None the wiser. One of them called me 'George,' two 'Lord Burford,' two 'my lord,' and the last one didn't call me anything. I'm not sure they know who each other are. They don't seem to be together, just sort of flocked—you know, birds of a feather. Anyway, I've split them up now."

"There are two old gentlemen, near the fireplace, also looking rather lost, so—"

"No," interrupted her father. "I don't want to know who they are. I don't care. Let somebody else take care of 'em."

Chapter Fourteen

About fifteen minutes later, Lady Burford approached Geraldine. "Have you noticed Dorothy?"

"She's almost unnoticeable," Gerry replied. "I've never seen anybody who is so close to not being anything."

"She hasn't left Clara's side for a second. And she's not spoken to anybody. But she can't take her eyes off you."

"Really? I hadn't noticed. What excellent taste she must have."

"Have a word with the poor girl, will you? I'll distract Clara."

"OK."

Lady Burford moved towards Clara, who quickly saw her coming and turned to meet her.

She took the Countess' hand. "Lavinia, how very, very good of you it is to lay on all this. To open up your beautiful home to so many strangers is a really gracious act. The girls and I are so grateful. Without you, I just don't know what would have happened."

"It's kind of you to say so."

"No, it's not kind at all. How could I say less? You and George are genuinely good people. I just wish there was some way we could repay you."

In spite of herself, Lady Burford found herself softening. Clara was certainly capable of great charm. She told herself that it was flattery, of course—but remarkably effective flattery.

"Really, er, Clara"—she always found using her Christian name something of a struggle—"there is really no need to think like that. We were very glad to do it. We were very fond of Florrie."

"I know, and she was so fond of you and George and Geraldine. She always spoke of you with the utmost affection."

The tactful thing to do would be return the compliment, but Lady Burford could not bring herself to utter this blatant lie. "She spoke a lot of you, too," she said.

If Clara noted the significance of the form of words, she did not show it. "Thank you, too, so much for allowing us to stay overnight. Dorothy is really quite excited about it."

Lady Burford was on the brink of answering with a phrase she had heard her daughter use: "You could have fooled me." But fortunately at that moment Clara suddenly realised that Dorothy was not at her shoulder. "Where is she?" she said sharply and started to turn round.

Hastily, Lady Burford put her hand on Clara's. "And tell me, how are you keeping?" she asked earnestly.

Gerry approached Dorothy with a broad smile. "Hello, I'm Gerry Saunders."

For a moment Dorothy looked terrified. Apart from the merest smattering of powder her face was totally devoid of make-up, and she was wearing a dress that looked as though it could have belonged to her mother. Gerry suddenly felt very sorry for her.

Dorothy gulped. "Y-Yes, I know. H-How do you do, Lady Geraldine?" She was gazing at her with something like awe.

"Oh, please call me Gerry, we are cousins of a sort, aren't we? And may I call you Dorothy—or is it Dorry? That's how Florrie always referred to you."

"Well, Agatha calls me Dorry. Grandmamma must have picked it up from her. But nobody else does. Mother doesn't like it."

"Then I'll call you Dorry, too, if I may. I think it's a very pretty name—much nicer than Dorothy." Gerry actually had no strong feelings either way, but if Clara was anti-Dorry, then she was going to be for it.

"Really?" Dorothy's face showed its first sign of animation. "Then I'll ask everybody to call me that in future."

Gerry blinked. She had often thought it would be nice to live in a world where everybody instantly followed her lead and took her advice on all matters, but now she had met somebody who was, it seemed, prepared to do just that, she was not at all sure she liked it. But she smiled again and said: "I was awfully sorry to hear about your grandmother's death. It must have been an awful blow for you."

"Well, we knew she had to go sometime, of course, but it was a shock all the same. I—I just wish I'd known her better, but I didn't get to see her all that often."

"I suppose with her living in Walton-on-Thames, and not getting out very often in recent years, and you living in—north London, is it?"

"Yes, Hampstead."

"Then it can't have been easy. I'm sure Florrie understood. She was terribly fond of you and Agatha, you know. I last saw her about three weeks ago and she was talking about you all the time."

This was a considerable exaggeration but, Gerry thought, a justifiable one under the circumstances.

Dorothy cast a somewhat furtive glance towards her stepmother, who was still being kept under tight rein by the Countess. Unnecessarily, in view of the babble in the room, she lowered her voice. "Aggie saw her more than I did."

"Did she?" Gerry was fascinated—not by the less-than-enthralling information that one sister had seen her grandmother more than the other, but by the fact that this had obviously to be kept from Clara.

"Yes, she used to go and see her every month or so. Usually on her motor bike."

"Aggie has a motor bike? What make?"

"A Norton. Five hundred cc."

"Gosh, I do envy her. I've always wanted a motor bike. I begged Mummy and Daddy for one years ago, but even Daddy put his foot down about that. I could get one now, of course, but I wouldn't want to worry them."

"Aggie took me for a ride on the pillion of hers once. It was really exciting. Mother had gone to the dentist," she added by way of explanation.

Gerry felt a surge of anger, but suppressed it. "I'd like to meet Aggie," she said. "Sounds as though we might get on."

"Oh, it would be lovely if we could all get together some-time!" But then she glanced again at Clara and added wistfully: "Though I don't suppose it will be possible."

"I don't see why not. Let's have a chat about it later and see if we can arrange something."

"Oh, can we really?"

"What?"

"Have a chat tonight."

"Certainly."

"It'll have to be after Mother's gone to bed. She always retires early. I'll have to go up with her, but I'll sneak back down. If—if it won't be keeping you up."

Gerry grinned. "Far from it. I am definitely not one who always retires early."

"No, that's what I thought—from what I've read." Dorothy was by the moment becoming more animated and talking more easily. "It's such a thrill for me to meet you, La—er, Gerry. I've wanted to for years. I've been such an admirer of yours. And even more since those murders, which you helped to solve."

Gerry endeavoured to look modest. "Oh, I didn't do much, really," she said, not thinking it necessary to mention the fact that until the very end she had been as baffled as everybody else.

"But you were nearly killed!"

Gerry raised her chin and squared her shoulders. "You have to be prepared for that sort of risk if you decide to get involved in murder investigations," she said nobly.

"And your fiancé—though he wasn't your fiancé then—saved your life."

Gerry's eyes went dreamy. "Yes, he was incredible."

"Perhaps you'd tell me all about it tonight, would you? There was so much that wasn't in the papers that I wanted to know."

"Yes, of course."

"Oh, I'll really look forward to it."

Gerry said: "And now I really must mingle for a bit. Have you had any lunch, yet?"

"No."

"Well, go and get something now. You really look as though—" She broke off, about to say, eyeing Dorothy's figure, "as though you need it." But she amended it to: "I'm sure you're hungry."

She took Dorothy by the arm and led her across to the buffet. "Now help yourself, and I'll see you later."

She moved away to talk to talk to somebody else. For once she really felt she'd made a hit. It was nice to have a fan.

◇◇◇

Stella saw that Gregory, who was standing alone, moodily munching a sausage roll, was eyeing her. She strolled over to him. He brightened visibly as she approached. "Hello, Gregory," she said warmly. "How nice to see you again."

"Er, very nice to see you, too."

"You haven't a clue who I am, have you?"

"I'm afraid not. But I'd very much like to." He eyed her appreciatively from head to foot.

"I'm Stella."

"Really. That's a lovely name."

It was as if he were talking to a small girl, she thought. "Which doesn't mean any more to you, I know. Stella Simmons, Henrietta's daughter."

"Ah, of course! You're the girl who went to America."

"And has come back again."

"How splendid. I'm sure America's loss is England's gain."

"Probably the other way round."

"I'm certain that's not true. In fact, I was wondering at the service who the exceptionally attractive and smart young woman was."

"And who was she?" Stella asked innocently.

"Why—" He broke off, with a chuckle. "I didn't realise that she was my—what, second cousin?"

"I believe so."

"Is that what the Americans call kissing cousins?"

"That depends on the cousins."

"Well, it's delightful to meet you at last."

"We did meet many years ago. At a wedding or a funeral, I can't quite remember which; I used to enjoy them both equally. I was only in my teens, then, and you'd just won your first election. I was thrilled to meet a famous Member of Parliament."

"What a charming thing to say. But surely a teen-aged girl couldn't have really been excited to meet a boring politician? Not a patch on a crooner or film star, eh?"

"Oh, better for me. I've always been fascinated by politics."

"Really? How very refreshing." Gregory was becoming more and more interested and edging ever so gradually towards her.

"Of course, I'm rather out of touch with the British political scene."

"You must be. So, whereabouts in America were you?"

"New York, for the past ten to eleven years."

"Indeed? That must have been very interesting. And doing what, precisely?"

"Oh, I couldn't possibly tell you *precisely* what I've been doing. But I earned a fairly honest crust as a journalist."

"And now?"

"Still a hack."

"Oh." An expression of wariness suddenly appeared in his eyes.

"On a fashion magazine," Stella added quickly. "I'm with *London Fashion Weekly* now."

"I see." He relaxed again. "Not a subject I know a lot about. Know what I like to look at, mind. Pity hem lines are so low at the moment, I must say."

Stella smiled. "I'm sure a lot of men agree with you."

"Then why don't you use your influence to get 'em raised a few inches, eh?"

"Oh, I've got no influence at all, Gregory. I just report. And I may not be doing that much longer."

"And why would that be?"

"I'm hoping to spread my wings a bit."

"I'd love to help you spread your wings, my dear." The hand not holding the sausage roll started to stray in the direction of her waist. Then he obviously thought better of it and let his arm drop to his side again.

"And I'm sure you've had lots of experience at doing that."

"I wouldn't put it quite that way."

"Well, my aim is to move into another branch of journalism. Politics, say. I want to meet the people who really matter."

"Indeed? Not many women political journalists around. In fact, I don't think there are any."

"There has to be a first, doesn't there?"

"Now that's an attitude I like. You know, Stella, I think you and I are going to get on."

"You know, Gregory, I was just thinking the very same thing."

"So, if there's any way at all I can help you..."

"That's so kind of you. I would really be very grateful." She looked at him from under half-closed lids. "And I might well take you up on that offer. Perhaps we could get together sometime and have a proper chat."

"I'd like nothing better."

"I'll really look forward to it."

She sensed it would be wise not to push her luck any further. "I must talk to some other people now. And I'm sure there are dozens who want to speak to you. I'm so glad to have gotten to know you properly."

"Likewise, likewise."

She touched his hand briefly and moved away. Would he be any use at all? She had met many types like him in New York. Probably all talk and no action. Still, you never knew. It was another contact, anyway. And in one respect she strongly hoped he *would* be all talk and no action.

One down. Later, Timothy…

Gradually the dining-room emptied. Lady Burford had let everyone know that they were free to explore Alderley's public rooms and most did so, a few preferring to stroll in the gardens, now at their best. Gerry showed some people the secret passage, which had been much featured in the papers at the time of the two murder cases. It was like one of the old open days, which they had not held this year. After his previous misgivings, Lord Burford was now clearly enjoying being the genial host and the Countess congratulated herself on her idea. A number of ghosts should have been laid today.

She was not, though, entirely happy at having had a funeral turned into what had become quite a festive occasion, and said as much to Miss Mackenzie.

"Oh, Lady Burford, please don't think that. I assure you, this is just what she would have wanted."

"Really?"

"Yes indeed. Shortly before she died she said to me that she didn't want any long faces at her funeral. 'Let people enjoy themselves.' Those were her very words."

"Thank you, Miss Mackenzie. That certainly makes me feel better. And I think most people are."

"I venture to say I believe Florrie is, too."

"We must hope you're right. In a way, it is pleasant to be commemorating a peaceful, contented death, after all those terrible violent ones."

Jean Mackenzie cleared her throat nervously. "Forgive my asking, but have you, or anybody else, witnessed any kind of phenomena since they occurred?"

"I'm sorry?"

"Well, those who die violently, particularly those who have been murdered, frequently do not rest easily. Quite often they, er, walk, as the saying is."

"You mean ghosts? Thankfully, no, nothing of that kind."

"Oh."

She seemed, the Countess thought, rather disappointed.

Chapter Fifteen

At three forty-five tea was served and shortly afterwards the taxis began taking those who were returning to town back to the station. By ten past four the last of them had departed, leaving just the eight beneficiaries remaining. With the reading of the will now imminent, these were all feeling various degrees of nervousness or expectation. Clara, Dorothy, Gregory, Timothy and Miss Mackenzie retired to their rooms; Penny, who had absolutely no interest in art, made Tommy, who had just as little, take her to look at the paintings in the gallery; and Gerry had a long chat with Stella, with whom she had struck up an immediate rapport. Later, they were joined by Tommy and Penny; the latter, seeming to have quite got over her initial distrust of Stella, questioned her eagerly about both life in New York and her opinions of the latest fashion trends.

At four forty Hawkins departed for the station to meet Mr. Bradley. The train was on time, and it was shortly before five that Merryweather showed the solicitor into the drawing-room, where the Earl and Countess were waiting.

He did not look at all as the Earl had expected, being a short-ish man, nearly bald, with thick horn-rimmed glasses, and given to quick, rather bird-like movements. Lady Burford offered him tea, but he refused. "Perhaps after the reading, if you would be so kind."

"You'd like to start straight away?" the Earl asked.

"Whatever is convenient to you, my lord, but there seems little point in delaying. I expect the legatees will be anxious to hear their fates. And as it will be a somewhat unusual occasion in several respects, I admit I am anxious to get it over."

"Hm, that sounds interesting. Very well. I thought we'd go to the library. There's a table there we can sit around. If we did it in here, people would be scattered all over the room. You'd practically have to shout."

"Splendid."

Lord Burford rang the bell and when Merryweather answered told him to ask the others to join them in the library. The Earl, the Countess and Bradley made their way there themselves. Lord Burford sat Bradley at the head of the table, and the solicitor opened his briefcase and extracted a sheaf of papers. Gerry and Stella were the first to arrive, followed quickly by Clara and Dorothy, Jean Mackenzie, Gregory, Timothy and finally Tommy and Penny. When they were all seated, Bradley looked round the ring of expectant faces and cleared his throat nervously. He seemed a little unhappy. "Before I read the will, there is something quite unusual that must be done. My client made a specific request that the proceedings be opened in a particular manner—a highly, er, unconventional manner, but one she was very insistent upon. I had better read the actual words of her request." He glanced down at the papers in front of him. "'I fear that there will have been much gloom and misery at my funeral and that at this moment everyone present is looking especially sombre. I wish to dispel that mood. So I request that before my will is read, everybody joins in singing *She'll Be Coming Round The Mountain*. I ask this because I have a firm hope that I may be doing that very thing—the mountain in question being Zion—just about then.'"

Mr. Bradley looked up at faces wearing expressions ranging from the blank to the aghast—and one face which bore a look of sheer delight.

"How absolutely topping!" Gerry exclaimed. "Good for Aunt Florrie! That's what I want at my funeral. I shall put it in my will, too. In a few generations it'll become a family tradition."

"I'm delighted you approve, Lady Geraldine. I don't know if anyone here feels capable of starting the piece in question. I have a made a note of the words." He held up a sheet of writing paper. "They are extremely simple, and I could make an effort, but if anybody else…" He petered out and looked hopefully around.

Now, much to her mother's disappointment, Gerry was not musical. As a little girl, she had gone through several piano teachers, who had left saddened and with their self-confidence badly shaken. There was, however, one good thing to be said of her singing voice: it was powerful. A friend of hers had once likened it to that of Ethel Merman. Greatly flattered by this comparison, Gerry had set about—mostly when driving her beloved Hispano-Suiza—perfecting what she believed was a first-rate impersonation of the young Broadway star. This she needed no encouragement to perform at parties, though she could not help noticing, and being rather hurt by the fact, that she was rarely asked to do an encore. Now, though, she suddenly realised that her big moment had come. "Gladly," she said happily. She took a deep breath, opened her mouth, and let them have it at the top of her voice.

"SHE'LL BE COMING ROUND THE MOUNTAIN, WHEN SHE COMES."

She could not have hoped to make a greater impact. Everyone round the table gave a noticeable jump, Clara adding a startled "Oh, my."

"*She'll be coming round the mountain, when she comes,*" Gerry continued solo, then stopped. "Come on. What's the matter with you? Can't you accede to an old lady's dying wish? Now let's start again. Follow me." She raised her hands and began conducting as she recommenced.

Tommy, with a broad grin on his face, was the first to join in, followed quickly by Penny, and after a few seconds by Stella.

The others opened and closed their mouths slowly, making vague humming and moaning noises.

The verse ended—after what to Lady Burford at least seemed an extremely long time. There was a sudden hush, which was broken by Mr. Bradley. "Well, thank you very much, Lady Ger—"

"*SINGING EYE-YAI-YIPPEE-YIPPE-YAI, YIPPE-YAI,*" Gerry bellowed. Lord Burford closed his eyes, as her supporting trio took up the refrain.

As the final "yippe-yai" faded, Mr. Bradley spoke hastily and firmly. "That was most spirited and I'm sure would have pleased my client immensely. She would not, though, have expected more than one verse and one chorus," (a murmured, "Hear, hear" from the Earl) "so I will now proceed with the reading of the will." With a decided air of disdain, he dropped his copy of the lyrics into a nearby waste paper basket and immediately became more businesslike.

"We are here for the reading of the last will and testament of my late client, the Honourable Mrs. Florence Saunders. If everyone is agreeable, I will omit the preamble, containing the various legal technicalities and provisos, appointment of and instructions to her executor, et cetera, and get straight to the bequests."

Timothy looked slightly disapproving, but didn't speak. "Jolly good idea," said the Earl.

"The will is dated just five weeks before her death, but I perhaps should anticipate any questions by saying that only a few minor alterations to her earlier will were made at that time, and they were mostly in the nature of comments, rather than actual changes in the provisions. Very well, to proceed. There are very adequate bequests to her servants, of which she informed them some time before her death, and to various charities: The Variety Artistes' Benevolent Association, The National Society for the Prevention of Cruelty to Children and the Royal Society for the Prevention of Cruelty to Animals. I have, of course, copies of the will, for anyone wishing to see the full details.

"I should explain at the outset that most of the wording of this will is my client's own. Now to the principal bequests." He began to read. 'To my dear great nephew, George, Twelfth Earl of Burford, I regret I am unable to leave the revolver with which Jesse James shot Billy the Kid or vice versa, which is no doubt what he would really like. But failing this, I give and bequeath the portrait of the Sixth Earl, painted by Sir Joshua Reynolds, given to my husband and me by his brother, the later Tenth Earl, on the occasion of our wedding, in the belief that Alderley is its proper home and where it will complement the portrait of the Fifth Earl by the same artist, which already hangs there.' "

Lord Burford raised his eyebrows. "My word, that is kind of her. I remember being told the story of that, but I had no idea she still had it."

"It's been in storage," Miss Mackenzie put in quietly.

"It will fill a gap in the gallery," said the Countess.

Bradley resumed reading. "'To Lavinia, Countess of Burford, in recognition of her numerous kindnesses over many years, I give and bequeath my Georgian sterling silver tea service, which I hope will supplement the similar dinner service she already possesses.'"

Lady Burford beamed. "It certainly will. That is most generous."

"'To my great-great niece, Lady Geraldine Saunders, who has always brought a sparkle into my life, I give and bequeath the diamond bracelet, which was my beloved husband's wedding present to me.'"

Gerry's face lit up. "She showed me that once. It's beautiful. Oh, thank you, Florrie, I'll treasure it always."

Bradley continued: "'To my great nephew, Timothy Saunders, I give and bequeath the seventeen volumes of the first edition of the complete works of Charles Dickens, in the sincere hope that it will encourage him to read something other than law books.'"

For the first time that day, Timothy's sculpted-like features seemed briefly to soften. "How splendid. I have always been meaning to read Dickens through from beginning to end, but to do it from the first edition of the collected works…more than I could have hoped.'"

"'To my great-great niece, Penelope Saunders, I give and bequeath the pearl necklace which was my husband's gift to me on the occasion of our thirtieth wedding anniversary, trusting that the husband she is so ardently seeking, and whom I am sure she will find very soon, will wish to give her a gift she will value as much as mine when and if she reaches her thirtieth anniversary.'"

For a split second Gerry thought that Penny looked a little disappointed, but she quickly covered it up. "Pearls? Oo, I haven't got any pearls. That's lovely." Her lack of any other reaction to the rather involved syntax of the paragraph suggested that she had not really grasped its meaning.

"You must take great care of them, Penelope," said her father. "Only wear them on very special occasions. They must be kept in the safe the rest of the time."

"'To my great nephew, Gregory Carstairs,'" Bradley started, but at that point came to the end of the page and he paused for a moment. Gregory was staring at him rather in the manner of a dog hoping against hope that he was going to be taken for a walk.

Bradley continued from the next page. "'…knowing of his deep interest in political history, I give and bequeath the Chippendale desk, which has for many years occupied the study of my late husband, and which was previously owned by both William Pitt the Elder and the Younger, and whose wisdom will I hope, through it, be communicated to him.'"

"Oh. Ah. Yes." Gregory's words came like a series of little explosions. "Most interesting. Great historical connections. I'm sure I'll be the envy of many of my colleagues. Capital." But his face looked rather grim.

"'To Miss Jean Mackenzie,'" Bradley went on, "'in gratitude for many years' devoted friendship and loyalty, I give and bequeath the sum of two thousand five hundred pounds, free of duty, together with the furniture from the room which she has occupied in my house and ten other pieces of furniture of her choice.'"

Jean Mackenzie gave a gasp. "Oh, how generous! How very generous! I never imagined… It will ease so many worries."

Stella, sitting next to her, patted her hand.

"The Testator adds two comments," Bradley said. "Firstly, 'I am putting her on her honour to give none of this bequest to any medium or psychic and warn her that if she does so I will have a serious bone to pick with her when we next meet, which I trust will not be for many years yet.'"

"How typical," Jean Mackenzie said. "Yes, indeed, I promise, Florrie."

"Secondly, the Testator says: 'Thank you for not peeking.'"

Jean's mouth fell open. "I—I—how did she know?"

"My client foresaw that question. I was to say to you: 'By your face, when you handled the envelope.'"

"Oh, what an amazing woman she was! I'm so glad now that I didn't. So glad."

"'To my great nephew, Thomas Lambert, I give and bequeath—'" Bradley cleared his throat. He seemed decidedly embarrassed. Tommy was leaning forward expectantly. "'I give and bequeath precisely nothing. He is a worthless young scoundrel, who doesn't deserve a penny.'"

There was a gasp round the table. Tommy's expression did not change, but his face drained of colour.

It was Penny who was the first to speak. "Oh, Tommy, darling, how awful! I'm so, so sorry." She put her hand on his. For practically the first time in his life Tommy was unable to speak. He just gulped and looked down at the table.

"My client's next words: 'It's all right, Tommy, that was a practical joke—one that you richly deserved to have played on you.'"

Tommy jerked his head up as Bradley continued. "I should explain that the last three sentences are not part of the will, but which Mrs. Saunders insisted I inserted at that point." He held up a sheet of notepaper. "I now revert to the will proper. 'To my ever-entertaining great nephew, Thomas Lambert, I give and bequeath the sum of fifteen hundred pounds, free of duty, in the hope if not the expectation that he will use it wisely.'"

Tommy gave his head a shake. His colour was returning. He managed a sickly grin. "The old b—the old dear. She really got me, there. Suppose I did deserve it, though. I really get fifteen hundred quid?"

"Of course you do, silly," Penny said. Bradley nodded.

"Gosh, that's hunky-dory." He seemed already to have got over the shock. "She needn't have worried. I've got some absolutely spiffing ideas."

"'To my great niece, Stella Simmons,'" Bradley continued, "'I give and bequeath the sum of fifteen hundred pounds, free of duty. It was a regret to me that I never visited the United States, but her most interesting letters over a number of years, and the stories she has entertained me with since her return, have made me feel that I really do know New York.'"

Stella looked delighted. "Oh, how swell of her! Unless this is a practical joke, too?"

"Most definitely not, Miss Simmons. I will continue. 'To my daughter-in-law, Clara Saunders, I give and bequeath the sum of one hundred pounds, free of duty. I give and bequeath the remainder of my property—" He broke off, for a strange sound had come from the direction of Clara. It was a sort of strangled squawking, like a person who had been gagged trying to call for help. Whereas Tommy had gone white, Clara's face had assumed a decided shade of puce. Her hands on the table had formed two bony fists and her eyes were bulging. Dorothy took her arm. "Mother, it's all right," she said urgently in a low voice. "Calm down. There's more to come. Please, Mother."

Clara raised one fist and for a moment Gerry thought she was going to hit Dorothy. But she merely brushed her hand off and, with what was clearly an immense effort of will, managed to get control of herself.

Bradley resumed hurriedly. "'I give and bequeath the remainder of my property jointly to my two beloved granddaughters, Agatha Saunders and Dorothy Saunders absolutely, feeling certain that in the event of their stepmother's present source of income ever proving inadequate, they will take care of her in whatever way they see fit.' That is all, my lord, ladies and gentlemen. The will is correctly signed by the Testator and witnessed by my two clerks."

He sat back and mopped his brow with his handkerchief. He seemed to have found the last ten minutes something of an ordeal.

Dorothy was looking dazed. "That's—that's very nice," she said. "But, I'm afraid I don't understand: what does 'the remainder of my property' mean?"

"It comprises cash, shares, the house in Walton-upon-Thames and the rest of her personal possessions, not otherwise bequeathed. I calculate the total value to be in the vicinity of sixty-five thousand pounds."

Dorothy's eyes grew so big that it looked as if they were going to take over all her face.

"By Jove!" muttered the Earl.

Gregory whistled softly and even Timothy looked startled.

Dorothy, who now looked on the verge of fainting, tried hard to speak. "Six—six—sixty-five?"

"At a conservative estimate."

"Congratulations, my dear," said Lady Burford warmly. "I am so pleased for you both."

"Yes indeed," added the Earl. "I must admit I had no idea…"

"I doubt any of us had," Timothy said dryly. "Allow me to add my congratulations."

All the rest then joined in, surrounding Dorothy, shaking her hand, or kissing her. The others had momentarily forgotten about Clara, who had not moved a muscle since Dorothy had last spoken to her. So it was a shock when she suddenly jumped to her feet, at the same moment shrieking at the top of her voice: "It's a conspiracy!"

It was like a volcano erupting. She stood there, quivering, and Gerry would not have been surprised to see smoke coming out of her ears. Then she started to speak, loudly and so quickly it was difficult to follow her.

"How dare she! One hundred pounds! To her own daughter-in-law! The woman who brought up her granddaughters, single-handed! It's an insult! But I know what's behind it. Her mind was poisoned against me, by all of you. You've always hated me. And you made certain I wouldn't get what was rightfully mine. Well, you'll regret it, eminent ladies and gentlemen. I know things about all of you, that I've kept secret—some for years, some just for weeks. Things that would make your reputations mud. Well, don't think I'm going to keep quiet about them any more. You just wait! You'll soon regret what's happened today."

And jostling aside those who were gathered round, Clara practically ran to the door and out of the room.

There was a stunned silence. It was broken by the sound of Dorothy sobbing. She looked tearfully round. "I'm so sorry. I'm so terribly sorry."

"You have nothing to apologise for, my dear," Lady Burford told her firmly. "You have done absolutely nothing wrong."

"But for Mother to talk to you all like that…"

"Your *step*mother is plainly overwrought." The Countess put a marked emphasis on the first syllable. "Obviously she did not mean what she said."

Dorothy got awkwardly to her feet. "I'm very much afraid she did," she said quietly. "Will you excuse me, please? I must go to her."

And stumbling slightly, she hurried from the room.

Gerry glanced round at the ring of faces. Was it her imagination, or did most of them at that moment look decidedly apprehensive?

"Poor girl," Lady Burford said, as the door closed behind Dorothy.

"Not exactly poor, Mummy," Gerry said. "Half of sixty-five thousand, after all…"

"You know what I mean. Anyway, let us hope that the money will enable her and her sister to gain their independence now."

"I am not at all sure that it will," Timothy said. "The woman seems to have a psychological hold over her. I know nothing about Agatha, but I fear Dorothy at least may have difficulty in breaking it. I would not be at all surprised if a good part of the estate found its way into Clara's hands before long."

"Oh, that would be terrible." The Countess looked at Bradley. "Can nothing be done to prevent it?"

"I'm afraid not, my lady. Inevitably, in view of the fact that they are no longer young girls, the bequest was made to them absolutely, not in trust. They can do precisely as they wish."

"Can you not put them in touch with a good financial adviser?"

"By all means, if I am asked to do so. But I am not the young ladies' legal representative."

"I think you're worrying unnecessarily," Gerry said. "From what I gather, Agatha has a good head on her shoulders, and is a lot tougher than Dorry. I think she'll take control now."

"I'm just staggered by the size of the estate," said the Earl. "I was always under the impression that Florrie wasn't all that well off. I never liked to ask her, but I did tell her on a number of occasions that if there was ever any help of any kind I could give, she only had to ask. I imagine she knew what I meant."

Miss Mackenzie cleared her throat in a ladylike manner. "If I may say so, Lord Burford, I am sure she did know. Your kindness used to please her very much. But she never needed to take advantage of it."

"I wonder where it all came from. I always understood that Great Uncle Bertie made some pretty disastrous investments."

"I think Mrs. Saunders—Florrie—would like me to explain. She would not want people to imagine that her late husband was financially incompetent. He did make some unwise investments, it is true, but apparently he also made some extremely shrewd ones. Moreover, she told me that he took out a very large life insurance policy soon after their marriage. So all in all she was well provided for. In addition, she herself had been investing, very cleverly, for a great many years. She seemed to have a real flair for it. Though, of course, even I did not know quite how big the estate was."

Tommy gave a guffaw. "I bet old Scary Clara would have been camping out on Florrie's doorstep for years, if she'd known just how much she was worth. Probably thought she was only going to leave a thousand or two, all told. Must admit I was hoping for a hundred quid at the most. Weren't you, Stella?"

"I had no idea what she was going to leave me. I'm just very touched to be remembered at all. After all, I hadn't seen her for eleven years, until a few months ago. She looked at Bradley. "What would fifteen hundred pounds be in dollars?"

"About seven thousand, five hundred."

"How sweet of her."

The Countess said: "I think it's time for tea."

When tea was over, Bradley had left and most of the guests had dispersed to their rooms or elsewhere, Dorothy reappeared. She handed the Countess a folded sheet of notepaper. "From Mother."

Lady Burford unfolded it and read:

My dear Lavinia,

Please let me offer my most sincere apologies for what must have seemed my extremely insulting words to you, Cousin George and Geraldine following the reading of the will. I wish to make it abundantly clear that it was not my intention for one moment to include you in the accusations which I made. Needless to say, I know nothing remotely detrimental about any of you, with whom I have always felt the closest friendship.

I regret that circumstances make it impossible for me to leave Alderley tonight. However, as it would be undoubtedly embarrassing for all concerned if I were to come down to dinner, I shall remain in my room for the rest of the evening. Perhaps, if it is not too inconvenient, a light meal might be served to me here? You may, if you think it necessary, inform your servants that I have an acute headache, which is indeed true.

With repeated apologies, I remain, your friend,

Clara.

Lady Burford looked up. "Please tell your stepmother that what she wishes can be easily arranged. I will also send some tea up immediately. And ask her if she requires aspirin."

"Oh, she has some, thank you. I'll tell her what you said." Dorothy scurried out again.

Lady Burford passed the note to her husband, who read it. "Well, at least she's got the decency to apologise to us, but doesn't say she's sorry for causing the rumpus in the first place. And you notice she doesn't withdraw a thing she said about the others."

"That's very noticeable. Do you suppose it's true, George?"

"What, that she knows their guilty secrets? I've no idea. Not likely, but I suppose it's possible she knows some. But that they all conspired together is obviously nonsense. However, I'm not going to worry about it. I reckon they're all quite capable of looking after themselves. By the way, didn't know Clara was your friend." He passed the note back.

"It's news to me, too, George."

Jean Mackenzie sat in her room and tried to think of her inheritance and what she would do with it. But a nasty, nagging little worry spoiled her full enjoyment of the prospect. It was those last words of Clara's. At first, she had not associated them with herself. But going over them again she had remembered that

Clara had said "I know things about all of you." *All* of you. Could the woman possibly know the awful thing that she, Jean, had done? It didn't seem possible. Unless Florrie had said something to her on Clara's one relatively recent visit. But that was highly unlikely. Florrie had thoroughly disliked Clara and told her as little as possible. But it could have been Agatha—Florrie could have told *her* and Agatha could have passed it on in all innocence to Clara.

Suppose Clara did know what she had done, and why she had done it? It didn't bear thinking about. It would, in Clara's rather vulgar phrase, certainly make her reputation mud. It must not be allowed to happen. She had built that reputation—for probity, honesty, truthfulness—over many years. She could not lose it now.

How, though, could she stop Clara? Would offering her money work? Two hundred pounds, perhaps, or three? It would be a big lump out of her inheritance, but worth it if it silenced Clara for good. But could she be sure it would? Suppose Clara came back for more? That's what blackmailers did. She might bleed her dry. And anyway, how could she approach Clara in the first place? "I'll give you two hundred pounds if you promise to keep quiet about"—when, perhaps, all the time, Clara did *not* know about it. Jean would be giving her the information.

Oh dear, why had she done that awful thing? She would surely be punished. However, it was no good crying over spilt milk. The important thing was to decide what was she going to do now.

Jean thought deeply for several minutes and eventually came to a decision. She gave a firm nod. Yes, she was going to go ahead. She was not going to back out now. Whatever the cost.

Chapter Sixteen

The menu at dinner that evening was superb: chilled watercress soup, poached salmon, roast saddle of venison, with redcurrant jelly, and Summer pudding, containing strawberries, raspberries and black cherries, served with cream. Nevertheless, the meal was a strained occasion. Perhaps it was the presence of Dorothy, who sat low in her chair, merely picking at her food, and when spoken to answered in monosyllables. Lady Burford had to resist a strong urge to order her to sit up straight and answer nicely when addressed. Of the others, Gregory seemed sunk in gloom, Stella distrait; Timothy at the best of times did not excel at light, dinner-table conversation, and Penny was preoccupied and apparently making valiant and unaccustomed efforts to think something through. Miss Mackenzie seemed decidedly nervous and was probably, the Countess thought, feeling rather out of place among a group of people who were all, however distantly, related to each other and all, as she would have described it, her social superiors.

Lady Burford, for whom hosting splendid dinner parties was one of the joys of life, was disappointed. This occasion was perhaps not so very grand—no dress clothes, for one thing, and no especially distinguished guests—but it was, nevertheless, the first for six months, and she had hoped for better.

Only Lord Burford, Gerry and Tommy were in good form, the latter prattling away about various fantastic business plans for which he might use his newly acquired capital. His schemes became more and more wild, and Gerry, realising that without their contributions the atmosphere would resemble that of a morgue, played up to him, adding even more bizarre ideas. Among the projects they came up with were tortoise farming in North Wales, a speech training school for parrots and a company producing reconditioned pencils from the glued-together stubs of old ones.

When they eventually ran out of ideas, the Earl decided to make a contribution. "I've got an idea." They looked at him enquiringly.

"Collapsible and expanding cufflinks."

Tommy stared blankly. "Sorry and all that, but I don't quite get the jolly old joke."

"I'm serious. I've got scores of cufflinks. Happened to mention once years ago that I was always not puttin' 'em in properly, so one fell out and I lost it, or else I kept breaking one of a pair, so I was always short. For ages after that I could practically guarantee gettin' a pair or two every birthday or Christmas. But I've never had a pair that it was easy to put in once you'd got your shirt on. I've never wanted a valet, and it takes me minutes sometimes, if somebody's not around to lend a hand. You want to invent some that are small enough to go through the holes easily, then when they're through, you just press a little button and they suddenly expand. You'd make a fortune."

"I'll certainly bear that in mind," Tommy said. He looked at Gerry. "Make a note of that, Miss Jones."

"Yes, sir."

When the ladies retired at the end of the meal, things were little better in either room. Tommy was out of his element in the company of what he thought of as three old buffers. A glass of vintage port and a cigar did loosen Gregory's tongue somewhat, though Timothy remained aloof and as unbending as ever.

The Earl concentrated on Gregory. "Congratulations on getting that Chippendale desk," he said. "I remember seeing it. Fine piece of work."

"Is it? I've never seen it myself."

"Yes, and in perfect condition, as I remember. Worth quite a bit, I imagine."

Gregory's ears almost visibly pricked up. "Really? Er, how much, I wonder."

"I wouldn't know, my dear fellow. I'm not up in antique furniture. But you won't want to sell it, will you? I mean, tremendous historical interest, and all that, owned by both the Pitts; absolutely fitting that it should stay in the family *and* be owned by an MP, what?"

"Oh yes, yes, of course. I mean, no, I wouldn't want to sell it. Of course not."

Timothy spoke for the first time. "Nothing would induce me to sell my set of Dickens, no matter how short of money I was."

"I am not short of money," Gregory said angrily. "I was simply wondering about the value for insurance purposes. Those of us on fixed salaries have to think about these things, not being in a position to charge exorbitant fees for our work."

"Perhaps those on fixed salaries should be careful to keep their non-essential expenses down to a minimum."

"Just what do you—"

The Earl broke in hastily. "Incidentally, wanted to say how much I appreciated your words at the funeral. Absolutely right, I thought: not too gloomy, but not too flippant either."

"Oh, thank you. One does one's best."

"Have some more port," said the Earl. He refilled their glasses.

Tommy, having drunk nothing so good before, sipped it appreciatively. He was beginning to feel more at home. "Must say, I do envy you fellows who can speak like that in public. I mean, if it's only a few people and everyone's feeling jolly I can chat away about anything."

"We would never have known," Timothy put in.

"No, I mean as long as I haven't got to talk about anything in particular, I'm fine."

"You would clearly make a splendid Member of Parliament. They are expert at talking about nothing in particular for hours on end."

"That from a lawyer!" Gregory sneered.

Lord Burford hastened to encourage Tommy; anything to keep the other two from getting at each other's throats. "So what's your problem, exactly, my boy?"

Tommy, who had really said all he had wanted to, ploughed on. "Well, I mean it's when it comes to talking seriously about a particular subject that I dry up. I mean, I was best man at a chum's wedding recently. Hundred guests and I was bally nervous. In the end it wasn't too bad, because I was able to spin 'em a few jokes. But you can't always do that, can you? I mean, you couldn't tell the one about the lighthouse keeper's daughter at a funeral, could you?"

"Oh, I don't know," said Gregory, "there are some people so totally without humour or warmth that they wouldn't recognise it as a joke at all."

"Shall we join the ladies?" said Lord Burford.

In the drawing-room, talk was not quite so stilted, this being largely due to the fact that Penny and Stella now seemed to be the best of friends and chatted together quietly, except for the occasional burst of laughter. However, Dorothy and Jean Mackenzie both totally failed to respond to Lady Burford's attempts to engage them in conversation, so that she was forced to talk to her own daughter. She would actually have been grateful for the company of Clara, who, as she remembered, conversed extremely fluently. Usually it had just been gossip—sometimes quite scandalous, but nevertheless, the Countess had to admit, often rather interesting…

She was, therefore, relieved when the men eventually arrived, followed by Merryweather and a footman with coffee. After this, the atmosphere lightened as people moved into smaller groups or pairs.

Penny moved up to Tommy. He grinned at her. "I say, this is all rather splendid, isn't it?"

"Mm. Tommy, I want to say something."

"I'm all ears."

"You mustn't be annoyed, but I don't think they're going to work."

"What aren't?"

"Some of your ideas. The pencils, for instance. It would take an awfully long time to stick them together. And I don't think you'd find glue strong enough to hold them. They'd break up again when you pressed hard."

Tommy just said: "Ah."

"And I don't think there are enough people who want to buy tortoises. The school for parrots could work, but it might take absolutely ages to teach just one to talk properly, and how much would people be willing to pay for the tuition?"

About to explain, Tommy wisely thought better of it. He just nodded thoughtfully. "Yes, I think you're absolutely right, Penny. I tend to get carried away, you know, but I can see, now you've pointed it out, that they're all rather impractical schemes. Thanks very much. You've got quite a head for business, haven't you?"

Penny flushed a bright pink. "Oh, do you really think so? It would be lovely if I had. It must be such fun to be a career woman, running your own company."

"I don't know that it's always much fun, actually."

"Oh, but it must be. Think of all that lovely money rolling in every week, and a private office and a secretary and letter headings and business cards with your name on: 'Penelope Saunders, Managing Director.'" She gave a wistful sigh. "You have got a bit of money now. You can try. I was hoping Florrie was going to leave me some, too, but all I've got is pearls."

"They sound lovely, though."

"But I'll hardly ever be able to wear them. They'll be shut up in Daddy's safe practically all the time. Of course, I might take them out sometimes, when he's away—I know the combination—but he doesn't go away very often and if I did it would be just my luck if they were stolen."

"But they'd be insured, so you'd have the cash value then, which is what you want. It would the best thing that could happen."

"Unless Daddy just invested the cash for me. In which case, I wouldn't see a penny."

"But it would be your money. You'll be of age in a couple of years. You could do what you liked with it."

"I wouldn't dare go against him. He'd probably cut off my allowance." She looked thoroughly miserable.

Tommy tried to cheer her up. "Tell you what, I'll steal them from his safe, sell them, and we'll split the proceeds."

A beatific smile spread over Penny's face. "Oh, Tommy, would you really do that for me?"

He was taken aback. The girl took everything you said perfectly seriously. Of course, given that she'd been brought up in a home without humour, it was hardly surprising. And in a way, he thought, it was kind of endearing. It made her seem so vulnerable. You felt you wanted to protect her. He said hastily: "Of course I would. But I think we ought to leave it as a last resort. If your father ever found out, he'd never forgive you, and you wouldn't want to risk that."

"I suppose not." Penny sounded doubtful.

"Tell you what," he said. "I won't start my own business without consulting you. You can be my adviser. Then when I get it up and going you can come and work with me. We can be partners. Or I'll be Chairman and you can be Managing Director; you can have cards printed and everything. Though I can't promise you a secretary, yet."

Penny almost jumped in the air with excitement. "Oo, Tommy that'll be absolutely divine!"

"Yes, won't it?" said Tommy, wondering what he had let himself in for.

◇◇◇

Timothy, sitting by himself on a large sofa, fastidiously sipping a cup of unsweetened black coffee, and looking disapprovingly at his daughter, as she talked to Tommy, glanced up as a shadow fell over him. It was Stella. "May I sit down?"

"Please." He made a gesture with his hand.

She did so. "I wanted to have a word with you."

"Oh? About what?"

The curtness with which he asked the question was not auspicious, but Stella carried on.

"I wanted first to congratulate you."

"On what?"

"On Penny. She's such a lovely girl."

"Oh, she's pretty enough, I dare say. But I cannot claim any credit for that."

"I didn't only mean that. She's has so much charm."

"I'm afraid she doesn't get that from her father, either."

"Well, there's one thing I'm sure she does get from him: she's smart."

He raised his eyebrows. "Are you serious?"

"Oh, she's not an intellectual. But she knows what she wants and my guess is she knows how to get it."

"I must admit I am surprised by what you say. She seems to me to live in a fantasy world much of the time."

"She day-dreams. What's the harm in that, at her age? She's also kind-hearted, totally without spite and devastatingly honest."

"You've summed her up remarkably quickly."

"Yes, but I've always been good at that, and we have to do it in my work. Sure, these are only my first impressions. Plainly you know her far better than I do."

"Sometimes I feel I don't know her at all. But I appreciate very much what you say, and on consideration I think you're probably correct. Perhaps I do tend to dwell too much on the negative side of her personality. No doubt because I worry about her so. "

"That's only natural. But I think you've done a great job, raising her on your own. It must have been hard."

"Well, her mother was there until she was nearly thirteen. It was terrible for Penelope, losing her then. I was proud of the way she handled it. But the past six years have not been easy. I knew nothing about teen-aged girls, really. Perhaps I've been too strict. She certainly thinks so. It's no secret that relations between us are somewhat strained at times. But girls of that age seem so vulnerable. One hears such terrible things. A few moments of recklessness and a life can be ruined. I've been so desperate to protect her that perhaps I've gone too far."

After the first few moments of suspicion, he seemed now relieved to be talking; probably, Stella thought, he normally had no one to unburden himself to.

"I was the only one able even to try and take her mother's place," he went on. "It wasn't as though she had an older sister or any aunts. Both my wife and I were only children, and her relatives are scattered throughout the country."

"You have at least one cousin, though, who is married, and living in London."

"Gregory? We never meet except unavoidably, on occasions such as this. Besides, his wife, Alexandra, is extremely aloof and very politically minded—the only reason, I'm sure, she married Gregory. She would have no interest in Penelope at all."

"I was chatting to Gregory this afternoon."

"I noticed." Timothy's manner was becoming slightly chillier again.

"He seemed very friendly."

"Oh, I'm sure he did. You appeared to be getting on famously."

"I was just making his acquaintance, really. Actually, I thought he might be able to help me. I'm hoping to make a career change. He's offered to lend a helping hand."

"I should be very cautious of Gregory's helping hands."

"Oh, I shall be extremely cautious of Gregory's hands: they may well want to help themselves."

For the first time since she had first seen him, Timothy smiled. "I can see that there are no flies on you—isn't that what they say in the United States?"

"Working as a journalist in New York City for nearly eleven years does help in that respect."

"I'm sure. I just wish that Penelope had someone as sophisticated and worldly-wise as you that she could look to for advice and help."

"Why can't she? I'd be delighted. Of course, we don't really move in the same circles."

"I'm sure that can be rectified. Look, perhaps you would care to come to dinner in a week or two. I'll make sure Penny's there—oh, I'm sure she'll want to be, anyway."

"That'd be swell. Thank you."

"Excellent. I'll look forward to it."

"And I have an idea. How old is she?"

"Nearly nineteen."

"When's her birthday?"

"The first of October."

"Why not throw her a party? Oh, I know not much is made of a nineteenth birthday, as a rule: people keep the big celebration for the twenty-first. But let this be an extra one—a sort of bonus. It'd be a thrill for her, I'm sure, and show her how much you care. I'd be pleased to help organise it, if you like."

Timothy nodded. "Yes, that is a very good idea. And I would certainly appreciate your help. I would not have the first idea how to set about it. In fact, you may find yourself doing more than merely *helping* to organise it, I'm afraid."

"That's fine by me. I'll enjoy it."

"The only trouble is that I suppose she'll want to invite Tommy. She's getting too close to that young whipper-snapper."

"Oh, Tommy's all right."

He said quickly: "I'm so sorry. I'd forgotten he's quite a close relative of yours, isn't he? Do forgive me."

"That's all right. He's only a first cousin. But I am fond of him. What have you got against him?"

"I'm sure he's quite without malice, but he just seems such a loafer, with absolutely no power of perseverance. He's had about a dozen jobs in the last four or five years. He's never going to amount to anything. He's the last sort of friend Penelope needs."

"He may just be one of those guys who takes a long time to find his niche. I'm sure he'll settle down—especially now he's got this money. I fancy he might pleasantly surprise everybody one day."

"I sincerely hope you're right. Because the more I criticise him, the more vehemently Penelope defends him. So it seems I'm going to have to tolerate him."

"I'm sure it's good tactics to try."

"Anyway, er, Stella, I'm really very grateful for your interest, and your offer. If there's anything I can do…"

"You know, Timothy, I'm very glad you said that."

"Indeed?" He looked slightly startled at the quickness and eagerness of her response. "Well, by all means, feel free."

"Now I know what you're thinking: first the offer to help and now the quid pro quo. But it's not that. I really do think Penny's a great kid, and I'll be glad to help her in any way I can. But I would like your assistance. If you say no, it won't make any difference as regards her. And no, to pre-empt your next suspicion, I am not looking for free legal advice. However, I do want to use you shamelessly to help further my career."

"In what way?"

"Would you let me interview you?"

"I'm afraid I do not understand."

"Well, as you may know, I'm a fashion journalist."

"I am afraid that if you are seeking my opinions on the latest fashions, I have to tell you it is something I know nothing about, and care as little."

"Well, we have one thing in common at least. While I know a lot about it, I'm coming to care about it as little as you do—or at least, writing about it professionally."

"That must make life rather difficult."

"Not really, just boring. Which is why I would like to break into a different branch of journalism, a more serious side. And I've been thinking that an interview with you, one of the country's foremost attorneys—" She broke off, with a laugh. "Sorry—foremost barristers, might well appeal to one of the weekly or monthly magazines."

"I find it hard to believe that any magazine would find me of interest. And I have to say that I deplore this modern tendency to build lawyers up as personalities, like film stars. Marshall Hall had a lot to answer for, great advocate though he was."

The reference meant nothing to Stella. But she carried on. "I'd place a bet that I could make your life sound a heck of a lot more interesting than you think it is. I mean, just your experiences of looking after a teen-age daughter unaided would make a fascinating story. But of course I wouldn't write about that. I was thinking more about your cases."

"No doubt of the more sensational ones?"

"Oh, of course. All the ones packed with jealousy, revenge, violence, blood, adultery."

"I'm sorry. That was ungracious of me. Which ones would you really want to write about?"

"The most interesting ones from a legal point of view. I'd also like to get your views about the law in general and the legal system—how you think it might be improved, for instance."

Timothy took a sip of coffee before saying: "Well, I certainly can see no objection to a serious piece of that nature. As a matter of fact, the editor of *The British Monthly* approached me some time ago, suggesting I wrote an article for him, along those very lines."

"Oh, then it seems I'm redundant, if you intend to write such an article yourself."

"Not at all, I turned him down. I just did not have the time. But I could certainly give you the facts and my opinions and you could write it up, if that is acceptable to you."

"Acceptable? It would be terrific. I'd have a market for the piece ready and waiting."

"I could get in touch with him, confirm that he is still interested and tell him the plan. You could then see him yourself and ascertain precisely what he requires in terms of length, general approach and so on."

"That's better still. Timothy, I could kiss you!"

He looked away quickly and cleared his throat. She realised the last words had been a mistake. "And you definitely would not write about me as a person?"

"Well, just a few basic details, perhaps. Give it a little human interest."

"I have to say that I dislike human interest."

"It does help sell papers."

"I suppose so."

"And it might be an idea to include a couple of anecdotes, just to lighten it a little. You must have had some amusing experiences in court."

"None that seemed amusing at the time; embarrassing rather. Later one can smile."

"Can you think of one in particular?"

"Well, perhaps, but I don't think it would—"

"Oh, I'd just love to hear it."

"You may not find it at all amusing."

"Try me."

"Very well. It happened many years ago, when I was an inexperienced young barrister. It was a case, strangely enough, involving a will. It was hand-written, not drawn up by a solicitor, but perfectly legal—if it were genuine. In it, the Testator left all his property to his only son, who had lived some distance away, and it omitted any mention of his daughter, who had lived with him and looked after him for a number of years. I represented the daughter, whose contention was that the will was a forgery by her brother, who had slipped it among their father's papers on one of his infrequent visits. The matter seemed easy enough to resolve, so we sent the will, and a letter, known to have been written by the deceased, to a professional graphologist by the name of William Jones, who in a written report stated that in his view the will was definitely a forgery.

"Came the time for me to call my expert. I said: 'My next witness is Mr. William Jones.' The usher put his head into the corridor, called out: 'William Jones,' a man entered and went into the witness box. I did what I normally did on such occasions, ran through his professional qualifications, prior to asking the first question—something along the lines of: 'Mr. Jones, you are a professional graphologist of many years experience, who has worked extensively with numerous police forces.' He did not say anything, just looked a little bewildered, but I assumed that he perhaps he hadn't often actually given evidence in court, and I carried on hurriedly: 'Would you be so good as to look at these two documents and say whether in your opinion they were written by the same person?' I passed the will and the letter to the usher, who handed them to the witness. He gazed at the papers for quite a long time, and then said, in a broad west country accent: 'Couldn't rightly say. They certainly look the same.' I was totally flabbergasted. I said: 'But Mr. Jones, you have had the opportunity to study these documents at leisure and examine them under magnification, have you not?' 'No,' he said. 'Never seen 'em before.'

"Well, you can guess what's coming. This was not my William Jones. This William Jones had been waiting to give evidence as a witness to a traffic accident in another court. It transpired he had been too nervous to correct me when I listed his qualifications, imagining he would be guilty of contempt of court."

"Oh, that's priceless. I love it. And I suppose at that very moment your Mr. Jones was indignantly denying that he'd ever been anywhere near a road accident." She threw back her head and laughed.

Seeming to find her amusement infectious, Timothy joined in. It was a strange and rarely heard sound, a sort of dry "hih-hih-hih-hih," all on the same note.

Standing not more than eight feet away, Penny spun her head and stared at him, an expression of astonishment on her face. She whispered: "Tommy, Daddy's laughing!"

Tommy had followed her gaze. Penny went on: "I haven't heard him laugh for years. Not since Mummy died."

Tommy didn't reply, and Penny plucked at his sleeve. "Tommy?"

He ignored her, took a few indecisive steps away from her towards Timothy and Stella. For a ghastly moment, Penny thought he was going to ask them not to make so much noise, but then he stopped and came back. He was wearing a strangely blank expression. "Sorry. You were saying?"

She repeated the words. "Oh. Well, good. That's fine." He seemed as surprised as she was.

Chapter Seventeen

At about twenty past ten, Dorothy slipped from the room, whispering to Lady Burford that she was going to say good-night to her mother. She returned in about ten minutes and drew the Countess aside.

"Could—could I ask you a very big favour?"

"Of course, my dear."

"Would you be very kind and look in on Mother? She really does want to apologise to you personally, but she's very anxious to avoid seeing anyone else, and wants to leave early in the morning. It would so ease her mind."

About to remark that she felt no obligation to go out of her way to ease Clara's mind, Lady Burford took in Dorothy's wan and quite haggard face and relented. "Very well. I'll go up now."

"Oh, thank you so much." Her gratitude was almost pitiable.

Lady Burford left the room. She came back in about seven or eight minutes. Dorothy immediately hurried across to her. "Well?"

"We've talked quite freely. Your stepmother did say some highly insulting things about members of George's—and your—family, and made some actual threats, which I told her frankly that I considered indefensible. She would not, however, apologise for that, and I believe she is truly convinced that some of them conspired against her. However, she has apologised handsomely for embarrassing George and me and Geraldine, as well as for any aspersions she seemed to have cast on us. I have accepted that apology and we left on relatively good terms."

Dorothy gave a big sigh of relief. "Oh, I'm so glad. Thank you."

"I asked her if she wanted any refreshments and she requested a cup of cocoa and a couple of digestive biscuits, which I have arranged to be taken to her."

"You're really so kind. I'm sure she'll sleep better now—oh, I don't mean because of the cocoa, but having spoken to you."

The Countess smiled. "You're a very loyal and dutiful daughter."

◇◇◇

It was shortly after this that the Earl made a short speech—one that he had delivered on a number of other occasions. "Just a word about our burglar alarm. It's unique and we think fool-proof. The one drawback is that while nobody can get in, no one can get out either, without setting it off. You'll find your bedroom windows will only open six inches. If you force them more than that—and, of course, you can do that quite easily in the event of a fire or some other emergency—or break the window or force an outside door, you'll trigger it. It can't be switched off but turns itself off automatically at six-thirty."

It had been a long, tiring day for all of those present, and a stressful one for some, and few felt like staying up late that night. By eleven o'clock only the younger people were still downstairs. They chatted for another quarter of an hour, before Tommy, Stella and Penny all went upstairs together, the girls leaving him at the top of the staircase and making their way together to their rooms in the west corridor. Gerry, who, of course, still felt wide awake, and Dorothy were left in sole possession of the drawing-room.

"Well," Gerry asked, "what's it feel like to be an heiress?"

"Wonderful—I think. I mean, I haven't really taken it in properly yet."

Gerry stood up. "Want a drink?"

"Oh, no thank you. I don't really drink alcohol very much."

"Hot drink? Coffee, tea?"

"A cup of tea would be lovely."

Gerry rang the bell, poured herself a glass of wine and sat down again.

Dorothy said: "You're not going to bed yet?"

"No, it's much too early for me. I'm a real night owl."

"Oh, good. I'm usually tucked up by this time, but I'm sure I couldn't sleep tonight."

"I'm not surprised. It's been quite a day."

A footman entered at that moment and Gerry ordered a pot of tea.

When he had departed, Gerry said: "You phoned Agatha, I suppose?"

"No. I meant to immediately after the reading, but then that trouble with Mother put it right out of my head. By the time I remembered, it was too late, because she was going out for the whole evening, until quite late. I might phone her last thing, if that's all right."

"Of course. She'll be over the moon, won't she?"

"I expect so. I mean, we were pretty sure we were going to get something, but nothing like this."

"Got any plans?"

"Not really. It'll depend on what Mother says."

Gerry felt a surge of exasperation. "It's your money, Dorry— yours and Agatha's."

"Oh, Aggie will probably be full of plans, when I tell her. She might even want to move into Grandmother's house. She'd like to be out of town, nearer the country. But I'm sure Mother wouldn't let me go with her, and she wouldn't want to move out of London. So I suppose I'll be staying in Hampstead."

"You must tell her what you want to do, and then just do it."

Dorothy looked doubtful. "I don't know if I could."

The tea arrived a few moments later. When she was sipping a very sweet and milky cup, Dorothy said shyly: "Do you still feel like telling me about the murders?"

"Yes, of course, if you really want to hear it."

"Oh, yes please!" She kicked off her shoes and tucked her feet up under her. "This is such fun."

It was amazing, Gerry thought, how much happier and more relaxed she was now Clara was not around.

"It's difficult to know where to start," she said. "You probably know most of the facts, from the papers. So why don't you just ask me questions?"

"All right." Dorothy was eager. "One thing I didn't understand is what made you decide, that first night, to go on watch in the corridor after everybody supposedly had gone to bed?"

"Just a general uneasiness. As you know, we had two foreign diplomats here, an American millionaire, his wife and her fabulous diamond necklace, a notorious jewel thief was active, and we had one guest who had virtually gate-crashed under very suspicious circumstances. I was sure something fishy was going on, and I just had to try and find out…"

"And the very next day he proposed to you," Dorothy said, with a sigh, a little over an hour later. "And you said yes. It's so romantic."

Gerry grinned. "Well, I hardly felt I could turn him down, after he'd risked his life to save mine."

"That's not the reason, though…?"

"No, no. I was quite certain by then. If he hadn't proposed, I probably should have."

"When are you getting married?"

"I don't know. We would have been married by now, but the poor darling had a death in the family, and that led to a lot of complications, which he had to go and try to sort out. Which is why I'm here at the mo—"

She stopped short and both girls gave a start as from somewhere in the house came the sound of a loud crash. It had a sort of metallic ring to it, as if someone had dropped a heavy tool box. Although muffled by the thick drawing-room door, Gerry realised that the fact they could hear it at all must mean it had been very loud. She jumped to her feet. "What on earth was that?"

She hurried to the door and pulled it open. Dorothy, after thrusting her feet into her shoes, joined her. For a second, all was silent, then came the sound of a woman's voice. It was shouting, sounding more angry than afraid, and definitely came from upstairs, but from which wing it was impossible to tell. They could not make out the words.

Dorothy gasped: "Oh, can that be Mother?"

"Let's go and find out," Gerry said.

She ran across the hall and up the grand staircase, Dorothy at her shoulder. They had nearly reached the head of the stairs before the shouting stopped. At the top, Gerry turned towards the east corridor and passed a room on her left, which was used for the storage of linen and where the upstairs end of the secret passage emerged. The next room was the last before the corner which led to the east corridor. She made to hurry on, but Dorothy stopped by it. "This is Mother's room."

"Oh." Gerry had not known which room had been allocated to Clara. "I think the voice came from farther away."

"Let me just check." Dorothy tapped on the panel. There was no response and she opened the door an inch or two and gave a loud stage whisper. "Mother? Are you all right?" There was still no reply, and she opened the door wider, groped for the light switch and clicked it on. Then she gave a muffled half gasp, half-scream and moved violently backwards, cannoning into Gerry.

Gerry stared past her into the room. The large double bed, sideways on to them in the centre of the wall on their right, was wildly dishevelled, the bedclothes half falling onto the floor. Clara was lying across the bed, her head hanging over the near side. Her face was nearly as white as the bed linen and her eyes, pointing fixedly at them, were totally lifeless.

Chapter Eighteen

Dorothy buried her face in Gerry's shoulder. Her voice came in hoarse whispers. "No. No. No." Gerry wanted to scream herself, but she just raised her hand and robot-like patted Dorothy on the shoulder.

Then there was the patter of footsteps, and suddenly her father was beside them. Gerry had never been so pleased to see him.

"What the deuce is going on?"

Gerry just pointed into the room. He gazed past her and made a sharp intake of breath. Then he went into the room. He gingerly approached the bed, bent and took the wrist of Clara's left hand, which was hanging down, nearly touching the floor. He clasped it for a few seconds, then let it go and straightened up. He turned round, looked at Gerry and slowly shook his head.

That second the Countess arrived. "What's wrong?"

Gerry said: "It's Clara. She's dead. It looks as though she's been murdered."

"Oh no! It can't be possible!"

"I'm afraid there's no mistake." The Earl's face was almost as white as the dead woman's. He muttered: "I feared something like this."

Dorothy was now sobbing uncontrollably, convulsions shaking her body.

Rapidly getting a grip on herself, Lady Burford said: "Geraldine, take Dorothy to her room."

"Yes, yes, of course." She said gently: "Come along Dorry," and tried to lead her away. But Dorothy suddenly resisted. "No. I must see her first, properly."

She pulled away from Gerry and half-stumbled into the room. She crossed to the bed and stood looking down for ten seconds, while the others watched. Then she turned and came back. "I—I think I would like to go and lie down now."

"Come along, then." Gerry put her arm round Dorothy's shoulder. "Er, which is your room?"

Dorothy pointed to the left. "The third on the right."

"Oh, next door to me." Gerry led her slowly along the corridor and opened the door of Dorothy's room. As she did so, she saw the door of the outside corner bedroom at the end of the corridor open and Timothy, dressing-gowned, emerging. She did not pause to explain the situation to him, but switched on the light, led Dorothy into the room and pushed the door closed behind them. Just inside, Dorothy suddenly resisted.

"What's the matter?"

"If Mother was—was murdered, the murderer's got to still be in the house, hasn't he?"

"Oh, I don't think—"

"But your burglar alarm. The Earl was saying earlier that no one can get out without setting it off."

Gerry bit her lip. It was, of course, true.

"Suppose he's in here?" Dorothy said, fearfully.

"I'm sure he's not."

"But why not? We must search. Will you look under the bed?"

"Of course."

She walked across to the bed and knelt down, while Dorothy went to the large wardrobe, stopped and took a deep breath, before reaching for the knob. In spite of her airy manner, Gerry did feel a slight *frisson* of apprehension as she lifted the bedspread and lowered her head. Just suppose...? But all was clear. She stood up at the same moment as Dorothy, with obvious relief, firmly reclosed the wardrobe door.

"Nothing," Gerry said, "and there's nowhere else in here he could be." The rest of the furniture consisted of a dressing-table and stool, a bedside table, one easy and one upright chair.

"I expect you think I'm terribly silly."

"No, I should have thought of it."

Dorothy sat on the bed, meticulously removed her shoes, then put her legs up and lay down.

"Can I get you some brandy?" Gerry asked.

"No, really, thank you."

"Or just a glass of water?"

"Nothing at all just now, thank you."

"I'll stay with you."

"There's really no need."

"I want to."

"Well, if you're sure. You very kind."

Gerry sat down herself in the easy chair. Her mind was in a whirl and she did not know what to say. Should she offer sympathy and commiserations? It hardly seemed adequate. Would apologies be more in order? Did any blame attach to her family? On two occasions they had had guests murdered under their roof. Now it had happened again. Was there anything she or her parents could have done to prevent it? Gerry closed her eyes. She suddenly felt very, very tired—something she was not at all used to.

Meanwhile, Lord Burford was explaining to a shocked Timothy what had occurred. Within a few seconds, they were joined by Gregory, Jean Mackenzie and finally by Tommy, to all of whom the situation had to be explained anew. Each of them, it seemed, had been woken by the crash and had got up to investigate.

"What the dickens caused that noise?" the Earl muttered. "There's nothing in there"—he pointed into Clara's room—"to account for it."

"I can tell you that," said Gregory. "I was closest to it. Tremendous noise. The door of your art gallery's open, and I looked in. It was that old suit of armour you've got in there. It's fallen over—pieces scattered all over the place."

Lord Burford looked totally bewildered. "Why on earth should he have gone in there? There's no way out that way. And he surely couldn't have knocked it over accidentally."

Before anyone could answer him they saw a sudden moving splash of colour at the far end of the main corridor. It was Stella and Penny, one in a sky-blue and the other a pink dressing-gown. They hurried towards the group, Stella calling out urgently: "Have you caught him?"

The Earl stared at her. "You saw him?"

"Yes, he was in my room."

"In *your* room?" It was Timothy who reacted first. He looked really concerned. "Did he attempt to harm you?"

"No. Something woke me, I opened my eyes and could just see the outline of a person poking about by the dresser. I yelled out something and he made a bee-line for the door."

"Thank God. But what a terrifying experience for you!"

"It was all over too quick to be terrifying, really. I kept on shouting, he ran out and I lost sight of him. I jumped out of bed and ran to the door. I was still shouting at the top of my voice—I read once that if you surprise a burglar it's best to make as much noise as you can—but he'd disappeared. Then Penny emerged."

Penny said: "I didn't see him. I just came out to see what Stella was shouting about. We decided the best thing to do was wake Daddy. Then, when we got to his room, we saw you all. What *is* happening?"

The Earl put his hands to his head. "Will somebody please tell them? I can't go through it all again."

Timothy drew the two girls aside and started talking to them in a low voice. Penny gave a little scream. Stella remained silent, but her eyes widened in horror.

The Countess said urgently: "George, we can't stand here all night like this. We must do something."

"Yes, yes, of course. Losin' my grip a bit, I'm afraid. Just all too damn familiar. Doctor, first, I suppose, then the police. Lavinia, could you telephone them?"

"Of course."

"I'll have to organise a search of the house. I'll rouse Merry-weather, and he can wake the footmen. There are three of them, but it's still going to take some time."

Gregory said: "Well, you can count on me to help."

"Yes, me too," Tommy said eagerly.

"Oh, thank you. Well, William, Benjamin and Albert are all strapping lads, and even Merryweather's no weakling, so we should be able to handle him."

Timothy turned away from the girls and was obviously about to speak. But before he could do so, Gregory addressed him directly.

"You'll probably be advised to keep out of it, dear cousin. I mean, *you're* not exactly a strapping lad, are you?"

Timothy's face remained expressionless but his complexion noticeably darkened. He moved towards Gregory and held out his hand. "I appreciate your being so concerned for my safety."

Clearly taken aback, Gregory hesitated for a second before taking the proffered hand.

Nobody afterwards could say precisely what happened next. With the speed of a striking cobra, Timothy pulled Gregory towards him, turned, put his left arm round Gregory's neck, bent his knees and drove back with his hips. The larger man's feet left the ground, he performed a graceful somersault in the air and the next second had landed on his back with a thump that shook the floor. Timothy said quietly: "I have been practising ju-jitsu for a number of years, and am a 3rd Dan."

As Gregory clambered awkwardly to his feet, the others gazed at Timothy speechlessly, the two girls with something like awe.

"Zowie!" Stella murmured under her breath, then softly to Penny: "Did you know he could do that?"

Penny, wide-eyed, shook her head. She whispered: "He goes to a gym twice a week, but I thought he just did physical jerks and things."

"He's quite a guy, your pa."

Meanwhile, as though nothing had happened, Timothy was addressing the Earl. "Naturally, I will take part in the search. You are convinced, I take it, that this villain is still on the premises."

"Um—what? Er…" He was uncertain whether or not to make any comment about what had happened, then decided it was better not to. "Can't see any other explanation. I explained about our security system. Merryweather locked up at about ten thirty—he always reports to me as soon as he's done so—at which time the alarm automatically switches on. So the fellow must have got in before that. Now, we'd better search in pairs: each of us go with one of the servants. You three chaps better follow their leadin', as they all know the house like the backs of their hands. I don't suppose any of you ladies feel like goin' back to bed?" He looked in turn at Jean Mackenzie, Stella and Penny. There was a vigorous shaking of heads.

"Right, then, I suggest you all go downstairs with Lavinia. Stay together and you should be quite safe. Now I suppose I've got to wake Merryweather and tell him the news."

Chapter Nineteen

Gerry jumped to her feet as a light knock came at the door, and Dorothy opened her eyes. Gerry hurried to the door. "Who is it?"

"Me." It was the Earl's voice.

She opened the door. "What's happening?" she asked.

He kept his voice low. "We've just completed a search of the house. There's no sign of an intruder."

Gerry's eyes widened. "Are you sure?"

"Absolutely. We've looked in every room, every recess, in every cupboard, under every bed. Even the secret passage."

"And he's certainly not in here."

"That's what I was going to ask you. It suddenly occurred to me."

"I checked under the bed and Dorry in the wardrobe. I suppose the alarm system *could* be faulty. I mean, nothing's absolutely infallible, so he could have got out."

"Possible, I suppose. No doubt the police will check it."

"You've called them?"

"Your mother will have done so by now."

"Where is everybody?"

"Downstairs. I'm just going to join them. I need a drink. Er, you'll stay here, I suppose?"

Gerry was about to answer when Dorothy joined them in the doorway.

"How are you, my dear?" asked the Earl.

"All right, thank you."

"Forgive my mentionin' it, but you haven't phoned your sister, have you?"

Dorothy shook her head. "I explained to Gerry, she was going to a party this evening. I meant to phone about half-past twelve. I think she would have been back by that time. But then—it all happened. Er, what time is it?"

Lord Burford glanced at his watch. "Just gone one thirty."

"She's sure to be in bed by now."

"But she'd want to be woken, wouldn't she?"

"She wouldn't hear the phone. It's in the hall, and neither Aggie nor I can hear it in our rooms. Mother's is the only bedroom it can be heard from. Of course, if you think I should try…"

"Well, it wouldn't do any harm, if you feel up to it."

"Oh yes, I'll come down now."

On the way downstairs, Gerry said: "She'll have been wondering why you haven't phoned."

"Yes, I expect so."

"I wonder why she didn't call here."

"I don't think she knows your number, actually."

"Oh, and of course, we're ex-directory, so she couldn't get it from Enquiries. Stupid of me. And it's so easy, too: Alderley One." She thought that to keep chatting away about trivialities might help a little to take the other girl's mind off the horror of the situation, but wasn't really hopeful.

She took Dorothy to the telephone room and waited outside while she made the call.

Lord Burford went to the drawing-room, where he found all the guests gathered. The women had been told about the result of the search, and everybody was looking rather grim as the full implications of this sank in.

Lord Burford crossed to the Countess. "Did you get through all right?"

She nodded. "Dr. Ingleby was out on a confinement, but his wife will notify him immediately he returns. I told her there was no great urgency, as there is nothing he can do. I also spoke to P.C. Dobson in the village—not going into any great detail. He was going to inform the County Police Headquarters in Westchester and then cycle here. I told him, too, that there was no hurry, as I knew you would want to complete the search before having to set off the alarm."

"Quite right, my dear. Thank you."

"And George—I'm so sorry. You were against this little house party from the start, I know. I talked you into it. And your worst fears have been realised. I feel very much to blame. But who could have anticipated that something like this could happen, again?"

"No need to blame yourself, Lavinia. I went along. Heaven help me, I went along."

◇◇◇

Dorothy came out of the telephone room in about three minutes. "No reply."

"Well, at least you can tell her you tried. What do you want to do now? Come into the drawing-room with the others?"

"No, I think I'd like to go back up to my room."

"Come on, then."

"No, Gerry, there's no need for you to come with me."

"Oh, but I don't mind, honestly."

"No, really, you've been marvellous, but I would like to be on my own for a while."

"If you're certain. Do you want anything?"

"A cup of tea would be nice."

"All right, I'll have some sent up."

"Thank you very much."

"Oh, and don't be startled if you hear an alarm bell shortly. We'll be opening the door to let the doctor and police in."

"Of course."

Dorothy ascended the stairs. Gerry watched her until she disappeared from sight, then pulled the cord of the nearest bell.

Merryweather arrived within seconds. He was fully dressed and as immaculate as ever.

"Merry, will you have some tea sent up to Miss Dorothy, please?"

"Certainly, my lady." He started to turn away.

"And Merry, thank you. For taking all this so wonderfully in your stride, I mean. Please thank all the servants. I'm so sorry you're having to go through it all again."

"That is quite all right, your ladyship. I, for one, am becoming quite accustomed to these occurrences."

Gerry joined the others in the drawing-room. For the next ten minutes, conversation was virtually non-existent. When one had said how terrible it was and how inexplicable three or four times, there seemed nothing more to say.

At last there came the sound of the doorbell. The Earl heaved himself to his feet. "That'll be Ingleby or Dobson."

He went out to the great hall, where Merryweather was approaching the front doors. He unlocked and unbolted them, and pulled one open. Immediately a deafeningly loud clanging shattered the silence.

It was Dobson who was standing in the porch.

"Come in, Constable," Lord Burford shouted above the din.

"Thank you, my lord." He removed his helmet, carefully and unnecessarily wiped his feet and entered.

The Earl went up to him and spoke loudly into his ear. "Come into the morning-room. Won't be so loud in there. It is morning, after all."

He led the way and when he had shut the door behind them the noise was considerably muffled. "What did my wife tell you, exactly?"

"Just that a lady had been found dead, my lord, and that it looked as though foul play might be involved."

"I think that's pretty definite. Her name is Mrs. Clara Saunders. She's a distant cousin of mine."

Dobson took out his notebook and slowly wrote down the name. "She would have been one of the mourners at the funeral, my lord?"

"Yes, she was the dead lady's daughter-in-law. D'you want me to go on?"

"I don't think there's much point, my lord. Better to wait until the CID arrive and give them all the details."

"So, what do you want to do?"

"I had better inspect the remains, my lord. There is not much else that I can do."

"Very well, I'll take you up."

They had just reached Clara's room when the alarm bell blessedly fell silent.

The Earl opened the door. "Nobody's touched anything, other, obviously, than the knob and the light switch."

Dobson went into the room, looked down at Clara's body for a quarter of a minute and then came out. He took out a pocket watch, glanced at it, put it away and wrote in his notebook, saying as he did so: "'Viewed remains of victim at two ten a.m.' Right, my lord, I'll just wait here until CID arrive."

"You don't happen to know who the investigating officer's going to be, do you?"

"It'll depend who's available, my lord."

"Yes, of course. I do hope it's—" He broke off. "Never mind."

He went downstairs again.

Chapter Twenty

It was just twelve minutes later when they heard the sound of car tyres on the gravel outside. Again the Earl went into the Great Hall. But this time when Merryweather opened the doors two men were standing there. The first was rather plump, had a drooping black moustache and a melancholy expression. He was wearing a raincoat and black bowler hat. With him was a tall, strongly built, brown-skinned young man.

Lord Burford gave a sigh of relief. "Wilkins! I'm so glad it's you."

Detective Chief-Inspector Wilkins came in, removing his bowler hat. "Why, thank you, my lord. That is extremely gratifying." He had a surprisingly deep and somewhat mournful voice, and did not sound in the least gratified. "It's not often people are pleased to see me. And I must say this is like coming home, if I may make so bold."

They shook hands. The Earl looked at the younger man. "Detective-Sergeant Leather, isn't it? How are you?"

"Well, my lord, thank you."

He turned back to Wilkins. "How much have you been told?"

"Very little, my lord. Just that there has been another regrettable incident here. Murder, I believe."

"Yes."

Wilkins made a tutting sound. "Dear, dear. Most unfortunate. Well, I can't say that I'm surprised."

The Earl stared at him in astonishment. "You're not? You mean you expected us to have another murder?"

"I wouldn't go that far, my lord. But twice I have been called to investigate murders here. You know the old saying, 'Never two without three.'"

"Bit superstitious, isn't it?"

"I am superstitious, my lord, I admit it. But I don't think that particular saying is superstitious. Two unusual occurrences in the same place, or involving the same person or persons, might well suggest some underlying cause leading to a third."

"The only underlyin' cause I can think of is that blasted gypsy's curse. I'm startin' to think there might be somethin' in it. Otherwise, it's such an incredible coincidence."

"Perhaps not, my lord. Let's wait and see." He lowered his voice. "And may I ask, my lord, do you have any film stars here this time?"

"No, nobody like that."

"Or oil millionaires?"

"No, just relatives. One of them's an M.P."

"Really?" He seemed to perk up a little.

"Thinkin' of your memoirs, were you?"

He was amazed to see the Chief Inspector actually blush, but before he could reply two more men appeared in the doorway. One was carrying a small case and the other a camera and a large accessory bag.

"Perhaps my fingerprint man and photographer could be shown the deceased, my lord?"

"Yes, of course. Oh, and one of the other guests reported an intruder in her room, lurking by the dressing-table. I don't know whether he'll want to check in there as well."

"Yes, indeed, my lord."

"Merryweather, will you take these gentlemen to the scene of the crime, and also show them where Miss Simmons' room is. And if I'm not here when the doctor arrives, take him straight up. I'll speak to him afterwards."

"My lord. Please follow me, officers."

He started towards the grand staircase, the two policemen at his heels.

"You're not going up to see the body, Wilkins?"

"Not yet, my lord. I don't like looking at bodies. I find it so depressing, so I always put it off as long as possible. I suppose I'll have to take a peek sometime." He sighed. "Not that it'll tell me anything. I would prefer it if you could list the *dramatis personae*, as it were, and give me an account of the events of the day."

The Earl led the way, to the morning-room, they sat down and Leather produced a notebook and pencil.

The Earl ran his fingers through his hair. "Difficult to decide where to start. You know we had a funeral here yesterday?"

"Yes, my lord. So a melancholy day on two counts."

"Well, the funeral wasn't too melancholy, actually. Quite a nice funeral, as funerals go. It was a great aunt of mine. The—the victim was a Mrs. Clara Saunders, the daughter-in-law of my great aunt."

Wilkins had rested his elbow on the table, with the palm of his hand supporting his chin. He closed his eyes and might have been asleep. The Earl eyed him doubtfully for a second before continuing.

Twenty-five minutes later the Earl sat back. "I think that's all I can tell you at the moment. Sorry, if it was a bit incoherent, but I don't think I left out anything of importance."*

Wilkins opened his eyes. "Not at all, my lord. It was extremely clear and comprehensive. Let me just see if I've got the names of your guests correct: Miss Dorothy Saunders, stepdaughter of the deceased; Mr. Timothy Saunders, KC; Miss Penelope Saunders, his daughter; Mr. Gregory Carstairs, MP; Mr. Tommy Lambert; Miss Stella Simmons; and Miss Jean Mackenzie, companion to your great aunt. All of these people, with the exception of the latter, being relatives of your great aunt, and indeed of your good self."

---

* Author's Note: He didn't.

Wilkins had made no notes or consulted Leather, and Lord Burford looked impressed. "That's it. Very distant relatives, of course."

"And some relatives can never be distant enough, can they? But all of these were beneficiaries under your great aunt's will. Now tell me, this unpleasant contretemps at the reading of the will, when Mrs. Saunders made these threats: do you think they were genuine? I mean, did she really know damaging facts about the other beneficiaries, and was she serious when she made her threat about exposing them?"

The Earl sighed. "I honestly don't know, Wilkins. It may have been just pique. And, of course, Clara was a great forager-out and collector of secrets. But I can't believe she knew somethin' damaging about each of them. One, perhaps, or maybe two. But if she did, then yes, I think she would have made sure the facts got known. I'm sure, though, that her accusation of some conspiracy between them to get her cut out of the will is absolute nonsense. Most of them barely know each other, as far as I can gather. Anyway, I'm certain none of them knew my great aunt was going to leave enough for it to make it worth anyone's while to try and cut Clara out."

"Now, about this search you made, my lord. You are absolutely certain no one could have been concealed in the house."

"Quite certain." He told Wilkins all about the search.

"And he couldn't have sort of dodged from one place to another, as you were searching?"

"We thought of that. We did it in a pretty systematic way. After we searched every room, Merryweather or I—he's got the only other set of keys—locked the doors that are lockable and one of the other searchers stuck sticky tape across the doors that aren't, so no one could get in to hide there without moving it, and obviously couldn't replace it after he was in. After we'd finished, we went back and checked every door. There were eight of us, and it took nearly an hour."

"That sounds like almost military efficiency. And it certainly seems conclusive. However, you do realise the implications of it, I'm sure."

"Only too well, Wilkins. Unless somehow the alarm was circumvented, or faulty, the murderer's one of my guests."

"And which of them do you fancy, my lord?"

Lord Burford jerked his head up. "You're asking *me*?"

"You're the nearest thing I have to an expert witness, my lord. You know them all, at least to a certain extent."

"Not well enough to commit myself on that score—especially after the other times, when all my early ideas were totally wrong. Anyway, how d'you know it wasn't me?"

"Oh no, my lord. One of the things Chief Superintendent Allgood got right last time was that you'd never murder one of your guests at Alderley. Wouldn't be the done thing, would it?"

"Is murder ever the done thing?"

"Some of your peers have thought so, my lord. And not only in the distant past."

"Just as long as you can clear it up for us quickly. You did wonders the other times."

"Oh, I had great deal of luck, my lord. Can't expect that to continue. I'm not sanguine, not sanguine at all."

At that moment Merryweather entered. "Dr. Ingleby has completed his examination, my lord, and would like a word with Mr. Wilkins."

"Show him in, Merryweather. Oh—unless you want to speak to him alone, Wilkins?"

"No, no, my lord, that will be quite all right."

Dr. Ingleby was tall, in his thirties, with a mass of ginger hair. He had been the Alderley medical attendant for a number of years and was also the assistant police surgeon.

Lord Burford stood up and shook hands with him. "Sorry to have had to drag you out, Ingleby."

"All part of the job."

"What can you tell us, doctor?" Wilkins asked.

"There'll have to be a post-mortem, of course, but cause of death almost certainly suffocation; there are small haemorrhages of the upper eyelids, blue lips and fingertips, slight contusions around the mouth—usual signs. It was very probably done with the pillow from the bed. There are what seem to be marks of her teeth on it."

"Would it have required considerable strength?"

Ingleby shook his head. "Not provided she was taken by surprise, asleep or just lying down. The murderer would have been able to throw their whole weight on top of her. She clearly put up quite a struggle and got her head over the side of the bed, but that wouldn't have prevented the assailant keeping the pillow clapped over her mouth."

"And the time of death, Doctor?"

"Between eleven thirty and twelve thirty, with perhaps ten minutes' leeway either way."

"It was about half twelve when we found the body," Lord Burford said.

"Did you touch her?" Ingleby asked.

"Just felt for a pulse."

"Did you notice if the skin was cold?"

"Hard to say. I just took her wrist between my thumb and forefinger. I'd say it felt fairly cold. But not icy, if you know what I mean."

"That's not a lot of use in narrowing the time of death further, then."

"But not before eleven twenty, doctor?" Wilkins said.

"Better say eleven fifteen, to be on the safe side. Look, I must go. I'll let you have my report."

"Thank you, doctor," Wilkins said.

"Would you care for a drink, or a coffee, Ingleby?" the Earl asked.

"Not just now, thank you. Good night." He went out, then put his head back round the door. "I didn't step on any of the cufflinks," he said, then went out again.

Chapter Twenty-One

The Earl and Wilkins stared at each other. "What did he say?" asked the Earl.

"That he didn't step on any of the cufflinks."

"What on earth did he mean?"

"I was just going to ask you that, my lord. You didn't see any?"

"No, but I only really looked at Clara."

"Well, I suppose we'd better go up and take a look-see."

"D'you want me to come along?"

"It might be helpful, my lord."

The went out and up the stairs. The photographer and the fingerprint man were standing outside the door of Clara's room, talking to Dobson.

"Finished, lads?" Wilkins asked.

The fingerprint man answered. "Yes, guv. Didn't take long. Hardly any dabs. The butler explained all the bedrooms were dusted and polished before the guests moved in. Three sets altogether, all women's by the look. One set in here and in the other room, nearly all on movable things—ornaments and the like. Obviously the maid's. She must have moved them to dust and polish and then put them back after. Then there are the dead lady's prints in here, and another's in the other room, no doubt the occupant's. Killer probably wore gloves."

"You'll have to take the maid's and Miss Simmons' prints, just to confirm it, but tomorrow'll be soon enough."

He stepped into the room and stood silently looking down at the body of Clara. Then he went close to the bed and turned round, to get a better view of her face. "A sad lady, I should imagine, my lord."

"I never thought of her like that, Wilkins, but you could just be right."

Wilkins gave a little shiver. "I hate murder. Never get used to it." He picked up the top pillow from the bed and handed it to the fingerprint man. "Take this with you, when you go. It could be the murder weapon. Doctor said something queer about cufflinks."

"Oh yes, they're all over the place. You can't really see them from this side of the bed—except that one." He pointed to a small square of gold touching the leg of the bed near the skirting board. "But if you go round…"

Wilkins did so. "My, my," he said, "how very rum. Come and look, my lord."

The Earl, who had remained in the doorway, joined him. "Great Scot," he muttered. There were cufflinks everywhere. Most of them were on the floor, but there were two on the chair, one on the bedside table, and three on the dressing-table.

"Did you count them?" Wilkins asked the fingerprint man.

"Only roughly, guv. We spotted about thirty. That's without moving anything, or making a proper search. I didn't dust them—would have taken far too long."

"Quite right. Any ideas, my lord?"

"Well, they're mine. At least, some of them are. I recognise that one, and that one, and one of those on the dressing-table. Which means they're probably all mine."

"*All* of them? Really? How remarkable." Then light seemed to dawn. "Oh, I see, collect cufflinks, do you, my lord, as well as firearms?"

"No. Well, not purposely. I get given 'em, and never throw any away. Stupid, really. There are a lot of single ones, which have lost their partners."

"Where would they normally be kept?

"In a little box in my dressing-room—the other side of the corridor, just beyond the stairs."

"Well, perhaps your lordship would be so kind as to take Smithson here and let him dust the box for prints."

"Oh yes, of course. Come along, my dear feller." He went out and Leather took the opportunity to enter the room.

"What d'you make of it, Jack?"

"To me, sir, it looks as if he's deliberately placed them away from the door, so that they can't be seen unless you come right in—except for that one by the leg of the bed."

"Well, some of them *can* be seen." Wilkins went back to the doorway. "Those three on the dressing-table, for instance."

"Yes, but they're not noticeable. I mean, if you just glanced into the room, you wouldn't remark on them."

"True. I reckon there's a simpler explanation, though."

"What's that?"

Wilkins made the movement of an underarm throw.

"Oh, you mean he chucked them in?"

"Yes, from the doorway. Threw them quite hard and most of them cleared the bed. Probably in a hurry."

"But why do it at all?"

"You tell me."

Leather's brow furrowed. "Some sort of symbolic act?"

"Symbolic of what?"

"Let me see. Links. Things linked together. A broken link. Many links, joining two people, now scattered, or thrown away. Or cuffs. Handcuffs. Restraint. Captivity. He's saying to the dead woman: all links between us have been discarded, you hold me in captivity no longer. On the other hand, of course, he's thrown them at her, or surrounded her with them. So perhaps he's saying the links binding us will always be there. You can never get away from me, even in death."

Wilkins pulled at his ear. "Bit of a contradiction there, isn't there?"

"Yes, well, either could be true. It's only a theory."

"Well, let's make another one on the same lines. A cuff can mean a sort of slap on the head. Links are seaside golf courses. So we could surmise that the deceased lady once hit somebody on a golf course, and this was an act of revenge."

Leather grinned. "OK, my effort was a bit far-fetched."

"I've got nothing against far-fetched theories. I've had a few that turned out to be right."

At that moment the Earl and Smithson returned. "Box quite empty," the Earl said.

"No dabs at all, guv," Smithson added. "Been wiped clean."

"That would mean they were definitely taken by the murderer, wouldn't it, sir?" said Leather. "Because he obviously expected us to be called in. Someone who'd just done it for a prank wouldn't have anticipated the box being dusted for prints."

"Yes, good point, lad."

Leather obviously felt that he'd redeemed himself after his theorising, and looked pleased.

Smithson said: "The only other unusual thing is that post-card, guv, on the bedside table."

Wilkins moved over and looked down at the white card. On it were written in big block capitals the words IN MEMORY OF MISS DORA LETHBRIDGE.

"This been dusted, too?"

"Yes. Nothing."

Wilkins picked it up and turned it over. The back was blank. "Would your lordship have ever heard of a Miss Dora Lethbridge?"

"No, not that I can recall."

"Oh well." Wilkins put the card in his pocket.

There was silence. Everybody was looking at Wilkins, who suddenly seemed to be far away and was staring moodily at the carpet. Then he came to himself and rubbed his hands together. "Right, so what shall we do now?" He looked round, hopefully.

It wasn't quite clear to whom the question was addressed. After a few seconds, Lord Burford took it upon himself to answer. "That's rather up to you, my dear fellow."

"Yes. Yes, I suppose it is." He looked depressed. Then he brightened. "Oh yes, the armour. Better take a look at that, I suppose."

"Lord, I'd forgotten all about that. Come along. I think it was Albert and young Tommy who checked in there during the search."

He led the way round the corner into the east corridor, the others following, like a retinue of attendants. The art gallery was half way along on the right.

Wilkins said: "I see there's an open fanlight over the doors. Accounts for the crash being heard so far afield."

"Yes, we were told years ago that it was a good idea to keep a flow of air through, particularly in the hot weather; helps stop the pictures getting warped or the paint cracking, or something. We keep the windows open a couple of inches, as well. I ought to lock the gallery at nights, really, but we've got so reliant on our alarm system that I don't usually bother. And, of course, the windows are barred." As he had been speaking, he had torn a length of brown sticky tape from the crack between the doors, thrown them open and turned on the lights. Now he stopped short. "Good lord."

He went in and the others followed him. They saw that the component pieces of the armour were strewn across the room for a distance of about ten feet. The wooden frame to which they had been attached was lying near to the small plinth on which the assembled suit had stood, just to the left of the doors that led to the gun collection.

The Earl crossed the gallery, the others behind him, and looked at the wreckage more closely. "The impact on landing seems to have snapped the cord that was attaching the parts to the frame. Wouldn't have expected that. Could have perished, I suppose. Must admit I haven't had the thing apart in donkey's years." He scratched his head and looked around. "None of it makes sense. If he came in here just to hide, he might have crossed to try and get in the gun-room, tried the doors and found them locked. But then why would he go to the left? You can clearly see that the windows are barred, so he couldn't have been looking for a way out."

"Might he have been thinking of trying to hide behind the sofa?" Leather suggested.

The piece of furniture in question, one of several chairs of various kinds placed around the room, for the benefit of people wanting to sit and study the paintings, was against the wall to the left of the plinth.

"Might conceal him from anyone in the right of the room," Lord Burford said, "but he could still be seen from the doorway."

"I'm not so sure, my lord. Smithy, go and crouch down to the left of it."

With an inaudible mutter under his breath, Smithson went across and did as Leather instructed. Leather backed to the doorway. "Can you make yourself smaller?"

Smithson shuffled back and to his left and bent his head. "That's about it, Sarge."

"No, I can't see him from here now," Leather said. "So it would conceal him from anyone just glancing in. Pretty useless sort of hiding place, though. OK, Smithy."

Smithson scrambled to his feet and came back to the centre of the room. "Perhaps he was groping about in the dark, and just cannoned into it," he suggested.

"But it looks as though it was knocked over with real force," said the Earl. "It obviously fell straight forward: there are no pieces to the side, so he didn't cannon into it from the right. And look at the way the pieces are scattered. If it had just toppled over gently, you'd expect them more or less to stay where they fell."

"Might have slid, my lord," Leather said. "The parquet blocks are very smooth and shiny."

"Mm." The Earl nodded. "Maybe you're right, Sergeant. I suppose that is the only logical explanation."

"Look at this, sarge," said the photographer. He'd wandered a little to the right and was pointing to the floor a few feet from the inner wall. The others, apart from Wilkins, joined him. Scattered around were a number of small pieces of shattered glass.

Leather crouched down for a closer inspection. "Looks like a broken wine glass."

"Shall I take a photo?"

"Might as well."

"Well, what do you think of it all, Wilkins?" asked the Earl.

The Chief Inspector, who had apparently rapidly lost interest in their conversation and was paying more attention to a painting of some horses by Stubbs than to anything else, seemed to pull himself back with an effort.

"I don't, my lord."

"Don't what?"

"Think. About this. It's another rum thing, like the cufflinks. There'll probably be a third. But I don't reckon this one's going to help us catch the murderer, so I'm not going to waste my time racking my brains about it for now."

"Prints, sir?" Leather suggested. Smithson gave a low groan.

"I heard that, Smithy," Leather said.

Wilkins shook his head. "It'd take ages, all probably to no avail. After all, any one of the guests might have come in here, quite innocently, and touched the armour, during the afternoon. Quite right to suggest it, though, Jack. But better take a couple of shots," he added, to the photographer, "just for the record."

When the man had done so, Wilkins addressed him and Smithson. "OK, you lads can clear off."

"Right, guv. Good-night." They started to move away.

"I think," Wilkins added. They froze in mid-movement. Wilkins concentrated for a moment, then he said, "Yes, all right, go and get a bit of kip."

They hastily departed, before he changed his mind again.

The Earl, Wilkins, Dobson and Leather followed them, Lord Burford this time locking the gallery doors. Then they made their way back to the main corridor. When they reached Clara's room, Wilkins said: "Dobson, you can collect those damned cufflinks. Try and make sure you get them all. When you've done that, you can vamoose, too."

"Right, Chief Inspector."

"What about prints on them, sir?" Leather suggested.

"They're so small you'd never get more than a tiny section of the print. Still, better be on the safe side, I suppose. Pick them up with tweezers, Dobson. I've got some here, somewhere." He started to search through his pockets. "Put them in a bag and give it to me or the sergeant. We won't bother to dust them yet, but we can if we need to later on. It'll mean, though, that Smithson'll have to take everyone's prints tomorrow, while he's here, just in case we do need them for elimination."

He found the tweezers and handed them to the constable.

"I haven't got a bag, sir."

"Oh drat it. I should have got one from Smithson. Chase after him, Jack."

"Why not just put 'em back in the box?" Lord Burford suggested.

"Good idea, my lord."

"I'll get it." The Earl hurried off.

"We can't do much more here now," Wilkins said. "But I suppose we'd better put the poor lady to rights. Come on, Jack."

They laid Clara straight in the bed, crossed her hands on her breast and covered her with the sheet. As they finished, the Earl returned and handed Dobson the box. Then the Earl, Wilkins and Leather went out, leaving Dobson to his task.

"Now, my lord, I suppose I'd better come down and have a word with your guests." The prospect seemed to depress him still further.

They went down the staircase. In the great hall, Wilkins paused before a large gilt mirror and carefully straightened his tie and smoothed down his hair. Lord Burford opened the double doors to the drawing-room and entered, Wilkins and Leather on his heels. Everyone looked at them.

The Earl said: "Detective Chief Inspector Wilkins would like a word. Wilkins, you remember my wife."

Wilkins went forward and bowed over the Countess' proffered hand. "Yes, indeed. How do you do, my lady?"

"Chief Inspector. I am pleased it is you. We are relying on you."

"And my daughter."

"Lady Geraldine."

Gerry smiled up at him. "Hello again, Mr. Wilkins. We can't go on meeting like this."

The Earl introduced him to the others. When he got to Stella, Wilkins said: "Ah, you're the lady who found an intruder in her room."

Stella nodded.

"Must have been very frightening."

"Surprisingly, not really. I was angry, more than scared."

"Nothing taken?"

"Not that I could see. There wasn't much of my stuff there, anyway: hairbrush and comb, make-up, sponge bag, things like that. Nothing remotely valuable."

"And that was just about the same time as the crash?"

"I think so. I wasn't conscious of actually hearing the crash, but it has to have been that which woke me."

"I heard it," Penny put in. "But I'm a very light sleeper. It was hardly any time after when Stella started shouting."

"It must have been within eight or ten seconds," Gerry added. "Dorry and I heard the crash, rushed to the door, and heard Stella start to shout almost at once."

Lord Burford moved on. "Miss Mackenzie, friend of my great aunt."

Jean Mackenzie took a deep breath. "Chief Inspector, I—" She stopped, then said quietly: "How do you do?"

The Earl completed the introductions, then said: "Right, Chief Inspector, if there's anything you want to say, the floor's yours."

Wilkins cleared his throat. "Just to confirm, ladies and gentlemen, that there seems no doubt Mrs. Saunders was indeed murdered."

There was little reaction to this until after a few seconds Stella spoke: "And by one of us, right?"

There was a gasp from the Countess. Gerry though shot an admiring glance at Stella. Miss Mackenzie gave a little cry of dismay.

Gregory said: "I say, steady on."

Timothy said: "A perfectly logical deduction."

Penny uttered a reproachful wail. "Daddy!"

Tommy assumed a sepulchral voice. "So who done it? Who done the foul deed?" He fell on his knees in front of Wilkins and held up clasped hands. "I am innocent, Inspector, I swear I am innocent. Have mercy. Think of my two wives and ten helpless children."

"Oh, stop playing the fool, man!" Timothy snapped irritably. "This is serious."

"Yes, I know. Sorry." Tommy sat back down, looking a little embarrassed.

Wilkins said: "There is at least the possibility that the alarm system is faulty and that an intruder did manage to escape without setting it off. We cannot get an expert to check it until tomorrow. There's not much point in doing anything further tonight, so as far as I'm concerned you can all go to bed now, unless there is anything any of you wish to tell me tonight."

He looked round. Miss Mackenzie opened her mouth as if to speak, then obviously changed her mind and closed it again. The others shook their heads. "Very well. I will, of course, be wanting to speak to you all later in the day. I trust there will be no problem for anyone in remaining here?"

There was a general shaking of heads. "It's confoundedly inconvenient," Timothy said, "but it is plainly unavoidable."

"And I'm afraid we're going to have to take your fingerprints tomorrow, for the purposes of elimination. They will, of course, be destroyed when the case is closed. Good night."

Wilkins backed towards the door, giving little nods of the head to everybody in turn, as if exiting from the presence of royalty. He went out. Leather, who had remained just inside the door, followed him. Lord Burford went out after them.

"That's a remarkable young lady, my lord," Wilkins said.

"Miss Simmons?"

"Yes. Just coming out like that with what everybody was thinking."

"She's a journalist. They tend to like things out in the open. Sorry about young Tommy."

"Think nothing of it, my lord. Everybody reacts in a different way when they're frightened. That's Mr. Lambert's way."

"Oh, by the way, you haven't seen Dorothy—the stepdaughter. She's still in her room."

"That'll keep till the morning."

"Good, good. Doubt if she's really up to it tonight. Oh, and it's just occurred to me: we've got no burglar alarm for the rest of the night. If one of those people is the killer, they could easily do a bunk."

"Oh, I hope they do, my lord, I really hope they do. Make my job a lot simpler. Easy to catch someone you know is guilty. Much easier than finding out who the guilty party is."

"But don't I remember your saying something last time along the lines of 'if you let a criminal out of your sight you might never see him again.'"

"A *criminal*, yes—a professional criminal. They've often made contingency plans to disappear in an emergency: money, false papers, clothes, stored somewhere safe. But none of these suspects are professionals in that sense; they'd all have the dickens of a job just to vanish without trace."

At that moment they saw Dobson descending the stairs. He was carrying the cufflink box carefully in both hands, came across and presented them to Wilkins like a votive offering.

"Thanks. Get them all?"

"I think so, sir. Can't be dead sure, of course, but I looked under the bed, behind the dressing-table, everywhere else I could think of."

"Good man." He turned back to the Earl. "We'll have to hang onto these, I'm afraid, just in case there *are* prints on them. Don't know how you'll manage tomorrow. I could lend you mine. Not such good quality, I'm sure, but—"

"Much obliged, my dear chap, but at the moment I don't feel I ever want to see another cufflink. I'll be happy to wear my sleeves rolled all day tomorrow."

"Very well, my lord. I don't think there's much more we can do now. We will return in the morning. I expect it would be convenient if we were not too early. About ten thirty, say."

"Oh, that's decent of you. I expect everyone will appreciate that."

"The ambulance will be coming to collect the body, so I'll tell them to leave it until about then, too. Well, good-night, my lord."

"Good-night, Wilkins, Sergeant, Constable."

Merryweather showed them out, closed and locked the doors. He turned round, with an almost indiscernible sigh.

"Merryweather, we'll put everything back a bit tomorrow morning. Breakfast about nine thirty be early enough. Tell the servants they can all sleep in a bit longer."

"Thank you, my lord. They will welcome that. I, however, will be rising at my usual hour."

"I'm sure you will, Merryweather, I'm sure you will. G'night."

The Earl returned to the drawing-room and explained the situation to the others. Slowly they trooped upstairs to their rooms. But it was a long time before anyone slept.

Chapter Twenty-Two

Dorothy crept almost furtively down the grand staircase. It was just gone seven a.m., but there was no sign of life and Alderley was enveloped in silence. It made Dorothy feel she must not on any account disturb the stillness. She reached the bottom and made her way along the short corridor that led to the telephone room. She reached it, turned the knob and pushed. The door didn't move. She pushed harder, but it was definitely locked.

Dorothy stood there irresolutely. It was vital she phoned Agatha now. It couldn't possibly be delayed any longer. She wondered if the room was always locked at night. But why? It seemed most odd.

Eventually, Dorothy returned to the great hall. Should she just go back to her room and wait there until she heard people moving about? Or wait down here? Or walk to the village and find a telephone kiosk? Dorothy's life was a series of such uncertainties, tiny in themselves but a never-ending source of worry for her.

Then she gave a terrific start as a voice behind her said quietly: "Can I be of assistance, miss?"

She spun round. "Oh! Mist—er, Merryweather. You startled me."

"I do beg your pardon, miss. I did not realise you had not heard me approaching."

"You walk so quietly."

"I know, miss, and I realise that on occasions it can be a fault, but seem unable to correct it. Lady Geraldine has remarked amusingly that I should go to evening classes and take clumping lessons."

"Please don't apologise. Normally, I would have thought nothing of it. But I am rather on edge."

"Perfectly understandable, miss, in view of the shocking occurrence. May I take this opportunity of offering my most sincere condolences?"

"Thank you. Thank you very much. Er, I need to make a phone call."

"I will show you where the telephone is, miss."

"No, I know where it is. I've just been there. But the door seems to be locked."

Merryweather's right eyebrow rose about an eighth of an inch. "How very strange. I have never known it to be so before. If you will kindly follow me I will investigate."

He led her back to the telephone room, turned the doorknob and pushed. The door opened.

Dorothy gave a gasp. "It *was* locked! I swear it."

Merryweather crossed to the phone and felt the receiver and mouthpiece. Then he put his hand on the base and nodded. "I would say the contraption has definitely been used within the last few minutes, miss. The earpiece and mouthpiece are very slightly warmer than the rest."

"Oh, Mr. Merryweather, how clever! I should never have thought of that. But I wonder why they locked themselves in. And where did they go?"

"There is a back staircase at the far end of the corridor, which leads to the first floor, miss."

"Of course, I remember seeing it. Well, I can call my sister now. Thank you."

"And may I get you some tea, miss?"

"Yes, please, thank you."

"Breakfast has been put back today, owing to the unusual—or perhaps I should not use that particular adjective—owing to the unfortunate circumstances, and the kitchen staff are not up yet. However, I would be happy to prepare something for you myself."

"That's very kind, but no thank you. Tea will be splendid."

Merryweather gave a slight bow and withdrew. Dorothy went to the telephone.

Needless to say, Gerry was the first of the others down, though it was ten o'clock when she breezed into the breakfast room and began helping herself to devilled kidneys from the heated sideboard. She was feeling excited and, probably alone among the occupants of Alderley, greatly looking forward to what lay ahead. During the last two cases she had made pretty much of a prize idiot of herself, totally failing to spot the murderers; and, worse, nearly getting herself killed and having to be rescued. She was determined that this time she really was going to solve the case. She was just starting her breakfast when Merryweather entered.

"Good morning, your ladyship."

"Morning, Merry. Seems I'm the first for once."

"Not quite, my lady. Miss Dorothy was down at seven a.m. She telephoned her sister, and asked me to inform you that Miss Agatha said she would set out on her motor cycle as early as possible, and hopes to be here at approximately eleven o'clock."

"Oh, good. She'll be able to look after Miss Dorothy and leave me free to pursue my enquiries. Where is Dorothy now?"

"After partaking of a cup of tea, she returned to her bedroom. She had not slept previously, but suddenly became somnolent and decided to try and obtain some repose before Miss Agatha and Detective Chief Inspector Wilkins arrive."

"Thanks, Merry." She gave a little cough. "Got a bit of a sore throat this morning. Miss Agatha's supposed to have tonsillitis. Hope I haven't picked it via Miss Dorry."

"I tend to doubt that one could so rapidly contract it via a third person, not herself showing symptoms, my lady. May I suggest you may have strained it yesterday during your full-throated rendering of *She'll Be Coming Round the Mountain?*"

"You heard that?"

"Yes, my lady, I happened to be on the terrace outside at the time—I had occasion to go out to speak to MacDonald about some flowers—and the library window was open."

She gave him a quizzical look. "I see. Very convenient. It was a dying wish of Great Aunt Florence, by the way."

"I surmised something of that nature."

"Is there anything that happens in Alderley that you don't know about, Merry?"

"I do my best to avoid that state of affairs, my lady. In the interests of the Family."

"So, perhaps you know who murdered Mrs. Saunders?"

"Unfortunately I do not. However, apropos of that, there was one rather unusual incident this morning, which might be of interest to you if you are concerning yourself with the elucidation of the mystery."

"You bet. Tell me." Gerry was all ears.

He explained about the locked door of the telephone room and how he had deduced that the telephone had recently been used.

"Well done, Merry!" she said when he'd finished. "You're obviously a natural detective. I can see I'm going to have to get you to help me on this case. After all, Bunter, Lord Peter Wimsey's man, often assists him in his investigations."

"I am slightly acquainted with Mr. Bunter, my lady; an admirable man, but I fear I do not share either his ability at or enthusiasm for ratiocination and criminology."

"Where's your spirit of adventure?"

"I have none, your ladyship."

He went out. Gerry pondered. Why should one of the guests not want it known they had made a phone call? After all, most of them would be likely to have people they would need to notify of their delayed return. So why try to conceal the fact?

The Earl and Countess were the next down, followed at few-minute intervals by the guests. If the atmosphere at dinner the previous evening had been strained, the tension this morning was almost palpable, with no one in the mood for talking.

At about ten twenty-five, the ambulance, which was to convey Clara's body to the mortuary, arrived. There was some discussion as to whether Dorothy should be awakened to witness the departure, but in the end it was decided it would be better if she were not. Everyone else gathered in the great hall and there was a solemn silence as the stretcher was carried downstairs and outside. Only Miss Mackenzie showed any sign of emotion, dabbing at her eyes with a handkerchief, but Gerry suspected this was a matter of form for her, rather than genuine feeling.

After this, nobody seemed quite to know what to do. People wandered from room to room, sitting down, flicking through magazines or books or just staring into space. Others went outside and mooched round, looking at the flower beds or just staring up at the house. It was as though everyone had retreated into a private world. Gerry had planned to engage each of them in turn in conversation and question them so subtly that they would not even realise that they were being interrogated; but their attitudes made this impossible. It was as if the spectre of the return of Wilkins hung like the sword of Damocles over the entire household, she said to herself, enjoying the mixed metaphor.

At last, at about ten forty, a police car rolled up the drive and stopped in front of the house. Wilkins and Leather alighted. Merryweather admitted them and showed them into the morning-room, where the family were waiting.

"Good morning, your lordship, your ladyship, your ladyship," Wilkins began, sounding rather liked a cracked gramophone record. He looked more cheerful this morning. "First of all, let me apologise for being late, but there were many things to attend to. Now, while Mr. Merryweather is here, could you tell me who it was who served the deceased lady refreshments in her room last night? It seems she must have been the last person, apart from the murderer, to see Mrs. Saunders alive."

"It was the maid Janet, Chief Inspector," Merryweather said.

"I'd like Sergeant Leather to have a word with her, if that is agreeable to you, my lady."

"Of course," said the Countess. "I trust she is in no way a suspect, Mr. Wilkins."

"Oh, by no means, your ladyship. And it is highly unlikely she will be able to tell us anything useful, but we have to go through the form. And perhaps afterwards the Sergeant could briefly speak to the other servants, just on the off-chance that one of them heard or saw something."

"Arrange that, will you, please, Merryweather?"

"Yes, my lady. And will you be requiring coffee?"

"Well, I for one only finished breakfast about twenty minutes ago," said the Earl. "And I imagine you'll be wanting to make a start straight away with your investigations, eh, Wilkins?"

"Actually, my lord, a cup of coffee would be most welcome."

"Oh, then, of course. I suppose we'll all have some. Help to get us back to the normal timetable, I suppose, at least."

Merryweather and Leather went out. "Better take the weight off your feet, Wilkins," said the Earl.

"Thank you, my lord." He sat down in a deep leather easy chair and gave a sigh.

"Tell me," Gerry said, "why do you rule out any of the servants being involved?"

"I asked Mr. Merryweather when I arrived whether any of them were new, and he said no, that they'd all been with you for at least three or four years, many much longer. They're all local people. I just cannot imagine one of them suddenly deciding to murder one of your guests. In fact, I have never come across a country house case in which any of the servants was guilty. It's true that some years ago there did seem to be a spate of cases all over the country, and in the United States, too, I believe, in which the butler turned out to be the villain, but that trend is long past."

"Oh, talking of butlers, Merryweather was telling me he did a piece of detection this morning." She narrated the story of the locked door.

Wilkins nodded. "Interesting," he said, not sounding remotely interested.

"Why would somebody do that, do you suppose?"

"Someone having a private conversation and didn't want to be interrupted, I imagine. Probably didn't hear somebody trying the door, finished their call and went back up to their room via the back staircase."

"Oh," Gerry said, feeling rather crushed. "Is that all?"

Just then William, the footman, entered with the coffee. When they were all sipping from steaming cups, Wilkins said: "Oh, by the way, my lord, you may be interested to know that there were thirty-nine of your cufflinks in the room."

"Good lord, never knew I had that many. Still, quite an evocative number, what?"

"Ah yes, your lordship is doubtless referring to the Church of England's Thirty-nine Articles of Religion."

The Earl looked a little awkward. "No, actually, I was thinking of *The Thirty-nine Steps.* You know, John Buchan."

"Oh, of course. I'm afraid I read very little crime fiction or thrillers."

"Too much of a busman's holiday?" Gerry asked.

"That's about it, Lady Geraldine."

"So, what do you like to read?"

Wilkins leaned back. "Well, I have very catholic tastes, but if I had to choose one author, I suppose it would be Dostoevsky—even though his perhaps greatest work is called *Crime and Punishment.*"

Gerry looked impressed. "Golly. I'm afraid I've never read anything of his."

"Oh, you should, Lady Geraldine. Amazing man: such insight, such power. I've read everything he wrote, I believe."

"In translation, I suppose?" she said dryly, feeling a little irritated.

Wilkins smiled. "I'm afraid so. I do try it in the original from time to time, but every other page I come across a word I don't know and have to stop and look it up, which does slow you down."

They all stared at him in amazement. The Earl said: "You read Russian?"

"Not very well, my lord."

"So you speak it, too, then?"

"After a fashion. Enough to get by."

"'Pon my soul. You show me up. I only speak a little French."

"I certainly found French easier to master," Wilkins said.

"Well, I must say, you're full of surprises, Wilkins." Lord Burford took out his pocket watch and glanced at it meaningfully. "Expect you'll be wanting to get on with your enquiries."

"I'm in no hurry, my lord."

"Oh, I was just thinkin' the guests will be gettin' a bit anxious."

"That's just it, Daddy, don't you see?" Gerry said. "Mr. Wilkins is deliberately keeping them waiting, simply to get them nervous."

"Oh." Lord Burford's jaw dropped a little. "I see. Is that really it, Wilkins?"

"I'm afraid Lady Geraldine is wise to me, my lord. The longer you keep people waiting, the more on edge they get, and the more on edge they are, the more likely they are to slip up, let something out they didn't mean to."

"But they may not all have anything *to* let slip out."

"Oh, my lord…" Wilkins shook his head reproachfully.

"Everyone's got something to hide, isn't that so, Mr. Wilkins?" Gerry said.

"Almost invariably, Lady Geraldine. And there is something I want to ask you."

"Oh dear. I'm petrified now."

"No cause to be. It's just that from what his lordship was telling me last night, you were with Miss Dorothy for an hour before the discovery of the body."

"More than an hour."

"And she didn't leave you even for five minutes?"

"Not for five seconds. I know what you're getting at, but it's out of the question. Mummy came down from talking to Clara. Dorothy was there then and she remained in the drawing-room until we heard the crash and rushed up to see what it was. I was at her shoulder the moment she first saw the body. She's absolutely in the clear. Anybody else might have killed Clara: Mummy, Daddy—"

"Really, Geraldine!" This from the Countess.

"She's right, my dear," said the Earl.

Gerry continued. "Even Merryweather might have gone against the trend and done it. Dorothy definitely didn't. Of course, I realise you can't take my word for that."

"Oh, I think I can, Lady Geraldine."

"But she and I might have conspired to do the murder together. After all, Clara did at first claim to know some appalling secret about *everybody* in the room. Perhaps I held her down, while Dorry killed her."

"Oh no."

"Why not?"

"Two against one? Wouldn't be sporting."

"Ah yes, the code of the Burfords." Gerry leaned back and lit a cigarette. "So, tell me, how would I murder someone?"

Wilkins considered. "With a gun: quick, clean and totally unambiguous. Probably in front of a number of witnesses. And not at Alderley, unless it was absolutely unavoidable."

"Yes, I think you're right. Though not even in Westshire. I wouldn't want to be in your jurisdiction."

"I appreciate that, Lady Geraldine."

He turned to the Countess. "Now, your ladyship, I wonder if you could kindly tell me just what was said between you and Mrs. Saunders when you visited her in her room?"

Lady Burford thought for a moment, and, without adding any significant details, gave a slightly fuller account of the scene than the one she had given to Dorothy the previous evening.

"Thank you, your ladyship," Wilkins said, when she had finished. "And did you get the impression that she'd been speaking the truth when she claimed to know discreditable secrets about all the other beneficiaries?"

"I really wouldn't like to say, Mr. Wilkins. She sounded convincing and she did make a point of finding out things about people." She shot a meaningful glance at the Earl.

He gave a sigh. "Yes, you'll have to know, Wilkins, that for some years Clara had been supplementing her income in a rather unsavoury fashion." He briefly explained about Clara's dealings with newspapers.

Wilkins nodded thoughtfully. "I see. Yes, quite unpleasant. Apart from that, I take it there is nothing any of you can tell me that might throw some light on this affair?"

The Earl shook his head. The Countess said: "I honestly don't think so. And naturally I have thought about it a great deal last night and this morning."

"Lady Geraldine?"

"You don't know how I'd love to say yes, Mr. Wilkins."

"Now, there's just one more thing." He reached into his inside pocket and brought out a somewhat grubby-looking piece of paper. "I've still got the little sketch map I made at the time of the egg cosy affair, showing which bedrooms were occupied by each person. The next time I rubbed out the names and filled the new ones in. Now I've rubbed those out, and I would be grateful if you could fill them in with the present names." He held it out.

"You do it, my dear," said Lord Burford.

"Certainly." She took it. "Does someone have a pencil?"

Wilkins handed her one and she started to write.

"It's a very rough plan," Wilkins said. "I'm sure the proportions are wrong and I haven't bothered with all the windows, and so on. But it's adequate for my purpose."

Lady Burford finished writing and handed it and the pencil back. Wilkins perused the plan. "Might I ask if there is any sort of order of precedence, as it were, in the allocation of rooms on occasions such as this?"

"Not really. Normally we will put members of the same family in adjoining rooms, but I decided to abandon the tradition in the case of Mrs. Saunders and her stepdaughters—a small symbolic act. The only other factor is that as it is slightly more convenient to be near the centre, we tend to put the older people there, and the younger ones towards the ends of the corridors. I made an exception this time in the case of Agatha and Dorothy. It somehow seemed more fitting that, as principal mourners, they should be closer to the centre."

Wilkins nodded. "I see, though, that Mr. Gregory Carstairs was given a room half way along the east corridor."

The Countess gave a sigh. "There was a slight problem. Mr. Carstairs and Mr. Timothy Saunders are not on good terms, so it was thought advisable to keep them as far apart as possible. Originally, in order to be more even-handed and not to give rise to suspicions of favouritism, I had intended to put Timothy in a corresponding room in the west corridor—the first one on the right, beyond the bathroom—with Miss Penelope in the room beyond, and Miss Agatha in the slightly larger corner bedroom, next to our suite. But when Miss Agatha did not turn up, it seemed rather absurd to leave that room empty, and I told the footman to put Timothy in there. That left the room originally allocated to him empty. I could have moved Miss Penelope into it. But I decided to leave her opposite Miss Simmons, as it occurred to me that two young women, spending a night in a room towards the end of a long corridor in a house which has recently acquired a somewhat notorious reputation, might both feel slightly more comfortable knowing that the room directly opposite was occupied." The Countess looked rather pleased with herself for this involved explanation.

Wilkins made a sympathetic clucking sound. "Who would have thought it would be so complicated? Rather like the allocation of beats to constables, which I had to deal with when I was in the uniformed branch. Certain routes are very much more popular than others, and some of the lads can get quite disgruntled if they're put on the less favoured ones too often. It requires a fair amount of diplomacy. Police constables can be as touchy as prima donnas sometimes."

"So can barristers and Members of Parliament, believe me, Wilkins," said Lord Burford.

Chapter Twenty-Three

Wilkins got to his feet. "Better get a move on, I suppose. And if I could kindly be informed when Miss Dorothy wakes, or her sister arrives…"

"I'll let you know," said Gerry.

"Thank you. Now, is there a room where I could interview the witnesses? We used the small music room last time, if that would be convenient."

"By all means," said the Earl. "Can't imagine anyone's goin' to want to play the piano today."

"I'll take you," Gerry said.

They went out. "I remember where it is, Lady Geraldine," Wilkins said, "but if you could lend me one of your servants to fetch each of the witnesses when I'm ready for them."

"I'll do it."

"Are you sure?"

"Yes, I'd like to. Who do you want to see first?"

"Miss Mackenzie, please."

"Really? Why her? In my book, she's the least likely—sorry. Nothing to do with me."

"Miss Mackenzie has something she badly wants to tell me. She nearly came out with it twice last night, in the drawing-room, but couldn't quite bring herself to. I think she will this morning."

"OK, I'll fetch her."

She hurried away, meeting Sergeant Leather in the great hall. "He's in the music room," she said, pointing.

"Well?" Wilkins asked when Leather entered.

"I've spoken to all the servants, sir. Started with Janet, but, as you thought, she couldn't tell me anything. She took Mrs. Saunders cocoa and biscuits in her room at around quarter to eleven. The lady was sitting in a chair, reading. Looked quite normal, no sign of fright or agitation. Janet just put down the tray, said good-night and left. She wasn't in the room fifteen seconds. And none of the others saw or heard anything. Most of them were in bed by then, and all were by the time the body was discovered. Albert, the footman, says he and young Lambert both went right into the gallery and had a good look round. He's willing to swear that then there was nobody hidden behind the sofa or anywhere else."

"Well done, Jack. Did they give you coffee?"

"Yes, and a very nice slice of rich fruit cake."

"Oh, I didn't get any of that."

"Something to be said for life below stairs. Oh, and Smithy's arrived. He's started fingerprinting the servants."

The door opened and Gerry entered. "I've brought Miss Mackenzie."

Jean Mackenzie, looking even more anxious than usual, came in, her eyes darting around the room, as if expecting to see some assailant waiting to pounce.

"And she says she would like me to sit in, if that's all right with you," Gerry added.

"Certainly, Lady Geraldine. Please sit down, Miss Mackenzie."

"Oh, thank you."

As she was doing so, Wilkins looked at Gerry, put his finger to his lips and then pointed at her. Gerry grinned and gave a nod.

The others sat down, Leather taking out a shorthand notebook and pencil.

"So, Miss Mackenzie, what do you want to tell me?" Wilkins asked.

She gave a gulp. "I have a confession to make."

"I see. Confession to what, exactly?"

"I have done something terrible. Really wicked."

"Really? So, why did you kill Mrs. Saunders?"

She gave a shriek of horror. "Kill? I didn't kill her."

"Oh, I do beg your pardon, miss. When you said you'd done something really wicked, I assumed it had to be murder."

"Well, it wasn't quite as bad as that, but the fact is I told a lie. And Mr. Bradley passed it on—in all good faith, I must emphasise—to Lord and Lady Burford. I do not think Florrie would have minded. She had no strong feelings either way. And I have been worrying in case she had said as much to Agatha, and that Agatha passed it on to Clara, so she would know I had lied. But I only did it because it did seem to be the Great Opportunity which I had been promised. Marion had said I would recognise it when it came. Well, of course, I had been wishing so strongly for just such a chance, and it seemed quite amazing that the opportunity should have presented itself in this way. I had thought at first that it was something quite different that was being suggested, but I soon decided that that would have involved spying in a quite underhand way, so it couldn't be that. I should, though, have realised that when it actually came it would never involve telling a lie, either. And the terrible thing is that if I had not sinned in this way, Mrs. Saunders—Mrs. Clara Saunders, that is, not Mrs. Florence Saunders—would be alive today."

All of this was said at a breathless pace and Leather's pencil had been flying across the paper. Wilkins waited for a moment for him to catch up, before asking: "But what precisely was this lie?"

"Oh, didn't I mention that? It's this. I told Mr. Bradley that Florrie had expressed a wish to be buried at Alderley. She hadn't. She hadn't said anything about where she wanted to be buried."

"And you said that because you believed this was the great opportunity you'd been told about? Why were you so sure of that?"

"Don't you see that even before last night there had been three murders here in the past twelve months? It is a well-known fact that souls who are murdered are often restless—unquiet. They are unable to Pass On. They remain confined to the site of their murder. They sometimes Walk. Of course, one would need to be a Sensitive actually to be aware of them. I'm sure, for instance, that were Mr. Hawthorne here, he would experience a Manifestation. I, to my great sadness, am not a Sensitive, but for so long I had been desperately wishing for a chance to come here and try an experiment, though it seemed totally impossible. Then Marion told me I was going to be given a great opportunity. A chance that is vouchsafed to few. 'You must seize the moment when it comes,' she said. 'Be resolute. Do not be afraid.'"

Wilkins broke in. "Just for the sergeant's record, could you tell us Marion's surname?"

"The same as mine, Mackenzie. She never married."

"So how did your"—he paused momentarily before guessing—"sister know about this great opportunity?"

"Well, they do, don't they? Know things, I mean, that we don't."

"Who do?"

"Yes, I'm afraid that may well be true."

Wilkins took a deep breath. "What may be true?"

"That there was a hoodoo on my whole enterprise."

"No, I mean who know things that we don't?"

"Those who are no longer in the body."

Light dawned in Wilkins' eyes. He nodded sapiently. "Yes, I suppose they do. When did your sister die, Miss Mackenzie?"

"We prefer not to use that word, Mr. Wilkins. My sister passed on nearly eight years ago. And in all that time she has never communicated before, which was what made it so exciting."

"And this was at a séance with Mr. Hawthorne, the medium?"

"A public meeting, really. He's truly wonderful. And the message was so direct: from Marion, for Jean. I couldn't think what it could mean, though I puzzled about it for days. Then Florrie passed on and that of course put it out of my head. But when I was talking to Mr. Bradley, he actually asked me if Florrie had ever said anything about where she wanted to be buried. And it suddenly hit me. If the funeral were held at Alderley, I felt sure, knowing how kind and hospitable they are, that the Earl and Countess would invite the mourners back to the house, and there just might be a chance, even if we were only here for an hour or so. So that's when I told my lie. Then we were actually invited to stay here overnight. It seemed to be working out so wonderfully and I honestly believed that I would be able to achieve a really important Communication with the Unquiet Spirits—or at least one of them."

"But what exactly were you planning to do? You said yourself that you're not a sensitive."

"No, but I had the next best thing: a ouija board. I've had really remarkable results with it in the past."

"But you didn't actually go ahead with your plan?"

"Oh, but I did. Last night."

"You did? When?"

"After everybody, except Lady Geraldine and Dorry, had gone to bed."

"In your room?"

"No, no. I wanted to get as close as possible to the actual site of one of the murders, and I knew that one had taken place in the room which houses the gun collection. Of course, I couldn't get in there, but the art gallery is very close to it. I went in there yesterday before the reading of the will, and I felt a definite coldness about half way along to the right as you go in—often a sign of a spirit's presence. And, remarkably, I'd actually been allocated a room across the corridor, which made everything very easy. It really seemed as though it were all part of some great Plan."

Wilkins stared at her. "You were actually in the picture gallery last night? What time?"

"It was just a minute or two before twelve when I went in."

"So it was you who knocked the suit of armour over?"

"Oh dear me, no. But I was there when it happened. It was terrible, really terrible—"

"Miss Mackenzie, just tell me precisely what you did and what occurred."

"I took my ouija board and a small glass, to use with it as a sort of pointer, into the gallery. Do you know how it is done?"

"I think so. You upturn the glass on the board, put your finger on the bottom, and it's supposed to move about of its own accord and point to the various letters."

"Exactly. I went to the cold spot and sat down on one of the upright chairs. I said a short prayer, that I would be protected from any evil forces, and then waited, trying to prepare myself mentally. I must admit I found it difficult to start. I was a little nervous, being alone, and so close to where a murder had been committed. It must have been about fifteen or twenty minutes before I felt ready. At first I put the ouija board on my lap, but it kept sliding about. So I put it on the chair and knelt down by it. I put the glass on it, rested my fingers on the glass and said: 'Is there anyone there?' And then."

Miss Mackenzie, who seemed to be quite enjoying herself now, paused dramatically. "Suddenly, without any warning whatsoever, the suit of armour just fell over. It made the most dreadful noise you can imagine. I literally jumped out of my skin. But I knew immediately what had happened. And it could hardly have been worse."

"What do you mean?"

"I had obviously raised an evil spirit or a poltergeist. It is something I have heard of happening, but it had never happened to me. I have to admit I was absolutely terrified. I grabbed the board and the glass and positively ran to the door. I dropped the glass, but couldn't stop to pick up the pieces. I did turn the light off as I went out, but I left the door open. When I got back to my room I was shaking like a leaf, positively like a leaf. I realised, of course, that this was a punishment for me, and a warning that no good can ever come of telling lies. Very shortly, I heard footsteps and voices outside. I would have stayed in my room, but, frankly, I felt the need of human company, so I went out, and then learned the terrible news."

Wilkins rubbed his chin. "Did you hear Miss Simmons shouting?"

"Yes, as I crossed the corridor, though I did not know it was her. I thought perhaps that somebody else was experiencing poltergeist phenomena, but it seems not. I just pray that there will be no recurrence here and that the manifestation was aimed solely at me, not at the house."

She turned to Gerry. "Lady Geraldine, I can only offer my most heartfelt apologies. I shamelessly took advantage of your parents' known generosity and I feel most terribly guilty."

"Miss Mackenzie, please don't reproach yourself too much. I think you're jolly plucky to have come out with it all like this. If you hadn't, no one would have ever known. And it was very suitable to have the funeral here. It was right that Florrie should have been buried at Alderley, as I know my parents both felt eventually."

"But I'm responsible for the murder. Clara wouldn't have been here if it hadn't been for me."

"You mustn't think that, Miss Mackenzie," said Wilkins. "This crime would have been committed somewhere. It arose out of that scene at the reading of the will—which would have occurred wherever the reading had taken place. What Mrs. Saunders said frightened somebody very much. And that led directly to her death."

"You do make me feel a little better, Mr. Wilkins. Thank you."

"Just one or two questions. Did you tell anyone in advance of your plans to hold a séance?"

"Yes, I told Tommy. He's always been most interested in psychic matters. I even invited him to take part with me, but he refused. I think he was a little nervous—and quite rightly, as it transpired. I have been warned that ouija boards are dangerous things, but I foolishly ignored the warnings."

"And you told him afterwards what had occurred?"

"Yes, earlier this morning. He was very concerned."

"Is there anything else you can tell us about last night?"

"No, nothing. I retired to my room quite early and stayed there, reading, until I went to the art gallery."

"Finally, have you ever heard the name Miss Dora Lethbridge?"

"No, never."

"Then that will be all for now. We may ask you to sign a statement later."

"Very well." She stood up.

"If you go with Sergeant Leather, he'll take you to our fingerprint man."

"It's all right," Gerry said, "I'll take her. And afterwards, a glass of sherry, eh, Miss Mackenzie?"

"Well, it is a little early for me, but it does sound very tempting. Tell me, Lady Geraldine, is your rector here an experienced exorcist?"

"I really wouldn't know."

"It might be advisable to find out. If not, I know a very good man." Her voice faded as they went out. Then Gerry put her head back round the door. "Who do you want to see next?"

"Who would *you* see next?"

She thought. "Tommy, I think—see if he confirms her story."

"Then Mr. Lambert it'll be."

"OK." This time she finally disappeared, closing the door.

Leather had put down his pencil with relief.

"Blimey, what a load of double-Dutch! I couldn't make any sense of it when she started, could you?"

"Not a lot, but we got there at the end."

"But wouldn't it have been quicker just to say you didn't know what she was talking about and ask her to spell it all out in words of one syllable? Instead of going all round the houses, trying to find out who Marion was without actually asking her, for instance."

"Oo, you don't ever want to let them know there are things you don't understand, Jack, unless it absolutely can't be helped. Things you don't *know*, yes, but you've got to let them see you take in everything they tell you right away. Besides, I'm a detective. I'm supposed to deduce things. Anyway, we're not in any hurry. This is a very nice place to conduct an investigation. And with luck they'll give us a very nice lunch."

Leather was flexing his fingers. "I'll be getting writer's cramp if they all go on at that rate."

"Get it all?"

"No. Not all the psychic claptrap, but enough, I think."

"You don't believe in poltergeists, then, Jack?"

"No fear. You don't, surely?" He took out a penknife and started sharpening his pencil.

"Dunno. Some pretty astute people have vouched for 'em. I've read some very weird accounts. And if it wasn't a poltergeist, how do you account for the armour toppling over like it did?"

"Could have been badly positioned on its plinth. Someone might have touched it yesterday afternoon, pushed it another half inch, so it was just on the verge of falling. Could have happened the first time anybody came in, opened and closed the door, caused a draught. Something like that."

"Mm. Maybe. Can't see it's got any connection with the murder, either way."

There came a cheerful-sounding, rhythmic tap-a-tap-tap on the door.

"Come in."

It opened and Tommy entered. "What-ho. Wanted to see me?"

"Yes, come in, Mr. Lambert."

With a not very successful attempt at nonchalance, Tommy strolled over to the table, sat down and leaned back. "Mind if I smoke?"

"Not at all, sir."

He took out a pack of Gold Flake, extracted and lit one. "Oh, sorry, have one?"

"No thank you, sir."

Tommy proffered the pack to Leather, who shook his head.

"So I'm in for the jolly old third degree, am I?"

"Hardly that, sir. Just a few questions."

"Fire away."

"Let's get a secondary matter out of the way before we start discussing the actual murder. We've been talking to Miss Mackenzie and we seem to have an eye-witness account of the armour falling over. I understand she told you about it."

"Yes. Quite spooky, eh?"

"Keen on psychic research, are you, Mr. Lambert?"

"What? No, not really. Just showed a friendly interest, you know."

"So much so that she told you about her plans beforehand, even invited you to join her."

"That's right. Not really my cup of tea, though."

"So you were in bed when the crash occurred, were you?"

"Actually, not exactly, no."

"Not exactly? Oh, you mean you were half in and half out, or sitting on the edge, prior to getting in?"

"No. Actually, when I say not exactly, I actually mean not at all, if you see what I mean."

"Not really, sir, you'll have to bear with me. So, where were you—er, actually?"

"I was in the art gallery, act—as a matter of fact."

"What, at the same time as Miss Mackenzie?"

"That's right."

"But she said she was on her own, that she'd asked you to take part but you'd refused."

"She didn't know I was there. I was sort of hiding."

"Sort of hiding where?"

"The far side of that sofa, to the left of the armour."

Leather looked up, an expression of deep satisfaction on his face, then quickly returned to his notebook.

"And she didn't see you?" Wilkins said incredulously. "I wouldn't have thought that sofa would have been big enough to conceal you, you being so tall."

"Well, I had to curl up into a pretty tight ball and keep absolutely still. I dare say if she'd looked straight in my direction she might have spotted me, and obviously she would have if she'd turned to the left when she came in. But she'd told me earlier about something she called a cold spot towards the other end and that was where she was going to set up the thingamy board. So I thought there was a fair chance she wouldn't see me."

"But what was the point?"

Tommy's embarrassment was becoming visibly more acute by the second. He took a nervous pull on the cigarette. "Look, this is bally awkward. I know it sounds awful, but the whole thing was a practical joke. On her, Miss Mackenzie. The truth is that I—I was responsible for the crash. I made the armour topple over."

"Is that so? I think you'd better tell us the whole story, Mr. Lambert."

"OK. Well, as I say, as soon as Mackenzie told me about her plan, I thought it would be a lark to give her a bit of a shock. I'd had a look in the gallery in the afternoon and I'd seen the armour and noticed the sofa and it occurred to me that if the armour came crashing down just when she was in the middle of her spook-hunt it might really give her something to think about, don't you know. Now I know it sounds dashed unkind, might have given her a heart attack, or anything, and I feel pretty ashamed of myself now. Anyway, what happened was that after I'd gone to my room at about twenty past eleven or so, I undressed, put on my pyjamas and dressing gown, and had a read and a smoke for half an hour or so. Then at about quarter to twelve, I got a length of string, went to the gallery and tied one end of it round the armour. I played the string out until it reached the far end of the sofa. Then I went back to the door, turned the lights out, made my way over to the sofa again, with the help of my lighter, and crouched down beside it. Then I just waited. After about quarter of an hour or so, Mackenzie came in, messed around for a bit and then started her 'Is there anybody there?' rigmarole. I thought that would be a good time to give her an answer, so I just gave the string a tug—and the armour went crashing down. It made an enormous noise, even made me jump. I heard Mackenzie give a shriek and go scuttling out. I waited just long enough to grab up the string and then hared it back to my room. That's about it, really. Sorry and all that."

Wilkins eyed him. "You must have realised you were going to wake up the household."

"Not really. First of all, I didn't realise quite what a big bang it was going to make. But the floor's very hard, and that gallery's a big place with nothing much in it, so there's a sort of echo. What's more, I knew how thick the walls and doors are here, but I didn't see the open fanlight over the door, which let the sound carry much farther. Oh, I thought it'd probably wake up Gregory the Great, who's got the room between Mackenzie and me, but that didn't bother me too much."

"Did you hear Miss Simmons shouting as you ran back to your room?"

"Yes—at least, I thought it was her—and I wondered what was up."

"It didn't occur to you to investigate?"

"For a second, yes. But she didn't sound frightened, just jolly ratty, as though she was having a big row. I had a girl friend once, who used to go on at me just like that sometimes. So I thought better to leave well alone. Anyway, I stayed just inside the door of my room, keeping it open a crack, and very soon after that I heard voices and general commotion, so I joined the throng outside Clara's room and found out she'd been croaked. Jolly upsetting."

He stubbed out his cigarette.

"Why didn't you tell us all this before, sir?"

"Well, it's pretty shaming. I was hoping it wouldn't need to come out at all. After all, it's got nothing to do with the murder. I did tell you as soon as you asked."

"Yes, and I want to thank you for being so frank with us now, Mr. Lambert. And talking of the murder, how well did you know the deceased?"

"Not at all. Yesterday was the first time we'd met. And we didn't exchange more than a dozen words."

"Yet yesterday at the reading, she said that she knew things about everybody there that would make their reputations mud, if they came out. She withdrew it later as regards the Earl and Countess and Lady Geraldine, but specifically refused to do so for the guests. So what do you reckon she knew about you?"

"Nothing, I'm sure."

"Got a clear conscience, have you, Mr. Lambert?"

"Well, not exactly. I mean there are things I wouldn't want shouted from the rooftops, obviously. But nothing that would make my reputation mud. Certainly nothing it'd be worth committing a murder to keep dark. I haven't got a criminal record, or anything."

"Three speeding tickets in the last five years. And fined two pounds for being drunk and disorderly in the West End on New Year's Eve."

"Ah. Yes, of course. You looked me up. But that is all, honestly. And they'd hardly make my reputation mud, or be worth Clara's while to spread around."

"So you think she was bluffing?"

"Must have been, in my case."

"Did you see her yesterday, after the scene in the library?"

"No, not for a second."

"Did you hear or see anything in any way suspicious or odd?"

"Not a thing. And I've really been racking my brains—what there are of them."

"Ever heard of a Miss Dora Lethbridge?"

Tommy shook his head.

"Well, I don't think we need keep you any longer, for now, Mr. Lambert." Wilkins repeated what he had said to Miss Mackenzie about a statement and fingerprints.

"Yes, of course. Only too glad to help in any way possible. And, by the way, does Mackenzie have to know—about what I did, I mean? Can you just let her go on thinking it was a poltergeist?"

"We'll see, Mr. Lambert. I won't reveal it unless it becomes necessary."

"Thanks."

"Perhaps you'd kindly ask Miss Simmons to step in next."

"Righty-ho."

Chapter Twenty-Four

Stella was the first person to enter the room with an air of complete confidence. She sat down, folded her hands on the table and smiled at Wilkins enquiringly.

"Miss Simmons, I'd like to talk first about this intruder in your room last night. You can give no description of any kind?"

She shook her head. "I was half asleep. It was almost totally dark. I was just aware of a presence, a kind of even blacker patch against the surrounding blackness, by the dresser. I think he'd most likely been using a flashlight or a match to see. I got the impression of a light going out just a split second after I opened my eyes. He probably put it out when he heard the crash, realising I might wake up."

"I see. When you awoke, he, or she, was by the dressing-table—"

Stella interrupted. "She? You think it could have been a woman?"

"Can you be sure it wasn't?"

She looked thoughtful. "No, I suppose not. I assumed it was a man. But if it was a woman, who could it have been? Let's see, Gerry and Dorry were downstairs, Miss Mackenzie was in the picture gallery—oh, she's told us all about it now—and Clara was dead. That only leaves the Countess, which is surely absurd, and—" She broke off.

"And Miss Penelope Saunders. You did say the intruder had vanished by the time you got to the door. Miss Saunders' room was right across the corridor from yours. And according to Lord Burford's account, you told everybody that she appeared almost immediately after you looked out."

"But that's screwy. Why on earth should Penny have been poking about in my room?"

"Why should anybody have been poking about in your room? Do we have to suppose they meant you harm of some kind?"

"You're not saying he was going to kill *me*, too?" She sounded incredulous.

"So you think your intruder was the person who killed Mrs. Saunders?"

"Search me. But if not, it means that two people were up to no good last night."

"For Alderley, that's nothing, I can assure you, miss. But when I wondered whether the intruder meant to harm you, I was thinking of something not quite so drastic."

"You mean one of the guys was after my virtue? Come off it!"

"Is it beyond the bounds of possibility?"

"I'd say yes. And I speak as someone not without experience. Tommy would be far too scared. I'd bet my bottom dollar that Timothy'd be absolutely horrified at the very idea. Gregory'd probably try it on if the time and place, and the woman, were right. He's quite a masher. But he's an MP, for Pete's sake!—and holding on by the skin of his teeth. He'd never risk the scandal. He'd be finished if it got out."

"He might have thought there was no likelihood of a scandal: that you'd welcome it."

For the first time, she looked doubtful. "Well, I guess I did flirt with him a mite. But only for my own ends, though keep that under your hat."

"He couldn't have known your real reason."

"Well, if that *was* his motive, why would he have been messing around by the dresser?" She shook her head decisively. "No, I'm sure that's not it. Think again, Mr. Wilkins."

"Well, you're the expert, Miss Simmons. So we're no nearer an explanation. You said there was nothing worth stealing there, and nothing *was* stolen."

"Oh, but there was."

"Eh?" For the first time, Wilkins looked surprised. "But you said last night—"

"I know. I only discovered it this morning. I didn't have a chance to tell you before."

"So what was it?"

"A tube of toothpaste," Stella said.

"A tube of toothpaste?" Wilkins looked totally bemused.

"Yes, and I can give you a description. About six inches long by an inch wide. White, with blue lettering. Answers to the rather unfortunate name of Dentigleam. Value, hard to assess, as about half the paste had been used but, at an estimate, perhaps sixpence. I haven't decided yet whether to put in an insurance claim."

"Are you absolutely sure about this, Miss Simmons?"

"Well it may have been slightly less than six inches long, and—"

Wilkins flapped his hands, and she stopped. "I mean, could you have just mislaid it?"

"No," she said firmly. "It was in a little draw-string toilet bag, with my toothbrush. I used it last night and left it on the dresser afterwards, rather than put it in my case, because I knew I'd be using it in the morning. When I went to get it this morning, the bag was open, the toothbrush was there, but the paste was gone."

Wilkins shook his head. "Rum. Most rum. It's not as though anybody could have mistaken it for something else, even in the dark. A tube of toothpaste doesn't feel like anything except a tube of toothpaste. However, again it doesn't seem to have anything obviously to do with the murder of Mrs. Saunders. So let's move on to that. How well did you know her?"

"I met her yesterday for the first time. We chatted, mainly about Florrie, for a few minutes in the afternoon. That's it. I'd heard about her, from Florrie, who saw her as the original wicked stepmother. I admit I thought she might be prejudiced, but after Clara's performance yesterday, I could believe anything of her."

"So when she said she knew something damaging about all of the other beneficiaries, what did you think she knew about you?"

"Nothing. I've been in the country for less than six months. I doubt Clara even knew of my existence. She couldn't know any of my guilty secrets."

"So you do have some guilty secrets?"

"That would be telling. No, my bet is that all that baloney, knowing things about all of us, was camouflage and she really had one of two people in mind."

"And which two would they be?"

"You're the detective, Detective."

"Oh, I'm never too proud to ask for help, miss."

"No, I'm not saying: wouldn't be quite cricket, what? Anyway, it's only a hunch."

"I take it that yesterday was the first time you'd met any of the others?"

"Apart from Jean Mackenzie and Tommy, yes. Tommy's my first cousin and I knew him quite well years ago, though he was only a kid then. Oh, and I met Gregory once, when I was in my teens."

"You must have felt a bit of an outsider."

"Not really. I'd kept in touch with Florrie by mail for years. When I came to, came home, one of the first things I did after I'd gotten settled in was look her up. She was as sharp as a needle and had a fantastic memory, and she filled me in on dozens of relatives. Also, of course, I'd read all about the earlier Alderley murders—they got pretty wide coverage in the New York papers, what with several big-shot Americans being mixed up in them, and there was quite a lot of stuff about the Earl and Countess and Gerry. So, all in all, I knew who I'd be meeting and just how we were related."

"So what can you tell us about last night?"

"Zilch. I didn't see Clara after the time she blew her top. I went up to bed at the same time as Tommy and Penny. I went to my room, undressed, took off my make-up, brushed my hair, put on my robe, went to the bathroom, washed my face and hands, brushed my teeth and so on, returned to my room and got straight into bed. It had been a long day and I was asleep in five minutes. The rest you know."

Wilkins nodded absently. He looked depressed again. Stella seemed to feel responsible for this. "Sorry," she said.

"That's all right, miss. I didn't really expect anything else. Oh, one more thing: does the name Miss Dora Lethbridge mean anything to you?"

"Not a thing."

"Thank you. Would you ask Miss Saunders to come along next, please?"

"Sure."

She went out.

Chapter Twenty-Five

Tommy was sitting on the terrace gloomily going over in his mind his decidedly embarrassing interview with Wilkins, when he saw Lord Burford come round the corner of the house. The Earl was carrying what Tommy at first took to be a bunch of flowers, but then saw that there were no blooms on them; it just seemed to be a mass of greenery. Next Tommy noticed that he was wearing a pair of brown kid gloves. For the middle of August this seemed extremely odd. Tommy kept his eyes fixed on the Earl as he got closer and a few seconds later was able to make out that what his host was carrying was a large bunch of nettles. Tommy stared at him in amazement, and at that moment Lord Burford looked up and saw him. He stopped short. "Ah," he said.

"Nettles," Tommy said, intelligently.

The Earl glanced down at them, as though until that moment he had been unaware of their existence. "Oh yes, yes."

"I thought so. I mean, can hardly mistake them, can you?"

"Suppose not. Make, er, excellent, er, soup—yes, soup, that's it."

"Really? Never tried it."

"Oh, you should. Very nutritious. I'm just going to give 'em to Cook."

"Give 'em a cook? Yourself?"

"No, no—give 'em *to* Cook—our cook, Mrs. Baldwin, to make into soup. Or something."

"Oh, right."

Lord Burford hurried off, moving more quickly than Tommy had yet seen him. He blinked. Very weird. He wondered if the strain was getting to the old boy. Perhaps he should say something. But to whom? Not the Countess. He couldn't face that. Gerry, perhaps. But it would need tact. Well, he had plenty of that. He got to his feet

Tommy found Gerry in the morning-room, writing furiously in a notepad. He sat down near her.

"Another lovely day, what?" he said brightly.

She nodded absently. "Mm."

"Eat a lot of nettle soup, do you?"

Gerry gave a little start. "*What* did you say?"

"Or should I say drink? Nettle soup. Like it, do you? Your family, I mean?"

"Nettle soup? Certainly not. Why the dickens should you ask such a thing?"

"Your papa. He says it's very good. Nutritious and all that sort of thing."

"Probably just something he's read. I don't believe he's ever tasted it in his life, unless it was in France during the war."

"Well, you're going to be having some soon, apparently."

"What on earth are you talking about?"

"He's just picked a big bunch of nettles, to give to your cook."

"Tommy, stop pulling my leg."

"I'm not, cross my heart and all that rot."

Gerry stared at him in bewilderment. "But it doesn't make sense. He never takes the remotest interest in anything like that. Just eats what's put in front of him. Mrs. Baldwin will probably give her notice in if he starts taking her peculiar things to cook."

"I did wonder if it was all getting on top of him, you know. All these murders. Quite natural."

"When was this?"

"Just a few minutes ago."

She stood up. "Then let's hope I can stop him before he gets to the kitchens. And, Tommy, if you *are* ribbing me…"

"Gerry, if I wanted to, I could do a darn sight better than this."

"Yes, I imagine you could. Sorry. And, Tommy, keep your trap shut, OK?"

"Oh, absolutely."

Gerry sped off.

There came a very timid knock on the door of the small music room. This time Wilkins got up and opened it. "Ah, Miss Saunders. Do come in. Would you care to sit down?" He might have been a particularly unctuous head waiter welcoming an old and valued customer.

Penny sat down. She looked terrified. She said: "I didn't do it."

"Didn't you? I'm very pleased to hear it."

She stood up again. "Can I go now?"

"Just a few questions, if you don't mind."

"Oh." She sat down again.

"So, who do you think did do it?" Wilkins asked.

"Gregory." The answer came immediately.

"Really? Why's that?"

"Because of what Clara said. She was going to expose him."

"She threatened to expose lots of people. I mean, why do *you* think it was Mr. Carstairs?"

"He's a horrid man. Daddy hates him."

"I see."

"And he's a Conservative."

"Is that bad?"

"Daddy's a Liberal, and he says the Conservatives are"—she screwed up her eyes and concentrated hard—"reactionary relics."

"Set a lot of store by your father's opinions, do you, Miss Saunders?"

"No!" Penny looked quite indignant. "I mean, not on important things like nail polish and cigarettes and night clubs. But he does know an awful lot about politics and things. And it was yummy when he threw Gregory down last night. Stella was really impressed."

"It didn't upset you too much, then, this murder?"

"No. I think it's thrilling. It's not as though anyone nice was murdered. She was a horrid woman. And she was awfully old, so she'd have probably died soon anyway."

"No doubt. So Gregory murdering Clara was just about the best thing that could have happened?"

"Well, I don't know about the *best* thing. But pretty good."

"But tell me, do you have any evidence that Gregory did it? Because, you see, we haven't, and we really need some."

"You can't just arrest him, then?"

"Not without evidence."

"It seems so silly, when we know he did it."

"That's the law."

"I'll tell Daddy it ought to be changed."

"Yes, you do that, Miss Saunders. But you didn't see anything?"

"I could say I did, if you like. Or would that be cheating?"

"Yes, that would definitely be cheating."

"Well, then, no, I didn't see anything at all."

"In that case, we needn't keep you any longer."

"Really?" She looked disappointed.

"I thought you wanted to leave."

"I did, but I didn't realise it was going to be such fun. Can I ask a question first?"

"Oh, I've just got one more first: have you ever heard the name Dora Lethbridge—Miss Dora Lethbridge?"

"I don't think so, no."

"Right, ask your question now."

"Do you think *Peepshow* might do another piece about this murder and put my photo in, as one of the Beauties Involved in Murder?"

"I don't see how they can fail to, Miss Saunders."

An expression of deep happiness came over Penny's face and she gave a little sigh, before getting up and starting for the door. Then she stopped and turned. "And it's OK if I tell everyone you know Gregory killed her, is it?"

Wilkins gave a start. "No! Definitely not, Miss Saunders."

"But I thought—" She stopped and a look of sudden understanding came into her eyes. "Oh, I see! You think if he knows we know, he might get away."

"Yes. That's it. And heaven knows who else he might kill in the process. You, your father, Tommy."

"Oh, golly, I never thought of that. All right, I won't breathe a word."

"Thank you, Miss Saunders. Could you kindly ask your father if he could join us, please."

"OK." She looked at Leather, who was still writing rapidly in his notebook. "You're very good at that, aren't you?"

Leather looked up. "Pretty good, I reckon, miss."

"Do you think you might like to be a secretary, one day? To a career woman, running her own company?"

"I don't think so, miss. I'm very happy in the police force."

"That's a shame. If you change your mind, let me know."

"I'll do that."

She smiled at them both radiantly and went out.

"Talk about dumb blondes!" Leather exclaimed, as the door closed behind her.

"Likeable, though."

"She's jolly pretty, I'll say that."

"I thought you would, Jack."

Chapter Twenty-Six

Gerry went first to the kitchens. There was no sign of the Earl. She engaged Mrs. Baldwin in conversation for a few minutes, on the pretext of seeking her advice about the menu for an imaginary proposed dinner party in her London flat. She cast surreptitious glances around, but nowhere was there any sign of nettles, nor did Mrs. Baldwin seem in any way bemused or disgruntled, so presumably the Earl had been delayed *en route.*

She thanked the cook and made her way to her father's study. She tapped on the door.

There was a couple of seconds' pause before her father's voice called: "Who is it?"

Gerry raised her eyebrows. That was an unusual response, for a start. "Me."

"Oh, hang on."

This time there was a full half minute's delay before he called: "Come in."

Gerry opened the door and peered somewhat apprehensively into the room. The Earl was seated at his desk, which was covered by an open copy of *The Times*. He had quite a guilty expression on his face as he stared enquiringly at her. "Er, what is it, my dear?"

"Daddy, what is this nonsense about nettle soup?"

"Oh. Well, supposed to be quite nice and good for one. Thought we might try it sometime."

"Tommy said you were going to take some nettles to Mrs. Baldwin."

"Haven't got round to that yet."

"Thank heavens. She'd have thought you were absolutely doollally."

"Don't see why. Traditional British dish. We ought to keep up these old customs."

"But why bring the stuff in here? That is it, isn't it?" She reached out and removed the newspaper. A big pile of already somewhat wilted nettles nearly covered the desk top. There were also two kid gloves and a pair of scissors. Gerry stared. Many of the leaves had already been cut from the stalks and themselves further cut into small pieces. "Why by all that's wonderful are you cutting them up?"

"Er, just thought I'd save Cook the trouble. Get them ready for the pot. Didn't want her or one of the maids gettin' stung. I had to wear my gloves."

Gerry took a deep breath. "Daddy, promise me one thing: don't take these to the kitchen. Mrs. Baldwin really wouldn't appreciate it. You know she can be as temperamental as any French chef and she might well be insulted."

"Oh, if that's what you think. I'll forget all about it."

"That would be a very good idea."

"Run along now, my dear. I've got a lot of things to do this morning."

Gerry refrained from asking what they were. She left the room with a baffled expression on her face.

◇◇◇

Timothy came into the room without knocking, walked quickly to the empty chair and sat down.

"I'm sorry to have kept you waiting, sir," Wilkins said.

"I imagined at first it was some kind of psychological ploy." (Wilkins looked hurt.) "Then after you asked to see Miss Mackenzie first, I decided you were taking us in the order of the degree of suspicion that is attached to us, working upwards. However, if that is the case, I fail to understand why you saw Lambert before my daughter. I cannot imagine that you consider Penelope a suspect in this case."

"Everyone is a suspect, Mr. Saunders. Some, of course, are more, er"—he hesitated—"more suspectable than others." He frowned, as though unhappy with the word, before continuing. "No, actually, we saw Miss Mackenzie first because she obviously had something she wanted to tell us. I understand you now know what that was."

Timothy nodded. "Highly bizarre."

"We saw Mr. Lambert next, as Miss Mackenzie informed us she had told him in advance of her plan, and we wanted his confirmation of that. Miss Simmons was possibly the only person actually to have seen the murderer, so it seemed sensible to talk to her next. In fact, it turned out she saw nothing. Then I spoke to Miss Penelope, as I imagined she might be nervous. Though that also turns out to have been wrong."

"I regret to say she seems to be quite enjoying the situation."

"Ah well, sir, the exuberance of youth, as they say. What a wonderful thing it is."

"I must say I never felt especially exuberant as a youth. May we get on now?"

"Of course, sir. Well, I don't intend to start questioning the best cross-examiner in the country. So I'll just leave it to you to tell me anything you think may be relevant, though I may have one or two points to clarify when you've finished."

Timothy bowed his head slightly. "Thank you, Chief Inspector, I appreciate the courtesy. I had best begin by saying that Mrs. Saunders' statement at the reading of the will regarding having damaging information about each of us was, in my case, totally incorrect. I do not say my life is an open book—no man's is—but that she possessed knowledge which, as she put it, could ruin my reputation is simply not conceivable. I therefore had no motive for killing her. As to the crime itself, I can offer nothing of value. I retired to my room a minute or two before eleven. The next thing I can tell you is hearing the sound of the crash. I looked at the luminous dial of my watch. It was precisely 12:28."

Wilkins interrupted. "How accurate is your watch?"

"Extremely accurate. I correct it every morning by the chimes of Big Ben on the wireless, and it is never more than thirty seconds out."

"Thank you, sir. Please carry on."

"There is little more to tell. I wondered whether I should go and investigate but decided that it was no concern of mine. A minute or two later, I heard raised voices and then did go to the door and look out. I saw a small group of people outside the room occupied by Clara. I joined them and learned what had occurred. Shortly afterwards, I assisted in the search of the house, accompanied by one of the footmen. When that was completed I went downstairs and gathered with everybody else in the drawing-room. I remained there until you came and spoke to us."

"I understand that before the search there was a little altercation between you and Mr. Carstairs, just outside Mrs. Saunders' room."

For the first time, Timothy looked a trifle discomposed. "Yes. I regret that now very much. It was most unseemly. He made a disparaging remark about my physical ability to handle myself in the event of some ruffian being discovered on the premises, and I could not resist showing him that I am more than capable. I am a third Dan in ju-jitsu, and am perhaps unduly proud of the fact. I should, of course, have ignored his sneers. I did apologise to the Earl afterwards."

"But not to Mr. Carstairs."

"Er, no."

"It seems quite widely known that you and he are not on good terms."

"That is so. But before you ask, it arose from something that took place fifteen or sixteen years ago, and which Clara could not possibly have known about. It can have no conceivable bearing on her murder, so I do not intend to talk about it. If Gregory should prove less reticent, then I shall, of course, give my side of the story."

"That's fair enough, sir. Just how well did you know Mrs. Saunders?"

"Hardly at all. I had met her only once, at her husband's funeral."

"And the young ladies?"

"The same. I feel guilty about not having kept in touch with them. Our fathers were very close friends, and, of course, my father was John's solicitor for many years and his executor. I had intended to use this opportunity to reacquaint myself with them, offer them any help or advice I can give. The trouble is that now they have come into such a large sum of money, they will assume that is the reason for my new-found concern for them."

"Oh, I'm sure they wouldn't think that, sir."

"I am a lawyer, Chief Inspector. People always think the worst of us. As I am sure that you, as a police officer, do."

"That usually depends on whether they're prosecuting or defending, sir. But to revert, there's nothing else you want to tell us about the events of last night?"

There was a perceptible pause. Wilkins looked at him and Leather glanced up from his notebook. Timothy's eyelid gave a twitch. At last he said: "There is nothing else I can tell you."

"I see, sir. So just one more question: do you know the name Miss Dora Lethbridge?"

"Ah, my daughter mentioned you asked her that. To the best of my recollection, I have never known anyone of that name."

"Then that's all, sir. Thank you."

Timothy stood up, gave another stiff little bow of the head and left the room.

"You let him off pretty lightly, didn't you?" Leather asked.

"For the moment."

"But there was obviously something he was on the verge of telling us."

"I know. I asked him if he *wanted* to tell us anything, and as you say, he plainly did. But he didn't know if he *should*. He decided not. I could have pressed him. But when a man like that makes up his mind there's no budging him. We'll get it out of him sooner or later, if we need to. Interesting answer he gave to the last question, too."

"About the mysterious Dora? I didn't spot anything."

"Read the question and answer."

Leather consulted his notebook. "'Do you know the name Miss Dora Lethbridge?' 'My daughter mentioned you asked her that. To the best of my recollection, I have never known anyone of that name.'"

"I didn't ask him if he'd ever *known* a Dora Lethbridge, but if he knew the *name.*"

"Think that means anything?"

"I think when anyone uses language as carefully as Saunders, KC, it nearly always means something."

"Want me to go and fetch Gregory the Great?"

"Yes, and make sure you treat him with all the deference and respect that befits a Member of Parliament."

Chapter Twenty-Seven

Gerry was feeling a bit disgruntled. Sitting in on the interview with Jean Mackenzie had been fine, but Tommy, Stella and Penny had all politely rejected her offer to accompany them during their interrogations. So her own investigation had come to a dead-end. Now she had the distraction of her father's odd behaviour. Perhaps she ought to tell her mother about it, just so that she could be on the watch for any other eccentricities.

She found the Countess in the morning-room, and was about to give an account of the Earl's behaviour when Merryweather entered.

"Bates has been on the telephone from the lodge, my lady. Miss Agatha Saunders has just arrived on her motor-cycle."

"Oh, thank you, Merryweather. Tell his lordship, will you; he is in his study, I believe. And show Miss Saunders straight in here."

The butler bowed and withdrew. "You were saying, dear?" the Countess asked.

"Nothing important. It'll keep."

The Earl joined them, looking, Gerry had to admit, quite normal, if a bit pre-occupied. She and her mother both noticed something that looked strangely like a grey sock protruding from his side pocket, but before either of them could say anything, Merryweather returned. "Miss Saunders, my lady."

Agatha positively strode into the room. She was wearing a fur-lined leather jacket, over a scarlet sweater, and jodhpurs. Her face was red from the wind. Lord Burford went forward and took her hand. "Hello, my dear. So sorry about all this. You have our deepest sympathy. It's shockin'. Feel terribly guilty."

"No, Cousin George, you mustn't, please. Nobody could possibly blame you."

"Nice of you to say so. You remember Lavinia and Geraldine?"

"Yes, of course. How are you, Cousin Lavinia? And you, Geraldine?"

They kissed. "We're very well. More important is how you are, Agatha?" the Countess asked.

"Oh, I'm OK. In a bit of a daze, still. Can't take it all in. All that money, and now our stepmother murdered. It's unbelievable."

"Is your throat better?"

"There was never anything wrong with my throat, Cousin Lavinia. That was my stepmother's little story, to account for my not being here. She won't have us all leaving the house at the same time. I'm sorry. But, tell me: how's Dorry?"

"She was devastated last night," Gerry said. "I stayed with her for some time, until she told me she wanted to be alone. We haven't actually seen her this morning. After she phoned you, she went back to bed. She told our butler that she'd been awake all night."

"I looked in on her about half an hour ago," Lady Burford said. "She was fast asleep. No doubt quite exhausted emotionally and physically."

"I'm not surprised. I'm amazed she didn't go completely to pieces."

"How much did she tell you?"

"Well, just a brief outline, really. I'll get all the details from her later. But I'm not going to disturb her yet."

"Will you have some coffee?" the Earl asked.

"Cousin George, that would be an absolute life-saver."

Gerry rang the bell.

"Do sit down," said Lady Burford.

"Thank you." She slipped off her leather jacket, sank into a chair and dropped the jacket on the floor. "Forgive the clobber, by the way. Only practical outfit for motor-cycling. I have bought some more suitable stuff, and I'll change shortly, if I may." She leaned back and hitched her left leg up, resting the ankle on her right knee, in a very masculine way. Unlike her sister, she seemed totally at ease and relaxed.

"You will be staying, I take it?" the Countess asked.

"If that's OK."

"Of course. We invited you and expected you yesterday, so we had had a room prepared. In the event I gave it to Timothy, but the one I had in mind for him is free."

"Thanks very much. I appreciate it, and I'd like to stay as long as Dorry does. I suppose exactly how long that is will depend on the police. They are here, are they? I saw a Wolseley outside that looked as though it might be a police car."

Gerry nodded. "They've been interviewing everybody."

At that moment, Merryweather entered with coffee. "Ah, you anticipated us," Lord Burford said.

When the butler had left, Agatha uncrossed her legs, sat up, groped in the pocket of her jacket on the floor and produced a packet of cheroots. "May I?"

"By all means," the Countess replied, hiding her surprise admirably.

"What are those like?" Gerry asked.

"Try one." Agatha proffered the packet.

"Oh, thanks." Gerry took one, casting an amused glance at her mother. She knew the Countess could not protest, without tacitly criticising their guest. Agatha lit it for her. Gerry drew on it, and concealed a grimace. "Interesting," she said.

"An acquired taste." She looked at the Earl. "So, what do the police think, do you know?"

"They've said nothing yet."

"But it does have to have been one of the household?"

"Seems so. They've cleared the servants. They know it wasn't Dorry or Gerry. And it seems they don't suspect Lavinia or me."

"I should hope not. And I'm sure it wasn't Miss Mackenzie. I've got to know her quite well, and I can't imagine a more unlikely murderess."

"Seems she's responsible for the funeral takin' place here at all," the Earl said. He recounted Miss Mackenzie's story, which she had confessed after emerging from her interview.

Agatha shook her head. "Who'd have thought it? Still, she'd have hardly admitted that if she *had* been the murderer, would she? So that just leaves the relatives, doesn't it? Gregory Carstairs, Timothy Saunders, Penelope Saunders, Tommy Lambert and Stella Simmons. Is that right?"

Gerry nodded. "Do you know any of them?"

"Not really. I seem to remember Timothy from Daddy's funeral, but I knew virtually nothing about the others before I started visiting Grandmamma. She loved to talk about all her relations, and I was glad to hear it, because we've never had much to do with the family. Which is why I cannot conceive why any of them could have had a motive for killing my stepmother. Though Dorry was a bit incoherent on the phone, she did say something about Mother threatening them all in some way. Could you tell me about that?"

"Well, that was a bit embarrassin', actually," Lord Burford said. He ran briefly through what had occurred, while underplaying the degree of Clara's anger and malevolence; she would, he thought, hear about that soon enough from Dorothy.

When he'd finished, Agatha stubbed out her cheroot. "Sorry about that. It's typical of Mother, I'm afraid. *De mortuis*, and all that, but she did have a fearsome temper and didn't take kindly to being slighted. Now, could you tell me just what happened last night, please? As I said, I only got a very sketchy account from Dorry on the phone."

Gerry took it upon herself to do this. When she had finished, Agatha was silent for half a minute, before saying: "Poor

Mother. Still, I suppose it's a better way to go than some long, lingering death." She looked round at them. "Perhaps you think I'm not showing enough filial emotion. Well, I'm not going to be hypocritical about it and pretend a grief I don't really feel. Mother and I were at loggerheads for years. She's not here to put her side of it, so I won't say much. She fed and clothed us well, when we were kids, and brought us up to be reasonably civilised human beings. And there was never any physical cruelty. But I don't think she ever loved us. And she—dammit all, I'm sorry, but I've got to say it—she used Dorry as an unpaid drudge. She tried to do the same to me. But I'm not as sensitive as Dorry and I stood up to her, and managed to a certain extent to live my own life. Dorry would never have done that. But now with this money, she may be able to make something of herself."

She suddenly seemed embarrassed by this outburst, coughed, gathered her jacket and got to her feet. "And, if it's all right, I'd like to go upstairs and change and freshen up now. And then I'll see Dorry. I can find my own way, if you tell me where my room is."

"Second door on the right in the left hand corridor," the Countess said.

"Thanks. And, I'm sorry, for all that. Very bad form, I know."

And Agatha hurried out. "Quite a character, what?" said the Earl.

"An unusual one, certainly," said the Countess. "I shudder to think what my mother would have said to me if I'd sat like that, even when I was Agatha's age."

"She's much more interesting than Dorry," said Gerry. "And she's got no pretence about her at all."

"I'm of the generation that considers there's a lot to be said for a little pretence sometimes."

"You don't like her."

"Oh, I don't say that. She's just not a type of young woman whom I am accustomed to."

Gerry stood up. "Well, must see how the investigation's going." She went out.

"George, what's that sticking out of your pocket?" the Countess asked.

The Earl looked down and hastily poked the grey shapeless object out of sight. "Oh, nothing."

"Of course it's something. It looks like a sock."

"Yes, it is. You know, when I'm trampin' round the estate I sometimes get my feet wet. Messing around by the lake, or crossing a ditch or something. Deuced uncomfortable. Thought if I carried a spare pair of socks with me, it would save having to trudge back to the house to change every time."

"But—but it hasn't rained for two weeks at least. The ditches must be quite dry. And why would you step into the lake?"

"Well, it's not for now especially. But if I get into the habit of keeping a pair in my pocket, they'll be there when I need them."

Lady Burford blinked.

"Anyway, must go and, er, look over the accounts." And he made off in the direction of his study.

The Countess stared after him.

Chapter Twenty-Eight

Leather opened the door, stood back and Gregory strode in. He started talking as soon as he crossed the threshold. "I must say at the outset, Chief Inspector, that I do not take kindly to being kept waiting so long." He sat down and folded his arms.

"Oh, but, sir, you must understand that in every case of this sort, we choose one witness whom we recognise as being the most important and reliable one. We always leave this person until after we have spoken to everybody else, so that we can use his testimony as a kind of benchmark by which to judge what the others have told us. You, as an MP, were the obvious one on this occasion."

Unexpectedly, Gregory laughed. "Nice try, Wilkins. A load of codswallop, but a nice try. You left me till last because I'm your number one suspect; that's it, isn't it?" It seemed to Wilkins that he was actually quite gratified at the idea of being Number One.

"No, no, sir. I must confess that I do talk codswallop from time to time, but I assure you I don't at this stage consider you any more suspect than several other people. I'd like to know indeed why you think that I should."

"Because of my position. Who, as much as a Member of Parliament, is susceptible to being ruined by the merest rumour of scandal, no matter how unfounded? A paid companion? A motor salesman? A fashion journalist? An eighteen-year-old flapper?"

"Perhaps a King's Counsel, sir."

"Not to the same extent. The press don't care about his private life, nor do his clients. It's not like an MP, with his constituents and his party whips breathing down his neck. As long as the KC doesn't breach professional ethics, or actually commit a crime, he needn't worry."

"So you think Mrs. Saunders may have been in a position to cause you embarrassment in this way, sir?"

"Yes, if her claim became public knowledge, it would be enough to set tongues wagging. Even though what she said was a total fabrication. In fact, her murder puts me in a worse position. If she hadn't been killed, I could have laughed it off, and if people looked as though they might be taking it seriously I could have issued a writ, and she would have been forced to eat her words. I can't do that now. Which is why, whatever it seems like on the surface, it is absurd that I should be considered a suspect at all."

"I can certainly see the strength of that argument, sir. But, tell me, why do you think Mrs. Saunders should have made that claim?"

"I haven't the foggiest. You'd do better to ask her stepdaughters. She claimed we were all in a conspiracy to do her out of her inheritance and deliberately slandered her to Florrie. It's ludicrous. I hardly know the others. It's years since I've seen George, Lavinia or Timothy. I've met Miss Mackenzie briefly when calling on my great aunt. Oh, and apparently I met Stella when she was in her teens, but I have no recollection of it. I barely knew of the existence of Penelope or young Lambert."

"And what can you tell us about last night, Mr. Carstairs?"

"Nothing, really. Went up at almost exactly eleven. Woken around twelve-thirty by the commotion. Got up, learned what had happened. Joined in the search. Went downstairs and waited for you."

"Do you have any reason at all, off the record, to suspect any one of your fellow guests of the crime?"

As with Timothy, there was a very slight hesitation before the reply came. "No."

"Are you familiar with the name Miss Dora Lethbridge?"

"Never heard of her."

"Well, thank you, Mr. Carstairs. I think that's all I need from you now."

Gregory stood up. "Look, how much longer are we going to have to stay here? I really need to get back to town."

"I can't keep you here, Mr. Saunders, if you decide to leave, but I would much prefer it if everybody remained one more night."

"You think you might clear this up by tomorrow?"

"Put it like this: if we don't, it could drag on for a long time, perhaps weeks. Plainly, I couldn't expect everybody to stay that long, so one more day would be the maximum I would ask people to remain. If one person left today, it would probably mean others would want to follow his example."

"Very well, I won't rock the boat."

"Thank you, sir."

Gregory went out.

Gerry saw her father leaving the morning-room and remembered she hadn't told her mother about the nettles. She decided she'd better get it over with and went back in, but before she could say anything the Countess forestalled her. "Oh, Geraldine, good, I wanted to talk to you. I may be worrying quite unnecessarily, but I have to tell somebody. I'm rather concerned about your father."

Gerry was suddenly alert. "What do you mean?"

"Well, he's behaving very oddly."

"Why, what's he done now?" She spoke sharply.

"'Now'? You mean you've noticed something, too?"

"Well, perhaps."

"Tell me, please," said the Countess.

"If you'll tell me."

"Very well. But you first."

◇◇◇

Five minutes later Lady Burford said: "Of course, your father has always been a trifle eccentric. And after all, some people do enjoy nettle soup, I believe, and carrying a spare pair of socks in one's pocket could be regarded as quite a practical idea. Nonetheless…"

"Putting them together," Gerry said. "And at this time, with policemen in the house and all of our guests under a cloud."

"Precisely. He is terribly upset by what's happened. In a way, it's worse than the other times because these people are all members of the family. Quite distant relatives, they may be, but they do all have Saunders blood, and some of them actually carry the name. Your father is totally without any personal pride or conceit, but he *is* immensely proud of the family, and now it seems one of its members is a murderer. I'm wondering if the blow has just been too much for him. And it's all my fault, really. I virtually insisted on having them here."

"Mummy, you mustn't think that. Daddy did fully agree eventually. No one could have foreseen what happened. And I think we are probably over-reacting. It could be he's just trying to take his mind off things. He does get these sudden crazes. Remember how he became an avid film fan, virtually overnight?"

"Cutting up stinging nettles in one's study, and deciding always to carry a spare of socks in one's pocket in the middle of the summer hardly fall into the same category. And if he wants to take his mind off things, why doesn't he go up and play around with his guns? That's what he's always done in the past when he's wanted to relax."

"Well, there's nothing we can do about it now. Unless you think you ought to call Dr. Ingleby to come and see him?"

"Oh no. Not for the time being, anyway. No, we'll just have to keep a close eye on him—both of us. And hope the guests don't notice anything."

"Tommy already has."

Before they could say any more there was a tap on the door and Agatha and Dorothy came in. Agatha was now dressed, the

Countess was relieved to note, in a very suitable tweed skirt and dark grey twin-set. Dorothy, who looked even paler than before beside Agatha's rubicund features, was still dressed in her funeral garb. Gerry remembered her promise to Wilkins and after a brief word hurried out.

Chapter Twenty-Nine

As Gregory went out, Gerry came in. "Just to let you know, Agatha Saunders has arrived and Dorry's up. They're both in the morning-room with Mummy, if you want to see them."

"I do indeed."

"Will you want me there when you talk to them, sir?" Leather asked. "If not, I'd like to go through my shorthand notes, check everything's readable, while what people said is fresh in my mind."

"That's OK, Jack, I won't need a note of what the Misses Saunders say."

He and Gerry went out, to find Merryweather waiting to inform him that he was wanted on the telephone.

"Ah. Probably the result of the PM. I'll join you in a few moments, Lady Geraldine," he said, and trotted off.

Having come off the phone, Wilkins was waylaid by Smith-son, who told him he had finished the fingerprinting. Wilkins sent him back to Westchester and then went to the morning-room. The Countess introduced him to Agatha and Dorothy, who were sitting close together on the sofa. Wilkins offered his sympathies. "I'm very sorry not to have had an opportunity to pay my respects earlier, Miss Dorothy," he said, "but it didn't seem necessary to disturb you."

Dorothy gave a nervous little smile. "That's quite all right."

"First of all I have to tell you that the post-mortem has con-firmed that your stepmother was suffocated."

Dorothy screwed up her face in horror and gave a shudder. Agatha squeezed her hand. Her face was grim. "And you've no idea by whom?"

"Not yet, miss, no."

"But by one of the people in the house."

"Unless we find that the alarm system was faulty, I'm afraid so."

The Countess interrupted. "Oh, I'm sorry, Mr. Wilkins, I should have mentioned that a man came by earlier and checked it. He said it's working perfectly and there's no sign of it's being tampered with."

"Thank you, my lady. It's what we expected, really." He looked at Dorothy. "I'm not going to make you relive the hor-rors of last night, miss. I've had a full account of what happened from Lady Geraldine, which I'm sure is completely accurate. But I would like to ask both of you about the accusations which your stepmother made yesterday. What do you think was behind them?"

They looked at each other. Dorothy spoke first. "She was terribly upset. She felt Florrie had slighted her in front of her relations."

"As, of course, she had," Agatha said. "Dorry's told me what she said in the will about Mother's income proving inadequate, and that she'd made a few changes in it recently. I reckon that could have been one of them. I told Grandmamma about Mother's little enterprise some months ago. I must say, though, I wish Grandmamma could have been a bit more diplomatic, tried to say *something* just a little nice about Mother and perhaps left her some token, a piece of jewellery, or something. Not that perhaps she deserved it, as she'd no doubt provoked and upset Florrie after Daddy died. We never saw our grandmother when we were children. But it would have avoided what sounds to have been a dreadful scene, and spared poor Dorry the embar-rassment."

"Do you think she really believed there'd been a conspiracy?"

Dorothy nodded. "I followed her up to her room and she was adamant that was what had happened. I didn't believe it, but I didn't argue."

"Your mother, though, must have made herself some enemies."

"Well, she did get a threatening phone call a few weeks ago." Dorothy said.

"Really? Tell me about that."

"It was somebody drunk and very abusive. He said she'd ruined his life and that he'd make her pay. I persuaded her to tell the police, but, of course, there was nothing they could do."

"You think killing her might have been an act of revenge, Mr. Wilkins?" Agatha asked.

"Oh, I doubt it, miss. No, I think the significance of her having enemies is that people the lady has exposed, like that caller, would often know whom they had to blame, would be extremely bitter and no doubt make this very clear to their friends. As a result, quite a lot of people—perhaps some of them in this house—would have got to know that when she threatened to expose somebody, she was genuinely capable of doing so. It wasn't just empty words. So this claim of knowing damaging things about her relatives: was that true?"

The young women again glanced at each other. Then Dorothy gave a little nod, as if prompting Agatha to answer.

She seemed to weigh her words before speaking. "She was only really interested in people well-known or wealthy or of high social standing. So the only two guests here whom she might have targeted are Timothy and Gregory. She may have discovered something about one or both of them, but I've never heard her mention either of them in any context. So my guess is that it was a shot in the dark. She thought there was a fair chance one or both of them might have secrets in their lives, so she just let fly. I think she included the others, just because she was so angry with everybody, and also didn't want anyone to think she just had those two in mind. That is, as much as she had time to *think* about what she was saying at all."

"I'm sure that's an extremely perspicacious analysis, Miss Agatha," Wilkins said.

"Sounds spot on to me," said Gerry. "And surely the important thing is not what Clara knew or didn't know, but what somebody *feared* she knew." She saw all eyes on her and smiled a little sheepishly. "Sorry, Mr. Wilkins. There I go again."

"No, you're quite right, Lady Geraldine. Which is why, if we don't clear it up quickly, it could take weeks—because it will be necessary to investigate each of the suspects exhaustively to try and discover if any of them do have a really big and clanking skeleton in their cupboard."

"Well, just as long as you do get him," Agatha said. "I may not have been at all close to my stepmother, but that doesn't mean I want to see the swine who held a pillow over her face escape justice, especially if he—or she—did it to cover up something shady in their own life."

"Well, I'll certainly do my best, miss. Now, there is just one more question, before we leave. Do either of you know of a Miss Dora Lethbridge?"

As one, they nodded. Agatha said: "She was our stepmother's mother—our stepgrandmother, I suppose you'd call her."

"We never knew her," Dorothy added. "She died before our stepmother married Daddy."

"I see. The answer so near at hand all the time. Was Lethbridge her maiden or married name?"

"Both," said Agatha. "Apparently she married a second cousin or something, also called Lethbridge."

"You don't happen to know the date of her death, do you?"

They both shook their heads.

"Or her birthday?"

The reaction was the same. "What's your interest in her, Chief Inspector?" Agatha asked.

"It's this, Miss Agatha." Wilkins produced a wad of papers from his inside pocket, ruffled through them and handed a card to Agatha. "That was found in your stepmother's bedroom. I was wondering if she was planning to insert it in one of those In Memoriam columns some papers carry. People mark the anniversary of someone's death, or their birthday. If her mother was born or died this month, or next, it would be an indication that might be what she was planning."

Agatha stared at the card. "I don't remember her ever doing anything like that, do you, Dorry?"

"No. But that's not to say she never did. I never read through those columns, so I wouldn't have seen it, if she had."

"And I suppose it's possible—if there was a particularly important anniversary coming up. Would it have been Dora's hundredth birthday soon?"

"She couldn't have been that old."

"Fiftieth anniversary of her death? No, that doesn't seem right, either. Anyway, why would she have been writing it here? Though I suppose it might have just occurred to her, and it was something to do. She must have been pretty bored, staying in her room alone all that time."

Dorothy held out her hand. "Give it me, a moment."

Agatha did so and Dorothy studied it closely. "I don't think this is Mother's writing."

"Are you sure, miss?" Wilkins asked.

"Not absolutely. It's difficult when something's all in capitals. But she always wrote an 'E' with a very short middle bar. There are"—she counted—"three 'Es' here, and in each of them all the bars are the same length. See?"

She passed the card back. Agatha nodded. "Yes, I see. But I never studied her writing all that closely, so I wouldn't know." She returned it to Wilkins. "I'm sure we could find out the dates Dora was born and died, if we went through Mother's papers."

"Maybe we'll have to ask you to do that. But it's probably of no importance. It's just one of those little points one likes to clear up." He got to his feet.

"You said you're leaving us now, Mr. Wilkins?" the Countess asked.

"Only briefly, my lady. The sergeant and I are just going to slip down to the village and get a bite to eat at the pub."

"Oh, please stay and have something here."

"Oh, that's very kind. An offer I didn't expect."

"I don't suppose you'll want to sit down with all the suspects—might be somewhat embarrassing. But if you don't mind lunching in the breakfast-room…"

"I think I can speak on behalf of Sergeant Leather when I say that will cause us no qualms at all, my lady."

"He's been in his study an hour now," said the Countess to Gerry later, "supposedly looking over the accounts. But he only did it a week or so ago. And now with a murder investigation going on here!" She stood up. "I've got to know what he's up to."

"What are you going to do?" Gerry asked.

"Just walk straight in as though I didn't know he was in there. Tell him I was looking for some writing paper or envelopes, or something."

"He might have locked himself in."

"I hope not. He's never done that. It would mean he wants to keep whatever he's doing a secret."

Lady Burford left the room and marched resolutely to her husband's study. Outside, she paused and listened. All was silent within. She took a deep breath, turned the knob, threw open the door and marched into the room.

The Earl, sitting at his desk, spun round with a start and stared at her, a positively guilty expression on his face.

"Oh, George, I'm sorry, I didn't know you were still here. Do you have any envelopes? I seem to have run…" Her voice tailed off as she took in the contents of the desk. Two half-empty bottles of ink, one blue, one red, stood each side of a small bowl, which contained a purplish liquid.

With a great effort of will, the Countess suppressed any sign of surprise. "What are you doing?" she asked casually.

"Doing? Oh, nothin' much. Just been makin' some purple ink. Mixed red and blue."

"I see. Any particular reason?"

"Not really. Just thought it would be a change. Gets a bit boring, always using blue for everything."

"I suppose it does. But couldn't you have bought a bottle?"

"Not likely to have any in the village shop. Would have meant sendin' someone into Westchester."

"Was it so important to have some now?"

"No, no. But had the red ink. So thought, might as well, you know."

"Of course." The Countess was running her eyes rapidly over the other things on the desk.

"What was it you wanted? Oh yes, envelopes." The Earl opened a drawer, withdrew half a dozen envelopes and handed them to her. "That enough?"

"Oh yes, plenty, thank you. I'll, er, leave you to it, then. Try not to spill any."

"No, I'll be careful."

The Countess went out.

◇◇◇

"Purple ink," said Gerry. "It's the sort of thing he'd usually think was rather vulgar."

"Well, of course, it is. But that's the least of my worries. There was something else extremely odd."

"What?"

"A thin strip of paper, with writing on it—big block capitals."

"Saying what?"

"I couldn't tell. It was backwards."

"Backwards?"

"Yes. Mirror writing. I didn't have time to work it out. For a moment I thought it was Russian, or some other language, but then I did recognise the word 'all'—'LLA,' with the 'Ls' the wrong way round."

"Anything else?"

"Not really. Well, there was a candle on the desk, which was a little unusual."

"But why should he want it there at the same time as he was mixing the ink?"

The Countess shook her head helplessly.

"Well, all we can do is just keep an eye on him."

"One of us can't always be with him, not with all these guests here."

"Talking of guests, I think I'll enlist Tommy's help."

"What do you mean?"

"Well, in spite of all outward appearances to the contrary, I believe he might be quite a reliable sort of cove. And as he knows something about it already, I think to take him into our confidence to a certain extent, and ask him to help keep an unobtrusive eye on Daddy, might make him even less inclined to gossip about either the nettles or anything else he may notice that's odd."

"You know him better than I do, so I'll leave it to you. But it's true I knew a number of young men like Tommy before the war. Quite vacuous on the surface. But a lot of them ended up leading battalions and winning medals."

Chapter Thirty

Wilkins leaned back in his chair, with a sigh. "Well, that was very nice."

He and Leather had just finished lunch, which had consisted of cold tongue, salad, new potatoes, with cold apple tart and cream for sweet. "Told you, didn't I?"

Leather, who had been hoping for something with chips and tomato ketchup, finished up his coffee. "Yes, it was OK. Could have done with a pint of bitter, though. So, what do we do now?"

"Well, we've finished here for the moment. Have to go and check up on a lot of things, but can't leave straight away, or it'll look as if we just hung on to get a free lunch."

"Which, of course, we didn't."

"What I really need to do is just sit and think. There never seems to be the time."

At that moment, Gerry entered. "Your HQ just phoned again, Mr. Wilkins. I took it. They said it wasn't important to speak to you, but to warn you that the early edition of the London *Evening News* is splashing the murder all over its front page. So we can expect swarms of reporters outside the gates very soon, I suppose. Heaven knows how they found out so quickly."

"Oh, I think I can guess, Lady Geraldine. I think you can, too, if you put your mind to it."

She furrowed her brow. "I don't think…"

"Your own personal mystery," Wilkins prompted.

She gave a start. "The early morning phone call! But who could it have been?"

"You should be able to work that out, too, if you're the detective I think you are."

Light dawned. "Of course! Right, I'm going to ask her, straight out. She's on the terrace, I believe."

"I'll be right behind you, Lady Geraldine."

Lord Burford dipped the paint brush in the purple ink and ran it down the length of the candle. Most of it immediately ran off, back into the bowl. "Dammit," said the Earl. It was being harder than he'd anticipated. The ink did not stick easily to the wax. After a couple more attempts, he took the candle by the wick, lowered it into the bowl and twirled it around before drawing it out. This time some ink at least stayed in place. He held it suspended over the bowl, spinning it round and blowing on it gently, until it had dried, then lowered it back into the ink and repeated the procedure. It took quite a long time, but eventually he laid the candle down on the desk and surveyed it proudly. Definitely a purple candle. Just what he'd wanted.

Then a little doubt began to niggle. It wasn't *really* a purple candle: just a white candle, inked to look purple. Suppose they could tell the difference? Oh, well, it couldn't be helped. It would have to do for now. He could always get a real purple candle later on. He took the strip of paper, with the mirror writing, wound it round the candle and held it in place with a small rubber band.

One more job nearly completed. Now he'd better knock off for a while and go and see how Wilkins was getting on.

"All right," Stella said. "It was me. I called a guy I know on the *News* early this morning. It was the chance of a huge scoop. But where's the harm? You couldn't have kept the lid on this much longer. Today or tomorrow you'd have had to issue a press statement. I just got in first by a few hours. And I didn't reveal the names of any of the guests, only that several well-known people were staying here. I didn't even give the name of the victim. I simply said a woman had been found dead, believed to have been suffocated, that the police were treating it as a case of homicide and that Detective Chief Inspector Wilkins of the Westshire police department was in charge of the investigation. Oh, and I did mention that a lot of cufflinks had been found scattered round the body. I thought that would give it a bizarre touch to hang the story on. If you'd asked us to keep quiet about it, I would have. But you didn't."

"I take your point, Miss Simmons," Wilkins said. "I should have done so. But, as you say, no real harm done, I suppose. No more phone calls, or telegrams, though, OK?"

"Understood, Mr. Wilkins."

He made his way back indoors, leaving Stella and Gerry alone. "Gerry, I'm sorry," Stella said. "But I don't think I've done anything to embarrass you or your parents. And look at it from my angle. I'm desperately trying to break into mainstream journalism. I've given the *News* an exclusive and several hours' lead over the *Standard* and the *Star.* They'll be cock-a-hoop. It's bound to put me in good with them. Now honestly, in my shoes, wouldn't you have done the same?"

Gerry, who was incapable of staying angry or feeling resentment for long, hesitated for a second, then smiled. "Probably."

"Oh, thanks for taking it like that. It's swell of you. I know there'll be reporters arriving. But it's not like a town house. They won't be able to get past the gates. So they won't bother anybody. Tell me, you've been helping the cops, I know: do you have any ideas yet as to who might have done it?"

"Nothing concrete. There is something at the back of my mind—something somebody said, or didn't say, or did, or didn't do—that at the time momentarily made me think 'That's odd.' But for the life of me I can't remember now what it was."

"You don't think it could have been Timothy, do you?"

"It *could* have been. Theoretically, it could have been practically anybody."

"But he seems such a non-violent type." She looked thoughtful. "Of course, there was the way he threw Gregory."

"Yes, those quiet, repressed people can sometimes snap, if they're provoked."

"You think he's repressed? You know, I think he's just shy and—outside the courtroom—rather unsure of himself."

"You may be right. I haven't seen a lot of him."

"Things aren't easy between him and Penny, apparently. She thinks he's too strict. 'No secret relations are strained,' as he put it. And that's probably an understatement. So one can understand it if he's a bit on edge."

"Must be difficult," Gerry said.

"I do hope it's not him. I kinda like the guy."

"I fancy it's reciprocated."

"Do you? Honestly? Why?"

"Oh, just the way he was talking to you last night. He lightened up a lot. He actually laughed."

"Which I don't suppose anybody's done since," Stella said.

"OK, Jack," Wilkins said. "We've done a bit more work since lunch, so we've justified staying on. We can go now. Let's tell his lordship."

They found the Earl in the drawing-room. "We've done all we can do here for the moment, my lord," Wilkins said, "and we're leaving now."

"So when will you be back?"

"Difficult to say. There's lots to do and we're a bit short of time. However, I believe you can help me."

"Certainly. What do you want?"

"Two things, actually. Sergeant Leather has to go up to London now." (Leather, to whom this was news, concealed his surprise admirably.) "And he needs to get on the earliest possible train. If we drive back to Westchester, the first one he could catch would be the two fifty-five, which wouldn't give him enough time in town to get everything done today. However, the twelve forty-five express will be leaving Westchester in about

five minutes, which means it will pass through Alderley Halt at
about five to one."

"D'you want me to have it stopped?"

"If you please. What is the procedure?"

"Oh, I just phone the chappie at the Halt—he seems to
be station master, ticket collector and signalman rolled into
one—and he signals it to stop. There's plenty of time. What was
the second thing?"

"You can tell me something about one of your guests; oh,
nothing confidential, a matter of public record, but a thing it
might take some time to find out."

"By all means. Anythin' to speed things up. What d'you
want to know?"

Wilkins told him. The Earl thought for a moment, before
giving him the information he wanted.

"Thank you, my lord. That's a great help. And it all means
that we'll be back tomorrow morning, if everything works out."

"Really? Oh, that'll be splendid. Do you think you may be
making an arrest then?"

Wilkins sucked air in through his teeth. "Well, *if* our enquiries
turn out as I hope, I shall then need to speak to several people
here again, and give them a chance to change their earlier state-
ments."

"You think *several* people lied to you?"

"At least three, quite possibly more. Once we've got them out
of the way, I think I may be making an arrest. But if we draw
blank in the next twenty-four hours, then I'm not sanguine, not
sanguine at all."

"Well, I'm not surprised, Wilkins. I mean, there are so many
mysteries, aren't there? That business of the cufflinks—"

"Oh, I know the explanation of that."

"You do? 'Pon my soul. What about the Dora Lethbridge
card?"

"I believe so, my lord."

"The stolen toothpaste?"

"I have an idea about that and hope to confirm it today."

"And the armour crashing down?"

"Yes."

"Then what the deuce is it you don't know?"

"Who killed Mrs. Saunders, my lord."

Chapter Thirty-One

"I'm wondering," Stella said, shortly after lunch, "whether it would be possible for Penny and me to get a ride into Westchester? If we're going to be here another twenty-four hours, we both need to buy a few things."

"Of course," Lady Burford said. "I should have thought of it myself. You must be thoroughly tired of those clothes."

"Well, they are starting to get a little crumpled, to say the least."

"I'll have Hawkins bring the car round straight away."

"Thanks very much. A shopping trip in a chauffeur-driven Rolls will be quite a treat in itself."

"Forgive my asking, but how are you both placed for cash?"

"Well, we're a bit short. I'm hoping I can find a store which will take a cheque."

"Don't worry about that. We have accounts at the two main stores, Harper's and Dawson's. Charge everything to us and settle up later, whenever it's convenient. Tell Penny the same. I'll telephone the two managers and instruct them."

"That's terrific. Thank you very much."

"It's the least we can do, considering the situation we've been at least partly responsible for putting you in. I wonder if anybody else would like to go. I don't imagine Agatha and Dorothy will want to leave here, but perhaps one or more of the men…"

Stella grimaced inwardly. A shopping trip with Gregory in tow was not what she had had in mind. She needn't have worried, however, as only Tommy, on hearing of Lady Burford's offer, decided to accompany the girls, though Timothy instructed Penny to buy him a shirt, plus some socks and handkerchiefs, while at the last moment Gregory requested Tommy to do the same for him.

The shoppers returned at half past four, loaded with packages. They reported—to the obvious delight of Penny—that they had been snapped on entering and leaving by the half a dozen photographers already gathered outside the main gates. The three then retired to their rooms to change. Stella emerged in a very plain light grey silk dress, of the kind which Gerry thought would be suitable for almost any occasion; while Penny had one in pale blue linen; both also had new shoes. Tommy sported a smart navy blazer and a pair of Oxford bags. Almost immediately Gerry cornered him.

"Yes, of course," said Tommy. "Glad to help. But what exactly d'you want me to do?"

"Just keep your eyes open and let me know if you see him do anything unusual. Or if anybody else mentions seeing anything. But don't let them know you're particularly interested."

"Do my best. Where is your papa now?"

"He's gone back to his study. He's been there ages. I wish I knew what he was up to."

"Can't you find some excuse just to go in and see?"

"I don't want him to know I'm checking up on him. There's a sort of unwritten rule nobody disturbs him when he's in his study, except for something really important. Mummy and I have broken it twice already today and I don't want to do it again. It's his sort of sanctum."

"I've never had a sanctum," said Tommy. "Nobody's ever felt they mustn't disturb me."

After Gerry had left him he sat thoughtfully for a few minutes. Would he be justified? Under normal circumstances, obviously not. Still, Gerry was clearly worried, and if the old boy *was* going off his rocker, somebody ought to know. He'd do it. He went outside.

Slowly, hands in pockets, he strolled round the side of the house. He gazed around him casually, kicked aimlessly at the turf and generally tried to give the impression of someone bored out of his wits. As he passed each window, he glanced quickly inside. He wasn't sure which room was Lord Burford's study. The first two clearly weren't, but as he passed the third he clearly saw the Earl, sideways on to him, seated at his desk.

Tommy stopped and stood for a few seconds, staring out over the park, then turned and looked up at the house, as though admiring the architecture. Slowly, he let his gaze drop, until he was looking straight into the study. The Earl was plainly engrossed in whatever it was he was doing and quite oblivious to being observed. Tommy, though, was unable to make out what was so engaging his attention. He strolled on a few paces, glanced around to make sure the coast was clear, then moved up close to the wall of the house, bent his knees and in a crouching position moved a couple of feet, until he was beneath the right corner of the window. The Earl had been facing to Tommy's left as he had looked in, so viewing from this side of the window should mean he would be out of Lord Burford's line of sight, even should he happen to glance out

Very slowly Tommy raised himself until he had a clear view into the room. The Earl was obviously working on something small, yet his movements were quite quick; it did not look as though he was repairing anything. A crumpled white handkerchief was lying on the desk, partly obscuring his hands.

Then the Earl gave his hand an irritated shake, sucked his finger, picked up the handkerchief and dabbed at his fingertip with it. Tommy could see that there were several small spots of what looked like blood on it. Lord Burford threw the handkerchief down again, this time in a slightly different position, giving Tommy a clear view of his hands.

For two minutes Tommy watched him in amazement, then moved clear of the window, straightened up, made his way back indoors and went in search of Gerry.

"He's bending pins," Tommy said simply.

"He's doing *what*?"

"Bending pins in half and putting them in a little glass jar. He must have done about a dozen while I watched. He kept pricking his fingers, but he didn't stop."

"Oh, lor." Gerry looked really worried now.

"Probably a perfectly logical explanation," Tommy said, encouragingly.

"Such as?"

"Well"—he groped for words—"I know: people make models out of things, don't they? You know, Taj Mahal out of matchsticks, and so on. Might be possible to do the same sort of thing with pins."

"Thanks for trying to help, Tommy, but do you really think...?"

"Perhaps not. So, what are you going to do?"

"There's nothing really I can do, short of calling the doctor, which Mummy's totally against."

"Are you going to tell her?"

"I'm not sure. I'll think about it."

"Well, if there's anything else you want me to do, just say the word."

He went out.

Gerry sighed. She'd really had hopes of solving this mystery single-handed, but her father's odd behaviour meant she had not been able to spend as long on the case as she had hoped. He had told her about Wilkins' progress report. It was certainly impressive. But—he had not yet identified the murderer. Which meant she still had time. It was just gone five. Nearly three hours till dinner. She must put that period to good use. She stood up and left the room.

Lord Burford furrowed his brow. That, surely, was just about all he could do here. Only two more jobs, but very simple ones. He opened the drawer of his desk, took out a ball of string and a pair of scissors and cut off two pieces of string each about a foot long. He took from the drawer two small glass jars, both nearly full of bent pins, and a pair of grey socks, bulging like miniature Christmas stockings. These he put in his pocket. He struck a match, applied it to the bottom of the candle for a second, placed the candle in the centre of an ashtray and lit it. Then he left his study, locking the door behind him.

◇◇◇

Gerry found Agatha and Dorothy sitting on the terrace, where Stella had been earlier. They were talking quietly, heads close together, but looked up as she approached and both smiled.

"May I join you?" Gerry asked.

"Please do," Agatha said.

Gerry sat down. "I've been feeling guilty that I've hardly spoken to either of you today. But I didn't really know what to say. How are you bearing up?"

They glanced at each other and Agatha answered. "I'm OK. It was much worse for Dorry than for me, of course. I'm shocked, obviously, but, as I said earlier, I'm not going to feign any great grief. And to be brutally frank—which I feel I can be with you, Gerry, as I couldn't with many people—I have to say I think it was one of the best things that could have happened for Dorry. Though not the manner of it, of course."

Dorothy looked distressed. "You shouldn't say things like that, Aggie."

"I don't see why not. It's a relief from servitude, petal."

"I don't feel it like that." She looked at Gerry. "I'm sure you, and everybody else, got a very bad impression of Mother yesterday. And I'm not going to pretend she was always easy. But she'd had a very difficult life. I'm sure she loved Daddy and then to lose him like that so soon after the marriage was a terrible thing for her. And she was left with us: two little girls whom she'd really hardly got to know. She could have washed her hands of us. She had no real obligation. She could have sent us to grandmother—"

"Wish she damn well had," put in Agatha.

Dorothy ploughed on. "She could have sent us to a home. But no, she took us on. She brought us up on her own. She sent us to good schools. She protected us. Money was always tight but she worked very hard. I didn't like all the things she did. But she did them because she had to and we never went short. Yes, she did become embittered, but I think she had cause. And I'll always be grateful to her."

Gerry felt a surge of guilt for all the uncharitable thoughts she had harboured about Clara. Someone who could engender such loyalty could not have been all bad. It made her more determined than ever to solve the case.

"I think that's wonderful," she said. "So there's certainly no doubt that you want this murderer caught, even though he or she might well be a relation?"

"Well, of course there isn't." Dorothy looked quite shocked.

"And don't get me wrong," Agatha added. "I didn't feel so well-disposed to our stepmother as Dorry did, but she didn't deserve to be murdered. So I don't want the bastard to get away with it." She bit her lip. "Sorry."

Gerry grinned. "Don't apologise. I've heard much worse. The reason I asked was that it occurred to me that if Clara *had* given any sort of hint that she knew something bad about one of the others, you might have been reluctant to tell Chief Inspector Wilkins about it. I'd be the same myself. I'd hate to make the police suspicious of someone, just on the basis of a casual word. But if there *was* anything, you could safely tell me. I'd promise not to pass it on to Wilkins, until I could find something additional to back it up. But it might just be the lead I'm looking for."

"Gerry," Agatha said, "if there was anything, we'd tell you like a shot. But she certainly said nothing at all to me."

"Nor to me," Dorothy said. "She was interested to know who the other beneficiaries were—we all were. And we discussed them. But all Mother said was things like Timothy was obviously very well off and it was a waste to leave him anything, and that Gregory probably wasn't short of cash either and she'd be interested in seeing what Stella was like. Things like that. And naturally we speculated on what we might get."

"I told Wilkins what I thought," Agatha said. "You were both there. Mother was bluffing. Only purely by chance, with somebody there she hit home. He believed the threat was genuine. And that meant Mother had to die."

◇◇◇

Next, Gerry went in search of Gregory. She eventually tracked him down in the billiard room, where he was knocking balls around the table in an aimless manner. He glanced up as she entered and put down his cue.

"Looks pretty heartless, I expect," he said.

"Not at all. We've all got to take our minds off things somehow."

"Just wish it worked."

"Must be getting you down,"

"Being chief suspect?"

"Oh, not *chief* suspect—just one of half a dozen."

"I'm under no illusions. Looking at the others, I've got to admit that *I'd* probably think I'd done it—if I didn't know I hadn't."

"Well, it's good you can joke about it."

"Must maintain the old stiff upper lip. Sure you feel safe being alone in a room with me? Don't think the other girls do. Stella was as nice as pie yesterday, but she's decidedly keeping her distance today."

Gerry didn't think it tactful to explain that, from what Stella had said to her, it was not the fear that Gregory was a *murderer* that was influencing Stella. She hoisted herself up onto the table. Gregory offered her a cigarette and lit it for her.

"Yes," she said. "It must be very nasty."

"I don't honestly believe they're going to try and pin it on me. But if Wilkins doesn't clear this up in a day or two, they're going to keep digging and digging—talking to my friends and colleagues, local party members, and so on. What I dread is that they'll never get proof and it'll just be left as an unsolved crime. The details are bound to leak out, and if just a few hundred people in my constituency decide I did it, my political career will be over come the next general election."

Gerry drew on her cigarette thoughtfully. "The only consolation I can offer is that, for all appearances to the contrary, Chief Inspector Wilkins is very smart. I'm sure he'll get to the truth. That is, if I don't first."

"Doing a bit of private detective work, are you?"

"Trying to."

"I didn't realise this was what they call a grilling."

"Oh, don't think of it like that. I am speaking to everybody, but I don't expect anybody to break down and confess, or slip up and give themselves away. I'm just trying to find out what people are thinking, or anything they might know. So if there's anything at all that *you* know which you didn't mention to Wilkins, you could tell me in strict confidence."

Gregory crossed to the mantelpiece, collected an ashtray, came back and put it on the edge of the table. "What sort of thing?"

"Any strange or odd behaviour, even if it apparently had nothing to do with the crime."

"Well, to be frank, just a few minutes ago I did see your father burying some small items outside, each side of the porch. Nothing to do with me, of course, but seemed rather, er, unusual."

It was all Gerry could do not to over-react. Somehow she managed to give a little smile. "Oh, that. Yes, it must have seemed odd. I can't explain now, but I assure you it's absolutely nothing to do with the murder. Feel free to tell Wilkins, if you like."

"No, no, take your word for it, of course. Anyway, neither you nor your parents are suspects."

"So did you see any of the suspects acting suspiciously?"

Gregory flicked some ash off his cigarette and carefully smoothed off the remaining loose ash against the inside of the ashtray. "Oh yes," he said.

Gerry gave a start. "You did?"

"Most decidedly."

"What? Who?"

"I can't tell you."

"But why—"

"Because I have absolutely no confirmation, no witnesses. It would be just this person's word against mine. And if I was to tell the police about it, the person could quite easily claim to have seen *me* acting suspiciously."

"Yes, but if you got your story in first, you'd have the advantage. If this other person did invent something about you, Wilkins would ask why they hadn't mentioned it before. They'd have a job to explain that."

"Not really. They could easily put it down to a reluctance to, er, sneak, as we used to call it as kids."

"Yes, I can see that, but I wasn't suggesting you tell the police at this stage: just tell me. I give you my word—"

"Naturally, I accept that without question, but I just cannot tell you, Geraldine. I'm sorry."

"As you wish. But this thing, whatever it was, it does give you definite grounds for suspecting someone?"

"No."

"But you just said—"

"Not grounds for suspicion. Knowledge. I know who killed Clara, Geraldine, know beyond all reasonable doubt. And as things stand at present, there's not a damn thing I can do about it."

Chapter Thirty-Two

Gerry found Timothy in the library. He was sitting extremely tidily, feet together, hands folded, reading a very thick book. He closed it when she approached and started to rise.

"Please don't get up," Gerry said. She sat in a chair opposite him, seeing with slight surprise that the book was one she had never seen before on ancient folklore and superstitions. He noticed her glancing at it. "It was on the table," he explained. "Just caught my eye. Quite interesting. Amazing what they believed in those days. Still do, apparently."

"Oh, there are some strange old customs still practised around here."

She realised as she said it that it was not the best form of words, given their present circumstances. "And I don't just mean murder," she added, making it worse.

He smiled frostily.

"I realise what a terrible situation for you this is," she said.

"It is not pleasant. One must hope that it doesn't continue too long. And although I know that Wilkins is an experienced officer, his manner does not inspire confidence."

"You shouldn't take too much notice of that. He's good. He does seem to be pretty baffled this time, though, I must admit."

"An alarming fact."

"Not for the murderer, though."

"No, indeed. The thought that he might get away with it is truly horrifying." Then he flushed slightly. "Oh, I realise you may think I am in fact hoping that the murderer does escape; in other words that I am myself he. And assuring you that I am not would plainly be quite pointless. Obviously, I am one of the chief suspects. Believe it or not, I have even found myself considering which of my fellow-counsel I might brief to defend me, if the worst should come to the worst."

"Did you choose somebody?"

"I could think of no one as capable as myself."

On the surface, the words suggested a breathtaking arrogance. But in fact they came across as a balanced, impassionate judgement.

"However," he continued, "I cannot really believe it will come to that. In fact, to me it is truly bizarre that anyone could even imagine me capable of murder."

Gerry decided on shock tactics. "I can imagine it," she said calmly.

There was no immediate display of indignation. Only his eyelid twitched rapidly three times. "Really? I admit to feeling disappointment. Under what circumstances, may I ask?"

"To protect Penny."

"Oh, I see. Well, yes, perhaps. I suppose most parents would kill to save their child's life."

"Or even perhaps to protect her reputation."

"Ah, I understand which way your mind is working: that it was Penelope who had some guilty secret, which Clara was going to expose."

"No, my mind's not working that way at all. I'm just trying to think how a policeman's mind might work."

"I cannot conceive of any police officer believing she could be guilty of anything which would make such a course necessary."

"Again, I can—just. A road accident, perhaps. Say she knocked down and killed someone. It may not have been her fault, but she panicked, and drove on."

"She doesn't own a car."

"She could have borrowed one. Suppose the accident was seen by someone who recognised her, and who also knew about Clara's little enterprise and passed it on to her. Penny could go to prison for quite a long time. You would be desperate to prevent that."

"I would certainly do all in my power legitimately to prevent it. But most decidedly not murder."

Gerry gazed at him. "No," she said at last, "I don't believe you would."

"Perhaps you think the less of me for it—consider that I should be prepared to kill in those circumstances."

"Not to kill just anybody. But perhaps to kill a person like that in such a situation might be legitimate."

"I cannot agree with you. However, we seem to have moved a long way from reality. Unless you believe some such course of events did actually take place."

"Good lord, no. I'm just pointing out how to someone like Chief Inspector Wilkins, with his experience, almost anything is possible."

"I take your point and I can see the logic of what you say. Nonetheless, I simply should not be a suspect. You see, I know—" He stopped.

"Know what?"

"It's nothing."

Suddenly Gerry knew what had been on his lips. "You were going to say you know who did kill Clara, weren't you?"

For the first time since she had met him, she saw him really startled. "What—what—?" he began, then took a deep breath. He obviously realised it was too late to deny it. "How did you know?"

Gerry couldn't answer this. Had it been intuition? Telepathy? Or merely the more prosaic fact that Gregory had said almost exactly the same thing? Resisting the temptation to reply "I have my methods," she just gave an enigmatic little smile. "Do you want to tell me about it—in confidence?"

"I'd like nothing better than to tell somebody, but I can't."

"Because you have no evidence."

"Yes."

"And if you were to say what you know, the person you accuse might well fabricate a story about you."

He stared at her. "This is remarkable. I can almost believe you have psychic powers."

"Nothing like that. It's simply logic. But you could tell me— not the police—and be sure it wouldn't get back to that person. It might just help me to get to the bottom of this affair."

He shook his head firmly. "If I tell anybody, it will be the police. I might have to do so eventually. But in the meantime it would be unfair to burden you with knowledge which you were honour bound to keep to yourself."

There was obviously no point in arguing with him. "OK. Don't forget, though, that if this person has killed once, they'll have no compunction about killing again. Having this knowledge, you yourself could well be in danger."

"That had not occurred to me, I must admit. But thank you. I shall be on my guard now. And I think you know I am well able to take care of myself."

◇◇◇

Gerry's brain had been in a whirl after she left Gregory; it was in a positive turmoil after she left Timothy. That they should both have come up with almost identical stories was incredible. Was one of them lying? Were they both lying? It was hardly possible to imagine that each had seen the other behaving suspiciously. So had they both independently seen a third person doing so?

Her cogitations were interrupted by Tommy. He wasted no time in preliminaries. "Something else to report."

She felt a stab of alarm. "What?"

"Nothing much, this time. He was just walking round the courtyard, tying knots in a piece of string, lots of them."

"When was this?"

"About twenty minutes ago. I saw him out of my window. And he seemed to be talking to himself. At least, his lips were moving. I couldn't hear anything. He could have been singing, I suppose."

"If Daddy's walking round the courtyard, singing to himself, when we've just had another murder in the house, things are really serious."

"Perhaps he was singing a hymn. You know, sort of private requiem, in memory of Clara."

"I'd much rather he was talking to himself," Gerry said.

"You didn't make me look too good in front of Geraldine, you know," Agatha said.

Dorothy stared at her. "What do you mean?"

"Well, here I've been telling everybody how badly she treated you, and then you come out with all that about how grateful you are to her, and how much you'll miss her. Makes me seem a pretty unfeeling bitch."

"Oh, Aggie, I'm sorry. I didn't mean to. It's just that when someone dies you've got to think of their good points, haven't you? And she did have some."

"How you can say that the way she treated you, I just can't understand. If she did have some good points, they weren't very obvious to me."

"But there's no need to come out with it. Not here. It's just not the done thing."

"Well, I've never been the one for doing the done thing, as you know. I believe in honesty."

"Absolutely agree with you," said a cheerful voice.

They both looked up sharply. It was Tommy, who'd approached without their being aware of him. "Sorry. Wasn't eavesdropping. Couldn't help hear what you said about honesty, though, and about not doing the done thing. I'm dead against doing the done thing. Positively an undone thing chap."

He cleared his throat a little awkwardly. "I just wanted to say one thing. Pretty pointless, really, sort of thing everybody'd say, but just wanted you to know, er, I didn't do it. Honestly."

"Never thought you did," Agatha said, gruffly.

"Dunno why. Could have done."

"Anyone can see at first glance you could never be a killer."

"Really?" Tommy looked a little disappointed. "Bit too wishy-washy, eh?"

Agatha hastened to reassure him. "Oh, I don't say you couldn't kill if it was necessary, in a war, say. But I can't imagine your murdering a woman."

"Ah." He seemed happier. "No, no, jolly well couldn't. Anyway, we all know who did it, don't we?"

"I don't," Agatha said. "I only got here today and I hardly know the others, so I'm not prepared to speculate."

"I am. Well, it's a process of elimination. Couldn't possibly be either of the girls or old Mackenzie. Timothy's far too cautious. No, it's got to be Gregory the Great. He's absolutely the type. Can't you just see him creeping into the room at night—"

"YOU INSUFFERABLE YOUNG BOUNDER!"

Tommy gave a start and spun round. Gregory was standing about eight feet away. His face was crimson and he was quivering with rage. "How dare you! How dare you blacken my name like that! I'll sue! I'll take every penny of that inheritance of yours. I'll ruin you. But first I'm going to thrash the living daylights out of you." He tore off his jacket and advanced on Tommy, his fists clenched.

Dorothy gave a scream and Agatha jumped to her feet. Tommy backed hastily away. His face had gone the colour of partly melted snow. He stammered.

"I say, frightfully sorry and all that. Only joking, you know."

"Joking? You can joke about a thing like this?" He continued to advance and Tommy continued to retreat, holding his hands up in front of him.

"Stop backing away, you young coward. Stop and fight like a man."

Tommy started to babble something, but nobody heard him because at that moment there was a further intervention. A small blue, pink and gold blur appeared, seemingly out of nowhere, and flung itself on Gregory. It was Penny. Like an avenging fury, she beat at his chest with both fists and tried to scratch his face. "Leave him alone, you beast!" she screamed.

Taken unaware by the onslaught, Gregory was forced to back away, but eventually he managed to grab her wrists.

"Whoa, whoa," he said, as if trying to calm an over-excited filly.

Penny squirmed and struggled unavailingly. "You bully!" she shouted at the top of her voice. "You—you Conservative!"

Agatha was standing indecisively, obviously quite at a loss to know how to react to all this. Dorothy had her hands clasped to her head and was rocking back and forth in her chair, making little moaning noises.

Tommy at last seemed to realise his situation: that he was being protected by an eighteen-year-old girl. He drew a deep breath and stepped forward. "It's all right, Penny, old thing," he said in an unnaturally low voice. "Thanks, but I can handle this." He took her gently by the upper arm. The back of his hand against her side could feel her body trembling violently. "Let her go, please," he said to Gregory. "She won't hurt you now."

Somewhat dubiously, Gregory released Penny's wrists. Tommy gently drew her aside. Then he slowly removed his blazer, folded it and handed it to her. "Will you hold this, please?"

He deliberately turned back his shirt cuffs and faced Gregory. "I'm not a violent bloke. But if this is your way of settling differences, I'm willing."

He clenched his fists and took up an exaggerated pose, left arm extended and bent upwards at the elbow, his fist level with his forehead, the other lower down; plainly a stance remembered from school boxing lessons. "Come on, then," he said,

If he was hoping the MP would back down at this stage, he was disappointed. "Right," said Gregory and moved forward. Tommy stood his ground and at that moment an ear-piercing shriek rent the air. It came from Dorothy.

"Stop it, stop it, stop it," she wailed. "I can't stand it! My mother was murdered yesterday. Have you no sense of respect? None of you?"

Agatha went to her and put an arm round her shoulder. She looked at the others. "She's right, you know."

Gregory slowly lowered his fists. "Sorry. Sorry, my dear. Lost my head. Bad form, in front of you and all that. Forgive me." He glared at Tommy. "Count yourself very lucky we're in the presence of ladies. I'm just sorry the days of duelling are over. I advise you to keep out of my way the rest of the time we're here." He looked at Penny. "And as for you, young lady, your father should give you a damn good spanking. Still, like father, like daughter, I suppose." He made a stiff bow to Dorothy and Agatha, picked up his jacket and strode off towards the house.

In a most unladylike gesture, Penny poked out her tongue at the retreating figure.

Tommy looked at the sisters. "My apologies as well."

"Me, too," Penny added.

Tommy offered his arm. "Shall we go and see if someone will give us a drink?"

"Oo yes, that would be lovely."

She tucked her arm in his and they strolled off.

It occurred to Agatha that in death her stepmother was capable of stirring up almost as much trouble as when she was alive. But she kept the thought to herself.

◇◇◇

"You were wonderful, Tommy," Penny said, "standing up to him like that."

"Well, thanks to you, got to admit. Couldn't let a girl fight my battles for me. I say, it was jolly sporting of you to stick up for me like that. Thanks awfully."

"I hate him," she said simply.

"Gosh, I wish duelling was still carried on, too. I bet I could make rings round him with a sword."

"Of course you could, Tommy. Or with a pistol."

He stopped, turned and looked at her. "Er, there's something I've got to say, old girl."

"What, Tommy?" Her voice and expression were eager.

"There's something you don't know about me. Fact is, that, well—I'm a Conservative, too."

Her eyes widened and he hastened to reassure her. "Oh, I don't mean I'm a member of the party, or anything like that. But I do vote for them. Well, I did once. Well, last time. Well, the only time I've voted, actually."

Penny blinked. "I see," she said slowly, clearly perplexed. "So, you think they're all right, do you?"

"Well, yes, not bad."

"Not reactionary relics?"

"Not especially."

She furrowed her brows in a deep frown. This was obviously a totally new concept, which took some grasping. "Are you going to do it again?"

"Probably. Haven't really given it a lot of thought yet. Couple of years to go, after all."

She looked relieved. Two years was an eternity. "Yes, of course. That's all right then. And I think it's very brave of you to tell me, Tommy. You didn't have to. You could have kept quiet about it and I'd never have known."

He smiled modestly. It seemed that nothing he could do was wrong. It was a rather pleasant feeling.

Chapter Thirty-Three

Gerry turned away from the window, to which she had hurried when she first heard Gregory's shout of rage and from which she had watched everything that went on. A completely new thought had come to her. Earlier, she had suggested to Timothy that he would be willing to kill to protect Penny. But she had just seen Penny, faced with a perceived threat to someone she cared for, turn in total fury and abandon on the source of that threat—even though the most damage Gregory had been likely to inflict on Tommy was a black eye. How would she have reacted had the threat been much worse, either to Tommy—or to her father?

If Timothy did have a guilty secret, it was quite possible Penny knew about it. If Tommy had one, she was at least more likely than anyone else present to know about it. And if she truly believed Clara had been about to make it public…

Gerry had not until now seriously considered Penelope as a suspect. But there was a remorseless single-mindedness about the girl which made Gerry realise that this had been a mistake.

But which of them would she kill for? Her devotion to Tommy was plain. But what could *he* have done that was so terrible that it had to be covered up at all costs? She came back to her earlier idea about a road accident. A hit and run. Tommy driving—and Penny with him. That was quite feasible. If someone had been killed and Tommy was proved to have been the driver, he would go to prison for a very long time. And for someone like Tommy to be shut up in Dartmoor or somewhere like it for many years would almost be as bad as a death sentence. (Of course, this line of thought put Tommy himself very much back in the picture as a serious suspect; but for the moment, she was concentrating on Penny.)

The trouble was that she just could not see Tommy being so carefree if he had something like that hanging over him. Even with Clara out of the way, there was always the possibility that the hit and run would come to light. Surely any decent person would feel a terrible guilt for the rest of their life: Gerry knew she would. And she still felt Tommy was basically a decent person.

No, of the two men in Penny's life, Timothy was by far the more likely to have something on his conscience—something that he might, in a weak moment, have confided to his daughter. Some professional indiscretion. Jury tampering or the bribing of a witness. Or more likely something not quite so blatant, some breach of the legal rules that the ordinary person might not think was too bad, but which would put a lawyer beyond the pale in the profession. Failing to disclose evidence—something like that.

One important thing to discover was just how much Penny cared for her father's welfare, how far she would be willing to go to protect him. If things were as difficult between them as Stella had said, it might be that she wouldn't care too much if he did come some kind of cropper.

Perhaps she could devise some sort of test to discover just how devoted a daughter Penny really was.

Gerry spent ten minutes in intense thought and at last came up with an idea. She would need two accomplices. Yes, Stella for one, and her mother would do for the other; she would only have to sit and listen. Now, what was the name of that book, and where was it? If she couldn't find it she was sunk—she had actually to have it in her hands at the time. Another fifteen minutes was spent unsuccessfully scouring first her room and then the library. Eventually, she found her mother writing a letter in her boudoir and asked her if she had seen it.

"Oh yes, I'm reading it at the moment," said the Countess. "It's by the side of my bed."

"Oh, terrific! Could you please bring it to the drawing-room straight away?"

"Am I to know why?"

"Eventually, Mummy, but it would take too long to explain now. I've got to find Stella." She rushed off. Lady Burford gave a little shrug to herself and made her way to her bedroom.

Gerry located Stella in her room, also busily writing. She could not help noticing that the page was headed "My Ordeal as a Murder Suspect."

"I want you to do something for me," Gerry said. "It's important. Could you bring Penny to the drawing-room in about five or ten minutes?"

"I guess so. Why?"

"It's a long story. Don't let her know I asked you to do it, come into the room without speaking, but do make enough noise for me to know you've arrived. Cough or something. And whatever you hear me saying, don't react at all."

"But what reason do I give her?"

"Oh, you'll think of something." She scurried towards the door again.

"Where is she?" Stella asked.

"I don't know," Gerry called, as she vanished, "but she can't be far away."

When Gerry got to the drawing-room, she found Lady Burford sitting meekly on the sofa, the book on her lap. Gerry grabbed it. "Wonderful! Now I must find a good passage." She sat down next to her mother and for two or three minutes she flicked frantically through the pages. At last she exclaimed: "Ah, that'll do. Page one-seven-five." She closed the book.

"Now what?"

"Tell me the plot of the book."

"But you've read it."

"Never mind."

"I haven't finished it."

"That doesn't matter. Just talk. And don't stop when you hear somebody coming in."

"Well, it's rather a hackneyed story. It's about this young girl, Isobel, who is left an orphan when her parents are killed in a rail crash and goes to live with an uncle and aunt, who live in this big, gloomy house in the middle of the Yorkshire Moors."

The Countess ploughed on until Gerry's sharp ears heard the click of the doorknob, followed by a rather theatrical cough. "Stop in five seconds," she whispered.

"Well, the girl doesn't know what to do. But then she has a surprise." Lady Burford stopped.

Gerry said loudly: "Oh, Timothy's a totally despicable character. Thoroughly deceitful and slimy."

There was a few seconds' silence in the room. It was broken, deafeningly, by Penny's voice. "I heard that!"

They both turned. "Oh, Penny—" Gerry began, but got no further.

Penny was staring at her, an expression of pure loathing on her face. "How dare you speak about my father like that! He's a wonderful man! He's—he's practically a saint. You're the despicable one, talking about him like that behind his back. I hate you, I hate you!" There were tears in her eyes.

Gerry jumped to her feet. "I wasn't talking about your father."

"Don't lie to me, you sly cat! I heard you say Timothy."

"I was talking about a character in a book! This book." She held it out.

"I—I don't believe you."

"I'll show you." She opened it and quickly found page one hundred and seventy-five. She handed it to Penny. "There you are: read the second paragraph."

Penny took it doubtfully and read aloud: "'I can't stand Timothy,' said Isobel. 'You're not alone,' Frank replied. 'In fact, I don't know anyone who's got a good word to say for him.'"

"There you are, you see," Gerry said. "I read it some time ago and Mummy's half way through it. We were just talking about it. I said despicable *character*, not *person* or *man*."

"Oh," Penny said blankly. The anger had drained from her face. "I'm sorry. I—I really thought…"

"Of course you did. I'd have thought the same. But I'd never talk about your father like that. I don't really know him. But I do know he's got a fine reputation."

"Yes, yes, he has."

"It's just a very weird, unfortunate coincidence. Come on, let me get you a glass of sherry." She moved with Penny to the far side of the room.

Stella came forward to join the Countess. "Do you have any idea what that was about?" she asked.

"Absolutely none, my dear. But one gets used to that, living with Geraldine."

"I think I'm beginning to get an inkling," Stella said.

"I don't intend even to try and understand." She frowned suddenly.

"Something wrong?"

"Not really. I just didn't know Frank felt like that about Timothy. I thought they got on rather well."

Chapter Thirty-Four

When Gerry went up to change for dinner, she was feeling very pleased with herself. She had proved one thing beyond doubt: however strained things had been between Penny and Timothy, in reality she idolised him. If looks could have killed, Gerry thought, she would be dead by now, simply for appearing to say something derogatory about him. If she had represented actual danger, would those looks have been converted into action? She was beginning to think it was very possible. The trouble was that her experiment hadn't really got her any further forward. No matter how sure she was that Penny would kill to protect her father, she still couldn't say that she actually had.

Nor had she yet remembered what it was that had struck her as somehow wrong. She'd heard that hidden memories were sometimes recalled in dreams. Before she went to sleep tonight, she must will herself to remember.

She had spoken now to practically everybody—well, with one exception. She hadn't had any really long conversation with Tommy since the murder. She couldn't think it would do any good, and didn't even know what she would ask him. But she supposed that for the sake of completeness she ought at least to go through the motions. There was still about forty-five minutes before dinner. He might be in his room.

She left her own room, went to the east corridor and tapped on his door. There was a cheerful call of "Come in."

He was lying on the bed, smoking and reading a new P.G. Wodehouse novel. He could almost be a character in it himself, she thought. There was definitely a touch of the Wooster about him.

He sat up when he saw her and swung long legs onto the floor. "Hello, Gerry. This is an unexpected pleasure. Take a pew." He indicated the room's only chair.

"Thanks." She dropped into it.

"Gasper?"

"Oh yes, please."

He gave her one and lit it. "Nothing else to report, by the way."

"Oh, good. But I didn't want to talk about that now. Tommy, do me a big favour."

"What's that?"

"Confess to the murder of Clara."

He grinned. "Like to oblige, and all that, but just wouldn't be true, and well, second George Washington, me."

"You think it was Gregory, don't you?"

"Ah, you heard about our little fracas?"

"Saw it through the window. Heard quite a lot. You stood up to him well."

"Eventually. In a bit of a funk, actually. Bad show all round, of course. Should have kept my mouth shut."

"Did you have any particular reason for accusing him?"

Tommy wriggled awkwardly. "Not really, I suppose. Just seems more the type than anyone else."

"Tommy, do you know anything at all that you didn't tell the police? Anything you could tell me, in confidence."

There was just a split-second pause before he answered. "No, not a thing."

It was enough for Gerry. She sat up and looked at him sharply. "You do, don't you?"

"No, no, honour bright."

"Tommy, second George Washington, remember?"

He had gone a little pink. "Nothing at all about the murder, truly."

"But something else?"

"Well, perhaps. It's just that, well, I'm pretty sure, no, I know, actually, that someone here's been telling whoppers. But please don't ask me who."

"I wouldn't tell anybody."

"It would put you in an impossible position."

"I could go to the person and ask them straight out."

"And how would you tell them you knew about it?"

"I wouldn't tell them."

"They'd know it came from me."

"Would that matter?"

"It would to me."

"But we're dealing with murder here."

"It's got nothing to do with the murder. I'm sure of it. When that's cleared up I'm going to tackle this person myself. But to do it now would only muddy the waters."

"And suppose the murder isn't cleared up?"

"Then I might have to tackle them anyway. But it will be. Gosh, it's not twenty-four hours yet. Give the rozzers a chance." He was silent for a moment. "I'll tell you what. Let me sleep on it. Then in the morning, if I feel up to it, I'll ask the person about it. And if they can't give me a satisfactory explanation, I'll tell you and you can tell Wilkins, if you like."

"Oh, that would be marvellous. But couldn't you do it tonight?"

"Rather not. It's going to be dashed embarrassing and I want time to work out what I'm going to say. And, er, afterwards, if I am satisfied everything's OK, then that'll be OK with you, OK?"

"OK," said Gerry.

On their way down to dinner, Timothy and Tommy met at the top of the stairs. Tommy gave a brief nod and started to hurry on down, but paused, with a slight tinge of alarm, when Timothy said: "Oh, a word."

"Er, yes?"

"Penelope's been telling me about what happened outside earlier. How you accused Gregory to his face of being the murderer and stood up to him and refused to withdraw when he wanted to resort to fisticuffs."

"Well…" Tommy began, but got no further.

"I just wanted to say, congratulations. Showed a lot of courage, moral and physical."

"Oh." Tommy was taken aback. Penny had obviously been shamelessly exaggerating. Perhaps he ought to put Timothy right as to what had really happened. But, no. One shouldn't contradict a lady. Not the act of a gentleman. So he just smiled deprecatingly. "It was nothing, really," he said.

Gerry woke with a start. For a moment she thought there was somebody in the room. But no. What—

Then it came to her. She remembered what it was that had been wrong. It had worked. She had concentrated on the problem before going to sleep, and it had worked. She sat up and turned on the light. What did it mean? It couldn't really be significant, after all. Could it? She thought hard.

The next moment she knew. She knew who had killed Clara. It had to be. It was the only answer. For seconds she couldn't take it in. There was still no way of getting proof. Except—except that one other person had to know. Somebody had been covering up. Could she somehow persuade that person to tell the truth? Obviously it wouldn't be easy. But she had to try. She looked at the bedside clock. Ten past four. She couldn't go back to sleep, not tonight, with this new knowledge. No, she had to act now and use all her powers to force an admission. She got out of bed, put on her slippers and dressing-gown and left the room.

Chapter Thirty-Five

"Wonder what time Wilkins'll be here?" Lord Burford said moodily.

He was picking at his bacon and eggs and for once *The Times* lay unopened beside him. It was 8 a.m.

"Extremely soon, I hope," said the Countess.

"'Course, he may just tell us he's drawn a blank."

"Well, at least he'll have to let them all leave and we can get back to something like normal."

"I sometimes think nothin' is ever going to be normal again."

At that moment the door of the breakfast-room was thrown violently open and they both turned towards it, A dark, pretty girl rushed across the room towards them. It was Gerry's maid.

"Marie, what on earth—" Lady Burford began.

"Oh, milord, milady, it is the Lady Geraldine. I cannot wake her! She is so still and white! Please, you must come."

They leapt to their feet. Lady Burford gasped: "Oh no!" and then followed the Earl, as he ran out of the room.

The Earl charged into Gerry's bedroom and ran across to the bed. Gerry was lying perfectly still on her back, only her head showing above the bedclothes. He put his hand on her forehead, then pulled back the sheets and grabbed at her wrist.

"Is she—is she…" The Countess, behind him, could not finish.

"I can't feel a pulse. Looking-glass, quickly!"

Marie ran to the dressing-table, grabbed a mirror and handed it to him. He sat on the edge of the bed and held it close to Gerry's mouth for a few seconds, then peered at it. "She's breathing."

"Oh, thank God."

The Earl swung round to Marie. "Find Mr. Merryweather, tell him what's happened and to send Hawkins for Dr. Ingleby at once. Hurry."

Marie rushed from the room. "And just pray he's not out," Lord Burford muttered.

"George, can you tell what's wrong?" The Countess was wringing her hands.

He shook his head. "Sorry, my dear."

"Is there anything we can do?"

"I can't think of anything. If we tried to force some brandy down her, or something, it might be absolutely the wrong thing."

"She's—she's still breathing?"

He again put the mirror to Gerry's lips. "Yes. But it's so shallow. Her chest's not moving at all."

The Countess fell on her knees beside the bed and took Geraldine's hand in hers. She closed her eyes and her lips started to move silently. With a restless, jerky movement, Lord Burford stood up.

A voice spoke from the doorway. "Can we help at all?"

It was Stella. She and Penny were standing close together, their faces horror-struck.

The Earl answered. "Oh. No, don't think so, my dear, thank you. You can tell the others what's happened."

"Yes, of course. Come on, Penny."

They went but a moment later there was the sound of hurrying footsteps and Merryweather appeared. "Hawkins is on his way, my lord. I instructed Marie to wait outside and bring the doctor straight up."

"Good, good."

The butler gazed past him at the wax-like figure on the bed. "Oh, my lord, this is terrible. But she must be all right, she must."

"It's out of our hands, Merryweather."

"May I remain, my lord?"

"Of course."

Merryweather sat down on an upright chair and fell silent. The Earl took out some cigarettes and lit one with fingers which trembled only slightly.

It was only a little over twenty minutes, though seeming to those in the room like twenty hours, before they again heard hasty footsteps along the corridor and Marie's voice saying: "In there, Doctor."

Ingleby appeared in the doorway and strode across to the bed. The Countess and Merryweather got to their feet. Lord Burford said: "We just found her like this, Ingleby, she was fine last night."

"Yes, her maid told me."

He put opened his bag and began his examination. He looked in her eyes with a small torch, took her pulse and blood pressure and then pulled back the bedclothes, put his hand under the crook of her leg, raised it and struck it sharply just below the knee with the side of his hand. To her parents' inexperienced eyes, there seemed a momentary delay before the lower part of her leg kicked up. Next, Ingleby gently turned her onto her face and closely scrutinised the back of her head.

At last he looked up. "Well, I can tell you what's wrong with her."

The Earl and Countess stared at him apprehensively.

"She's been knocked unconscious."

"*What?*"

"There's a big lump on the back of her head."

"You—mean somebody just crept into the room and hit her?"

"I can't say whether they crept into the room, but she's certainly been hit with some heavy object." He turned her over again onto her back.

"The murderer," Lord Burford whispered. "She's been going round questionin' everyone, hoping to solve the case before Wilkins. Oh, why couldn't she have left well alone!"

"Will she be all right?" Lady Burford asked fearfully.

Ominously, it seemed to them, Ingleby avoided a direct answer. "I would ideally like to get her head x-rayed, but I think it's probably safer not to move her, at least for the time being."

"But she will regain consciousness?" Lord Burford said.

"Prognosis is notoriously difficult in the case of head injuries. She will either recover spontaneously, or—" He stopped.

"Or what, doctor?"

"Sink deeper into a coma."

"And—and if that happens?"

"It could be days, or weeks."

"Or longer?"

"It's possible."

"You're saying she could be in a coma, for months, or years."

"Let's not think that far ahead. Twenty-four hours will tell. If she has not come round by then, I will have her removed to hospital and get some x-rays taken. We should then learn more about the extent of the damage and be able to make a more accurate forecast."

"Is there nothing you can do now?"

"I'm afraid not. It's just a question of waiting and keeping her under observation."

The Countess sank down slowly on the bed. "Oh, dear Lord."

"I'm very sorry I can't be more helpful. But I can say that in the majority of head injury cases the patients do recover spontaneously." He glanced at his watch. "I wish I could stay longer. But unfortunately I have another emergency awaiting me. I will look in again later. If Hawkins could take me home to collect my car…"

The Earl shook his head. "Have Hawkins take you wherever you need to go for the rest of the morning. We won't be needing him."

"Oh, that's extremely kind. Thank you. Just keep her comfortable and warm." He hurried out. Merryweather unobtrusively followed him.

The Earl and Countess looked at one another. Her lips trembled. "Oh, George."

He put his arm around her shoulder. "Bear up, my dear. She'll be all right. Gerry's a Saunders. She'll pull through."

"She put the wind up somebody," Stella said. "She must have been getting close to cracking it, and the murderer realised that and decided to silence her before it was too late. No doubt thought he'd killed her."

"*He?*" Tommy queried.

"OK, I know we're none of us in the clear."

Penny gave a gasp. "You don't think the police would suspect me, do you?"

"That cop suspects everybody. If the Archbishop of Canterbury was here, he'd be a suspect in Wilkins' eyes. And I figure we're all capable of violence."

"Oh crumbs. Do you think he'll hear about yesterday—me and Gregory?"

"Afraid so, honey. Sorry and all that."

The three of them were in the morning-room. Tommy, seeing Penny was distressed, quickly changed the subject. "Talking of Gregory the Great, he's conspicuous by his absence this morning. Don't suppose he's done a bunk, do you?"

"No, I saw him from my window, mooching about down by the lake," Stella said. "Must realise he's still the number one suspect and wants to keep out of the way."

"And where's your father?" Tommy asked Penny.

"He's in the library, catching up on some paper work. He says he knows he's a suspect, too. It's idiotic! If everybody knew him like I do, they'd never think for a second he could do anything like that."

"Who else is missing?" Tommy said. "Oh, Mackenzie. Anybody seen her today?"

The girls shook their heads. "I wonder if anybody has?" Stella said. "Gosh, I hope she's all right. If she'd seen the attack on Gerry, and the murderer saw her, she could have been attacked, too. I think I'll go and check."

She left the room, went upstairs, made her way to the east corridor and tapped on Jean Mackenzie's door. She was relieved when she heard her voice call "Come in."

Miss Mackenzie was sitting in a chair by the window. There was a book on her lap but it was closed. She looked alarmed when she saw Stella. "Is there any news?" Stella saw that for the third time in two days her eyes were red.

"No, not yet. You know what happened, then?"

"Yes, Geraldine's maid told me."

"We wondered if you were all right. Is something wrong?"

"Oh, Stella, I feel so guilty."

"What about?"

"What's happened to Geraldine. It's all my fault."

"How on earth do you figure that?"

"You all know about the lie I told—that Florrie had asked to be buried at Alderley. It came about as a result of what I now see was my obsession with mediums and séances and that sort of thing. I'm giving all that up. However, it's too late to undo the damage I have done. At first I blamed myself for Clara's death, but the Inspector assured me that after she'd made that threat at the reading, she would have been murdered wherever it had taken place. But that's not the case with this wicked attack on Geraldine. It wouldn't have happened if the reading had taken place somewhere else."

Stella went across to her and took her hand. "Look," she said, "Gerry was thoroughly enjoying herself. She knew there was danger involved. Dorry was telling me the afternoon of the funeral how Gerry had been saying to her that you have to be prepared for that sort of risk if you get involved in murder investigations. She herself would be the very last one to blame you."

"You're very kind, my dear, but if that lovely girl—if she, she, dies, I'll never forgive myself."

"This brooding all on your own is not good," Stella said. She drew Miss Mackenzie to her feet. "Now come on down to the morning-room. There's only Penny and Tommy there, and you know how you say he always cheers you up."

"Oh, really, I don't think so."

"I insist. And you can talk to us about Florrie. You knew her better than anyone, and she must have told you some wonderful stories over the years. I know I'd love to hear some."

And she led the older woman, still protesting a little, from the room.

Chapter Thirty-Six

Nearly three hours had passed, during which Gerry had not stirred. The Earl and Countess had hardly spoken or moved, except when three times Lord Burford again put the mirror to Gerry's lips, afterwards giving his wife a brief reassuring nod. Then, a little after eleven, there came a light tap on the door.

It was Merryweather. "No change, my lord?"

"Not yet."

"Chief Inspector Wilkins is here, my lord."

"Oh, I can't see him now."

"He wishes to come in, my lord. He says it is important."

"What? Oh, very well."

Wilkins entered the room almost on tip-toe. He bowed his head stiffly to the Earl and Countess.

"'Morning, Wilkins," said the Earl. "'Fraid I can't talk about the case now."

"No, of course, my lord. This is appalling, really appalling. I can't say how shocked I am." He gazed down at Gerry, shaking his head slowly. Then he looked up. "I've been given the details by Mr. Merryweather and Marie. I understand you think the attacker came in here during the night and did this?"

"Seems obvious."

"With respect, my lord, I think not."

"Eh? What d'you mean?"

"May I ask if anyone has touched Lady Geraldine's bedroom slippers this morning?"

The Earl looked down at them. They were placed neatly side by side, close to the bed. "No. Why d'you ask?"

"They're the wrong way round, my lord. Right on the left and left on the right. If Lady Geraldine had just lifted her feet out of them as she got into bed, they could not have got in that position. Which indicates to me that she was lifted into the bed. Either the slippers fell off, or the attacker snatched them off and let them drop, and then afterwards straightened them, without realising that they were in the wrong positions relative to each other."

"Good gad."

Lady Burford spoke for the first time. "He's right, George. Something has been worrying me as wrong ever since we've been sitting here. Her dressing-gown." She pointed to where it was draped on a hanger suspended from a hook on the back of the door. "She never hung it up at night—just laid it across the bottom of the bed. And during the day it was always hung in the cupboard."

Lord Burford said slowly: "So she was up in the night."

"Yes, my lord. Elsewhere in the house. About her investigations, no doubt."

"And actually identified the murderer?"

"We can't say that for sure. It's possible she uncovered a secret that someone other than the killer of Mrs. Saunders might have been desperate to prevent coming to light. Now, forgive me but I must get on. My investigations are complete and when I arrived I took the liberty of asking Mr. Merryweather to gather all the guests in the drawing-room. I must join them."

"You've solved the case?"

"Let's just say I have logical and coherent explanations for everything that occurred, though at this stage I cannot be certain there are not equally logical alternative ones. And the attack on Lady Geraldine is an additional complication, which I cannot as yet fit in. Anyway, my lord, I felt it only right to tell you of my plans. I don't suppose under the circumstances you yourself will want to be there."

"Not really, Wilkins, not really. Not at all sure I can face up to it."

"I hate to ask you, my lord, but I really do need you there, just for part of the time. There'll probably be something I want you to do."

"I see. Well, suppose I ought to be there, really. But I don't like leaving you here on your own, Lavinia."

"Go, George," said the Countess. "Ask Marie to join me. I'm sure she would like to. I'll let you know the moment there's any change."

"Very well. What is it you want me to do, Wilkins?"

"I'll explain on the way down, my lord."

"Come along, then."

He started to move to the door, then suddenly stopped and turned. "Lavinia, it's no good, I've got to tell you. I'm partly to blame for this."

"George, what do you mean?"

"I could have prevented it, but for my laziness and stupidity. I can't explain now, but I had to get it off my chest."

He made for the door again, inside which Wilkins was standing waiting for him. As the Earl passed him he muttered something, almost under his breath. Wilkins raised his eyebrows, gave a little shake of the head and then made to follow him. But the Countess called after him. "Mr. Wilkins!"

He came back. "Yes, my lady?"

"What did my husband say as he passed you?"

"I think he was just talking to himself, really, not to me at all."

"But what did he say?"

Wilkins looked decidedly embarrassed. "It was rather odd."

"Mr. Wilkins, please."

"He said, 'Should have had a real purple candle. Rosemary, too.'"

◇◇◇

Wilkins caught up with the Earl on the stairs. "All I want you to do, my lord, is, if you are shown a pair of cufflinks, to identify them as your own."

"Even if they're not?"

"Oh, they will be. So say they are, even if you don't actually recognise them."

"Very well."

Merryweather was standing outside the drawing-room, as though on sentry duty. He opened the doors as the Earl, Wilkins and Leather, who had been waiting in the hall, approached and went in. Like those of spectators at a tennis match, eight pairs of eyes swung towards them in unison. Gregory was standing by the huge fireplace and Tommy half sitting on and half leaning against a table just inside the window. The rest were seated, Timothy and Penny on one sofa, Agatha and Dorothy on another, Stella in an easy chair and Miss Mackenzie, as if in penance and recognition of her own perceived lower social status, in a hard upright chair against the wall.

Timothy got to his feet as they entered. "George, is there any news?"

"No, no change."

"Penelope and I are appallingly shocked, needless to say. You do both have our heartfelt sympathy and prayers." He sat down again.

"Thank you," said the Earl, gruffly. "Appreciate it."

"I'm sure that goes for every one of us," said Gregory.

"Absolutely," added Tommy. Gregory shot him an angry glance, as if he objected to having Tommy agree with him.

"I guess not quite *every* one," Stella said dryly.

Miss Mackenzie gave a shocked gasp and there was no one who did not look embarrassed.

It was Wilkins who broke the silence. "A very perceptive comment, Miss Simmons. Lady Geraldine was certainly attacked by somebody at present in this house. Needless to say, I rule out the servants."

He moved to the centre of the room. There was a sudden air of authority about him that had been totally absent before. Leather and the Earl remained standing just inside the door.

"I'm sorry to have to ask you all to come together, like this," Wilkins said. "But there are questions I need to ask most of you, and I want everyone else to hear the answers. We need some interplay, some cross-fertilisation, as it were. I'm hoping one person may be able to add something to another's answer or comment, or possibly refute it."

He paused, before continuing. "According to Dr. Ingleby, Mrs. Saunders died after eleven fifteen and we know she must have been killed before twelve thirty. That, obviously, is the key period. There were, apart from the murder itself, a number of very strange incidents during that time. I'd like to look at those in turn. The most obvious of them was the armour falling over. Miss Mackenzie, who was present, was totally unable to account for it."

He swung suddenly on Tommy. "However, you were able to give me a perfectly logical explanation of it, Mr. Lambert."

Tommy gave a start. His mouth opened. "Uuuhhh," he said.

"Perhaps you'd be so good as to share that explanation with everybody now, sir."

At last Tommy found his voice. "I say, Wilkins, this is jolly unsporting. I told you that in confidence."

"I promised it wouldn't be revealed unless it became necessary, sir. It is necessary now. Perhaps you'd prefer it if I recounted it."

"Well, if you must, I suppose," Tommy said grumpily. He lit a cigarette.

Wilkins addressed the room at large. "Mr. Lambert explained that he was responsible. He had decided to play a practical joke on Miss Mackenzie, tied a piece of string round the armour, hid behind the sofa, and when she commenced her session with the ouija board, pulled the armour over."

Jean Mackenzie stared at Tommy in horror. "Tommy! I can't believe you did such a thing! You frightened me out of my wits."

He was red-faced. "I know, and I'm awfully sorry. It was an idiotic thing to do. It was just meant to be a prank, but it was quite out of place, I see that now. I didn't mean to scare you so much. Do forgive me."

"I'm not at all sure that I can," she said stiffly. "I'm gravely disappointed in you."

"It was a pretty mean sort of trick, wasn't it, Mr. Lambert?" Wilkins said. "Rather uncharacteristic of you."

"All right, don't rub it in."

"Very well. Anyway, that's one of the mysteries solved. Now to turn—oh." He broke off. "One small point first: where did you get the string?"

Tommy looked blank. "Eh?"

"The string you used to topple the armour: where did you get it?"

"Oh. I usually carry some with me, you know."

"I see. So there's a ball of string in your case now, is there?"

"No, no, not a ball. I just carry a length, you know, a few yards. Never know when it might come in useful."

"So you still have it, do you?"

"No, think I left it in the gallery, actually."

"No, you didn't, Mr. Lambert. You said you only stayed long enough to gather up the string, before hurrying back to your room. Presumably you thrust it in your dressing-gown pocket."

"Suppose I must have."

"And no doubt it's still there."

"Er, no. I remember now. I threw it away."

"When?"

"Can't quite remember."

"Why did you throw it away, if you always carry a length, in case it comes in useful?"

"Well, I realised that if it was found it might give the game away: you'd realise what it had been used for."

"So you must have thrown it away before you told the Sergeant and me the story yesterday morning. You had nothing to conceal from us after that time."

"That's right. It was early yesterday."

"Where did you put it?"

"Oh. Jolly good question. Waste basket, I suppose."

"Which one? Where?"

"Sorry. Shocking memory, you know."

"Oh well, we can always ask the servants. I'm sure any of the maids would remember finding several yards of string in one of the waste baskets."

"Oh, I remember now. Actually, I burnt it."

"You did what?"

"Set fire to it with my lighter. In my room. And scattered the ashes out of the window."

"Let me get this straight, sir. Because you feared that if we found a length of string in your possession we would immediately realise it had been used to pull the armour over, early yesterday morning you burnt it, threw the ashes out of the window—and completely forgot having done so until this moment."

Tommy grinned weakly.

Wilkins gave a sudden shout, which caused everyone in the room to give a start. "Oh, come on, Mr. Lambert! Let's stop this farce, shall we? You no more pulled that armour over than I did. For one thing, with your height, you'd never conceal yourself properly behind that sofa. Smithson, who's four or five inches shorter than you, could only just manage it. Again, the armour fell straight forward, away from the wall. If your story was true, it would have toppled sideways, no doubt hitting the sofa. And don't say you rearranged the pieces before you left the gallery, because you've already said all you did was gather up the string, the non-existent string, I should say."

"Oh, steady on. Why would I confess to a mean trick like that, if I hadn't done it?"

"For a very good reason, Mr. Lambert. The armour fell at almost exactly the same time that Miss Simmons woke to find an intruder in her room. You realised that claiming responsibility for the armour incident would give you a perfect alibi."

"But why should I need an alibi?"

"You didn't, no more than anybody else in the house. Just to say you were asleep in bed would have been perfectly natural, and I couldn't reasonably have expected anything else. Unless, that is, you had reason to think that you could fall under particular suspicion, that perhaps Miss Simmons had caught a glimpse of the intruder and might mention that he looked like you. After all, your appearance, even in silhouette, is highly distinctive: you're very tall and thin and no one else here looks remotely like you. The previous night, Miss Simmons had said she'd not seen the intruder. But suppose she was playing safe and was just waiting to tell me privately the next morning that she had seen you? So you needed a stronger story, apparent proof that you were nowhere near her room at that time. Miss Mackenzie's experience with the armour was a godsend to you and you quickly saw how you could use it to your advantage. Now, Mr. Lambert, I'm going to give you one last chance: tell the truth. If you didn't kill Mrs. Saunders and attack Lady Geraldine you have nothing to fear. But if you keep up this ridiculous story, then I shall have to assume the worst."

Tommy licked his lips. Then he sighed and shrugged. "OK, you're right. No, I didn't topple the armour. It was me in Stella's room."

Only two people reacted, and in very different ways. Jean Mackenzie beamed. "Oh, Tommy, I'm so glad." He gave her a sheepish smile.

Stella, on the other hand, looked decidedly frosty. "And perhaps you'd explain just what you were doing there, Tommy. And why in tarnation did you steal my toothpaste?"

"I didn't mean to steal it, Stella. I only meant to look at it. But I'd just got my hand on it when you woke up and I ran out still holding it."

She stared at him in bemusement. "You wanted to look at my toothpaste? Are you loco, or something?"

"Yes, I'm sure we'd all be interested to know just what fascination Miss Simmons' tube of Dentigleam held for you, Mr. Lambert," Wilkins said.

"I—I really only wanted to know whether she used tooth-paste at all."

"Oh, so my teeth looked dirty, did they? Well, have a good look. Do they look dirty now?" She bared them at him in a mirthless smile.

"No, no, they're fine," he said hastily. "Very white. But, well, they're not perfect. They're not a hundred per cent straight."

"Oh, I'm so sorry if they offend you!"

"What I mean is they're obviously natural."

"Well, of course they're natural!"

"But they shouldn't be, should they, Mr. Lambert?" Wilkins said quietly.

Tommy shot him a surprised glance. "No," he said. "You see, my cousin, Stella Simmons, had all her teeth extracted after rheumatic fever, when she was in her teens. She wore false ones always, after that. And if your teeth are natural, it means you're not Stella at all."

Chapter Thirty-Seven

For a good five seconds, she said nothing and showed absolutely no emotion. Then at last she gave Tommy a very small smile. "So, maybe you're not loco," she said. "Perhaps you'd better finish your story before I say anything."

Wilkins realised she was giving herself a little time to think, but he didn't intervene.

"OK. Well, I was only a little kid when Stella had her teeth out, but when I heard about it I was fascinated. I'd never known anybody young who had false ones. They were something for grandparents. I longed to ask her to take them out and show me, but when I mentioned this to my mother she was horrified and told me I was on no account ever to mention them to Stella. I'd more or less forgotten about it, but then, after dinner, the first night, she laughed and I saw her teeth properly for the first time. And then it all came back to me. I was shaken. They looked so obviously natural, and all the false teeth I've seen have been absolutely perfect—too perfect. You can nearly always spot them. It occurred to me that perhaps in America now they're deliberately making them a bit crooked, just to make them look natural. But one thing I do know is that ordinary toothpaste is no good for false teeth; it doesn't get them white. People use special denture cleaner. I thought if Stella was using one of those, it would show that her teeth were false and everything was OK. But if she was using ordinary toothpaste—well, it wouldn't *prove* her teeth were natural, but it would be a pretty strong indication. And, well, that's it, really."

"Didn't it occur to you just to ask me straight out?" she asked.

"Yes, but I funked it at first. Thought there might be some perfectly normal explanation, and that I'd make myself look the most awful idiot. But after I'd found you *were* using ordinary toothpaste, I made up my mind to tackle you. And I would have done if it hadn't been for the murder. I mean, someone had crept into a woman's room at night and suffocated her. How could I admit to anybody that same night I'd crept into another woman's room and then run out when she'd woken up? It would look as though I was a homicidal maniac, hunting for another victim. Besides, you'd have either denied you were an impostor, in which case I'd be pretty sure you were lying, or admitted it. Whatever, I'd be almost bound to tell Mr. Wilkins, and it would obviously make you the number one suspect. And I didn't want that to happen because I was quite sure you weren't the murderer."

She raised her eyebrows. "I'm flattered. What made you so sure?"

"You were fast asleep when I went into your room. I could tell from your breathing and the way you suddenly woke up. I couldn't believe that anyone, except a hired assassin or a gangster, could murder someone and then go fast asleep. Even if they were absolutely without conscience, they'd surely lie awake for hours, thinking about it, wondering if they'd left a clue or something. Anyway, I decided just to keep mum for the time being and see how things panned out. Anyway, that's just about bally well all." He turned to Wilkins. "Sorry and all that, Chief Inspector. But I didn't really lead you astray, you know. I knew I was innocent and that Stella was, so I just stopped you being distracted by red herrings."

"Very considerate of you, sir, I'm sure. Anyway, I think it's high time we heard from Miss—whatever her name is."

◇◇◇

"It's Julie Osborne," said the girl they'd known as Stella. "I'm an actress, and American born and bred. I come from a little town in the Midwest that nobody'll have ever heard of so I won't name. I always loved amateur dramatics and usually played leads in our little local society. About twelve years ago, I went to New York, to try and make it as a pro. After a couple of years living on bread and cheese, I started to get pretty regular work. Nothing big time, but I got by. Then about four years ago I was invited to a party by a guy who said there was someone he wanted me to meet. I hoped it was going to be some big-shot producer, but no such luck. It was Stella. This guy thought we were remarkably alike and wanted to see us side by side. Well, it was true. I mean, we weren't doubles, but we were the same height, same figures, same colouring and so on. Naturally, we got talking and found we had a lot in common. We were roughly the same age, we were both orphans, with no brothers or sisters and our only relatives various uncles, aunts and cousins, to whom we weren't particularly close. We'd both come to the Big Apple to try and make our fortunes, she as a journalist, me as an actress.

"We hit if off, and after a few months decided to share an apartment. We were different in many ways: different opinions, different tastes. But on the whole we got on OK, and it was convenient. The landlady was a bit short-sighted and often couldn't tell which of us was which. Stella used to talk a lot about her aristocratic relations in England. She was mighty proud of them, bit too proud sometimes, to be quite frank. But I got to know quite a lot about them over three or four years. The only one she kept in touch with, though, was her Great Aunt Florrie. She used to write her regularly, telling her all about life in New York, and she let on she hoped to inherit some money from her one day. I was interested in Florrie, seeing that, like me, she'd been on the stage and had come from a pretty poor background, and I got Stella to tell me all about her. Oh, I should also mention that we were listening to some lawyer talking on the radio one day about how important it was that everyone should make a will, even if they didn't have much to leave. So just for fun, really, we made wills in each other's favour."

It seemed to Wilkins that this was a well-prepared and rehearsed statement, one she had been expecting to have to make at some time. She continued.

"Then last fall, two things happened at about the same time. Stella's magazine folded and she found herself out of a job, and I broke up with a guy I'd been dating for about six months. Also, for some time I hadn't been doing too well professionally. Parts had been getting very thin on the ground. We both had the blues pretty bad and to try and cheer ourselves up we decided to drive down to Atlantic City for a short vacation. About half way there, we took a little diversion, to have a look at the scenery. We were on this dirt road, and Stella was driving. It was her car—I didn't have one. We rounded a bend and suddenly there was this truck, coming towards us, much too fast in the centre of the road. Stella had to swerve violently. She lost control and we hit a tree. She was killed outright. How these things happen I don't know, but I just had a few cuts and bruises. I was in hysterics, of course. The truck didn't stop but luckily a guy on a motor bike was about fifty yards behind us, had seen the whole thing, knew we weren't to blame for the accident and that I hadn't been driving. He checked that I was all right, then rode on to call the cops and an ambulance at the first phone box.

"Well, I'm not proud of what I did next, but I'm not too ashamed, either. I was at a dead end, professionally and personally. I had nothing to keep me in America. I saw a chance for a fresh start in a new country—a country where I would have a number of influential and wealthy—quote—'relatives' and a new profession. I know a lot about fashion, quite as much as Stella did, and I could use her very good references. I can write—I've had a few pieces in a New York theatrical magazine—so I was pretty confident I could hold down a similar job in this country. So I simply switched purses with her. There was a lake nearby, and I put everything with my name on it in my case, weighed it down with a couple of rocks and threw it in the lake. When the police arrived I gave my name as Stella Simmons and told them I didn't know the dead woman's name, that she was a hitch-hiker

I'd picked up, and when I'd got drowsy she'd offered to take the wheel and I'd let her. It was a bit unlikely, perhaps, but they had the biker's evidence that the truck driver was wholly to blame for the accident and that I hadn't even been driving, so they had no reason to doubt me or hold me.

"Anyway, when I eventually got home I kept out of the landlady's way—we often didn't see her for days on end. During the next couple of days, I scoured all the papers, to make sure the accident wasn't reported: 'Mystery Woman Killed. Journalist Escapes in Fatal Car Crash,' type of thing, but it had happened out of town, out of state, even, and there was nothing.

"I spent time practising Stella's handwriting and signature, and learning to imitate her voice—luckily, she'd once made a recording of it in one of those booths. When I thought I'd got the voice right, I made a recording of myself, and played the two records one after the other. It was OK. I spoke to the landlady, keeping my distance, identified myself as Stella, and told her that Julie had decided to move out and wouldn't be returning, and gave a week's notice for myself. Then I phoned every one of Stella's friends I could think of—I had her address book—identified myself as her and told them that as I had lost my job I was returning to England straight away. None of them questioned that I was Stella. Afterwards, I called a lot of my own friends, telling *them* that I was going west to try and make it in Hollywood.

"Stella had kept dozens of clippings from the papers about the two earlier murder cases you had here and there was a lot in them about Alderley and the Earl and Countess and Geraldine and I went over those again and again, more or less memorising them.

"I also spent a long time in front of the mirror, trying to make myself up to look as much like Stella as possible. My nose is a bit bigger than hers, and my mouth a bit wider, but on the whole it was a pretty good likeness. I was aware my teeth weren't perfect—that doesn't really matter if you're just a stage actress and not in movies. I couldn't really remember how Stella's teeth were.

She didn't show them a lot. Strangely enough, even though we shared a bathroom for nearly four years, I never knew she wore dentures. I guess she must have been pretty self-conscious about it. Anyway, as soon as I'd got the likeness as good as I could I went to Stella's bank, drew out all the money—three hundred and seventy odd bucks—and closed the account. That was the most nerve-racking part, but they didn't question it. Unfortunately, of course, I had to leave my own money in my checking account, but that was less than a hundred dollars and I had drawn out some cash to take on the vacation. I gave most of Stella's clothes to the Salvation Army, but sold a few quite nice pieces of jewellery she had. A few days later I sailed for England, using Stella's passport—I don't have one of my own."

Julie was now clearly enjoying telling her story, and had her audience riveted. She paused to light a cigarette and then continued.

"I went straight to London, got myself a room, and started job-hunting. *London Fashion Weekly* was the second paper I applied to. Luckily, the woman who interviewed me there had subscribed to Stella's old New York magazine for years and was familiar with her work. She offered me a job straight away.

"As soon as I got settled in, I went to see Great Aunt Florrie. She accepted me without question and was really thrilled to see me. I visited her regularly after that. I was nervous at first in case I slipped up over anything, but it was OK. I knew a fair bit about the family from listening to Stella. And Florrie, like me, had read all there was to read about the Alderley murders, as well as hearing about them from Gerry, and she loved to talk about them. In addition, of course, having supposedly been out of the country for nearly eleven years, I could legitimately ask about all the other members of the family, so I was soon pretty well primed for when I did meet any of them. Most of the time, though, I just talked to her about New York. She really loved hearing about it. I'll never feel guilty about deceiving her in that way. I gave her a lot of pleasure during those last six months or so of her life, and she never knew that Stella was dead, which would have upset her terribly. I grew really fond of her. She was a great old girl, and I shed a few tears when she died."

She stubbed out her cigarette. "That's about it, Mr. Wilkins. I want to apologise to everybody—especially to you, Tommy. It's rotten for you to have to learn about Stella's death in this way. You were the one person I was really nervous about meeting, which is why I never contacted you after I arrived in England. I was sure relieved after the funeral when you said you would have recognised me anywhere. That really sealed my credentials."

Tommy gave a wry grin. "I hadn't seen Stella since I was about thirteen, and you do look awfully like I remember her."

"Anyway, thanks for not snitching on me—until you had to. Well, Detective, am I under arrest?"

"No, Miss Osborne. Not yet."

"That sounds ominous."

"Well, you've committed a number of crimes, miss, both here and in the United States. It'll obviously be necessary for us to notify the authorities there."

"I don't think they're likely to seek my extradition. After all, what did I do? I gave a false name to the cops, told them I didn't know the name of the dead woman, and—quote—'stole' some money and jewellery of Stella's, which would have all come to me under her will, anyway."

"That's as may be. But there is the little matter of attempting to obtain money by false pretences in this country."

"Oh, you mean my inheritance. Well, actually, I think not." She picked up her handbag from the floor, reached into it and took out a folded sheet of paper, which she handed to Wilkins. "That's a copy of a letter I sent to Mr. Bradley, immediately I got his wire notifying me that I was a legatee under Florrie's will—he has the original, of course."

Wilkins took it and read it. Stella looked round the room. "In it, I tell him in confidence that I will not accept anything which I am bequeathed in Florrie's will. I add that I want, nonetheless, to attend the funeral and the reading."

Wilkins handed the letter back to her. "Yes, that's roughly what it says. However, as I understand, you said nothing at the reading about refusing the bequest."

"No, why should I have? I didn't figure it was anybody else's business. But I said nothing about accepting it, either. I never mentioned anything about having plans for the money. And I think Mr. Bradley will confirm that I asked him what fifteen hundred pounds *would be* in dollars—not how much it *was* or *will be*, which points to it being of just academic interest."

"Very subtle, Miss Osborne. But then again, there's nothing legally binding in that letter. You could have easily changed your mind—if you hadn't been found out."

Timothy spoke. "What Miss Osborne may or may not have done or intended to do in a hypothetical situation is itself hypothetical and therefore irrelevant. It is my opinion that the existence of that letter would make it virtually impossible to succeed in a charge of attempting to obtain money by false pretences. If such a charge were brought, I would positively relish the chance to defend her against it."

Julie's face lit up. "Why, thank you, Timothy. I really appreciate that."

"Well, it won't be my decision," Wilkins said. "And I'm not really concerned. I should warn you, though, miss, that there is no getting away from the fact that you did enter the country under a false name, using somebody else's passport. Even if no other charges are brought, you are very likely to be deported."

"We would fight such a move most vigorously," Timothy said, and, except perhaps the Earl, who clearly was not really taking in the proceedings, nobody present missed the use of the plural pronoun. "But even if we should lose," Timothy continued, "Stella—er, Julie—er, Miss Osborne could always marry a British subject and so obtain British citizenship, meaning she could not be deported. I feel it quite probable that that could be arranged, in fact, I can guarantee it, if she so wishes it." He went very red, took out his handkerchief and blew his nose vigorously.

Penny was gazing at him in amazement. She gave his hand a squeeze. He gave hers a hurried and somewhat awkward pat.

"Timothy, I don't know what to say." Julie spoke dazedly.

"Good," said Wilkins, "and I suggest you don't try to think of anything. I am investigating a murder and I would like to get on with that."

"OK," Julie said. "Just one thing: I am in the clear, as regards the murder, I take it?"

Wilkins regarded her coolly. "Whatever gave you that idea, Miss Osborne?"

She went white. "But, but after what Tommy said about my being asleep…"

"Why should I believe Mr. Lambert? He's lied from the start. You could have cooked the whole story up between you."

"Oh, I say!" said Tommy.

Wilkins ignored this. "Anyway, we've cleared up the business of the stolen toothpaste. I now want to turn to the matter of the 'Dora Lethbridge' card, or I should say the '*Miss* Dora Lethbridge' card, because that 'Miss' is important."

He turned to the two sisters. "Miss Agatha, Miss Dorothy, perhaps you wondered why I asked for you to be present this morning, as I realise it must all be painful for you. The reason was that I am going to divulge something that cannot be kept secret, concerning your stepmother, something which I don't believe you know. I had meant to talk to you privately before convening this little gathering, but the attack on Lady Geraldine disrupted my plans, and I decided the best thing I could do was make sure that at least you did not hear it *after* everybody else."

Agatha answered. "Very considerate of you, Mr. Wilkins. I'm intrigued, must admit."

Wilkins addressed the room at large again. "The reason for that card, with its use of the word 'Miss,' was to indicate the writer's knowledge that Dora Lethbridge, Clara Saunders' mother, had always been 'Miss' Lethbridge, to the end of her life. In other words, she had never married. That, of course, means that Clara Saunders was illegitimate."

"I don't believe it!" Agatha exclaimed. Dorothy gave a little gasp.

"I'm sorry, but I can assure you it's true," Wilkins said. "Sergeant Leather visited Somerset House in London yesterday and saw her birth certificate. The space for the father's name is blank. I'm quite certain no copy of that birth certificate will be found among Mrs. Saunders' papers, that she destroyed it many years ago. The story of her mother marrying a cousin of the same surname as herself was obviously invented by Mrs. Saunders to account for the fact that her mother's maiden name, which she might have to give on occasions and which might appear on various documents that other people would see, was the same as her own maiden name."

"She would have been absolutely horrified at the thought of that coming out," Agatha said.

"Precisely," Wilkins said. "It made her extremely vulnerable. When she saw that card, I'm sure she would have realised its significance: that somebody else in the house knew of her shameful—as she would have thought it—secret and that it was a coded warning not to reveal somebody else's secret or the same thing could happen to her.

"I asked myself who of those present could conceivably know the secret. I felt sure her step-daughters didn't, as I could not imagine her being able to exercise such control over their lives—particularly over Miss Dorothy's life—if she had known they were in a position to make it known more widely."

"She certainly couldn't," Agatha said. "Golly, I wish I had known. I wouldn't have let on, of course, but she wasn't to know that. And I could certainly have put a stop to her money-making enterprises."

"So" Wilkins said, "who could have known? Perhaps his lordship, but that was unlikely and even if he had, I feel sure he would have kept it absolutely confidential. I considered each of the other beneficiaries, but could think of no way in which any of them could have found out about it. With one exception." He looked at Timothy.

"Mr. Saunders, your late father was Mr. John Saunders' solicitor and executor. No doubt he had access to many family papers and was privy to many family secrets. Some things he may have discovered perfectly properly but inadvertently and, while not divulging them, thought it necessary, as a lawyer, to keep a written record of them. Illegitimacy, with all the legal ramifications that has, would certainly be such a thing. You, I take it, would have been responsible for going through your father's papers after his death and would certainly have come across any such record. All of which means that you are the only person here who could have known that Mrs. Clara Saunders was illegitimate—and so written that card. I should warn you that, although it is written in block capitals, we have obtained a photostat copy of a passport application you filled out a few years ago, also in block letters, and the lettering is identical, as I'm sure a graphologist would confirm."

Chapter Thirty-Eight

Timothy's eyelid twitched twice, but he did not hesitate before answering. "Very well, Chief Inspector. Your deduction is quite correct. I found out about Clara's illegitimacy in precisely the way you assumed. And I did write that card. It was, as you say, a warning to Clara about what might happen if she was to reveal other people's secrets. You may consider it to have been a cowardly act, and it is true, I could have spoken to her face to face. But that would have been less effective; she could be virtually certain that I would be honour bound not to reveal anything learnt in the course of my professional duties, or by my father in his. So it wouldn't matter too much to her that *I* knew. However, there are others here about whom she could feel no such confidence. So I considered it wiser to leave her uncertain about the identity of the writer of the card, thus hoping to ensure she would keep quiet about *any* secrets she might have."

"And that was just a gesture of goodwill, was it, sir: a wish to save your fellow beneficiaries any possible embarrassment?"

This time Timothy did hesitate for a moment before saying: "No, not entirely. I did have occasion to believe it possible—well, it was no more than a suspicion, really—that Clara possessed something which I did not wish seen by anybody else. It concerned no crime, and the exact nature of it is irrelevant, so I am not prepared to say what it was."

"You don't need to, sir."

"Thank—" Timothy began.

"It was this, I imagine," Wilkins said. He reached into his pocket, brought out what was clearly a six by four inch photograph and, very carefully, so that no one else, not even Penny, could glimpse it, held it out for him to see.

Timothy positively blanched. "May—may I ask where you obtained that?"

"It was in Mrs. Saunders' handbag," Wilkins said, putting the photo back in his pocket. "So in fact your suspicion of her was quite correct. I suggest it was far more than mere suspicion. You knew she possessed this photograph and presented a real threat to you."

"No, she did not possess that photograph, at least, not for any length of time."

"I beg your pardon, sir?"

"I believe that to be a photo which was locked in my briefcase, in my bedroom here. There is a slight mark in the top left-hand corner. If I am correct, the date I received it, 10th July, is written in pencil on the back."

"Yes, that's correct, sir. May I ask why you were carrying it with you?"

"Because I feel happier when I know where it is. But I hadn't checked on it since I arrived here at Alderley."

"So what you are suggesting, Mr. Saunders, is that some time on the day of the funeral, after her outburst at the will-reading, probably while you were having dinner, Mrs. Saunders—oh, I can't go on using the name 'Saunders' all the time, it's too confusing. I'll use first names from now on. Where was I? Oh yes: you say Mrs. Clara went into your room, searched it, found some means of picking the lock on your briefcase and abstracted the picture."

Timothy nodded. "And if that is what happened, she must have lighted upon it purely by chance; there was no way she could have known it was there. The fact, then, that she took it, means that she did not previously have a copy—she would not have needed another. Which in turn means that she could not have used it to ruin my reputation and that when she made her threat at the will-reading she was not threatening *me*, after all."

"But you *believed* she was, sir, that's the important point. And when you went up to your room that night, you discovered the photo was missing. Perhaps the briefcase had been moved or left open. You knew Mrs. Clara had had the run of the first floor for several hours that evening, while the rest of you were downstairs, and that she was virtually the only person who could have taken it. You decided to confront her. You went to her room and demanded it back. She refused, you lost your temper and killed her. Then you panicked. You didn't dare stay long enough to search for the picture among her things and you hurried back to your room. That's what happened, isn't it?"

"No! Nothing like that." Timothy shook his head vigorously. He took out his handkerchief and dabbed at his lips. He cleared his throat. "I'll tell you what did happen. I went upstairs at about 11 p.m. and straight to my bedroom. I undressed and then went to the bathroom next door. As I was leaving it, I saw someone coming out of Clara's room. I was surprised, but at that moment not unduly so. They didn't see me, just turned away and went round the corner into the east corridor."

"And that would have been around ten or fifteen minutes past eleven, sir?"

"Yes."

"Please carry on."

"When I returned to my room, I found that somehow what I had seen had unsettled me. It seemed to me in retrospect that there had been something hasty and rather furtive about that person's movements. I wondered if the purpose of the visit could be something to do with Clara's threat. That caused me to start worrying whether she had had me in mind when she made it. I tried to read but I couldn't concentrate. I wasn't able to get Clara's words out of my mind. It was then I thought of a warning message. I always carry a little writing case with me and I keep a few postcards in it, as well as writing paper and envelopes. I spent some minutes composing a suitable form of words and then made my way to her room."

"What time was this, sir?"

"I cannot be precisely sure. Probably between eleven forty-five and eleven fifty."

"Carry on."

"I meant just to push the card under her door. But the door fits very tightly and it wouldn't go under. There was no light coming through the keyhole, so I decided to risk going in. I left the door open behind me an inch or two, which gave me just enough light to see the position of the bed and not to bump into anything. I crept across to the bed and put the card on the bedside table. Everything was absolutely silent. I suddenly realised it was too silent. I have exceptionally sharp hearing and I should have been able to hear her breathing, but I couldn't. I became alarmed. I took a chance and switched the bedside lamp on. I saw Clara, just as you saw her later, Chief Inspector: lying across the bed, plainly dead, almost certainly murdered, and obviously by the person I had seen leaving the room. It was a frightful shock and I have to admit I did panic. I should, of course, have raised the alarm immediately, but my only thought was that I might be suspected. After all, what reason could I give for having gone to her room, after she was asleep? So I decided to return to my own room to try and think what I should do. I opened the door very cautiously—and actually saw the same person as before going down the stairs. I waited until the coast was clear, and hurried to my room. Then I remembered the card, which in my confusion I had left on the bedside table. It would serve no purpose now Clara was dead, might mislead the police, and—most important from my point of view—would almost certainly have my fingerprints on it."

"There were no prints on it," Wilkins said.

"No, later I remembered that before I went into Clara's room I noticed that the card had got quite dusty and dirty from my efforts to force it under the door. So I gave it a wipe all over with my handkerchief. Thereafter, I must have only held it by the edges, though I wasn't conscious of doing that. I knew I had to get it back, and I was also trying desperately to think of some way of directing suspicion onto the person to whom it belonged. But I had absolutely no proof of what I had seen earlier and if I mentioned it to you, it could easily seem that I was simply attempting to divert suspicion from myself. Moreover, I would have to explain why I was up. It occurred to me that if I could put something belonging to that person in Clara's bedroom, that might point the police in the right direction. George's talk about cufflinks at dinner gave me the idea. If, while that person was still downstairs, I could obtain one of his cufflinks and leave it by the body, that might do the trick. This person—"

Wilkins interrupted. "Mr. Saunders, this constant talk of a person is nonsensical. Concealing things doesn't do your credibility any good. Now, tell me who it was you saw."

"Very well. It was Gregory."

Wilkins looked across to where the MP was standing by the fireplace, but he didn't react in any way.

"Carry on, Mr. Saunders," Wilkins said.

"There is little more. I took a chance. I went to his room. It was still empty. I took a cufflink and left it in Clara's bedroom. I should point out that everything I did was intended to further the ends of justice."

Gregory came forward slowly. "No doubt my learned cousin expects me to splutter a lot of indignant denials. But why should I? Yes, I looked in to see Clara on my way to bed. To tell you the truth, I felt a bit sorry for her. She'd been bitterly disappointed and humiliated by the will and on top of that had made a complete fool of herself. She'd been stuck alone in her room all the evening, and I just wanted to show her that as far as I was concerned there were no hard feelings. I think she was grateful. We chatted for about five minutes. When I left her, she was perfectly well and I think a little more cheerful. The idea that there was something hurried or furtive about my movements is the fantasy of an over-active imagination."

"What did you talk about?"

"I commiserated with her, said I didn't think Florrie meant to insult her, but was relying on the girls to see she was all right—nonsense, of course, but one has to say something—and that Florrie was very old and getting perhaps a little eccentric, and that she mustn't take it to heart. She thanked me, congratulated me on my few words at the funeral, said how kind Lavinia had been, and so on."

"Her threats at the reading weren't mentioned?"

"No, I thought it was well to stay clear of them. As I was leaving, she did say she was very sorry about everything. A bit ambiguous, but that must have been what she was referring to."

"And this was at about ten or fifteen minutes past eleven?"

"I suppose so. I couldn't say precisely."

"Why didn't you mention this before?"

"Suppose I should have done. But I thought about it carefully and decided that it was quite irrelevant to your investigation. So I asked myself, why complicate things? Might look suspicious if I said I'd been to her room."

"Not nearly as suspicious as keeping silent about it, sir."

"I can't see it as suspicious. I went into her room while she was still up. I left openly, without even looking round to see if I'd been observed. I didn't creep into her room in the dark, for the purpose of leaving a frightening anonymous note, and then run like a scared rabbit back to my room and sit quaking in my shoes, without telling anyone, when I found her murdered—which is what Timothy says he did. He then goes on to say, simply on the grounds of seeing me leave her room half an hour earlier, that I was 'obviously' the murderer. This from a reputedly top rank barrister. Let's all hope to heaven he never sits on the bench. He'd be another Judge Jeffries!* Worse, in fact: at least Jeffries never actually killed anyone with his own hands."

"How dare you!"

Timothy positively bellowed the words. He jumped to his feet and strode towards Gregory, who took a hasty step backwards.

---

* Notoriously cruel British "hanging judge" of the Seventeenth Century.

Leather quickly and silently strode across the room, until he was standing a foot or two behind Timothy. Wilkins reached into his pocket, produced a boiled sweet, unwrapped it, popped it in his mouth, folded his arms and watched interestedly.

"You murderer!" Timothy shouted, seemingly totally out of control. "You did kill her, you blackguard! She knew all about your kept woman in St. John's Wood. She was going to tell the papers. You went to her room to try and threaten or bribe her out of it, and when you couldn't you killed her."

Gregory's face took on the colour of ripe beetroot. "Liar!" he yelled. "It was your drunken orgy she was going to tell about."

"*Drunken orgy?* What the devil do you mean?"

"What else does that photo show?"

Timothy's eyes bulged. "How do you know what that picture shows? It was you—you sent it!"

He started to make a lunge at Gregory. But Leather was quicker. In a flash his right arm had gone round Timothy's neck and his left under Timothy's arm and he had the lapels of his jacket in a firm grip. Timothy made a series of convulsive movements, desperately trying to break the hold, but without success. "Give it up, sir," Leather said quietly. "I'm a fourth Dan."

Timothy tapped the back of Leather's hand, and Leather immediately released him

Timothy coughed, then swung round to Wilkins. "Ask him. Ask him how he knows about that photo."

"No," Gregory positively snarled. "Ask him why he's so desperate to pin the murder on me."

The next second they were shouting at each other again. Hardly a clear word could be picked out.

Wilkins raised his hands. "Gentlemen, please."

They ignored him. "Please, please," he repeated, but there was no effect.

Wilkins took a deep breath. "SHUT UP!"

His low, resonant voice filled the room. Gregory and Timothy both gave a start and at last fell silent.

"Thank you," Wilkins said. "I would remind you, gentlemen, that we are all guests of Lord Burford, whose daughter is at this moment lying unconscious upstairs, perhaps fighting for her life. Is this appropriate behaviour?"

They both had the grace to look guilty.

Timothy spoke first. "No, it is not and I'm sorry. I rarely lose control, but the situation is somewhat exceptional."

"I apologise, too," Gregory said. "My only excuse is that it is hard to remain calm when you can see the possibility of being charged with murder."

"Very well," Wilkins said. "Let's see if we can get to the bottom of what did happen that night. Mr. Carstairs, Mr. Timothy has said he planted one cufflink in Mrs. Clara's room. I suppose it was you who planted the other thirty-eight?"

"Don't know what you're talking about, Wilkins."

"Then let me make it simpler. When did you first notice one of your cufflinks was missing?"

"None of my cufflinks is missing. Only brought one pair with me and I'm wearing them. See." He pulled down his shirt cuffs to reveal a pair of gold links.

"I wonder if you would show those to Lord Burford, sir."

Apparently with some reluctance, Gregory crossed to the Earl and held out his wrists. Lord Burford peered at the links. "Why, those are mine. Recognise them anywhere. But do hang on to them, by all means. Now, please all excuse me. I must get back to Gerry." He hurried out of the room.

"Seems pretty conclusive, sir," Wilkins said. "But before you comment, I want to say one thing to both you and Mr. Timothy. You've both concealed things and hindered my investigation. If you hadn't done so, the case might have been solved before this. And I warn you that if there are any more lies or concealments I shall have no hesitation in charging you with obstructing the course of justice, which would do neither of your careers any good. Now, the full truth, if you please, sir."

"All right." Gregory seemed suddenly to have shrunk an inch or two. He sat down on the arm of an easy chair and ran his fingers through his rather sparse hair. "I went upstairs about a minute after Timothy and stopped in to see Clara, exactly as I told you, and afterwards went on to my room. I got all ready for bed but I couldn't settle down and after about fifteen minutes I decided to go and help myself to a drink. I put on my dressing-gown and went downstairs. Geraldine and Dorothy were in the drawing-room but I didn't feel correctly attired to join them. I knew there were some drinks kept in the billiard-room, so I went there and had a Scotch and soda—well, two to be quite accurate—and smoked a cigarette. I stayed down there about fifteen or twenty minutes, and then started back upstairs. I had nearly reached the top when I saw Timothy in the act of closing Clara's door. He had his back to me and hadn't seen me. There were dim lights in the hall and in the corridor, but nothing on the stairs, so I retreated half a dozen steps, until I was more or less in shadow. The next second I saw him practically run across the top of the staircase, going towards his room. I imagined he'd been trying to persuade her to keep quiet about whatever it was she knew about him. Well, I wanted another word with her myself—"

Wilkins interrupted. "Why, sir?"

"What?"

"You'd had a reasonably pleasant conversation with her earlier, parted on good terms, so why did you want to see her again? Was it because *your* attempt to persuade her to keep quiet had failed and you wanted another go?"

Gregory hesitated. "Not exactly. I hadn't tried to persuade her to keep quiet earlier, but I admit I did try to pump her. She was like a clam, though. I don't believe now she knew anything at all, but at that time I was convinced she did, and I decided it would be worth one more try to find out what, and what she intended to do. I had assumed she'd be asleep, but now it seemed clear she wasn't. I tapped on her door but there was no reply. That surprised me, because it was less than a minute since Timothy had left. I knocked a bit louder and when there was still no answer I opened the door. The light was out and I began to think this was rum. I turned on the light and, well, you know what I saw. I needn't bother to tell you my emotions. I closed the door behind me but apart from that just stood there, more or less rooted to the spot, trying to think, for five or ten minutes. It was plain Timothy had killed her—or else why wouldn't he have raised the alarm immediately? I was going to do so myself, but then I wondered if somebody might have seen me going in there earlier. I had absolutely no proof that I had left Clara alive and well, or that Timothy had been in there after me. What was more, as an MP, I would obviously be the far most likely person to want to cover up any so-called guilty secret. But I just couldn't concentrate, with Clara lying on the bed like that, staring up at me. I had to go back to my room, to work out what to do.

"Almost as soon as I got there, I noticed something. When I'm staying in a place for just the one night, I don't usually bother to put my clothes away overnight. I'd brought a clean collar for the next day, of course, but no spare shirt, and I'd thrown it over the back of a chair. My tie, this black tie, had been on top of it. Now it was on the floor. Somebody'd been in there. I had a look round, to see if anything was missing—and at once noticed that one of my cufflinks, which I'd left half in the cuffs, ready for the next day, was gone.

"I realised in a flash what had happened. When I had seen Timothy leaving Clara's room, he had not at that moment killed her. He must have done it *earlier*, and then tried to think of a way to divert suspicion. He'd no doubt seen me going downstairs, slipped into my room, pinched one of my cufflinks and hidden it in Clara's room. When I saw him leaving, he'd just done that."

"This is the most—" Timothy began, but Wilkins silenced him. "Mr. Saunders, please, I'll come back to you in a moment. Let Mr. Carstairs finish." Timothy gave a resigned shrug and sat down again on the sofa.

"For minutes I just couldn't think what to do at all," Gregory continued. "I couldn't go back and look for it. It might take half an hour, or I might never find it. But I couldn't let the police find one cufflink, my cufflink, in Clara's room. Then it came to me. If I could camouflage my link with lots of others, it wouldn't be recognised, wouldn't stand out. I remembered what George had been saying at dinner about having a good many pairs. So I went to his dressing-room and took them all—and gave the box a wipe over with my handkerchief. I kept the pair I'm wearing for myself, went back to Clara's room, opened the door and just threw them in. No doubt you think I've misled you, Chief Inspector, but I would say I was unmisleading you, even though it was confusing for you. If you had found that one cufflink by Clara's body, you would have been convinced I was the murderer. All I was doing was getting myself out of what I believe nowadays is called a frame-up. Well, that's just about it."

"I don't think so, sir."

"I'm sorry?"

"Didn't you attempt to do a little framing yourself?"

"What do you mean?"

"The photograph. Mrs. Clara never stole that from Mr. Timothy's room. She would have had no earthly reason to think he would be carrying anything compromising with him. Anyway, while she may not have been averse to a little bribery, I don't believe she was actually a thief. What do you say, ladies?" He looked at the sisters.

Dorothy shook her head. "No. Mother would never have done that."

"I agree," Agatha said. "Everyone knows I was under no illusions about her, but she wasn't a criminal, for heaven's sake. Besides, I think she would have been far too afraid of being caught."

"She knew she'd behaved very badly earlier," Dorothy added, "and she would never do anything that would make people think even worse of her, if it ever came to light."

"Thank you. My thinking exactly. No, you're the only one who could have done that, Mr. Carstairs. Now please remember what I said: I want the full truth."

"All right. Yes, I did."

"Why, you unmitigated cad!" Timothy shouted.

"Tit for tat, Timothy, tit for tat." He looked at Wilkins. "You must remember, Chief Inspector, that I saw him leaving Clara's room, and then discovered he had tried to frame me for the crime. I knew I had to put the police back on the right track. It was after I'd taken the cufflinks that it occurred to me to plant something of *his* in Clara's room. But it seemed impossible, as he was still in his room. But just as I was leaving George's dressing-room, I saw a shaft of light appear in the corridor from Timothy's door opening, and I dodged back in. I kept the door open a fraction of an inch, and watched him go past. I peered after him and saw that he went down the staircase. I guessed that, like me, he needed a drink. I knew that would give me a few minutes, so I hurried into his room. I couldn't see anything at first that would be suitable, on the dressing-table or bedside table. I had a quick rummage through his overnight bag, but there was nothing there, either. Then I saw his briefcase."

"And you forced the lock," Timothy interrupted angrily.

"No, it was unlocked."

"It wasn't—oh." Timothy stopped short. For the first time he looked a little awkward. "I must have forgotten to lock it after I took my writing-case out. And later I had other things on my mind."

"Such as murder," Gregory sneered.

"Mr. Carstairs, please!" Wilkins said exasperatedly. "Just carry on with your story.

"I had a rummage through the briefcase. And, no, I did not look at any of the papers in there. They were of no interest. I was looking for something like a fountain pen or propelling pencil, something that might easily fall out of a breast pocket if you were bending over somebody suffocating them with a cushion. But then I saw the corner of a photograph. I took it out and looked at it. I could hardly believe my luck. I hurried back to Clara's room and put it in her handbag. In my haste, I forgot the cufflinks, which were in my pocket, until I'd got back to the door. So, as I said, I chucked them from the doorway then went back to my room. It had only been about seven or eight minutes from the time I left it. And that, Wilkins, is the truth, the whole truth and nothing but the truth."

"Thank you, sir. Mr. Saunders, do you have any comments?"

"At this time just one. When he saw me as he was coming up the stairs, I had not in fact been *in* Clara's room at that time. I had intended, as well as leaving the cufflink there, to retrieve the postcard, but as I was opening the door, I heard a slight sound from the east corridor, which could have been another door opening or closing. No doubt it was Miss Mackenzie, on her way to the art gallery, but I didn't know that then. So all I had time to do was throw the cufflink in blindly, before practically running back to my own room. When I got there, I suffered a quite severe attack of palpitations and had to sit down for five or ten minutes. Then I did decide I needed a drink, went downstairs and had a brandy, and then returned to my room, where I remained until I heard the commotion."

"And that is everything you have to tell us, Mr. Saunders?"

"Yes, but I do have a request."

"And what would that be?"

"Perhaps this is not the best time, in the middle of your interviews, but I feel it may be the last opportunity, the last time we are all together. I would like you to show that photograph to everyone else."

Wilkins raised his eyebrows. "Are you sure, sir."

"Quite sure. I do not want everybody indulging in much fruitless speculation as to its nature."

"As you wish." Wilkins looked round the room, then took a few steps towards Julie and held it out to her.

There was a marked apprehension in her eyes as she took it and glanced down at it. Then her face changed. However, anyone who had expected an exclamation of disgust or horror was surprised.

She looked up. "Is this it? Is this all?" she asked blankly.

"All?" echoed Timothy.

"But it's totally innocuous!"

She looked at it again. It showed Timothy lolling back in a chair. He was in evening dress, with his collar askew, and was wearing a barrister's wig sideways. He was holding an upturned champagne bottle to his mouth. On his lap, her arm around his neck, was an extremely attractive brunette.

"Yes," Julie said, "I think everybody should see this." She handed it back to Wilkins.

He took it round the circle. Miss Mackenzie frowned with slight distaste, Agatha and Dorothy showed no emotion. Tommy started to give a grin, which he quickly stifled before handing it back.

Timothy meanwhile was talking, very quickly. "I want to explain what happened, though I don't expect every one here will believe me. A few weeks ago, I went to a one-day legal conference in Oxford. It was to carry on into the evening, and I'd arranged to stay the night in my old college. After the events had finished, I was persuaded, somewhat against my better judgment, to go out for a drink with a few others to some club. It seemed a perfectly respectable place. I had one drink. And that is all I remember until I woke up in bed at home the next morning. How I got there from Oxford I have no idea. I must have let myself in, because none of the servants did; they were extremely surprised the next morning to find me home. They had heard nothing, perhaps not surprising as they sleep on the top floor, but neither had Penelope, whose bedroom is next to mine."

"Some dirty rat slipped you a Mickey," Julie said.

Timothy stared at her. "I beg your pardon?"

"A Mickey Finn. A drink spiked with some fast-acting sedative."

"Ah. Is that what they are called? Yes, no doubt. The photo arrived in the post a couple of days later. You will have seen that my eyes are closed. I realise it could be assumed that I was blinking, due to the flash. Actually, I was asleep or unconscious at the time. How it was arranged for my arm to be up, holding the bottle, I cannot explain. I was extremely perturbed. But I did not like to ask any of the fellows who were there what had happened, because I did not wish them to be aware of my ignorance. I was half-expecting some kind of blackmail demand, but there has been nothing. It has nonetheless caused me severe disquiet."

Wilkins was looking at the picture again. "I think the business of your arm and the bottle can be easily explained. Someone crouching down behind the chair, holding your arm aloft. A piece of thread attached to the bottle and it being dangled by someone standing on a chair, so that your hand was actually merely resting against it. I daresay if the picture was enlarged sufficiently the thread might become visible."

"Do you really think so? I must certainly try that. It would prove, wouldn't it, that the whole thing was a frame-up. That would be wonderful…" His voice tailed away. Then he looked at Julie. "You said it was quite innocuous. No doubt in theatrical or journalistic circles that would be the case. But imagine if a copy of that were sent to the Lord Chancellor, when he was considering my possible elevation to the bench. Or, almost worse, if it appeared on the front page of some scandal sheet immediately after my appointment was announced."

"I can almost see the headline," Tommy put in. "'Sober as a Judge.'"

"I can imagine worse than that," Timothy said.

Chapter Thirty-Nine

"Right," Wilkins said, "having got that little diversion out of the way, let me just run through your combined testimony. Mr. Carstairs visited Mrs. Clara, stayed about five or ten minutes and then went to his room. Mr. Timothy saw him leaving. Some time later, he himself went to her room and put the postcard beside the bed before discovering the body. When leaving, to return to his own room, he saw Mr. Carstairs going downstairs. Shortly afterward, he abstracted Mr. Carstairs' cufflink from *his* room, returned to Mrs. Clara's room, was alarmed by a sound, threw the cufflink in and hurried back to his room, where he remained. Mr. Carstairs, on his way upstairs, saw him, went to Mrs. Clara's room himself, saw the body, and after another ten minutes, returned to his own room, when he discovered his cufflink missing. He made his way to the Earl's dressing-room, took all the cufflinks he found there and was about to leave when became aware of Mr. Timothy going downstairs. He went to Mr. Timothy's room, found the photo, went back to Mrs. Clara's room, put the photo in her bag and scattered the cufflinks, before finally returning to his own room. Is that it?"

"Congratulations, Chief Inspector," said Timothy, "a remarkably accurate summary of my movements."

"And of mine," said Gregory. "So what does it tell you?"

"It tells me that, rather surprisingly, you're in total agreement. Neither of your accounts contradicts the other's. Only your assumptions differ. Nothing in Mr. Timothy's account proves his own innocence or Mr. Carstairs' guilt. And vice versa."

He scratched his head. "It's all very confusing. I think I'm going to have to move away from what happened in the night, to the following morning. Several quite noteworthy things occurred then, though you are probably not aware of them. The timing of them is important. And I need some help in working that out." He took a notebook from his pocket and opened it. "Miss Osborne, you were first down, I think."

"I believe so."

"What time would that have been?"

She screwed up her eyes. "Let me see. A few minutes before seven."

"And you went immediately and phoned your friend on the *Evening News.*"

"Uh-huh."

"How long did the call take?"

"Well, they were a minute or two finding him, but when he came on I was able to give him the gist of the story in about four minutes."

"So six minutes would be a fair estimate?"

"I guess so."

"You didn't hear Miss Dorothy trying the door?"

"No."

"And afterwards you returned to your room by the back stairs?"

"Yes, it was quicker."

"And then it would have been five, six, seven minutes past the hour?"

"Around that."

"Thank you. That's very helpful." He made a brief entry in his notebook and then turned to Dorothy. "Miss Dorothy, what time did you come down?"

"Just a minute or two after seven."

"And you also went straight to the telephone room, found the door locked, returned to the great hall, and told Mr. Merryweather about it."

"Yes."

"So it would have been about ten past by the time you eventually got through to her?"

"I suppose so."

"And how long did your call last?"

"Oh, I really couldn't say."

"Well, let's try to work it out. You told her first, of course, about your stepmother—that she was dead, murdered, almost certainly by one of the guests."

"Yes."

"And no doubt she had a number of questions."

"Yes."

"Did you mention Mrs. Clara's outburst at the will-reading."

"Just briefly, an outline."

"So all that would have taken three minutes, at the very least, I should imagine."

"I should think so."

"And, naturally, you then told her about your inheritance."

"Of course."

"The money and the house, how much it was all worth?"

"Does that seem terribly heartless?"

"Not at all, miss. But it would have taken another minute or two. And then you asked her to come and she said she'd be here as soon as possible."

"That's right."

"Does that agree with your recollection, Miss Agatha?"

"Pretty well."

"So that means we can say the call took a minimum of five minutes, probably longer. Are we agreed on that?"

They both nodded.

"That's very strange," Wilkins said.

"What do you mean?" Agatha asked.

"Well, according to the telephone people, there were two calls put from here at about that time, both to London. The first one lasted approximately six and a half minutes—Miss Osborne's to the *Evening News*. The second call lasted precisely eleven seconds. Perhaps you could explain just how you managed to impart all that information in just eleven seconds, Miss Dorothy."

The room had been quiet before Wilkins' last question. Suddenly it seemed even quieter, the silence to become almost palpable. It was as though everyone had stopped breathing.

It was Agatha who broke it. "Oh, must be some mistake."

"I don't think so, miss. I saw the supervisor, looked at their records. They don't get things like that wrong; and after all, they were bang on as regards Miss Osborne's call. No, the call took only eleven seconds because you *already knew everything that had happened*. You were here at the time. And you killed your stepmother."

Chapter Forty

"That's—that's absurd!" Agatha exclaimed. "Everybody knows I wasn't here. The house was searched from top to bottom."

"Yes, but Miss Dorothy's room was searched only by her and Lady Geraldine. Lady Geraldine told her father that she looked under the bed, while Miss Dorothy looked in the wardrobe. You were concealed in that wardrobe, as Miss Dorothy knew—and so made sure that only she looked in there. You'd been there since the afternoon. That morning you had ridden to Alderley Village, changed somewhere into a long black dress and a hat with a veil, attended the funeral and come back here with all the other guests. There were no doubt a number of ladies dressed in exactly the same way. You were totally anonymous. Everyone had free time in the afternoon to explore the house. At some stage, Miss Dorothy had whispered to you the location of her room. You simply slipped in there and got in the wardrobe, which is a very capacious one. There you remained—Miss Dorothy no doubt supplying you with refreshment from time to time—until late that night, when you went to your stepmother's room and smothered her. You believed all the other occupants of the house, except for Lady Geraldine and your sister, downstairs, were in bed. You couldn't have known that Miss Mackenzie, Mr. Lambert, Mr. Carstairs and Mr. Timothy were all up and about on their various adventures, and you were amazingly lucky not to have run into any of them, particularly Mr. Carstairs or Mr.

Timothy. After the murder, you returned to the wardrobe. Following the discovery of the body, your sister looked in on you briefly, with Lady Geraldine actually in the room. Later, they both left and then Miss Dorothy returned alone.

"When PC Dobson arrived and the alarm was set off, you were able to leave the room, Miss Dorothy no doubt leading the way, to make sure the coast was clear, go down the back stairs and exit the house by one of the side doors or French windows. You returned to your motor-cycle, changed your clothes again and rode home, arriving probably just in time to take Miss Dorothy's call and almost immediately start on the return journey."

Agatha regarded him coolly for a few seconds before replying. "You're a clever little bugger, Wilkins, aren't you? Well, I could deny it all, but I don't suppose it'd do any good in the long run."

"I must warn you, miss, that—"

"Oh, you can skip all that about anything I say being given in evidence. Yes, it's all true. I set out on my bike on Wednesday morning, shortly after our stepmother and Dorry left by train. I stopped in the woods just outside the estate, changed my clobber, and walked to the church. When we got here after the service, I tagged on to a bunch of old girls, none of whom I knew from Adam. Cousin George even came and spoke to us at one time. It was a devilish long wait in that wardrobe. I didn't get out of it until about half past ten. Then I went to the door, opened it an inch and stood waiting, just inside it, with the light off. I had to know when people had gone to bed. Of course, it was far from certain, even then, that I'd be able to go through with it. If people had drifted up to bed, one at a time, over a period of an hour or so, I just wouldn't have had the time. Luckily, everyone except Dorry and Gerry came up in the space of about thirty minutes. I could only go by listening, and couldn't be absolutely sure they were all up. I just waited until it got quite quiet, but it was still quite a risk. Of course, if I'd known how many people were still up and scurrying around I'd never have chanced it. Also, if Gerry had wanted to turn in a bit earlier, I'd have had to scrap the whole thing, because Dorry had to be with her every second until the body was found.

"Afterwards, I went straight back to the wardrobe. The armour crashing over was a shock. I couldn't think what it could be. Hadn't anticipated that, of course, but it was lucky in a way, because it meant the body was discovered a bit sooner, so I was able to get out of the house much earlier than otherwise.

"You're absolutely right about what happened afterwards. I have a key, which belonged to Daddy, to the doors in the outer wall of the estate, so that was no problem. I had to go home, because it would have been thoroughly unnatural if I hadn't come here—so there had to be a record of a call put through from here to our house; otherwise, how would I have learnt what had happened? I was just bloody stupid not to have told Dorry to stay on the line a bit longer. Reckon it was my only mistake. And I want to make it absolutely clear that this was entirely my idea and I forced Dorry to help me, blackmailed her, in fact."

"Blackmailed her?"

"Yes, for her own good. You see, she's got a secret, too. Oh, nothing too terrible, but our stepmother had been using it against her for years, in order to keep Dorry her virtual slave. Just this once, I used it, too. Because I knew that as long as our stepmother was alive, Dorry would never be free. It's ironic that if we'd only known about our stepmother's secret, she could never have treated Dorry as she did: if *she'd* talked, *we* could have talked. Grandmamma's money might have made a difference, too, but probably not: Dorry would never have broken away. Which is why I decided to go ahead, even after I learned about the inheritance. Anyway, as I say, I started planning it a long time ago. Oh, and by the way, that threatening phone call Stepmother received: Dorry didn't know it at the time, but it was me on the line."

"What was the purpose of that?"

"There were two, one quite legitimate. First, I hoped it might scare her into giving up her little game altogether. But, looking ahead, I also thought it might be a good idea to implant the idea that she had an enemy who had threatened her, and have the police officially notified of it. A waste of time, as it turned out: it didn't stop her, and you quickly quashed the idea that she'd been murdered in revenge by one of her victims."

"So it was part of a long-term plan? Tell me more about that."

"Stepmother often used to go away and take Dorry with her, both as a sort of messenger and maid, and leave me behind. So when I started thinking about it, I decided the best way would be to follow them on my bike one of these times, do the job and come back. There were several trips when for various reasons it turned out not to be possible. But Grandmamma's funeral was perfect. I remembered a lot about the house from when we came here as kids, and there were pictures and floor plans in the papers at the times of the other crimes, so it was all quite easy to work out. Naturally, I had no intention of coming to the funeral *as myself*, but when Florrie told me I had to stay behind I argued with her, just so she wouldn't think I was up to anything."

"Now, what about the attack on Lady Geraldine?"

"I'm really sorry about that. I like Gerry. It was purely a spur of the moment thing. I was in Dorry's room, talking, when Gerry came to the door, saying about how she knew who the murderer was and accusing Dorry of knowing as well, and covering up. I was behind the door. I just panicked, snatched up a bronze statuette and hit her. Thought I'd killed her, actually. Should have done a bunk as soon as I knew she was still alive, but that would have meant saying good-bye to the money, so took a gamble."

"A gamble that she'd die. You hoped she would."

"No! Just a gamble that she wouldn't remember what had happened. Anyway, that's immaterial now, isn't it? I suppose you'll want me to 'accompany you to the station,' as they say in books?"

"Both of you."

Dorothy, who had sat as though frozen and totally expressionless since Wilkins' last question to her, gave a little strangled cry. "Don't worry, petal," Agatha said, "it won't be for long, for you."

He formally cautioned and put them both under arrest, and he and Leather led them outside, Dorothy sobbing silently.

In the hall, Agatha said: "Mind if I have my leather jacket? Rather fond of it. It's in the cloaks cupboard."

Leather went to the cupboard and came back carrying the coat. "Thanks." She started to put it on. "Bit hot for it, today, but easier than carrying it. Oh, must make sure I've got my cheroots." She put her hand in the pocket. The next moment a small snub-nosed automatic was pointing straight at Wilkins.

Dorothy gave a gasp of horror. "Aggie!"

Leather took a step towards Agatha. Wilkins said sharply: "No, Jack," and he froze.

"Right," Agatha said calmly, "let's all go outside. You two stay close together."

They slowly made their way out onto the gravel forecourt in front of the house. A police car was parked there, a uniformed constable standing near it. He gave a start when he saw what was happening. "You, over here," Agatha called.

"Do as she says," Wilkins told him and he joined them.

Agatha's motor-cycle was standing where she had left it the previous day. She backed towards it, still keeping the pistol trained on Wilkins.

"This is useless, Miss Agatha," he said. "You haven't got a chance."

"Well, I haven't got a chance any other way. And I don't relish the prospect of being hanged."

"It may not come to that."

"Oh, just life imprisonment? Not a tempting alternative, thanks all the same. Now, lie down on the ground, all three of you."

Slowly, they did so. Agatha mounted the motor bike. She looked at Dorothy, who was wringing her hands. "Aggie, don't do this, please."

"No choice, petal. Sorry to leave you in the lurch, but you'll be all right. Get a good lawyer, you can afford one now. Put all the blame on Aggie."

She started the engine, thrust the pistol in her pocket, gave a wave and roared off, sending a shower of gravel into the air.

Wilkins, Leather and the constable scrambled to their feet. Wilkins pointed at Dorothy. "Keep an eye on her," he ordered the constable. "She's under arrest. Come on, Jack." They ran to the car, Leather jumping behind the wheel.

By the time they had got moving, Agatha was already two hundred yards down the drive and in a few more seconds was out of sight. "Whew, she's going at a lick," Leather muttered. "Still, the gates are closed. She'll have to stop for the lodge-keeper to open them." He put his foot down hard.

It was about fifteen seconds before they heard the sound of the crash.

Half a minute later, they skidded to a halt near the heavy wrought-iron gates and jumped out. The motor-cycle lay on its side, the front wheel buckled, the handle-bars askew. Agatha lay motionless a few feet from it. The lodge-keeper, Bates, was standing, gazing down at her in absolute horror. He looked up as they approached. "I—I heard the bike coming and came out to open up. She had to have seen they were closed. But she didn't try to stop. She must have been doing sixty or seventy when she hit them. If I'd been just a bit quicker…" He buried his head in his hands.

"It's not your fault," Wilkins said. "She knew what she was doing. Go and phone for an ambulance, there's a good chap."

"What? Oh, right." Bates half stumbled into the lodge.

Wilkins knelt down and felt Agatha's pulse. Then he looked up and shook his head.

"Suicide, you think?" Leather asked.

"Yes, she preferred this to the rope. And who can blame her?" He reached into the pocket of Agatha's jacket and drew out the pistol. He got to his feet and put the muzzle of the gun to his head.

"Don't—" Leather began, in alarm.

Wilkins pulled the trigger. There was a barely audible click.

Leather gave a gasp. "Unloaded, all the time! How did you know?"

Wilkins put his hand into his side pocket, took it out and displayed several small cartridges.

"You took them out?"

"Yes, had a rummage through the pockets of her jacket as soon as I arrived. Just a precaution, really, but after the last case here I certainly wasn't going to arrest anyone without making sure first they weren't armed."

"So you knew then that Agatha was the murderer?"

"No, no. I thought she was the most likely, but I had no proof. And several of the others had questions to answer, things to explain. Let's say I would have been surprised if it hadn't been Agatha, but not flabbergasted."

"But when you found the gun in her pocket…?"

"Could have been quite innocent. She was a woman who roamed around on a motor-cycle, on her own. Quite natural if she felt she needed some protection. Daresay she had a permit for it."

"But we could have stopped her getting away!"

"I know, Jack."

"You wanted her to make a run for it?"

"She obviously couldn't get far and I thought there was a good chance she'd end it like this. I hate sending someone to the gallows, and I've never sent a woman. Would haunt me always, if I did. Not that I feel sorry for her, mind. Would have done. Clara was a real monster, and killing her seems to have been a totally unselfish crime, done solely for Dorry's sake. But the attack on Geraldine changed everything. Agatha Saunders was a dangerous woman and if she'd got away with this one, killing would always have been an option for her when anyone posed any kind of threat, or even inconvenience, eventually. So it's better she's gone like this." He reloaded the automatic. "Not a word about this, eh?"

"No, of course not."

Wilkins put the gun in his pocket. "Now we've got to go and tell Dorry."

"I should never have gone along with it," Dorothy said tearfully. "It was very, very wrong of me. But Aggie was always so forceful. It was all her doing, really. She planned every bit of it. And I am weak. I've always found it easier just to do as I'm told. And I suppose even up to the last minute I didn't really believe in my heart that she would go through with it. When I opened Mother's door that night and saw her lying dead, it was terrible. But, of course, it was too late, then. I had to protect Aggie. But I swear I never, never knew she was going to hit Gerry. That was the most awful shock. So although I don't know what I'll do without Aggie, I am glad in a way it's ended as it has. Though I suppose I'll have to go to prison. But, it won't be for long, will it?"

"That's not for me to say, miss."

"Oh dear, I don't think I could stand it for very long. You want me to come with you, now?"

"Go with Sergeant Leather, miss. I've got a few things to clear up here. Send a car for me, Jack." Leather gave a nod.

"Do we have to go past the—the crash?" Dorothy asked.

Leather shook his head. "No, miss, there's a track that leads to the Home Farm and then out onto the road. You'll be taking that route."

"Thank you."

Wilkins watched silently as Leather led Dorothy to the car, put her inside and got in next to her. The car moved off. Wilkins watched until it was out of sight, then turned and went back indoors. Merryweather was still standing outside the drawing-room.

"Are they all still in there?"

"Yes, Mr. Wilkins. I did not know whether you had finished with them, so I took the liberty of saying you wished them to remain for the time being. I hope that was correct."

"Yes, thank you. I must tell them what's happened."

He opened the door and went in.

Five minutes later, Wilkins said: "So the case is closed, and you are all free to go. You'll be pleased to know I've decided not to bring any charges of obstructing the police, concealing evidence, or anything of that nature."

"I for one am very grateful, Chief Inspector," said Timothy. "And I would like once again to tender my apologies for my behaviour."

A quiet murmur of assent went round the room.

"What about me?" Julie asked.

"I won't be detaining you, miss, but I'm putting you on your honour not to leave your present address in London. No doubt you'll be hearing from the Metropolitan Police in due course."

"Of course. Thank you."

"One more thing I want to say to you all. A lot of secrets came to light in this room earlier. Nobody will hear about them from me or Jack Leather. And I think you'll all be wise to bear in mind that if one secret leaks out, others are likely to, as well. So I suggest you keep your traps shut."

The doors behind him burst open and the Earl came rushing in. His face was an expression of pure joy. Merryweather, his face wreathed in smiles, was just behind him. "She's come round!" the Earl positively shouted. "Gerry's come round!"

Chapter Forty-One

Wilkins said, "Oh, my lord, that's wonderful news."

Timothy said: "Splendid, splendid."

Gregory said: "Attagirl!"

Tommy said: "Absolutely ripping!"

Julie said: "Oh, that's swell."

Penny said: "How lovely!"

Miss Mackenzie said: "Praise the Lord!"

"Thank you, thank you, all. She just suddenly opened her eyes, saw her mother, said, 'Hello, Mummy, what time is it?' and went straight back to sleep. But she was breathing normally, after that. Ingleby arrived a few minutes later. He's left some tablets for her but he says he thinks she'll be fine." He looked round. "Where are Agatha and Dorothy? I must tell them."

"There's something you need to know, my lord," said Wilkins.

Having brought the Earl up to date and said his good-byes, Wilkins left the room. He found Gregory waiting for him. The MP was looking a little embarrassed. "Oh, Wilkins, just wanted to congratulate you. Terrible business, really tragic. But you handled it superbly. And thanks for what you said about everybody keeping quiet about anything that came out. Save me a bit of embarrassment, I must admit. Actually, I've realised the young lady's not much more than a gold-digger, so I'll be severing my connection with her—if I can just think of a way without putting her back up, which might be tricky."

"I don't see why it should be, sir."

"Er, how d'you mean?"

"Well, if she's a gold-digger, no doubt she believes you're very well off. You need to disabuse her of that belief."

"Easier said than done. Only last week, she asked me if I was hard up, and I assured her I wasn't."

"Why did you do that? Would have seemed an obvious way out."

"I know. Pride, I suppose. Anyway, she'll never believe me if I plead poverty now."

"Then you've got to convince her."

"Yes, but how?" He seemed to be hanging on Wilkins' words.

"Well, I've never been in such a situation, but if I were you I should leave a bill unpaid."

"I'm sorry, I don't…"

"A small bill, from some big company or organisation, who won't miss it. Ignore all their follow up demands, until they write threatening legal action, or better still, until you actually get a summons. Pay it immediately then—apologise, urgent constituency business, family bereavement, etc. But keep the letter. Take it with you next time you visit the young woman, and leave it somewhere about the flat, where it could have fallen from your pocket. When she finds it and sees you're being sued a few pounds, you won't have to convince her you're hard up. She'll either confront you, when you can admit it, or more likely you'll find she'll be severing her connection with you pretty quickly."

"Wilkins, that's brilliant! I'll do it. Thanks very much. Anyway, must go and pack. Good-bye."

He shook hands hurriedly and ran up the stairs. Wilkins looked after him. If Leather had been here, he thought, he'd have asked why his chief had bothered to help get Gregory Carstairs off the hook. But you never knew when it might be useful to have an MP in your debt.

Wilkins noticed that Timothy and Julie were standing in the porch, chatting quietly. "Nor a KC, if it comes to that," he said under his breath, and went over to them. "Miss Osborne, I'll make a bargain with you."

"What's that?"

"Give me your word that first thing next week you will go to Scotland Yard and confess to having entered the country illegally, and I'll forget to include it in my report to my Chief Constable. It should help."

Her face lit up. "Oh yes, of course I promise. That's terrific. I don't know how to thank you."

"You have my word, too, Wilkins," Timothy said. "I'll go with her. It's much appreciated."

"Mr. Wilkins," Julie said. "Do explain one thing. Why did you question me so about my call to the *Evening News*? I've been racking my brains to think why it was important."

"It wasn't important. I did it to get the Misses Saunders off guard. If I'd just turned on them suddenly and started asking about their conversation, they'd have certainly realised I was on to something. And it only needed them to say that Dorry had just gabbled out a few words and then rung off, and I'd have been sunk, because I didn't have a bit of concrete evidence. But as I questioned you first, they weren't wary when I started on them. It seemed simply routine. Also, it gave the impression that I didn't know how long your call had lasted, so it didn't occur to them that I'd know how long *they* had talked."

"I see. Gee, there's an awful lot to this detective business, isn't there? Tell me, when did you first suspect I wasn't really Stella?"

"From the start it occurred to me that your speech was almost totally American in vocabulary, phraseology and accent. Granted Stella Simmons had lived in New York for nearly eleven years and would obviously have picked up many Americanisms, but I couldn't think she'd have lost all her Britishness. I also noticed that when we talked, you used the words 'When I came to'—and then changed it to 'When I came home.' I guessed what you'd been about to say was 'When I came to England.' I think the clincher was when you referred to the Westshire 'Police Department,' rather than 'Police Force' or' Constabulary.' Yesterday I went to the village in Worcestershire, where Stella had been brought up—I got the name of it from the Earl—and saw the local doctor, who's been in practice there for over twenty years. He remembers the family well. I was still puzzled by the business of the toothpaste, though I thought it must be something to do with proving or disproving your authenticity. When I asked the doctor about Stella's teeth, he told me they'd all been extracted when she was in her teens. He recalled it clearly, because she had been so upset. Then everything fell into place."

"You could have accused me outright of being an impostor on the terrace yesterday. I might have admitted it."

"Or you might have denied it, and it could have taken weeks or months to prove it either way. Until I had the doctor's testimony—and for all I knew, he might have been dead—there'd have been only Mr. Lambert's word that Stella had ever had her teeth extracted; it would be virtually impossible to find the dentist who had done it after all this time. No, I wanted to get all the business of the toothpaste and the postcard and the cufflinks and the armour out of the way at the start. Besides, it's a bit of an idiosyncrasy of mine that I like to find things out for myself, rather than being told them. It gets on Jack's nerves sometimes."

"I bet you're a dab hand at crossword puzzles, aren't you?"

"I must admit it gets the day off to a good start if I can complete *The Times* one over breakfast."

Timothy blinked. "You *finish* it—over *breakfast?*"

"Not always, sir. Only mostly. Well, I'd better go out and wait for my car. Hope if we meet again it's under pleasanter circumstances. Good-bye."

He strolled out into the sunlight. He found Penny already there, staring thoughtfully out over the park, and went across to her. "Leaving now, miss?"

"Yes, there's a train at two thirty. Hawkins is taking us. He thinks he can squeeze us all in."

"Your father and Mr. Carstairs won't like that very much."

She smiled absently.

"Answer me a question, Miss Saunders, or two actually."

"What?"

"Why did you arrange to have that photo taken of your father?"

Penny went crimson. "I—I didn't—what—how?"

"How did I know? Well, as Miss Osborne pointed out, the picture was so bland. Anyone really wanting to damage him would have made it a lot more compromising. No blackmail demand followed it. Then again, someone, probably two people, brought him home and put him to bed. Your father seems to have imagined he got home under his own steam, but that's very unlikely. It was obviously the early hours of the morning. And you can't draw up in a car or taxi, let yourself into a house, carry an unconscious man upstairs, undress him and put him to bed without making a fair bit of noise. You said you're a very light sleeper; so why didn't you, in the room next to his, wake up? Also, when I was showing the picture round earlier you kept your head down and looked thoroughly unhappy and didn't ask to see the picture, even after Miss Osborne said it was quite innocuous. That confirmed my earlier suspicion that you'd seen it before."

Penny gave a sigh that seemed to come from the depths of her soul. "I never intended to blackmail him, of course. He wasn't even supposed to see the picture. The silly chumps were just supposed to give it to me. Only they couldn't resist sending him a print. I was mad with them."

"One of the silly chumps being Mr. Lambert?"

"Crumbs, no. He knew nothing about it. It was a couple of young lawyers, who loved the idea of playing a trick on a top KC. When I suggested it to them, they jumped at it. There wasn't supposed to be a girl in the picture, though. That was their idea. And I didn't know they were going to drug him. They're keen photographers, and I simply asked if they could fake a picture that made him look drunk. That was all."

"And what was your reason?"

"To have a sort of bargaining counter, to keep by me. He's so strict. And he disapproves of Tommy and he'll never agree to my marrying him. I just wanted something I could use if it really came to a deadlock. But it was a stupid idea, and I'd never have gone through with it. I've destroyed the negative already. And I'd no idea he'd been worrying about it, all these weeks. I thought he would have just thrown the photo in the waste-paper basket and forgotten about it. I've been feeling awful for the last hour. And he's sure to go on worrying."

"Then let's see if I can put his mind at rest. Tell you what, I'll write to him in a week or two, saying I've discovered who was responsible, that I cannot give him the name, but that the negative and all the prints have been destroyed and I guarantee he'll hear no more about it."

"Oh, that's wonderful! He'll think you tracked down the criminal and somehow frightened him off. He'll be awfully grateful."

"Oh yes, I suppose he will."

"But why aren't you going to tell him it was me?"

"I feel very kindly disposed towards you, Miss Saunders. Apart from Miss Mackenzie, you're the only one of the guests who didn't tell me a single lie."

"Really? Oo, I must tell Daddy that."

"And I suggest you think of some other way of persuading him to be a bit less strict."

"Well, actually, I've got high hopes of Julie. He seems really keen on her, and he doesn't mind she's not Stella. We're good chums already and I think she'll soften him up."

"I hope you're right, and I wish you every happiness. By the way, I didn't know you and Mr. Lambert wanted to get married."

"No, Tommy doesn't know yet, either. But he will soon. Oh, what was the other thing you wanted to ask?"

"Just why you pretend to be the typical dumb blonde of fiction and the films, when in your own way you're obviously a very smart young lady."

"Well, Tommy'd never marry anyone cleverer than himself. And though he's absolutely adorable, he hasn't got the world's greatest brainbox. So I've got to be pretty dumb, for the time being."

At that moment, the adorable one emerged from the house, carrying a small overnight bag, just as a police car rolled up.

"My transport," Wilkins said. "Back to the station and a lot of paperwork, I'm afraid. Well, good luck, Miss Saunders."

"Thank you for everything, Mr. Wilkins. You were wonderful." She stepped forward and kissed him lightly on the cheek.

Wilkins reddened a little, gave an awkward little bow and hurried to the car. Penny waved as it moved off.

Tommy came across to her. "New boy friend, Penny?"

"Oh, he's sweet, Tommy, don't you think?"

"Well, not exactly the word I'd use, not after the way he put me through it."

"It was your own fault, you silly boy, telling all those fibs about playing a practical joke on Miss Mackenzie and pulling down the armour."

"I know. But everything's OK now. I've apologised to Gregory for what I said and he's promised not to sue me for slander. And I've thought of an absolutely spiffing idea for a company. It'll be called Get Your Own Back, Ltd. It's really up my street. What happens is that if anyone's had an absolutely rotten deal from somebody, their boss, say, or a boy friend or a girl friend, they come to me and I pull a prank on the culprit, just like I did to the Hodges. Then if the client's happy, he or she pays me: ten, twenty quid, perhaps even fifty for a really super wheeze. He's got to pay, because he knows that if he doesn't I'll do the same sort of thing to him. Of course, I'd have to make absolutely sure first that the client is in the right. And I wouldn't do anything to really hurt anybody, just give 'em a very uncomfortable and embarrassing time. It really fits my talents. What d'you think?"

"Tommy, it's terrific. It could really work."

"And I wouldn't need much capital to get started. It'd hardly eat into my fifteen hundred quid at all."

"Don't you mean fourteen hundred and fifty three?"

"Oh. You guessed. Forty-seven?"

"Mm. Is it a bookie?"

"Yes. I put fifty quid, which I didn't have—over the phone—on this absolute cert. It came in fourth. I've been horribly worried. But it's all right, you needn't lecture me. I've learnt my lesson."

"Good."

"So we're in business?"

"Well, I'm sorry, Tommy, but I really don't think I can be the Managing Director."

Tommy hid his relief. "That's OK. Be a—a consultant. That's it. All you'll have to do is just keep your eyes and ears open and when you hear anybody moaning about how badly someone's treated them, just point them in my direction. I'll pay you commission. Then when I come up with a wheeze I'll run through it with you and you can tell me if there are any flaws, or suggest refinements, and so on."

"Oh, that sounds perfect."

"Topping! I'll put your name on the letter heading. I'll even get you some cards. 'GET YOUR OWN BACK, LTD. Miss Penelope Saunders, Special Consultant.'"

"*Special* Consultant? Oo, that's even better. Tommy, this is so exciting."

"I think I can come up with a better name."

They turned round. It was Julie, who had approached, unheard.

"What's that?" Tommy asked.

"'Get Even, Ltd.' That's what we say in the States. It's shorter and snappier."

Tommy nodded thoughtfully. "Yes, I think you're right. Penny, your first consultation. What do you think?"

"Mm. I like it."

"That's settled, then. Oh, and I've got something for you, Julie."

He put his hand into his pocket and took out a crumpled tube of toothpaste. "This is yours. I put it in a vase in one of the empty rooms and just retrieved it."

She threw up her hands in mock delight. "I'm overcome! I thought I would never see it again. I've been devastated." She clasped it to her breast. "But it's come home! I shall keep it always, as a souvenir. Tommy, you've done the decent thing."

"One tries to, don't you know."

"But seriously, Tommy, I want to apologise again, for impersonating Stella. I know you were very fond of her. I don't mind about the others but I feel fooling you was pretty mean."

"No, it's all right. I was fond of her a long time ago. But I'm not sure she was all that fond of me. I mean, she never wrote— just Christmas cards. Not even birthday cards, even though I sent her one regularly for years. And I'm beginning to think all those letters to Florrie were for only one reason, really."

"Well, I have to say she never showed much affection for her. She was always saying things like, 'Oh lord, I suppose I've got to write to Florrie again this week. Crashing bore.' It used to kind of rile me, sometimes."

"Well, I don't blame you for what you did. I think it took a lot of spunk."

"That sure makes me feel better. Timothy actually said that while he could not approve of what I did, it demonstrated considerable initiative. I guess I'm pretty lucky all round."

"Guess we all are," said Tommy.

Jean Mackenzie took a last look around the room, then, carrying her small suitcase, made her way towards the stairs. She had just reached them when she saw the Countess leaving Gerry's room. She hurried across to her.

"Oh, Lady Burford, any further change?"

"No, she's still sleeping very peacefully and normally."

"How wonderful. A real answer to prayer."

"Yes, indeed."

"I have been feeling so guilty, having in a way been responsible for bringing Agatha to this house."

"Please don't think like that. Only Agatha was responsible."

"I still find it so hard to believe that she should do such terrible things. She was a strange girl in some ways, and most outspoken in her language. But I was nonetheless fond of her. It must have been some inherited—oh, inherited from her mother's family, of course—some kink of the brain, perhaps, for which she could not really be blamed."

"I find it difficult to think like that, I must admit."

"Oh, naturally, naturally. We cannot know, of course. We must simply commit her to God's infinite mercy."

"Yes, well, we all need that."

"I would like to thank you for your great kindness, and for making me feel so much at home here, in spite of the unusual circumstances."

"Not at all. It's been a pleasure having you. We are all grateful for your kindness to Florrie over many years."

"Thank you." She went slightly pink. "Would you consider me terribly impertinent if I offered a small piece of advice?"

"Not at all."

"Please don't think I've been spying, but I spent a lot of time yesterday simply sitting, staring out of the window. And I saw Lord Burford twice, once carrying a large bunch of nettles, and later burying some small items each side of the porch. It was obvious, of course, what he was attempting." She broke off and frowned before saying thoughtfully: "I wonder if he tried bent pins or nails, as well."

For a moment Lady Burford was at a loss for words. Here was somebody who seemed to find her husband's behaviour not at all odd. She had to try and find out more. "I wouldn't know. But, er...he did mix blue and red ink to make purple."

"Purple ink? I don't quite... Oh, wait. Yes, I think I see. He had some candles, no doubt."

This woman was miraculous, thought Lady Burford. "Well, one candle. And later, after Geraldine was attacked, he did say it should have been a real purple candle."

Miss Mackenzie nodded sapiently. "He's right, of course. But I honestly don't think it would have made any difference. Do tell him that. It may set his mind at rest."

The Countess moistened her lips. "He—he also said Rosemary should have been here. But we don't know anyone called Rosemary. At least, I certainly don't. I keep asking myself, if George does, why should he never have mentioned her?"

Miss Mackenzie smiled. "Oh, I shouldn't be concerned about that. I'm sure he was not thinking of any female friend. But the advice I wanted to give was that these things are not really a good idea. Far better to have a word with your rector."

The Countess had considered the possibility of consulting the doctor, but the idea of consulting the rector had not entered her mind. But she gave nothing away. "Yes, I'm sure you're right. I'll tell George. Thank you." She suddenly felt very indebted to Miss Mackenzie and groped around in her mind for some way to show it. "By the way," she said, not without a slight qualm, "I'm sorry your experiment was spoiled. If at some time you would like to come and try again, we would have no objection."

"Oh, that is very kind of you, Lady Burford. But no, thank you all the same. I shall never touch a ouija board again. In fact, I'm giving up all that sort of thing. I realise I have been very gullible. I shall always be interested in psychic research, but I won't let it take the place of true religion in future."

"I'm sure that's a wise decision."

"And now I really must go. The car will be coming round. Thank you again, and good-bye."

"I'll come down with you," said the Countess.

They descended the stairs. A moment later, Timothy came out of his room and started towards the stairs himself. As he did so, Gregory appeared around the corner of the east corridor. They saw each other at the same time, both slackened their stride for a second, then continued to advance. At the top of the stairs they stopped. Both spoke together.

"Look—"

"I—"

"You first," said Timothy.

"Well, just wanted to say, very sorry. For my suspicions and the way I acted. Idiotic, really, but sort of lost my head. Frankly, in a blue funk, to tell you the truth."

Timothy gave a quick nod. "I know. I have never behaved in that way before. Quite irrational. But it was a unique situation. So I apologise, too."

"Perhaps we should, er, bury the hatchet. After all, it's many years since it all started and we're not getting any younger."

"Yes, I agree. Let bygones be bygones."

"I had nothing to do with that photo being taken, by the way."

"No, I realised afterwards that you couldn't have."

"Might I ask, what you said about St. John's Wood: how did you know…?"

"Oh, I was lunching at my club one day—the Reform. There were some chaps talking at the next table. Couldn't help over-hearing them. One of them seemed to be an MP and he was telling them about one of his colleagues who was paying the rent for 'a little bit of fluff,' as he put it, in St. John's Wood. In the next few minutes it came out that the man he was talking about was a Tory, married, had a small majority, and sat for a strongly non-conformist West Country rural constituency. I realised all of it applied to you. I have to admit that later I browsed through *Who's Who* and a couple of parliamentary reference books, and found that you were the only one who fitted the bill."

"I see. No idea anybody knew. Actually, I'm going to end it—or rather, I've thought up quite a subtle way to make sure she does. It's been pretty nerve-racking. And, after all, I do like Alex. Wouldn't want to lose her."

They went down the stairs and outside.

Chapter Forty-Two

It was Saturday morning and Wilkins was in his office, working on his report, when his phone rang and he was told, by an impressed girl on the switchboard, that there was a call for him from the Earl of Burford.

"Ah, Wilkins," said the Earl, when he got through, "sorry to bother you again, but wonderin' if you could come out to Alderley some time today."

"Oh, my lord, not another—?"

"Great Scot, no! Nothing wrong. It's Geraldine. She wants a chat with you: to compare notes, as she puts it. She's got to stay in bed for a couple of days and she's not a good patient, is bored stiff and frankly is driving everyone crazy. She's been nagging me to phone you."

"My lord, I'll be delighted. I've been hoping for a word with Lady Geraldine myself."

"Splendid. Come around four, if that's all right."

Gerry was sitting up in bed, wearing a pink bed jacket. Apart from the fact that a bandage completely enveloped her head above the eyebrows (in spite of Dr. Ingleby assuring her it was not necessary, she had insisted upon this), she looked quite ridiculously healthy.

Wilkins went across to the bed. He was carrying a large bunch of red roses.

"Oh, are those for me?" Gerry asked, unnecessarily. She took them, held them to her nose and breathed in deeply. "How lovely! Thanks awfully."

"Rather superfluous, I'm afraid," Wilkins said, looking round the room. There were about eight large vases, all filled with flowers of every conceivable colour.

"Oh, you can never have too many flowers. Marie, put them in water, please. And we'd like some tea in about half an hour." She handed the roses to the maid, who left the room.

"Sit down," Gerry said, pointing to a chair, and Wilkins did so.

"How are you feeling, Lady Geraldine?"

"Terrific. It's barmy, making me stay in bed, but Ingleby's a bit of an old woman. Up tomorrow, though, thank heavens. But let's not talk about me. I've got absolutely millions of questions. I've only had a second-hand account of things."

"From his lordship?"

"No, he didn't take it all in, by any means. Actually, from Merryweather, who was outside the door throughout and just happened not to have closed it properly. But there's a lot to be filled in. So, please."

"Well, first of all I've got to admit that at the beginning I made a bad mistake. I briefly considered the possibility that Dorothy had done it, but as soon as you gave her a cast-iron alibi, I decided that the murder had to have arisen out of the scene at the will-reading: that Mrs. Clara's threat had frightened someone, who decided she had to be silenced before she could spill the beans. In fact, the murder had been planned well in advance and Mrs. Clara's outburst had nothing to do with it. But it was a big stroke of luck for the girls, because for a while it stopped me looking for any other motive. I kept questioning them about whether their stepmother had ever mentioned having some dirt on any of the other guests. And I'll say this for them. They could have taken advantage of the situation to try and divert suspicion on one of the others: said yes, Clara had mentioned knowing something disreputable about Timothy or Gregory. But they didn't."

"When did you first realise your mistake?"

"I don't think there was one moment. But one thing about Dorry puzzled me from the start: why she hadn't phoned her sister earlier? I mean, they'd inherited a large fortune, which was going to transform their lives. The first thing she'd want to do would be call her sister and tell her. OK, immediately after she learned about it, she was distracted by Clara's tantrum, and had to go up and try and calm her down. But even when she'd done that it couldn't have been much more than six o'clock at the latest. Agatha was (supposedly) going to a party in the evening, but Dorry had an hour or two in which she could have at least tried to get in touch with her. But she didn't. The same thing applies at the end of the evening: you can't be sure what time a person is going to get home after a party, but in such a situation I'd certainly ring them at about eleven or half past—and keep trying. But she stayed with you—as, of course, she had to—all the time. It did sow the seed in my mind that perhaps she wasn't being entirely above board with me."

"Yes, I thought it was odd. But nothing more than that, of course, at that stage."

"There was something else: Agatha referred to the killer having held a pillow over her stepmother's face. As far as I could discover, she had never been told it was a pillow. Of course, it's a reasonable assumption, but it could just as easily have been a cushion or a towel or something. I decided at the time it was probably just a lucky guess. I was still working on the belief that the murderer was one of the other beneficiaries. After I'd interviewed them, I knew that most of them had lied to me, the possible exceptions being Miss Mackenzie and Penelope. But I was sure that all of them were capable of having done it. I was already fairly certain, from the way she spoke, that Stella was an impostor. I didn't believe Tommy's story about the armour for a moment and the fact that it gave him an alibi for the time of Stella's intruder made me virtually sure that that was him. He was the only one who'd known her at all well years previously and I wondered if he had spotted she was a fake and was trying to prove it. The stealing of the toothpaste clearly suggested something to do with her teeth, but that's as far as I was able to take it. I'd marked Timothy down as the likely source of the postcard, as soon as I learnt who Dora Lethbridge was. It occurred to me that the use of the word 'Miss' was meant to indicate she had never been married, and there was a subtlety about that which suggested a lawyer to me. I couldn't think, though, that he'd leave the card *and* scatter the cufflinks, so that left Gregory as the likely culprit as regards them. Anyway, that was the position when we left here yesterday lunchtime."

"So what did you do the rest of the day? What were those enquiries you were pursuing elsewhere?"

"I sent Jack up to London. First of all he went to Somerset House and obtained a copy of Clara's birth certificate, which showed that she was almost certainly illegitimate. I also wanted to see what Timothy's block lettering was like, and I thought the best source would be some official form he had filled out. I phoned the Passport Office, asked them to look him up and ten minutes later they rang back to say that he had made an application for a passport a few years previously. I asked them to do a photostat of it and informed them that my sergeant would pick it up. I'd told Jack to phone after he'd finished at Somerset House and I left instructions at headquarters for them to tell him to go and get the photostat. Then I went up to Worcestershire."

He told her what he had told Julie the previous day. He went on: "By then I'd confirmed many of my suspicions and theories but I still didn't know for sure who the murderer was. I'd ruled out Miss Mackenzie and Penelope, and almost, but not quite, ruled out Tommy and Stella. That left Timothy and Gregory. All the time, though, at the back of my mind those two little facts about the sisters—the delayed phone call and Agatha's knowing about the pillow—must have been nagging away. I woke up thinking about them yesterday morning. It was the phone call that worried me most. I was on my way to work, asking myself,

'Why didn't she call earlier?' And then it suddenly hit me. There was a possible reason—that Dorry had already spoken to her sister, face to face. Which would mean Agatha had been in the house all along. I realised how she could have got in unobserved and where she could have hidden."

Gerry gave a grimace. "Actually in the room with me! And I didn't have a clue."

"No way you could have, Lady Geraldine. Anyway, that left the question of the early morning phone call—obviously necessary because there had to be a record of a call to their home: it would be unthinkable that Dorry wouldn't phone her *eventually*. And, of course, Agatha had had to go home after the murder, in order to answer it."

"It also gave her a sort of alibi, didn't it? I bet that if you'd made enquiries in Hampstead, you'd have found a neighbour or postman or milkman who saw her leaving in a hurry on her motor-bike early that morning."

"More than likely. But this all meant that the call could have been very brief—just long enough for Dorry to tell her that nothing untoward had happened since Agatha had left and that she could start back straight away. I wondered if it was possible that they had slipped up and forgotten to make the call long enough. I turned round and went straight to the telephone exchange. They showed me their records, and there it was: call from Alderley 1 to their Hampstead number, starting at 7.09 a.m., lasting for 11 seconds."

"And that's when you knew Agatha was guilty."

"Not knew. She was now obviously a very strong suspect, but so were Timothy and Gregory. That's why I needed them all present when we went through the events of the night, as that might show up some blatant discrepancies in someone's story which would clearly point to his guilt. But actually it didn't. When I finally got Timothy and Gregory, as well as Tommy, to tell the whole truth, their accounts dovetailed remarkably well. And that was when I knew."

"Marvellous," Gerry said. "But you say you didn't work out how Agatha could have done it until you were actually on your way to work yesterday morning. What time was that?"

"Oh, around eight-fifteen, I suppose. Why do you ask?"

Gerry looked smug. "Because that means I beat you to it, by about four hours."

"Really? Congratulations, Lady Geraldine."

"You see, Aggie made one other mistake. I didn't spot it at the time, though I knew there was *something*. About four o'clock, I woke up and remembered what it was. When she first arrived, Aggie spent about a quarter of an hour with us. Then she said she'd like to go up to her room and asked which one it was. Mummy told her. She said that after she'd freshened up she'd go and see Dorry. *But she didn't ask which was Dorry's room.* Of course, she could have asked one of the servants, but the natural thing would have been to ask the location of both rooms at the same time. I wondered if Dorry could have told her when they spoke on the phone. But it was inconceivable to me that, with everything else on her mind, she would have mentioned that. Can you imagine it? 'Oh, Aggie, Mother's been murdered, and we've come into sixty-five thousand pounds, and I've got a nice room, almost opposite the top of the stairs'? I thought to myself that the obvious explanation for Aggie's not asking where Dorry's room was, was that she already knew. And then, just like you, everything came to me in a flash. All those unidentified ladies in black veils at the funeral, free to roam the house during the afternoon. So easy just to stay behind when everyone else had left. Only where I was stupid was at first it didn't occur to me that Dorry had been in it from the start. I imagined she'd only discovered afterwards what Aggie had done, and had simply been covering up for her. I just had to go and see Dorry at once and confront her. But before I'd got out more than a few words—wham. After that, as they say, I knew no more."

"Well, you did very well, Lady Geraldine. You've got the natural makings of a detective. I'm just sorry you weren't in at the dénouement."

"No, no, it was horrible seeing people being arrested the other times and I would have hated to see it happen to Aggie and Dorry. You know, for a while earlier today I found myself feeling quite sorry for Dorothy and worrying about her."

"Oh, I shouldn't worry too much about that young woman."

Something about his tone made Gerry glance at him sharply. "Are you thinking what I'm thinking, Mr. Wilkins?"

"What would that be, Lady Geraldine?"

"Well, she seems such a natural victim, a pushover for anyone who wants to use her or manipulate her. And apparently being virtually blackmailed by Clara over this guilty secret—and I suppose we've all got a pretty good idea of what that must have been. But I can't help remembering that hour or two when she and I were together downstairs. She seemed really happy, and totally engrossed by all I had to tell her about the other cases. And yet she knew that at that very time her sister was murdering their stepmother."

"She says she never believed Aggie would go through with it."

"But she knew Aggie was *planning* it, and at the very least there was a chance she'd do it. Even when we first met here, after the funeral, she virtually arranged that she and I should stay down and have a chat after everyone else had gone to bed. And when the time came, she made sure she was with me every second. Yet, she didn't seem even slightly anxious. And later, going on about how she would always be grateful to Clara. Aggie at least wasn't a hypocrite. But Dorry could have stopped the murder, as soon as she knew about the inheritance, which was obviously going to change everything—just told Agatha it was off, and Agatha could have walked out of the house, pretending to be one of the funeral guests, who had lost count of the time. Again, when I knocked on Dorry's door and called out that I had to speak to her about the murder, Aggie must have got an inkling I was on to something and gone behind the door immediately. Didn't Dorry wonder why? Didn't she see her pick up the statuette? No, I'm sure she knew just what Aggie was going to do. Then, helping Agatha carry me in here, putting me to bed and leaving me, without attempting to let anybody know. I could have died in those four hours before Marie found me unconscious."

Wilkins nodded. "And then she let Agatha take all the blame, and after she's killed she's only really concerned about what's going to happen to her, and she wouldn't get a long sentence, would she? No doubt within a few months she'll have a cell to herself, she'll be a trusty with all sorts of privileges, and all the wardresses will be saying what a pity it is that such a nice, lady-like, gentle person should have to be there."

"And I suppose in a year or two she'll be out. With sixty-five thousand pounds in the bank—plus interest."

"Oh, I wouldn't be so sure of that. When it comes to trial, I'll emphasise all the points we've just made, as I'm sure the prosecutor will. Miss Dorry could be in for quite a shock. She won't do life, of course. I don't say she deserves to. I don't believe she planned the murder—that *was* sister Aggie's work. But she's not the used innocent she pretends. I reckon about eight years would be satisfactory, from my point of view."

"I just hope you're right," Gerry said, fingering the back of her head.

Chapter Forty-Three

"Well, Wilkins, we have to thank you yet again," said Lord Burford, when the Chief Inspector was saying his good-byes.

"We are greatly in your debt," added the Countess.

"Not at all, your ladyship. Very pleased to have been of service. A complex case. But its occurrence here not such a coincidence as your lordship at first assumed."

"How d'you mean?"

"Agatha had decided to kill her stepmother whenever the opportunity arose. The funeral provided the first such opportunity. And the funeral would not have taken place here had it not been for the earlier crimes. It was those murders which made Miss Mackenzie so eager to conduct her experiment here and tell her little fib about your great aunt's wishes. So the location of this crime resulted directly from the earlier ones. It was a simple matter of cause and effect."

The Earl nodded. "Yes, I see. Good point."

"And I have to say that in one respect this was the most satisfying case I have ever handled."

"Really? What respect was that?"

"For the first time in my life I was able to tell both a Member of Parliament and a King's Counsel to shut up." A quite dreamy expression came over his face. "It was a moment I shall long remember and cherish."

Lord Burford chuckled. "So shall I, Wilkins, so shall I."

◇◇◇

When Wilkins had left, the Countess said: "George, it's wonderful about Geraldine, but it's almost as good that you seem quite your old self, too. I was so worried about you."

"Worried about *me*? Why?"

"Well, you were behaving extremely oddly: picking bunches of nettles, carrying spare socks around with you, making purple ink, burying things outside."

"Oh. That. Yes. I see." He looked decidedly embarrassed.

"What were you up, to, George?"

He coughed. "Well, suppose I can tell you now. Fact is, I was trying to break the curse."

"What curse?"

"That old gypsy's curse. Thought perhaps all these dreadful things happenin' here, might be something in it, after all. Found this old book about folklore in the library. Lots in it about black magic. Full of ways you can undo or nullify curses and hexes. Some of 'em quite disgustin', actually. But some of the others didn't seem it would do any harm to try. One of them was to take a lot of nettles, cut them up into small pieces and stuff them into things they call poppets—sort of effigies, made of cloth. Best I could do was a pair of old socks. Then you bury them one each side of the porch. Another was to put a lot of bent pins or nails into glass jars and bury them as well. Then there was one where you take a purple candle, write 'All blocks are now removed' in reverse on a strip of paper, fold it round the candle and then let it burn out. Only I didn't have a purple candle, so I dipped an ordinary one in purple ink. Then some say you've got to rub oil of rosemary on it, and I didn't have any of that, either."

Lady Burford gave a slight start. "Rosemary?"

"Yes. Why?"

"Nothing. Go on." She gave an almost imperceptible sigh of relief.

"So all in all I wasn't too sure of that one. The last one was simpler: you just tie a length of twine in dozens of knots and say, 'Tie and bind, tie and bind, No harm comes to me or mine' and bury that. Anyway, I buried two of each, a poppet of nettles, a jar of bent pins and a length of knotted twine, one each side of the porch. Then, of course, Gerry was attacked, so it didn't seem any of it had worked and I thought it was because I hadn't done it properly. But then she got better, so perhaps there was something in it, after all. What do you think?"

"What do I think? George, it's pagan!"

"But a curse is pagan, isn't it? So why not fight fire with fire?"

"Well, you worried Gerry and you worried me. And you had young Tommy thinking you were out of your mind. We must make sure he learns what was really going on. And Miss Mackenzie saw some of the things you were doing, and guessed what it was about. She seems to be something of an expert. I told her that you'd said it should have been a real purple candle and she said to tell you that you were quite right, but it probably wouldn't have made any difference."

"Really? Well, glad of that, anyway."

"She suggested we have a word with the rector. I didn't know what she meant at the time, but I do now. If you really believe Alderley is cursed, we could ask him to come and perform, well, not an exorcism, it's not haunted, after all, but a blessing or a service of cleansing. But I'm sure he'll be willing to arrange something. That will be the Christian thing to do."

"Yes, fine idea, Lavinia. Will you speak to him? More in your line than mine."

"Yes, I'll see him after church tomorrow. Now something else. That armour is still scattered all over the picture gallery."

"Oh, I know. There just hasn't been time to clear it up so far." He looked at his watch. "I'll go up and make a start on it now."

"You'll do it yourself? Isn't it quite a complicated job?"

"I'm sure there's nobody else here can do it. And I'm darned if I'm going to call in somebody from a museum, or something. No, I know a bit about armour. I think I can manage all right." He went out.

The Countess leaned back in her chair and gave a sigh. So all was explained. But what had George been thinking of? Nettles, bent pins, purple candles. Really, if it wasn't so ridiculous, it would be quite funny. In fact…

The Countess smiled. Her lips twitched. She gave a little chuckle. The chuckle turned into a laugh. The laugh became louder. Lady Burford laughed as she had not done for years.

In the gallery, the Earl stared at the various components of the suit of armour, trying to recall just what would be the best way to set about putting them together. Doing it on his own could take quite a time. He was going to need some help. He went out and made his way back along the corridor, towards the main staircase. But before he reached it, he saw his butler coming towards him, stopped and waited until Merryweather reached him.

"I've just been looking at that armour," the Earl said. "I'm going to start puttin' it back together."

"Strangely enough, my lord, I was looking at it only ten minutes ago, and was intending to remind your lordship of the situation."

"I'll need a hand, though. So if William or Benjamin aren't doin' anything vital at the moment, send one of them along to the gallery, will you?"

"I shall be very happy to assist your lordship."

"Really? It'll mean some crawlin' about the floor, you know."

"Quite within my capabilities, my lord."

"Well, if you're sure, come along then."

He turned and began to retrace his steps towards the gallery, Merryweather accompanying him. A thought struck the Earl. "You know, we never did find out what caused it to fall over. That young scallywag Tommy confessed to it. But seems he didn't, after all. So, who did?"

The merest ghost of a smile appeared momentarily on the butler's august features. "Perhaps Miss Mackenzie's original belief was correct after all and it was indeed a poltergeist, my lord."

The Earl chuckled. "Don't believe in 'em."

They had reached the double doors of the gallery. About to go in, Lord Burford suddenly stopped dead, causing Merryweather very nearly to bump into him. Both men stared into the room. In a strangled whisper the Earl uttered just two words. "Good gad."

The suit of armour was standing on its plinth, intact and perfectly reassembled.

Long seconds passed. At last, Lord Burford gulped. He seemed to have difficulty in speaking. "Not—not two minutes ago that was all over the floor. There was an hour's work to put it back…"

His normally pink complexion had become very pale. He turned and gazed at Merryweather uncomprehendingly.

The butler's face, by way of contrast to his employer's, had gone a dingy grey. He stared at the suit of armour. "There—there seems to be a piece of paper stuck under the visor, my lord."

"What? Oh, so there is." The Earl looked around, then, somewhat hesitantly, crossed the gallery, lifted the visor and gingerly extracted a sheet of crumpled note paper bearing a dozen or so lines of writing. He stared down at it and his eyes bulged. Merryweather gazed at him expectantly. Lord Burford looked up at him, his face a blank mask. "It's the words of *Comin' Round The Mountain.* Bradley's notes. He threw this away. How the deuce…?"

Merryweather gulped. "You think possibly the Honourable Mrs. Florence Saunders, my lord…?" His voice, too, tailed away.

"Great Aunt Florrie? You think *Florrie* knocked the armour over—just for Miss Mackenzie's benefit? And put it back again? But, good gad, she's dead. It's not possible. Is it? Is it possible?"

With a sharp click, that sounded like a gunshot in the stillness, the visor of the suit of armour fell shut.

The Earl gave a convulsive start, Merryweather a slightly more controlled one. For a full ten seconds neither of them spoke. It was the butler who found his voice first. "My lord, may I suggest we retire downstairs immediately and that you allow me to fetch you a stiff whisky and soda?"

At last the Earl pulled himself together. "Merryweather, you may indeed. And for once, you're going to join me."

"Thank you, my lord," said Merryweather.

To receive a free catalog of other Poisoned Pen Press titles, please contact us in one of the following ways:

Phone: 1-800-421-3976
Facsimile: 1-480-949-1707
Email: info@poisonedpenpress.com
Website: www.poisonedpenpress.com

Poisoned Pen Press
6962 E. First Ave. Ste 103
Scottsdale, AZ 85251